To Whitney

WORD OF HONOR
a novel

by
John Edgell

For His Pleasure
John Edgell
Romans 5:1

A REALMS OF LIGHT BOOK

**Text Copyright © 2002 John A. Edgell
All Rights Reserved**

Dedicated to the Wagner Scifi-fantasy Writers Group (1994-2002)—mentors, critics, and friends—and Agnes Lawless Elkins, copyeditor and friend, and Sue—dear wife and proof reader.

Pronunciation Guide Appendix at End

Chapter 1

In the reign of King Xzadrk
743 FBK (From the Beginning of the Kingdom)

An ashen-faced, down-in-the-mouth young boy trudged the narrow, shadow-laden streets of Zwexdrof as dusk settled over the realm of Xzwendaria. Carts rolled by, raising swirls of dust, while stoop-shouldered men plodded the wooden walkways.

"A hard day's work," complained one of the men.

"Humph! You think you had a hard one!" grubbed another.

The boy followed at their heels but paid them no mind. He shadowed another farther on. When the men in front of him passed an opening between two buildings, the boy's sky blue eyes darted this way and that. As the men continued along the walkway, he casually stepped into the darkened alley, leaned his back against the wall, and waited. After a time he heard the squeak of a door and then footsteps on the boardwalk. He turned and peeked around the corner, showing just one eye. "Yep, that's him," he whispered, as if to the building against which he pressed his face.

A tall, dark-haired man wearing nice-looking clothes had stepped from the bakery three doors down.

The boy noted the man's broad smile. "Well, he won't be smiling for long," he mumbled.

A leather pouch hung heavily on the man's belt, an easy take for the typical purse snatcher, but the young thief took no notice of it. However, he did notice the growl that broke the silence of the dark alley. He grimaced, and his hand went to his stomach. Over the last two days he had eaten only a few stale pieces of cracker. He fixed his eyes intently on the loaf of bread in the man's right hand. Just a few more steps and the man would be even with him. He would snatch the bread and disappear into the gloom of the alley.

Unknown to the boy, the man was aware of his presence. Having previously seen the boy watching him, he had inquired of the locals and learned that the boy was an orphan who had turned to thieving in order to get by.

As the man had walked into the bakery, he had seen the boy slip from the street into the shadows of the alley. The purchase took but a few minutes. When he came out with the hot loaf of bread in hand, he was aware of the boy peeking around the corner and was certain of the boy's intent.

As the man passed the alley, the boy lunged for the bread. But as his fingers touched the outer crust, the man pulled the bread away and popped him a blow to the shoulder with his elbow. The boy tumbled face first off the walkway onto the dirt road. He tried to rise, but a large foot pressed the small of his back, forcing him back to the ground. He squirmed vigorously, and then a hand wrapped around the nape of his neck. The foot released his back and he felt himself being lifted from the ground.

The man set him on his feet but did not loosen his grip. "Young man, your thieving will eventually land you in the king's dungeon." The man looked into the boy's panic-stricken eyes. "And if a month in the dungeon doesn't reform you—and it won't—when you're caught a second time, you'll be sent to the mines of Xzendr and hard labor for five years." The man shook his head. "Who knows? It might do you good."

The boy fought with tears—and lost.

"I can't do anything right!" He mumbled the words more to himself than the man who held him by the neck. "Can't even do a decent job of stealing a meal."

The man laughed inwardly, but maintained a grim facade. "Did you ever consider that you might have more success asking for bread than stealing it?"

The boy looked up at the man with water-filled eyes and told him he was afraid to ask.

"Why?"

"'Cause when I ask I get laughed at and pushed away," said the boy. "Last time I asked for a meal, a woman spit in my face and chased me off with a broom. But I fixed her. Took a pie from her window that night." His eyes strayed to the ground. "But I stay away from Barr Street anymore."

As the man loosened his grip he could feel the boy tensing to run. "Well, I tell you what," he said, holding the boy more loosely, "Ask and I'll give you this hot loaf of bread. But only if you ask." The man dropped his hand from the boy's neck.

The boy hurriedly stepped away but did not run. He gazed at the man questioningly, distrustfully. It took great effort, but finally he forced the words through tightly drawn lips. "Can I have that loaf of bread you are carrying?" The boy waited, his eyes measuring the man, his stomach rumbling impatiently.

The man smiled and tossed the loaf of bread to the boy, who moved farther away and tore at the crust with his teeth.

The man started to walk away, then turned back. "By the way," he said, "if you choose to accompany me to my home, you can sleep in a warm bed tonight." He looked toward the sky and frowned. "A storm is brewing to the west. Rain will be pounding the street to mud by morning. You could use a roof over your head, couldn't you?"

The boy continued to gnaw at the bread. He made no attempt to answer the man though he gave him a skeptical glance.

The man repeated his offer, turned on his heels and headed down the darkening street. A lamplighter shuffled by, ignoring the boy.

The boy stared at the lamp the lighter carried and thought about how nice a warm hearth and bed would feel. He hadn't slept in a real bed in ages! But could the strange man be trusted? He shrugged a shoulder and followed at a safe distance, his mind working anxiously. Why is he being kind to me? Could he be baiting a trap? I'll bet he's a slave trader. No sir, I'll not be sold into slavery for a loaf of bread!

The boy felt puzzled when he found himself in the middle of Zwexdrof standing before a huge building made of polished marble. At the top of a long stairway, statuary lions guarded the door. A narrow, well-kept, greensward encircled the building. The boy's face twisted to a frown. He had always stayed a safe distance from the temple because he knew Baruch would not be pleased with him.

The man's stopping to worship? The boy scratched his head and grimaced, then chucked the last piece of bread into his mouth.

The man went up the steps and entered the temple.

The boy looked around. The street was empty. He felt uneasy—out of place. He desperately wanted to distance himself from the temple, but his curiosity would not let him. Taking a deep breath, he scampered up the great stone stairway to the massive front doors of the temple and stole inside just in time to see the man enter a side chamber off to the right. The boy slipped into a shadowed corner and waited. Twenty minutes later, the man reappeared dressed in priestly robes.

The boy let out a quiet whistle. When the man turned his eyes in the boy's direction, the youngster turned white and pressed himself hard against the wall, hoping the man could not see him.

"It is time for the evening sacrifice." The man smiled at the boy. "When I am finished, I will show you to your quarters. I won't be long."

The boy sank to the floor, his heart racing. Deep inside he felt a sense of relief—of hope. And hope was something he had not felt for a long time.

An hour or so later, the two sat before a warm fire in the living quarters of the temple. The boy, still leery, cast the priest a bewildered gaze.

"My name is Thaxndar." The priest smiled gently. "And your name?"

The boy hesitated but finally blurted, "My name is Kanderxn. I go by Kander—sort of." He shifted a shoulder. "Actually, there ain't anybody who knows my name."

"Your name has a nice ring to it. Tell me, Kander, what happened to your mother and father?"

The boy's eyes went wide.

Thaxndar reached out and touched the boy's shoulder. "I have seen you around and have inquired a bit here and there, and I understand you are an orphan. And by the way, I was aware that you were following me and presumed you would try to steal the bread."

Kander pulled away from Thaxndar's hand. He frowned deeply. "Phooey! I can't even follow a person without giving myself away. I can't do nothin' right!"

Thaxndar grimaced. He should not have told Kander that he had been aware of his presence in the alley. He didn't want to discourage the boy. "How old are you, Kander?"

The boy scowled and squinted toward the vaulted ceiling. He pulled down one finger, then another until he had pulled them all down. "Ten," he declared with an air of pride.

Thaxndar smiled and nodded. "Now," he pressed, "about your parents?"

Kander jacked his shoulders. "Never had a father," he said. He forced a wan smile, and his voice went heavy with sadness. "That's the one thing I always wanted, a father. But never ever did I have one, not one at all. And then. . ." Tears rose to Kander's eyelids, and he looked at the ground. ". . . then, 'bout a year ago, my ma took sick and died. We lived in a room over on Hovel Street. Ma called our place 'The Cellar.' Don't know why. But when Ma died, old Dorkin kicked me out, an' I been gettin' by on my own ever since."

A tear wet the priest's cheek. He wiped it away before the boy could see it. "Kander, how about letting me be your father?"

The boy looked at him askance.

"I thought you always wanted a father," said the priest.

Kander cocked his head to one side and gazed at Thaxndar. "Why should you want to be my father?" He grimaced and shook his head. "If you were a good priest, you would hate me like everyone else does."

"Hate you?" The boy's words stunned Thaxndar. "Why should I hate you?

Guilt sheeted Kander's face. "Humph! You're a priest, aren't you?"

"Yes, I am a priest. But why should I hate you, Kander?"

"My mother told me that one of Baruch's laws is never to steal," said Kander. He lifted his hands out to the side, palms upward. "I've stole lots of things. I even tried to steal your bread, and you a priest and all. If you steal and do other bad things, Baruch hates you. And since you're his priest, if you were any good, you would hate me too."

"Kander! Kander!" Thaxndar stepped closer and gently grasped the boy by his shoulders. "Baruch does not hate you because you have broken his laws. Sure, when you do something bad, you disappoint him, but I assure you, he still loves you. Kander, the laws Baruch has laid out are for our good. If we break them in one way or another, we or others suffer. Because he loves us, he does not want to see us suffer or cause others to suffer."

"But a lawbreaker is condemned." Kander pulled away from Thaxndar's hands.

"True, Baruch, also known as the Majesty or the Presence, is holy, and we are not. The bad things we do come from our fallen state and make us unclean before him," explained the priest. "But Baruch has provided for our cleansing. Kander, if you will admit that you have done bad things and come to him with a sacrifice, he will grant forgiveness."

Kander's shoulders slumped, and his voice quivered. "But I have no sacrifice to bring." Tears edged the boy's words.

"Give him yourself," said the priest.

The boy's eyes exploded with fear.

Thaxndar grinned. "No, Kander, I do not mean that," he reassured. "Baruch does not accept human sacrifices. But you can give yourself as a sacrifice by serving him here in the temple. And if you will accept me as your surrogate father, I will provide you with a sacrifice to bring to him." He raised his eyebrows and waited. "So, what do you say?"

The boy's eyes sparkled as he cast Thaxndar a huge smile.

Chapter 2

At the Temple in Zwexdrof
745 FBK

*K*ander gazed out at the city thinking about how much his life had changed. Thaxndar's words came to his ears, but they did not register.

THUMP! THUMP! THUMP! Thaxndar's pounding his table startled Kander out of his reverie. He refocused his attention.

"It is a beautiful day, Kander," said the priest, "but the history of our land is important."

"People, and dates, and places. . ." Kander shook his head. "I just don't see what is so important about it."

"History is a record of good choices and bad, the people who made them, and the consequences of those choices. Hopefully, understanding history will help *you* make right choices and avoid bad consequences." Thaxndar got up from the table and went to the window. He sat on the ledge and faced Kander. "At the least, history will help you understand this day in which we live—why things are the way they are."

With a scowl creasing his brow, Kander leaned back in his chair. "You were telling me about Xzadrk."

"So I was," said the priest. "Xzadrk was twenty-nine years old when the people crowned him king after the death of his father. That was in 681."

"Is the date important?" asked Kander.

"Only relatively so. It gives structure to the flow of what we are talking about." Thaxndar stretched out a hand toward the city. "Anyway, our good people held Xzadrk in high regard because he walked in the ways of Xtrakan, the first king of Xzwendaria."

"But before Xtrakan became king, wasn't Xzwendaria known as Fairlander?" broke in Kander. "Why was it Fairlander before and Xzwendaria after?"

"Good question." Thaxndar folded his arms across his chest. "You see, in the waning years of what was called Fairlander, the kings of the realm turned their hearts away from following Baruch. They disavowed his laws and did as they pleased."

"So how was the transition made from being Fairlander to being Xzwendaria?" asked Kander. "I mean why change the name of the realm?"

Thaxndar smiled and nodded. "Well, the last king of Fairlander was Elthexn the Great, a man both proud and oppressive. In his day Baruch appeared to an artisan named Xtrakan and told him that he was going to judge the nation because of the sins of its kings. He also said that he must pursue knowing him with his whole heart. And so he did.

"That same year Baruch stirred the hearts of the people to rise up against Elthexn the Great. They hanged him on the gallows outside his palace on which he himself had hanged many an innocent man. The people were so ashamed of what their realm had become that when they sought out Xtrakan and crowned him king, they changed the name of the realm to Xzwendaria." Thaxndar rubbed his chin and asked, "And what is the meaning of Xzwendaria?"

"Land of Great Joy or Renewed Joy." Kander grinned broadly. "See. . .and you thought I had not been listening."

"I am glad that you were." Thaxndar stood and gave Kander a mock bow. "Now, let us continue. A year after Xtrakan was crowned king, Baruch again appeared to him and promised Xtrakan that as long as his heirs turned their hearts toward him, he would bless them and their land."

Thaxndar paced back and forth in front of the window. "On the other hand," he continued, "Baruch also promised that if Xtrakan's heirs turned their hearts away, then he would turn his back toward them and not his face. And Xtrakan bowed his head and replied, 'So be it, Lord.' And for more than six hundred years his heirs looked to Baruch again, whom they also knew as the Majesty or the Presence, and they were blessed.

"When Xzadrk became king, Heferndal was high priest." Thaxndar paused in his pacing and looked at Kander. "By the way, Heferndal died in 740—and no, you do not need to remember the date—and I was appointed high priest. For the previous seventeen years I had been Heferndal's assistant.

"Anyway, Xzadrk heeded the wisdom of Heferndal and has listened to me." He stopped and turned toward Kander. "That is, except in the matter of Nefarious Reach to the north. Against my advice, Xzadrk established diplomatic relations with our northern neighbor and recently invited their emissary to his court.

"As you know," Thaxndar went on, "Xzadrk has a fifteen-year-old son, an only son named Zandirxn. I have observed that Nefarious Reach's ambassador, Xvardris, who is from Athos, has made a point of befriending Zandirxn. He appears to be encouraging the boy's defiance of his father and indulgence of his baser desires, although the king denies it. Furthermore, I know that Zandirxn does not seek Baruch's face. He has not once darkened the door of this temple except when state affairs have demanded it." Thaxndar stopped again and focused his attention on his student. "The truth is, Kander, I believe that slowly and surreptitiously Nefarious Reach is reaching out with the intent of usurping the throne of Xzwendaria."

Kander leaned forward, placing his elbows on his desk. "But isn't Nefarious Reach north of the Ardent Sea and east across the North Labyrinth Mountains, so it's pretty much inaccessible?"

The corner of Thaxndar's mouth pulled back into a slight smile. "Yes, and until 650 it was a sparsely settled territory under Xzwendaria. But because of its inaccessibility, Xzadrk's father paid little attention to that distant territory. In 650 the Pagyns invaded the territory, and by the time word reached the king, the Pagyns had built a powerful fortress at Athos and the Temple Tenebrous as well. Xzadrk's father sent ships and warriors to assail the fortress, but they returned badly beaten. So Xzadrk's father named the usurped northern territory Nefarious Reach. And for years bad blood flowed between Xzadrk's father and Werfhx, the declared king of what had been a territory of our realm. But I also must say, in truth, Werfhx was but a puppet of the priestess of the Temple Tenebrous."

"Do they worship Baruch?" asked Kander.

"Humph! Most certainly not! They are worshippers of Bayl." Thaxndar sat on the ledge of the window again. "Now to complete the lesson: Werfhx died just a year before Xzadrk ascended to the throne of Xzwendaria. Werfhx the Second took his place and pressed for better relations between the two countries. Xzadrk is a peaceable man, and not heeding counsel, he agreed with Werfhx that hostilities should cease, that they were not in the best interests of either country. And so with a stroke of ink, he relinquished the northern territory to the Pagyn invaders. And it was just last year that Wazrxna became the priestess of the Temple Tenebrous and, for all intents and purposes, the priestess ruler of Nefarious Reach.Furthermore, I understand it was Wazrxna who instructed Werfhx the Second to send her personal attendant, Xvardris, to represent Nefarious Reach at Zwexdrof in Xzwendaria."

"If the territory became Nefarious Reach, then what is Amity?" asked Kander.

"Ah! Amity. . .the land of friendship." Thaxndar nodded. "Yes, one and the same. The Pagyns do not acknowledge the offensive title of Nefarious Reach given them by King Xzadrk's father. They do indeed demand to be recognized as the Realm of Amity. "

Kander puckered his brow. "Is Xvardris really all that bad or dangerous? After all, he is just an ambassador."

"An ambassador with a mission," snapped Thaxndar. "I am confident he has been sent here with his wonderful smile and charming ways to win the hearts of the people of Xzwendaria and to prepare the way for the Pagyns to usurp the throne."

Thaxndar stood up, his face sheeted with anxiety. He waved the back of his hand at Kander. "Enough for one day!"

When Thaxndar left the room, Kander walked to the window and looked out over the city. *I wonder what it will all come to*, he mused.

Chapter 3

The Village of Netrag in the Northern Territory
706 FBK

Before Kanderxn was born, events were taking place that would eventually impact his life and the destiny of the realm.

Two men with gray beards and leathery wrinkled faces sat in a dark corner of the Red Leaf Inn. They were alone, so they could talk freely.

"I tell you, Dollfig, the king may have cast off the title of Nefarious Reach and recognize this here northern territory as the Realm of Amity, but whatever this place is, it ain't any longer a friendly sort of place to live."

Dollfig cast an anxious glance around the room. "Barkus, ifn ya' wanna' talk about safe, this ain't a safe conversation."

The other man grimaced. "Ain't no one listening, Dollfig. And what makes me mad is that those Pagyns didn't invade with weapons in their hands. They just pushed in on us with smiles, kindness, and promises of friendship—and there ain't all that many of us. So we just let it happen."

Dollfig nodded. "Yeah!" He looked around cautiously before speaking further. "But once they got themselves moved in among us, those Pagyns rose up like a terrible giant awakened from slumber. They has imposed their Pagyn law on us, and crushed any voices of opposition. They has even banned belief in Baruch. 'Tis a travesty, Barkus."

"Aye, and mark my word, Dollfig, one way or another the Pagyns are going to silence that young couple out the way who keep yappin' about taking a stand. Don't they know that folk around here have families?"

The other man smiled and shook his head. "Those two got pluck if nothin' else. But yer' right. If they keep talkin' about Baruch, they'll pay the pie man sure."

At the sound of horse hooves on the road, both men fell silent. After the horses passed by, Barkus whispered to Dollfig, "Must be Pagyns, since no one else is allowed astride a horse."

"Gives me the creeps," said Dollfig, "them ridin' through town this time of night. Makes one wonder what the scoundrels are up to."

Warzella heard the riders coming. She had had run-ins with Pagyn riders in town, and living alone, she feared the worst. She threw a shawl about her shoulders and ran out the back door fully intending to hide in the woods until the threat of the Pagyns had passed. But in her hurry, she stumbled and fell. Her heart pounded in her chest. The hoofbeats drew near. She crawled to a stand of bushes and watched in horror as masked Pagyn riders circled the home of the young couple who lived next door. Her hand went to her mouth to silence a scream as bowstrings twanged and she watched the young couple die hand in hand in the doorway of their home. The men threw torches, and flames began to devour the house. Then as suddenly as they had come, the riders rode off into the night.

Warzella stared at the flaming house, afraid to move. Then above the crackle of the flames, she heard the cries of the couple's small child. She had watched the child for the couple on numerous occasions.

"Brokre!" she wailed as she ran toward the burning house. And careless of the flames, Warzella dashed inside. She held her nose and mouth and hurried to his room. One of the Pagyn torches had landed by Brokre's bed. The flames that lapped at the child crackled like Pagyn laughter to her ears. Brokre screamed in terror as his clothes ignited. Warzella whipped her shawl around him, snuffing out the flames. Then, with Brokre in her arms, she stumbled through the inferno and out into the night.

Warzella's arms and legs were red and sore. Her hair was singed, and her nightgown smoldered at the fringes. Although badly burned, Brokre was alive and safe, and that was all that mattered.

Warzella suffered deeper wounds when the town folk found out what she had done, for they did not praise or encourage her. Rather, they mocked and railed at her. A dear friend called her a "stupid woman!"

"Foolish girl! You'll bring a curse on us all!" spat the usually kindhearted and jovial baker.

"Whose house will be next?" cried the blacksmith.

"The child is cursed like his parents!" shouted a neighbor woman.

"Destroy the child!" yelled another.

So with the town folk at her heels, holding little Bokre to her breast, Warzella fled into the woods—into darkness. She spent the night hiding in a brushy depression. But when dawn peeked through the trees, she hurried eastward toward Prauge. She whispered to the child, "I will keep you safe, Brokre, and you will grow up to be a great man. Just you wait and see!"

The Cities of Belem and Avard in Xzwendaria
717 FBK

Wilgrin had just turned seventeen. He sat, fishing pole in hand, on the edge of the dock next to his grandfather, Fragn, a crusty old seaman with weather-wrinkled skin and a head and face of gray, bushy hair.

"Gramps," Wilgrin said, "I heard a fellow talking about queens the other day. He said there used to be queens here in Belem." He gave the old seaman a sidelong glance. "So tell me, Gramps, what are queens?"

The old man looked at the boy from beneath his bushy eyebrows. "Well, I suppose yer' old enough to be knowin' about such things as queens," he rasped.

"Yeah, well?" said the boy.

The man ran a hand through his hair as he began. "Well, knowing about queens begins with the Realm of Amity, which as you know, is not the friendly land it claims to be. It was, as the king's father had so aptly named it, Nefarious Reach. And Nefarious Reach's tentacles had wormed their way into Xzwendaria long before that fella Xvardris arrived at court."

"What's that got to do with queens?" asked Wilgrin.

"Listen, and you'll find out!" gnarred the old man. "Now, not only was slavery introduced to the Realm of Xzwendaria, so was what they call moral perversion."

"Who calls what 'moral perversion'?"

"That's what I'm tryin' to explain!" huffed Fragn. "You see, when merchant slave-ship sailors visited Athos, people introduced them to Pagyn perversions." The old man held up a hand. "Don't ask any questions. Just let me finish. Anyway, the sailors visited dark dens of wantonness where male prostitutes seduced them. And a number of the slaves they brought back to Belem and Avard were female prostitutes. Some of the prostitutes were what the sailors called 'queens,' because they practiced their prostitution woman with woman."

Wilgrin's eyes went wide. "And the king allowed it?"

Fragn shook his head. "It was all kept hushed up at first. But the perversion grew here in Belem and Avard as well, and in time word of it did get to the king. They say he went into a fit of rage at the very thought of such perversion being practiced in Xzwendaria. 'From this day forward all such practices are outlawed!' he declared, and he put his seal to the decree. Furthermore, he said that anyone breaking the law would pay with their lives!"

"Pay with their lives?" questioned Wilgrin.

Fragn nodded. "Yep, anyone practicing perversion was to be hanged."

"So what happened?"

"Well, a number of women from Belem and Avard had no inclination to forgo their perverse ways. But they feared the king's edict and all . . . and the gallows, of course. So they fled east into the wilderness, determined to find a place where they could establish their own brand of Utopia."

"So did they?" asked Wilgrin.

The old man shrugged. "Don't know. The queens disappeared and have never been heard of since."

The end of Fragn's pole dipped toward the water, and the conversation ended for the moment. However, once the fish was in the bucket, Wilgrin's curiosity returned.

"So, Gramps, what's so bad about all that kind of stuff you call 'perversion.'"

Fragn gave the boy a look of disgust. "Well, let me tell you a little story, and you can figure it out from there."

Wilgrin smiled at the old man and waited for him to begin.

The old man checked his bait and then told his story. "That same year, 717, a child named Nedrn was born here in Belem. The child's father, a fellow sailor, engaged in perverse acts. He was married to a fine woman, but still he sought out male prostitutes. He loved the thrill of wanton pleasure. And as Nedrn grew, his father came to his bed and forced him to participate in things I won't talk about." He looked sidelong at the boy. "So don't be askin'! Anyway, Nedrn's father's perversion led to him getting some kind of disease, and the man died a terrible death. Well, the disease took hold of Nedrn and affected the poor boy's mind. He went mad, he did, and in 739 he fled stark naked from family and home. Ran off to somewhere, and no one has seen him since, though rumors say he haunts the wild places of the realm. That's the kind of thing perversion will do to ya, boy. And there are those who'd have us just accept it."

Wilgrin started to speak, but Fragn cut him off. "Enough for one day. Let's get back to fishin."

Wilgrin smiled and turned his attention to his pole.

The Cities of Belem and Avard in Xzwendaria
733 FBK

*T*he fat, flabby-jawed man turned from the window and grinned at his wife. "People grubbed when the Pagyns brought slavery to the territory, but by the stars, ya' never heard me complain."

The man's wife scowled. "Humph! Well, ya better get the price ya' was askin,' that's all I've ta' say. And there had better be no trouble. You know as well as me that slave tradin' is illegal in Xzwendaria."

The man's eyes sparkled. "I told you, woman, the Pagyns see that the local officials at Belem and here in Avard get their share of coin, so there'll be no snags."

Fourteen-year-old Trevr watched from the next room as a man with beady eyes and a wicked smile approached the house. Trevr's father met the man out on the porch. Trevr could see their mouths moving but could not hear their words. He shook his head as his father held out his fat hand, into which the wicked-looking man dropped six silver coins. "Always conniving," Trevr muttered to himself.

Moments later, Trevr heard footsteps. As he turned from the window, his mother's coarse hand grasped his shoulder. She dragged him stumbling to the porch and pushed him toward the strange man.

The man grabbed Trevr by the arm and led him out of the yard, past a paintless picket fence where a group of children waited, their faces empty of emotion and their eyes distant. Trevr's eyes went wide when he saw that they were all attached to a chain. Only then he noticed the cart with an anvil on the back.

"Clang! Clang! Clang!" Tears streaked Trevr's cheeks. Once his shackles were in place, the man pushed him toward the other children. Another man linked him to the long chain that ran between the children, and then they trudged down the road.

As Trevr stumbled along behind a small blond-headed girl, he smiled. The girl reminded him of one of his sisters. He was the tenth of twelve children. His mother, Belka, had made her living on the streets. Trevr sighed. Neither he nor any of his brothers and sisters had any idea who their real father might be. But none of them claimed the fat man who sat in his big overstuffed chair and collected the money brought in by their mother.

Hendrk was not only lazy and uncaring when he drank, which was most of the time, but he also was mean to the boys physically and to the girls in other ways. So Trevr felt like he had been sold from evil into evil.

At the port city of Athos, the center of slave trading in Nefarious Reach, Trevr watched as the man with the wicked smile held out his hand and ten silver coins fell into his palm.

He made a good profit, Trevr mused to himself.

Trevr found that a man named Trader Trent had bought him. Trent ran the black market slave trade in Xzwendaria from a large warehouse on the wharf. Trader Trent was a robust man, bald, and wore a black business suit and gold watch, which impressed Trevr. Trent seemed pleased with him and put him on the block early.

"The boy is strong, healthy, and has good teeth," Trader Trent explained to the auctioneer. "He should bring a good price."

Even though he was being sold, Trevr felt proud, for he had indeed brought a good price—twenty silvers. Trevr glanced at Trader Trent. The man's thumbs were stuck in his suspenders, and he was smiling broadly.

Rough hands jostled Trevr aboard a merchant ship docked near the trading block and thrust him down into its dark bowels. Other unseen hands chained him to a post.

Trevr peered into the blackness. He could smell other slaves nearby, and now that the clang of his chains had fallen silent, he could hear them breathing, some wheezing, and some crying. Trevr had already cried all his tears.

Captain Kavadren had Trevr hauled up out of the ship's hold at Belem. As he was pushed toward the gangplank, he heard the first mate ask the captain, "Goin' ta' have 'em made inta' eunuchs before you sell them, right?"

The captain responded, "Well, we certainly don't want 'em defiling our women, do we?" And so a new fear gripped Trevr's heart.

Fear had gripped him ever since a chain had banded his ankle. But when he faced the laughing man with wild eyes and a long razor-sharp knife, he felt absolute terror. A terrible sense of loss ripped at his insides for weeks thereafter. But through it all, he refused to shed a tear.

After his wound healed, the process of being bought and sold continued. In a dingy warehouse on the south of Belem, thirty silver coins dropped. Captain Kvadrn closed his purse strings and pushed Trevr into the arms of his new master named Egrnal, a government official from Aynek.

"You're my nephew." Egrnal dug his fingers into Trevr's shoulder as he spoke. "Your parents died when you were young, and you have come to work for your mother's brother. From this moment on, your name is Tagrt. If you tell anyone otherwise. . ." Egrnal, a powerful man, let go of Trevr's shoulder and whacked the side of Trevr's head with the back of his hand, laying him flat on his back.

Trevr glared at his master but held his tongue.

Egrnal peered down at him. "Ya' understand me, boy?"

Egrnal raised horses for the king. He put Trevr to work cleaning, grooming, and finally breaking horses. Although Trevr worked hard to please his master, Egrnal treated him harshly. Even the most insignificant error would loose the man's wrath. On one occasion, Trevr broke a worn saddle strap.

"You worthless fool!" shouted Egrnal.

"It was wore out," defended Trevr. "Besides, I can repair it."

"Don't answer back to me, boy!

Egrnal's fist flew quicker than Trevr could dodge. Lights flashed in his head. Egrnal's other fist took his wind. After five or six punches to the face and body, Trevr's knees buckled. As he lay half-conscious in the dirt, Trevr swore to himself that when the opportunity presented itself, he would run away.

The strap had broken when Trevr was cinching up the saddle of an extraordinary gray dappled mare that he had just broken for Egrnal. The king had come to the ranch and chosen the dappled mare to be his personal riding horse.

Egrnal's abuses continued, so a month after the beating,
extending blankets and curtains to the ground, Trevr climbed

out his window. He took Egrnal's best saddle and a bedroll from the tack room, along with what supplies he could muster. Then mounting the king's dappled mare, he headed east into the mountains.

Chapter 4

*T*he year Xvardris arrived at Xzadrk's court (745 FBK), Prince Zandirxn turned fourteen. During his growing-up years, the impetuous young prince had stuffed his heart full of resentment. He had felt henpecked by his straight-laced mother and neglected by his always "busy with court business" father. In those early years, Prince Zandirxn held his feelings in check. But his frustration and anger spilled out following his fourteenth birthday.

One day Xvardris found the young prince sauntering, head down and sulking, along a palace hallway.

"And why does the king's son wear such a scowl upon his handsome young face?" chided the charming Pagyn emissary. He laid his arm across the boy's shoulders and gave the prince a gentle squeeze.

The boy recoiled from Xvardris' touch.

"I'm tired of Jentrxn's lectures about learning to be a proper heir to the throne!" spat Zandirxn. "Being a prince is boring! I'm tired of books, and learning, and manners, and . . . and I want to have some fun for a change!"

"A prince should have fun!" agreed the Pagyn ambassador with a wink. "After all, life was meant to be enjoyed. And who should enjoy life more than a prince? Having fun is a prince's right. Why, if you were a prince in the Realm of Amity, you would not be down in the mouth—not at all. In Amity a prince has influence and rules his own destiny. He does as he pleases, not as some second-rate court advisor pleases." Xvardris jacked a shoulder. "But then, you are not a prince in the realm of Amity, so I suppose you will just have to endure your unfortunate circumstances as best you can."

"I wish I were a prince in some other realm!" shot back the disgruntled boy. "What's the good of being a prince in my father's court? He doesn't even know I exist."

"My young friend," Xvardris cajoled, "your father is a good man. Busy, but a good man nonetheless. With the weight of state affairs on his mind, you can't expect him to have time for you. You are a prince, Zandirxn, so act like a prince. Take charge of your own life! Determine your own destiny!"

"I wish it were that simple," whimpered the boy.

"Ah, but it is that simple," said the ambassador. His eyes shifted this way and that, sentinels looking for spies. "I am throwing a party at my villa tonight. Why don't you join my friends and me and find out what it's like to have fun?"

"I would love to go to your party," groused Zandirxn, "but I am not allowed out at night. And my mother would never let me visit your villa. She thinks you're a wretched Pagyn and has told me to stay away from you."

Xvardris laughed and placed his hand on the boy's shoulder. This time he was not rebuffed.

"Old prejudices die slow deaths, my lad," said the ambassador. "But come to my party, and find out for yourself how a wretched Pagyn lives. Like I told you, you must take charge of your own life."

"But my mother. . ."

"Your mother does not have to know where you are going or even that you are out. You're a prince, Zandirxn. If you must, tell your mother you are going to your quarters, then sneak away and come to mine. If you really want to have fun, you'll find a way. It's up to you, my prince."

"I do want to have fun," responded the boy. He kicked at the marble floor in disgust. "And after all, I am a prince!"

"That's the spirit, lad!" Xvardris laughed and gently slapped the boy's back. "Now you're sounding like a true prince." He and gave the young prince a somber look. "Being a prince means being smart, Zandirxn. And being smart means keeping your tongue. I wouldn't tell anyone of this conversation. If Jentrxn or your mother were to get wind of what has passed between us, I'm sure they would make your life even more miserable than it already is. Let these words that have passed between us remain a secret between two men of rank. And if you are missed tonight, tell them you went out on the town, but tell them no more than that, for if they were to learn that you had visited my villa—so much for having fun!"

That night at Xvardris' villa, the young prince had more fun than he had ever had in his life. He drank wine and played fascinating games of chance. But what he liked best was the dancing. As he watched the Pagyn women dance, he became intoxicated with desires he had never before experienced. More! he told himself. I must have more!

The first party led to a second. The second led to a third. And each party brought the young prince further and further into the grip of the Pagyn ambassador. Zandirxn became addicted to the ambassador's offerings. He became dependent on Xvardris to supply his every desire.

As time passed, Jentrxn, the king's trusted advisor, discovered what was happening, but too late to redeem the boy's soul. Rebellion had already fully penetrated the heart of the young prince. Jentrxn brought the boy to his father and accused him of scheming disobedience, lying to cover his tracks, and collusion with the enemy.

"The ambassador is not an enemy, " argued the prince. "We have friendly relations with the Realm of Amity, so I saw nothing wrong with visiting the ambassador's villa. I've only been there a time or two. The visits were harmless!"

The king listened with an impatient scowl etched in his face.

Jentrxn drew in a skeptical breath and shook his head. "Another lie! According to my sources, and they are reliable, visiting the ambassador's villa has become an obsession with you, Zandirxn."

"And why should my father believe 'your sources' and not believe me?" said the prince angrily. "Your sources are jealous courtesans whose singular purpose in life is to get me in trouble. I tell you they are the ones who are liars!"

"Wretched child!" shot back the king's advisor.

"Come, come, Jentrxn," interrupted the king, "aren't you carrying this whole affair a bit far? The good ambassador has been most helpful since he came to court. He has been both prudent and discreet in all our negotiations. He has given me no reason to distrust him. He is both professional and astute, as well as being sensitive to our ways. Zandirxn can learn much from the ambassador. In fact, Xvardris has told me that he has been seeing the boy in order to subject him to a deeper understanding of diplomatic affairs. You are too suspicious, Jentrxn. Ease up on the lad. He has much to learn before he becomes king of Xzwendaria."

"That is the truth!" The king's advisor shot the boy a disapproving look. "But I fear that what Zandirxn learns from that Pagyn will not benefit him or the kingdom."

King Xzadrk laughed.

"Enough! Enough!" he declared. "I have heard all I want to hear of this matter. Away with both of you! I have more important things to see to. Send in the minister of mineral resources, Jentrxn. We must not keep him waiting any longer. We apparently have a thief stealing from my mines at Xzendr. Now that is a matter worthy of my time."

Zandirxn held back the delight he felt at the exasperation he saw in Jentrxn's face. He breathed a sigh of relief as he left his father and Jentrxn and sought refuge in the marbled halls of the palace. He had dreaded the confrontation with his father, but the meeting had turned to his advantage. Now he could freely pursue his relationship with Xvardris without fear of recrimination, thanks to the alibi provided by the Pagyn ambassador. That Xvardris had lied to his father did not bother the young prince at all. In fact, all that mattered to Zandirxn was that the parties would continue, and the fun would go on.

He laughed in Jentrxn's face when he came out from the king's chamber to receive the minister of mineral resources. And that was the end of the boy's relationship with wisdom. The young prince gave himself utterly to folly—with his father's unwitting approval.

Chapter 5

Zandirxn's excessive appetites soon craved more than Xvardris' parties offered. A month before the prince's seventeenth birthday, he trekked from the Pagyn ambassador's villa to the palace and saw a beautiful young woman. As she passed by, he gently reached out and caught her arm. "Excuse my brashness," he said with a playful lilt to his voice. "But I simply have to meet you. May I ask your name?"

The girl's face turned red, and she pulled away. "My name is Patrexna," she said in a cautious tone.

Zandirxn bowed slightly. "Well, Patrexna, I am Prince Zandirxn."

Patrexna's eyebrows raised and she blushed even more deeply. She dared a sheepish smile. When he smiled back, she looked at the ground, avoiding the boldness of his gaze.

Zandirxn ran his eyes over the girl's body, and desire flared from a spark to a blazing flame. "How old are you, Patrexna?" He reached out and touched her hair.

"Sixteen," she whispered.

"The age of innocence," he responded softly. The prince lifted her chin, forcing her to meet his eyes. He spoke softly. "Patrexna, have you ever. . .you know, done things with a boy?"

"Of course not!" she stammered and looked away.

"That is a good thing," he murmured in return. He let his hand move to her shoulder and run gently down her arm. "I meant no offense, Patrexna. Would you walk with me? It is lonely being a prince. I could use a friend right now." He reached out and took her hand.

Her whole body shuddered at his touch, but she did not pull away. "What will my friends say when they find out I have walked hand in hand with a prince?"

"Yes, what would your friends say? And to whom?" mused the prince in a pensive tone. He put a finger to his lips. "And for that very reason, you must not tell your friends. This must remain your secret and mine. If my father, the king, were to hear that I was walking about the city holding hands with a common girl of the streets. . . . Well, I'm sure you understand."

"Oh, I do! I do!" said Patrexna. "I guess I was not thinking."

The prince laughed. "Yes, this night must remain a secret. . .always a secret."

As the sun slowly slipped toward the horizon, Zandirxn and Patrexna walked the byways of the city talking about his life at court—romanticized, of course—and her life and family. The prince patiently charmed the young girl with kind gestures and sweet words while holding his fiery inner passions in check.

Time found them walking a lonely path that meandered alongside the Xzwendar River in the greenbelt on the south side of the city. When they came to a wooded area, Patrexna noticed a breeze moving the leaves of a stand of poplar trees. "The fluttering leaves create such a magical aura," she said. "Isn't it wonderful?"

"Indeed, it is," responded the prince. Still holding her hand, he headed off the path. "Now, let me show you the loveliest meadow in the kingdom."

Patrexna's eyes danced with joy, as she hurried along beside him. They passed through the stand of poplars and came to a beautiful flowered meadow. Patrexna gasped in awe. "Look! Over there beyond the meadow, a weeping willow. Isn't it beautiful?"

Zandirxn's eyes were not on the willow tree.

When Patrexna turned and met his gaze, fear gripped her breast.

There in the loveliest meadow in the realm, Prince Zandirxn picked the realm's loveliest flower, cast it on the ground, and defiled it. When he rose from his vile deed, he laughed and walked away.

Patrexna watered the crushed flowers beneath her with tears.

Several months later, in the very place they had first met, Patrexna confronted Zandirxn as he made his way once again to Xvardris' villa. He tried to ignore her, but she caught him by the arm. "My lord, I am with child," she said in a hoarse whisper. Her hopeful eyes sought his.

The young prince's face turned red with rage. "Who have you told?" he grated.

"No one, my lord!" she gasped, and began to weep.

"Stop it!" Zandirxn grabbed her by her hair and jerked her head to one side. "If you tell even one soul that I am your child's father, you are a dead woman!" Sneering, -he pushed her aside and walked away.

When Zandirxn arrived at the ambassador's villa, he drew Xvardris aside and told him about Patrexna. "The wretched wench bears my child," he complained. "What do I do now?"

Xvardris laughed, putting his arm around the prince's shoulders and moving off to a quiet corner. "It is no great matter," he said. "I have an illegitimate child of my own. But tell me, does anyone else know about your relationship with the girl, or that she is pregnant with your child?"

"No, no one," said Zandirxn. "Why?"

"It is best if no one knows," responded Xvardris. As he removed his arm from around the prince, he gave his shoulder a gentle squeeze. "Worry about it no more. I will take care of the matter."

"Does that mean. . . you know?" asked the prince. Guilt sculpted his face.

Xvardris met the boy's eyes. "Yes, it does, Zandirxn. Does that bother you? Or perhaps you would rather have the girl and child haunting you from the shadows?"

"No, not at all," returned the prince with a forced laugh.

Zandirxn returned to the party. The ambassador watched the prince thoughtfully until he disappeared among the guests. He shook his head. *He's actually relieved at the idea of having the girl killed*, he thought. *He is a despicable creature. And he has become utterly incorrigible as well.*

That same hour Xvardris sent for his slave, Zanzxra, the Black Assassin. But while he waited for Zanzxra to arrive, he changed his mind about killing the girl. He smiled wickedly. Perhaps a living child is even better than a dead child, he mused. Then an idea took form, and a wry smile crossed his face. I have a better assignment for my slave.

When Zanzxra arrived, Xvardris gave him detailed instructions. A scowl registered the Black Assassin's disappointment. "There will be other opportunities," Xvardris assured him.

His slave showed no further emotion. He turned on his heels and left.

Far from Xvardris' villa, Patrexna made her way up the stairs of the temple, leading a goat for sacrifice. It was all she had to give.

Thaxndar accepted her sacrifice and prayed for her.

Kanderxn saw the girl enter the temple, and struck by her beauty, sought a vantage point from which he could watch her undetected by Thaxndar.

Whew! he whistled silently from behind a partition of latticework covered with ivy. She is the most beautiful girl I have ever seen!

But as he completed the thought, Thaxndar's words and the girl's response arrested his attention. He had not intended to overhear her confession. He knew he should slip away, but curiosity overpowered his sense of guilt.

"Would you like to tell me about it, Patrexna?" asked the priest. "It might help if you share your burden. Carrying such a weight all alone can be an awful strain."

"If I share what tears at my heart, you must promise to tell no one," begged the girl.

Kanderxn swallowed hard. He could not bring himself to do what he knew he should. He pressed back into the shadows remaining utterly silent, except his heart pounded so loud that he thought surely he would be found out. In fact, in order to hear their conversation over the noise of his heartbeat, he had to stick his ear to the latticework. He felt pangs of guilt but listened anyway.

Back at Xvardris' villa, Zandirxn was enjoying himself, and Patrexna no longer had any place in his thoughts. Three of the ambassador's slave girls were fawning over him. What followed the fawning is not for lips to tell or ears to hear. But Zandirxn felt no sense of remorse or guilt.

When the prince had had his fill of perverse entertainment, one of the slave girls brought him a goblet of wine.

Xvardris watched from behind a curtain as the indulgent prince guzzled it down.

The young prince wiped his mouth with the back of his hand. He sighed. "Well, it's late, and I've. . .I've got to get back to the palace," he slurred. Grinning, he tossed the golden goblet to a slave girl and excused himself with a promise to return the next night. Another slave girl took his arm and walked him to the gate and partway down the street.

"I feel sick," complained the prince. He tried to shake the cobwebs from his head. "Too much wine. . .and maybe too much of you and your friends."

"You can never get too much of us, can you, my lord?" said the slave girl. She suddenly stopped in her tracks, and her face went sober. "I must return to the villa. Xvardris will be angry if he finds that I'm gone."

"I'll be all right," said Zandirxn. He gave the girl a groping embrace, bade her farewell, made a tipsy sort of turn, and staggered up the road. The slave girl watched with a knowing smile.

Suddenly, a black-clad arm reached out and pulled the prince into the shadows. Before Zandirxn could cry for help, the man's cudgel brought darkness.

The next day, when Zandirxn awoke, he felt sick to his stomach, and his head throbbed. Above his right ear, he found a nasty lump."I was mugged!" he wailed. When he cried out, he became aware of a knifing pain between his legs. He groaned as his hand sought the source of the pain. "Blood?" he whimpered. As he gazed at the red wetness on his hand, his eyes rolled back in his head, and he passed out again.

Zandirxn found his father and told him about the mugging. "I'll bet it was a slave trader who tried to carry me off!" The boy shook with anger. "It may be against the law, but you know as well as I do that it still goes on."

Zandirxn did not tell his father that he had been made a eunuch. He got rid of the bloody clothes and told no one.

"Why am I walking like this?" he responded to his father's questioning. "The wretched mugger kicked me in the kidneys! The pain is terrible!"

"I will call for the healer," said the king.

Zandirxn's eyes went wide. "See a healer?" He shook his head. "No, father, I do not need a healer. I'll be fine."

Xzadrk ordered his elite guard to find the person who dared accost the prince of Xzwendaria, but the prince could tell them nothing helpful. Their search proved futile.

The prince was not seen in public for more than a week. At court a genial Xvardris inquired about him and was told that he was not feeling well.

"Do greet him in my behalf and express my concern for a speedy recovery," offered the ambassador in a solemn tone. He turned away, his eyes alight with mirth.

Chapter 6

Zandirxn returned to his normal activities a changed man, somber and withdrawn. No fits of frivolity, no obnoxious boldness. He kept to himself and said little.

Xvardris sought out the young prince. "Zandirxn, I have not seen you in days—nearly two weeks, actually." The ambassador maintained a gentle, compelling tone. "I suppose you are aware of the rumors."

Zandirxn looked away. "What rumors?" he muttered.

"Oh!" Xvardris let his eyes go wide. "Well, on the one hand, people are saying that you have some dread disease. On the other, word has it that some ruffian assaulted you. I am in the dark as to the truth of the matter."

"I don't have any terrible disease! I was mugged and beaten," complained Zandirxn. "It was terrible. I've never hurt so bad in my life!"

"Well, you're better now," chimed Xvardris brightly. "And I must say, Kardis, Vilkina, and Beldara have missed you. In fact, Kardis has been worried sick about you. I'm throwing a party tonight. Why don't you come?"

"No," protested the prince. He shrugged a shoulder. "I cannot come. I wish I could, but no, not tonight."

"Come, come," mocked Xvardris teasingly. "That is not like you, Zandirxn. There is surely something you are not telling me."

Zandirxn's face went red. "It's nothing," he grated.

Xvardris pressed him yet further. "I thought I was your friend, Zandirxn. Perhaps I was wrong." He turned to walk away.

"Please don't go!" said the prince. Then fighting back tears, he told Xvardris everything.

"I am stunned!" The ambassador put his hand to his brow and then shook his head in feigned disbelief. "That is terrible! But. . .it's not the end of the world."

"Humph!" was the extent of Zandirxn's reply.

"I must say," continued Xvardris, "it is a good thing I changed my mind about the girl."

"You mean you didn't have her. . . You know. . ."

Xvardris smiled and shook his head. "She is alive," he assured him.

Zandirxn breathed a great sigh, as if a weight had been removed from his back. "So I will have an heir to sit on the throne someday!" he crooned.

There was loathing in the ambassador's glance, but he covered it quickly. "The girl being so pretty and heavy with child, I could not bring myself to do her harm. It just was not in me. I'm not that kind of man, Zandirxn."

"Are they at your villa?" The princes's eyes flashed with urgency.

"No, they are not here in Zwexdrof. That would not do." Xvardris raised an eyebrow. "I sent her away. But she and the child are being well cared for."

"You must bring her back immediately. I will marry her and claim the child as my own."

"My prince, do not be so hasty." The ambassador cast Zandirxn a reproving gaze. "Bringing her back would create an instant scandal. Your right to the throne might even come into question. No, they cannot safely return until after you are king. In fact, it is imperative that no one know of their existence until you have the kingdom in hand."

Zandirxn clenched his fists, and fire danced in his eyes. "But who knows when that might be?" he chafed.

"Patience, my prince." Xvardris touched a gentle hand to his arm. "Your father grows old. Our. . . your day will come."

"Humph! He grows old too slowly!" spat the prince, oblivious to Xvardris' slip of tongue.

The ambassador nodded and again encouraged patience.

A grimace creased Zandirxn's brow, and he shook his head dejectedly. "I don't even remember her name." He glanced at Xvardris. "Where did you send her?"

"It's best if you do not know," said the ambassador. He laid a hand on the prince's shoulder. "Trust me in this. I have only your welfare in mind, Zandirxn."

"But why should I not know where she is?"

"What you do not know, you cannot accidentally tell. And what you cannot tell cannot be used against you," said the ambassador curtly. He was growing tired of the conversation. Nor did he tell Zandirxn the girl's name.

The young prince was not happy with the arrangement, but he had no choice but to accept it.

"Now, what about that party at my villa? Good food, wine, and dancing women. It will lift your spirits."

"I suppose," caved in Zandirxn.

Kardis, Vilkina, and Beldara met Zandirxn at the villa door. The slave girls did not mind that he was a eunuch, and in spite of his embarrassment, they soon had him reveling in new perversions.

Chapter 7

With the passing of each day, Zandirxn felt more and more driven to take his rightful place as king of Xzwendaria.

Xvardris outwardly encouraged patience. "Look, Zandirxn, your father is getting old, and one of these nights as he sleeps on his couch he will simply quit breathing."

Xvardris repeated the statement on numerous occasions like a mantra, and the words echoed to distraction in Zandirxn's mind. "He will simply quit breathing. He will simply quit breathing. He will simply quit breathing."

And Xvardris, smiling knowingly, watched the young prince struggle with his thoughts.

On the event of his twenty-fifth birthday, Zandirxn lay on his couch late in the evening musing on his misfortunes since he had forced himself on the young girl, whatever her name. He grimaced. Ascending the throne would put all those miserable trials behind him. "I deserve to be happy!" he grumbled aloud. "I'm not getting any younger, and my father doesn't seem to be getting any older. At sixty-six he's as lively and strong as he was at forty. He'll never die! What does Xvardris know?" He lay there arms crossed while his angry eyes attempted to pierce the ceiling above. "It isn't fair!" he whined. "He should have died last summer!" That was the summer his mother had died, but he had shed no tears for her. And I'll shed even fewer for Father!

And at that moment a wicked thought broke his pensive mood. "Hmm. Yes, he will simply quit breathing," he whispered to himself. His eyes suddenly took on the appearance of a wild animal hungry for prey. A sardonic smirk creased his face. He slipped from his couch and stole to his father's bedchamber. He reached out a trembling hand and turned the handle. Holding his breath, he slowly pushed the door open.

Xzadrk lay on his back, his chest rhythmically rising and falling—a wheezy inhale and a noisy exhale.

Zandirxn, his sweat-beaded face contorted as if holding back laughter, slipped into the room, took a pillow from a couch near the door, and stepped cautiously toward his father's bed. But when Xzadrk moved an arm and made a loud snuffing noise, Zandirxn started, his face went white, and his hands quivered. "What if he wakes up and finds me standing over him with this pillow in my hands?" he whimpered to himself. Then, like a craving hellcat, he pounced.

His father's eyes opened, and Zandirxn met surprise mingled with sadness. Then the pillow came between.

From that moment to the day he died, whenever Zandirxn closed his eyes, he saw his father lying lifeless on his bed staring up at him. But he felt no remorse or regret, only guilt. And now, as he quietly fled his father's bedchamber, he sneered and muttered, "The throne is mine at last! I, Zandirxn, am king of Xzwendaria!"

The people of the realm were stunned at the news that King Xzadrk had unexpectedly died in his sleep. They mourned the loss of their beloved king, while lamenting the rise of Prince Zandirxn to the throne. And they also shuddered at the thought of the influence the ambassador from Amity would have on their young monarch. For in spite of Xvardris' ability to mesmerize kings and princes, the vast majority of the people were not charmed and did not trust him.

Zandirxn's first official action after his coronation was to get rid of his father's advisors, especially Jentrxn. And although Xvardris was still the ambassador of Amity, Zandirxn provided him with chambers and quarters at the palace, and Xvardris became the young king's closest advisor. However, all was not well between the king and his chosen advisor, for when Zandirxn became sovereign of the realm, he also became obstinate and autocratic. He called for his advisor and faced him with grim determination. "Xvardris, you will immediately return my mistress and child to Zwexdrof." He grated.

"Your mistress?" chided Xvardris. "You mean the woman you raped, don't you?"

Zandirxn's face went red. "You'll watch your tongue, Xvardris! You may be my advisor, but I am king of this realm." His face contorted to a caustic sneer, and he leaned back in his throne and crossed his arms. "You will return the woman and child immediately!"

Xvardris bowed slightly. "My lord, I will send for them at the appropriate time."

The king jerked forward. "Now is the appropriate time!" he barked.

Xvardris laughed, turned his back, and walked away. However, to mollify Zandirxn's anger, Xvardris gave him the three slave girls, Kardis, Vilkina, and Beldara, who distracted the king sufficiently to provide an uneasy peace in the palace.

Further, in return for Xvardris' gift of the slave girls, Zandirxn allowed him to build a temple to Bayl. The people protested loudly, but the king ignored them. In truth, he hoped his gesture of goodwill would be revisited in kind by the ambassador, that he would return Patrexna and his child. However, that was not to be.

And so the Black Chancel, as it was to be called, began to be built in Zwexdrof. From the apex of a hill that overlooked the city, its dark presence would eventually cast a menacing shadow that would cause the people to tremble with fear.

Thaxndar came before the king and expressed people's concern at the building of a Pagyn temple.

The king laughed and spat on the floor. "They are my people, not yours, priest. Are you jealous for your position?"

"Jealous for my position?" Thaxndar shook his head. The corner of his mouth upward. "No, my king, I am jealous for Baruch whom you have forsaken in order to build a temple to a false god. Furthermore, it is forbidden for the kings of Xzwendaria to maintain concubines, and you have taken three."

"You speak of Baruch, and yet when I enter your temple, I see no god. Perhaps Bayl who will inhabit the Black Chancel is the true god and your so-called Majesty, the false. And as for concubines, I am the king and I will do as I please."

The priest shook his head. "No, Zandirxn, you are not a king. You are little more than a selfish, manipulated despot."

Zandirxn came from his throne, teeth gnashing, and his body trembling with anger. He pointed a quaking finger toward the door. "Leave this chamber and never return. If I ever see your face again, I'll clamp you in an iron mask and chain you to a wall in my dungeon."

After Thaxndar left his chamber, the king enacted a new law that negated the old law concerning concubines. "There!" he declared, lifting his chin proudly. And from that day on, he sneered at any mention of Baruch.

Kardis, one of the king's slave concubines, had visions of marrying Zandirxn and sharing his throne. However, Xvardris stood in the way of her ambition. Kardis, aware that the ambassador was using the king as a puppet, shared dark secrets with Zandirxn. "You know that Xvardris intends to usurp your throne, don't you? He told me as much himself," she whispered. "And I don't suppose you are aware that he is the one responsible for your, uh, unmanly condition?"

Zandirxn's face went white. Now the king was not a wise man, but he was clever enough to realize that what Kardis told him was true. The reality of it jolted him into a fit of madness. He hurried to his throne room and demanded the ambassador's presence.

"I don't know whether I should banish you from the kingdom or have you executed!" The king's voice quavered with anger. "Your days of influence are over, Xvardris. You are finished. Do you hear me? Finished! No one uses me and gets away with it! No one!"

Xvardris smiled and jacked an eyebrow. "Powerful words, my lord. Yes, powerful words."

"Do not mock me, Pagyn! " Zandirxn came to his feet. Fire flashed in his eyes, and hate contorted his face. "I am king of this realm!"

Xvardris gave a slight nod. "Yes, and you have but one heir to the throne." The ambassador's smile faded. "Oh, by the way, your illegitimate offspring is a boy." He shook his head. "It interests me that you never asked and that when you spoke of him, he was always just the child. He means nothing to you, and yet that he is your only heir does mean something to you, doesn't it? And he is in my hands, Zandirxn. And should anything unfortunate happen to me, he will die." Xvardris grinned and gazed at the king.

The color drained from Zandirxn's face, and his body went limp. Slowly he sank back into the safety of his throne.

"That's better, Zandirxn." The ambassador grinned broadly. "I think we shall get along just fine now that we understand each other. You sit on the throne. I rule the kingdom. A rather nice arrangement, don't you think? So from this time forward, I will make all decisions that relate to state affairs. "

Tears coursed down Zandirxn's cheeks. He turned his head and closed his eyes to rid himself of Xvardris, but from the darkness his father stared back at him. He grabbed at his hair and cried out. His eyes shot open again, and he shuddered.

Xvardris scowled. "You never will grow up, will you?" he muttered.

Zandirxn glared at the ambassador but said nothing.

"You know, Zandirxn, duping you was the easy part of my plan, other than the fact that you were a despicable creature to have to fawn over. But thankfully, I no longer have to pretend to like you."

Xvardris turned and walked out of the throne room. From behind him, he could hear the king snuffling in self-pity and mumbling something about revenge.

Chapter 8

After telling Thaxndar the details of her situation, Patrexna had agreed to tell her parents as well. She also said she would return the next week and let Thaxndar know how it had gone. But one week became two. Two weeks became three. Another week passed, and concerned for the girl's welfare, the priest went to her home. Thaxndar knocked on the plain wooden door.

A man with unnatural pouches darkening his eyes and a frown creasing his brow, answered. It was obvious to Thaxndar that the man was grappling with deep disquiet. Yet, as the man's eyes took in Thaxndar's priestly robe, his countenance glimmered with hope. "Markta, it's a priest!" he called over his shoulder.

Markta came running. Thaxndar noted that in spite of her years, she was a lovely woman. Still, lines of distress marred the beauty of her countenance.

"Jorfindel, have they found our Patrexna?" Hope rode the edge of her voice. She turned to Thaxndar. "Is she all right?"

The priest smiled but hesitated in his response.

The old man and woman heard what he did not say. Hope drained from their eyes. Fresh tears trickled down their cheeks.

"Your daughter came to me four weeks ago," said Thaxndar.

"Why did she come to you?" questioned Markta.

"Didn't she tell you?" Thaxndar raised a bushy eyebrow.

"She said nothing about having visited a priest."

Despair edged Markta's voice. "It has been that many weeks since we last saw our Patrexna," interjected Jorfindel. "She had not been herself for more than a month, but I cannot imagine that she would run away without so much as a word to Markta or me. Where would she go? Surely something terrible has happened to our poor Patrexna. Why else would she not come home?"

"Before she left the house that morning, she said she had something important to take care of," put in Markta. "She took her pet goat and headed up the street. We have not seen her since."

"We've inquired of the city guard," fretted Jorfindel. "They told us that they found nothing that would tell them where she might have gone but they would contact those who might know where she went. When I opened the door and saw you standing there, I thought perhaps you had come to tell us that she had sought refuge at the temple."

"Jorfindel, our Patrexna would not run away!" wailed Markta. "She carried some weight on her heart. Remember how she said that she loved us and that her sadness had nothing to do with us? She said it was just something she had to work out. Our Patrexna would never run away!"

Thaxndar laid his hand softly on her trembling shoulder as she sobbed. He did not tell Markta and Jorfindel that he too felt certain the girl had not run away. He suspected treachery, probably at the hands of King Zandirxn. "I'll do what I can to help you find your daughter," he said.

"Please! Please!" they pled through their tears.

Thaxndar left Jorfindel and Markta and went straight to the palace. Once again he confronted the prince.

Zandirxn mocked the priest for his gullibility and claimed ignorance. "I suppose every girl in Zwexdrof has illusions of meeting a prince and carrying his baby. You have a scandalous imagination. I know nothing of this girl you speak of nor does Xvardris know anything of her." He took a deep breath, leaned forward on his throne and glared at the priest. "And furthermore, I told you I never wanted to see your face again."

He desperately wanted to have the priest thrown in his dungeon, but what if Baruch was real? He leaned back. "My dungeon longs for your flesh, but I feel gracious today. However, priest, do not press me further."

"The girl has disappeared. Her parents grieve for her." Thaxndar ignored Zandirxn's threat. "What have you done with the girl, Zandirxn?"

The prince's face turned red, and his knuckles went white as he pushed himself up from his throne. "Don't press me, priest! I don't know what has become of your street urchin. But I do know that you have overstayed your welcome. You found your way in; now find your way out!"

A scowl crossed Thaxndar's face. This time he detected an element of truth in the prince's words.

He stared fixedly at the prince. "As you wish," he said.

Zandirxn grimaced and turned his gaze off to the side at an ornately painted wall. Ignoring the priest, he flicked the back of his hand toward the door.

Thaxndar's shoulders sagged as he left the prince's chamber with Patrexna's disappearance remaining a mystery. He rehearsed the conversation in his mind and wondered why Zandirxn made a point of the fact that Xvardris knew nothing of the girl. "Zandirxn knows far more than he is admitting to," muttered the priest. "And it would appear that the Pagyn ambassador had something to do with Patrexna's disappearance." When Thaxndar returned to the temple, he sought out his young aide.

Kanderxn had nearly reached the far end of the long temple corridor when he heard the echo of footsteps behind him. He turned to find his grim-faced mentor hurrying toward him. He waited.

"Kander, there is a girl named Patrexna who came to me here at the temple sometime back," said the priest as he caught up with him.

Kanderxn had never told Thaxndar of his eavesdropping in the temple sanctuary. Nor did he tell him now. He had brought a sacrifice, and he considered the incident behind him. The color drained from his face. How did he find out? he wondered. But aloud he simply mumbled, "Yes?"

"She has disappeared, and her parents are worried sick about her. I would like to enlist your help in finding her."

Kanderxn tried not to show any outward sign of the relief he felt. "I'd be glad to help," he responded. He was more than willing to accommodate Thaxndar in any way he could. He felt like it would somehow help absolve him of his error in judgment. Besides, he might get to see the young beauty again.

"Xvardris, the ambassador for Nefarious Reach may have had something to do with the girl's disappearance," explained Thaxndar. "You must tell absolutely no one that you are looking for Patrexna. If those who took her knew that you were looking for her, you might disappear as well, and I would not like that."

Kanderxn hiked a shoulder and gave Thaxndar a helpless look. "But I have no idea where to begin looking for her."

"You can begin by watching the ambassador's villa. But be careful!" said Thaxndar. "And I'm sorry I cannot tell you more, but I assure you, finding the girl is of utmost importance."

Outside the temple, Kanderxn allowed a wry smile. That he knew more than Thaxndar realized gave him a feeling of importance but also a sense of urgency. He feared for Patrexna, but even more so for her child who was heir to the throne of Xzwendaria.

Wearing shabby clothes, Kander hung around the ambassador's villa begging alms. The people who came and went treated him with disdain, and yet many were generous with their coins. Others apparently complained, because after several days, a burly guard took him by the cuff and gave him a shove toward the road. "Away with you, ya' wretched beggar! You've bothered people quite enough!"

After a day or two of begging farther down the street, he returned. They endured his presence for a few days and then shooed him off again. However, when he wandered back down the street near the villa a day later, it became obvious the guards' patience was wearing thin. "Yer a persistent fool, aren't you, ya' Spunger?" complained one of Xvardris' watchdogs.

Kander begged from a distance while moving closer each day. But by the third day, he was too close, and the Pagyns threatened him with bodily harm.

One guard poked a spear at his chest and declared in a gruff voice, "Listen, Spunger, I understand that you have a livin' to make, but you had best find somewhere else to make it. If I see yer' face anywhere near this gate again, you'll be suckin' water at the bottom of the Xzwendar River!"

"You can't do that!" complained Kanderxn. "Beggars have rights, you know."

The guard pushed the tip of his spear into Kanderxn's chest, drawing blood.

A second guard stepped forward and gave Kander a shove, causing him to fall. "We execute beggars in our country, and legal or not, we'll do it here too! Now off with ya!"

The first guard prodded him to his feet with his spear. Kander stumbled away from him. The guard laughed and then growled, "You been warned; now don't come back."

"Drat, I'm not learning anything by watching the Pagyn's villa," Kander grumbled to himself. He set off to other parts of the city. Perhaps back-alley information would prove more productive. He mingled with the rest of the city's beggars and bums. Nothing! He took the guise of the tradesmen that frequented the inns. Again, nothing! He took his begging money and bought a peddler's cart. He pushed his wares and pried for information on just about every street corner in Zwexdrof but to no avail.

Kander reported back to Thaxndar. The priest smiled patiently. "Keep looking," he told Kanderxn. And so he relentlessly searched for Patrexna, yet without uncovering even the smallest of clues. As far as he or Thaxndar could tell, she had simply vanished from the face of the earth.

Then in 760 FBK, more than five years after Patrexna disappeared, the complexion of things in Zwexdrof, and for that matter, in all Xzwendaria, changed. Tragedy struck the realm! And it was in the midst of the upheaval that Kanderxn got his first inkling as to what had become of Patrexna and her child.

Chapter 9

King Zandirxn despised pompous dignitaries, along with making decisions about meaningless projects in far-flung cities, none of which benefited him in any personal way. Furthermore, he hated the tedious task of signing documents.

So one evening, as was his habit after a boring day of doing things a king is required to do, he feasted on roast boar, smoked duck, and other favored delicacies. Then, once he had eaten his fill, again as was his habit, he called Kardis, Vilkina, and Beldara to his bedchamber that he might in turn feed his carnal appetites to what degree he was able.

In the midst of his perverse sporting, he called for wine. Vilkina and Beldara glanced at each other and giggled. A somber-faced porter brought a wicker-covered bottle and the king's silver chalice. Beldara poured the wine, winked at Vilkina, and handed the chalice to Kardis to give to the king. Kardis was the king's favorite of the three slave girls, and he would only drink from her hand. She lifted the cup to his pursed lips. He took a slurping sip, then opened his mouth, and she poured a stream of wine into his throat. When the chalice was empty, he wiped his mouth on his arm and fell back on his pillows laughing raucously. "Now, this is living," he bellowed.

As the king spoke, Xvardris stepped from behind the curtain that divided the king's bedroom from his dressing chamber.

The king lifted his head. His eyes went wide, and his laughter died. His mouth twisted to a sneer. "How dare you invade my private chamber? You are not invited to this party. Leave us!" he growled.

Xvardris cast Zandirxn a roguish smile and made no move to leave.

Zandirxn pointed a slightly wavering finger at the ambassador. "I... am the king, and I command... you to leave my bedchamber... at once!"

Xvardris continued to ignore the king's command.

"Zandirxn, what was it like the night that you killed your father?" The ambassador raised his eyebrows and glowered at the naked potentate. "Did he wake up before you killed him? Did you see the terror in his eyes? I presume you suffocated him. Or was it poison?"

Xvardris shifted his cold eyes to the king's empty chalice. Vilkina and Beldara sniggered like small children. Kardis looked from Xvardris to the chalice, and her eyes went wide with horror.

Zandirxn too stared at the empty cup. His panic-stricken gaze shifted to Xvardris. "You wouldn't dare!" His voice quavered as he spoke. "I am the king!"

"What you are is a fool. And I have grown weary of you."

With fists clenched, fire in his eyes, and rage contorting his face, Zandirxn rose from his pillows. However, just as his feet hit the marble floor, his tremulous body stiffened. He clasped his hands to his chest. Terror sheeting his face, he opened his mouth to speak, but no words came. He convulsed once, twice, and then fell back on his bed, eyes gaping blankly at the ceiling.

Kardis wept.

Vilkina and Beldara broke into defiant, mocking laughter—their hatred satisfied.

"Kardis," said Xvardris, "do you weep for the king or for yourself?" His voice resonated coldness. "When Zandirxn became king, it seems you let ambition distort your sense of loyalty. It grieves me that you conspired to undermine my efforts and position. Not a bright choice, Kardis." He sighed and glanced down at the dead king. "You know, the poor fool even talked of having me executed." His fiery eyes shifted back to meet the eyes of the now trembling slave girl. "That wasn't your idea was it, Kardis?"

"Of course not, Xvardris!" she whimpered. "I have always been loyal to you. He forced the information out of me. Really he did. They'll tell you!" She looked to Vilkina and Beldara for help.

Their faces were lined with contempt.

"Fill the king's chalice with wine," ordered the ambassador.

Vilkina giggled and picked up the chalice. She held it out to Beldara, who with a likewise cheerful countenance poured the sweet, red liquid into the king's silver cup.

"No, Xvardris, please!" begged Kardis. "I'll do anything for you, anything!"

Xvardris nodded to Vilkina. She held out the cup.

Kardis backed away, refusing to take the chalice.

The stoic ambassador grimaced. "So you'd rather face Zanzxra," he commented calmly. The assassin stepped from the shadows. Blood lust leached from the dark eyes that looked out from the black mask. The blade of the long knife he held in his huge hand sparkled menacingly.

"It is up to you, Kardis." The corner of Xvardris' mouth twitched upward to form a smirk. "The chalice or the Black Assassin?"

With hot tears running down delicate red cheeks, Kardis reached out and took the chalice from Vilkina's hand. Her whole body trembled as faltering fingers wrapped around the neck of the chalice. Drops of red wine splashed from the cup to fall like drops of blood on the king's naked form. Kardis didn't notice. Her sad eyes looked at Xvardris, then at Vilkina and Beldara who glowered at her with disdain. She avoided looking at the assassin. She closed her eyes, shutting them all out, lifted the cup to her trembling lips, and drank. Moments later, her pretty young form lay draped across the king.

Vilkina and Beldara tittered with glee. "Wretched girl!" they each declared in turn. However, their thoughts did not dwell long with the dead, for they were anxious to receive the reward Xvardris had promised.

The ambassador cast them a passing smile as he turned to leave the room.

"What of our reward?" Beldara squeaked expectantly.

Xvardris stopped. He slowly turned and faced the slave girls. His eyes effused coldness. "Was not watching them die reward enough?" he said.

The slave girls' faces blanched with disappointment. They had expected more. Their eyes pleaded.

The ambassador of good will smiled kindly. "Very well," he said.

Instantly, Beldara and Vilkina's dismay turned to silly giggles.

The ambassador turned to the hooded assassin who stood beside the door with knife in hand, dark eyes watching. "Zanzxra, you are their reward. They know too much. Dispose of them as pleases you."

The next morning word that the king had gone mad (of course, the people were confident he was mad to begin with), had killed his concubines and then himself spread through Zwexdrof like a wind-driven fire. But the most stunning news of all was the fact that Xvardris, the Pagyn ambassador, had declared himself king of Xzwendaria. And although the people disdained the ambassador, his usurpation of the throne would go unchallenged, for during the previous two years, while Zandirxn had played at being king, Xvardris had surreptitiously moved his own people into positions of authority and influence in the palace and the city. Furthermore, Xvardris barred Thaxndar and Jentrxn, priest and advisor to the king's father, from entering the palace.

So with two draughts of wine, the Pagyn invaders took Xzwendaria for themselves. Zandirxn drank the first cup while still a prince—a draught that destroyed his soul, and as king he drank the second cup, which cost him his life.

Chapter 10

Kanderxn's search for Patrexna eventually took him away from Zwexdrof. He reasoned that Xvardris was not so stupid as to confine the heir to the throne in Xzwendaria, let alone in Zwexdrof. He further reasoned it likely that the Pagyn ambassador had shipped Patrexna across the Ardent Sea to Athos. Thus, Kanderxn's search took him to the Xzwendarian port cities of Belem and Avard.

Wearing the blues and whites of a sailor, Kander wandered the waterfront at Belem, frequenting places seamen haunted when they weren't hoisting sails. And as in Zwexdrof, he found himself pursuing one dead-end lead after another. Nothing, he complained to himself.

News came of King Zandirxn's death and Xvardris' rise to power. Kanderxn grimaced in disgust along with the sailor who told him. However, he was not surprised at the turn of events. He had long expected Xvardris to usurp the throne. To him it had simply been a question of when.

Kander's search for Patrexna and the heir to the throne of Xzwendaria took on more urgency than ever. He left Belem and headed northeast to Avard. Again he learned nothing. He had spent three weeks in Avard and had no idea where to look next. I have wasted six months, he carped. It irritated him that on the morrow he would return to Zwexdrof and have to tell Thaxndar he had failed in his quest.

He pushed open the doors of a dank inn called the Sailor's Rack. He walked in stoop-shouldered and with his head hanging low. He had been there more times than he could count. This would be the last.

After ordering a meal, he noticed a sailor he had not seen before. He shrugged a shoulder, took up his food, strolled over, sat down across from the man, and struck up a conversation.

"Sailor?" The man shook his head. "Never been on a ship in my life," he laughed and winked at Kander. "Name's Burggen. Yours?"

"Kanderxn. So what do you do?" asked Kander. "Your clothes say you're a sailor."

"Will be a sailor, but until last week I worked for the Viper Run Horse Train. Yep, worked for 'em for the last ten years. Did maintenance at Yep's Station." The man ran a hand through his hair. "Had enough of all that heat. Decided I needed a change. So tomorrow I ship out on the Red Dawn."

"Well, at least out on the frontier you didn't have to put up with the wretched Pagyns that have been swarming about the realm recently," jibed Kander. He let his gaze wander around the room, hoping to spot a sailor to pump for information about slave trade with Athos—someone who might have seen Patrexna.

"In the whole ten years, I only saw two Pagyns," responded Burggen. Kander paid him little attention. "Tw'er about five years ago. They were escortin' to somewhere the most beautiful young woman ya' ever did see. I remember 'cause she were so pretty and 'cause I couldn't imagine takin' a pregnant woman out into the Savage Lands." The man cut a broad grin. "But then, they were with Pegran so they probably fared all right."

The sailor's story regained Kanderxn's attention. He leaned forward on the table. "So who is Pegran?"

Burggen laughed. "Pegran is Andrapegran the Second. He's a rogue."

"A rogue?" Kanderxn jacked an eyebrow.

"He's a loner that wanders the Savage Lands living as he pleases, where he pleases, comin' and goin' when he pleases." The corners of Burggen's mouth turned upward. "Not that anywhere out in the Savage Lands could be very pleasing, if you know what I mean."

"Seems a strange setting for Pagyns and a pregnant girl."Kanderxn tried to keep his tone conversational. "Any idea where were they headed?"

Burggen shook his head. "Thought so too," he said, "so I sneaked a look at their manifest. They were takin' the horse train clear to Luxurd Station, which is the end of the line. Where in a horse's hiney they might have gone from there is beyond my imagination. Nothin' but desolate wilderness beyond Luxurd. The way I figure it, her husband were an uppity-up at the mines who had sold out to the Pagyns, and they were taking her to him." He shook his head again. "Not where I'd be wantin' my wife ta' have a baby!"

As Kander left the Sailor's Rack, excitement surged through his veins, yet he was angry with himself. "I never do anything right!" he muttered. "Been looking in all the wrong places. Five years wasted because I was looking in the wrong direction. Drat!" Still, he was now anxious to get back to Zwexdrof and report his find to Thaxndar.

As Kanderxn set his feet to the dusty road leading from Avard to Zwexdrof, Thaxndar once again walked the cobbles connecting the temple with the king's palace. This time the spurned priest gained entrance, for he had sent a sealed letter in advance. When he arrived at the palace gate, a dour-faced Pagyn guardsman met him and immediately ushered him into Xvardris' presence.

The usurper king set aside his business of the moment and excused his advisors and attendants. The priest of Baruch and the usurper king faced each other alone.

"So what is this foolishness?" demanded the usurper king. He extended Thaxndar's letter crumpled in his closed fist. "There is a legal heir to the throne? Ridiculous! Evidently, you were not aware that a number of years ago Zandirxn was waylaid by slave traders. They castrated him. Eunuchs do not have children. So don't start rumors that can't be substantiated. If an heir exists, produce him!"

"You can refrain from playing ignorant, Pagyn." Thaxndar set his jaw, and his eyes shone with the cold glint of steel. "You know about the girl-Patrexna. What have you done with her and her child?"

Xvardris' response was a guttural growl and his own bladed glare.

"On behalf of the people, I demand that the rightful heir be returned to the throne of Xzwendaria!" A slight smile touched Thaxndar's grim countenance. "Pagyn, you no longer have a place in Xzwendaria. And I warn you, if you refuse to relinquish the throne, the people will rise up and take it from you!"

Xvardris stared at the priest, shook his head, and chuckled quietly. He turned his back on Thaxndar, slowly walking away. After a moment, he turned again. A sneer cleaved his face. "Valiant words, Priest!" His brow hunkered down. "But I tell you this: If the people so much as raise a finger, there will be a blood bath such as has never been known in the annals of Xzwendarian history."

"Yes, you do control the army, don't you, Pagyn?" Thaxndar nodded. He then lifted a finger. "But remember, the army is made up of men who are loyal, not to you, but to the kingdom. When they find out that there is a legal heir to the throne, they will turn their weapons on you and your henchmen, not the people. If there is blood flowing in the streets, it will be Pagyn blood!"

Xvardris scowled and grated his teeth, but his demeanor became more subdued. Head down, he paced back and forth. Suddenly, the usurper stopped, and his fiery gaze shifted from the floor to the priest.

Thaxndar watched with a fixed stare and did not back away.

The usurper king took a deliberate breath. "You know, priest, everything was going fine until you came along." He bit his lower lip momentarily and looked toward a distant window. A storm was brewing outside. Time passed slowly. Finally, Xvardris turned again. The corner of his mouth twisted slightly upward. "Very well, I am willing to consider your demand. However, I must have assurances. If I restore the heir to the throne of Xzwendaria, what happens to me and the other Pagyns in the land?"

"You will be deported beyond the northern territory, for that too must be restored," said Thaxndar.

"No." Xvardris grimaced and shook his head. "I will restore the heir only on the condition that we are allowed to return to Athos. I will give you Xzwendaria in exchange for the territory. You will recognize the Realm of Amity as a legitimate nation. Otherwise, I will take my chances."

Thaxndar did not want blood spilled in the streets, neither Xwendarian nor Pagyn. Although he resented having to do so, he agreed.

They spent the next hour working out a timetable and an agreement that allowed King Xzadrk's advisor, Jentrxn, to become regent until the heir should come of age.

When they were finished, Xvardris shrugged and forced a conciliatory smile. "Well, I tried," he said.

"Yes, you tried," responded Thaxndar, "but thankfully, you did not succeed."

Xvardris tilted his head slightly in acknowledgement. "From your perspective," he muttered. "But tell me, Priest, how did you find out about the heir? I thought I had taken care of all the loose ends."

"Patrexna came to me at the temple shortly after she discovered she was with child," said Thaxndar. "In fact, your henchmen must have kidnapped her after she left the temple and before she got home."

"But why did you wait so long to come forth with the information?" Xvardris' scowl deepened and ran his hand through his hair. "After all, it's been five years."

"She told me in confidence," explained Thaxndar. "But when Zandirxn died and you took the throne, I had to reconsider the matter. I agonized over it but decided that the continued sovereignty of the realm could not be ignored. That is no small matter. However, what transpired five years ago must be revealed to the people of Xzwendaria and the rightful heir restored to the throne. Tomorrow begins a new era for our nation."

Xvardris sighed, his face drawn. "It is late. Please leave me," he said. "I would enjoy my last night as king. Tomorrow, priest, tomorrow."

Thaxndar nodded slightly then left the usurper's chamber.

The priest gone and the shutting of the door still echoing through the room, Zanzxra stepped from behind a loosely draped purple curtain.

"See that he talks to no one," commanded Xvardris. His fiery eyes still attended the door by which Thaxndar had left. "When he gets back to the temple, kill him. Then set the temple on fire. Tomorrow I will have Dindrikin and his men rip it stone from stone until it is level with the cobbled streets that surround it!"

The Black Assassin's lip twitched as if he might smile, but his face remained somber, his eyes emotionless. He bowed, turned away, and followed the priest into the city.

Xvardris left the palace and went to the Black Chancel in search of the Ten Reapers. After giving five of the ten instructions, he returned to the palace and his chamber.

As he entered, a figure stepped from the shadowy recesses. Light from the cressets fell on a face delicately formed, yet hard as the broadsword's blade that lay on Xvardris' table. The woman's eyes shone black and deep. Long ebony hair streaked with gray hung front and back down to her waist. She wore a dress of fine coal-black silk with little silver etchings that shimmered like stars in the night sky. The red jewel that appeared to be implanted in her forehead flashed like fire, as did her eyes.

"I wondered why you weren't at the chancel," commented Xvardris.

"What of the heir?" the woman demanded.

"I sent five of the Ten Reapers to destroy the child. The darklings will see to him and his mother." Xvardris shifted uncomfortably under the gaze of the priestess. He despised her and at the right time would set the darklings on her as well. "You need not worry yourself, Wazrxna, as you know the darklings are merciless and efficient. They have no conscience."

Wazrxna knew the darklings well, better than Xvardris, still her frown remained. "That may be," she said, "but Xziland is a long way off."

Xvardris waved a hand dismissively. "They will get there soon enough. The heir is as good as dead."

"So you say. But what if others know about the heir?" Wazrxna held his eyes, not turning her gaze aside.

"There are no others." Xvardris stared steadily back at her, trying to exude an air of confidence. "Even the men who escorted her to Xziland are no more. Zanzxra took care of them."

"It is a long journey, Xvardris. Along the way, many must have seen the girl."

Xvardris jacked a shoulder. "Of course, but that was all they saw, two Pagyns escorting a girl out into the Savage Lands." Xvardris once again waved a dismissive hand. "They may have thought it strange, but they had no way of knowing that she carried the heir in her womb. No, all they saw was a girl traveling east."

Wazrxna twisted her cold face into a smile that had no warmth. "You have done well, but remember, you sit on the throne of Xzwendaria at my behest and in my behalf. Do not get ambitious, Xvardris." Her smile vanished as she studied his face, then she added, "I would caution you—ambition is a deadly disease."

"I'm no fool, my sovereign." Xvardris bowed submissively shifting his eyes away from hers. "I do your bidding. When you speak, it is done."

As Xvardris bowed before the Pagyn priestess, Thaxndar bowed before Baruch in the temple sanctuary. Intent on his prayers, he did not hear the leather-shod feet of the assassin as he came down the aisle. There, at the altar of sacrifice, with the name of Baruch on his lips, Thaxndar died.

The Black Assassin sneered as he looked down on the blood-stained priest whose blank eyes stared toward the ceiling. "Tonight you were the sacrifice!" he grated. Then he turned to the lampstands, and moments later, flames lapped at curtains, wood panels, and all that was burnable. "A feeble, helpless god!" mocked Zanzxra as he slipped down a shadowed alley and made his way back to the palace.

Later, in the darkness of the night, as Zanzxra turned on his couch seeking sleep, his closed eyes envisioned Thaxndar kneeling by the altar. He saw his own sneer, the flash of his blade, the blood, the fire. And out from flames and shadows, he saw the priest's glazed eyes gaping at him. He started in his sleep when the dead priest's lips moved: "Baruch. Baruch. Baruch." The name of Baruch echoed in Zanzrxa's head. He slashed with his blade at the flaming body again and again shouting, "Stop! Stop!" Still, the dead priest's lips sent forth Baruch's name. The Black Assassin came up off his bed in a cold sweat. Shaken to the depth of his being, he paced the night away, afraid to return to his couch.

Chapter 11

Men with long, weary faces, women carrying unseen burdens, and noisy children trudged the cobbled streets of Zwexdrof alongside horses, donkeys, two-wheeled wagons, and four-wheeled coaches—a normal snarl of cloppity comings and goings for midday. Swarthy soldiers moved through the crowd, their dark, beady eyes peering at faces and into the backs of carts and carriages.

Kander walked close behind a fishmonger as he passed through the Great Gate, hoping the guards would think he was the merchant's helper.

"Move it along!" shouted the gatekeeper after snatching a fish from the monger's supply. The fishmonger glared at the guard but kept his tongue.

Kander scurried by and melted into the crowd. However, he had not gone far when someone came up beside him, took his arm, and whispered, "The city is not safe for you. Keep your face hidden as much as possible and stay close." Another man brushed against his right side. "Best thing is to act like chums," he urged.

The two men moved Kander along the street while talking loudly, laughing, slapping him on the back. As they approached a public house, they suddenly whisked him into the darkened alleyway between graying buildings. "Hurry along!" urged one of the men. They made their way deeper into the darkness.

"Jentrxn is regent of the new underground government," whispered the other man. "He told us to watch for you."

"The door to your left," said the first man.

Jentrxn, who had been King Xzadrk's advisor, sat at an old oak table. Other somber-faced men sat around the table with him. When he became aware of Kander's presence, Jentrxn looked at him and smiled, but there was no sparkle to his eyes, rather a deep sadness.

"What's with all the secrecy? Why have I been brought here?" Kander looked over his shoulder at his escorts. A scowl crossed his face as he turned back to Jentrxn. "I need to see Thaxndar."

The room became uncomfortably silent. The men sitting around the table glanced at Jentrxn and then at their hands, the table, or a distant wall. They refused to look at Kander. Dread ripped at his stomach.

"I'm sorry, Kander." The regent met Kander's questioning eyes. "Thaxndar is dead. A beggar named Thedrx saw the usurper king's assassin leave the temple the night Thaxndar was killed and the temple torched. We understand that the assassination took place shortly after Thaxndar had left the palace. He told me before he went that he had some important information to confront the usurper with. He said he would tell me more the next day. He never got the chance." Jentrxn sighed deeply. "Apparently, that information cost him his life."

Anger sheeted Kander's face. He drove a fist to the palm of his hand. "Drat!" His eyes filled with unwanted tears, and he dropped into the nearest chair. "If only I had not been looking in all the wrong places!" he grated. "If I had returned with news of the girl sooner, he would not have died!"

One of the men laid a hand on his shoulder.

Jentrxn leaned forward. "Don't be too hard on yourself, Kander. But tell me, of what girl do you speak? What salient matter was Thaxndar aware of that cost him his life?"

Kander had been staring at the floor. He looked up. "The heir," he said.

Jentrxn's eyes went wide. "Zandirxn had an illegitimate son?"

A pall of silence once again engulfed the room.

Taking a deep breath, Kander looked from one man to the next. Finally, he grimaced and nodded his head. "Yes, he had a child," he acknowledged.

"Can't be!" someone whispered. Then others joined the denial.

Jentrxn raised his hand. Silence returned. He tilted his head toward Kander, who in turn told them the whole story, even the part he had kept from Thaxndar. "And as far as we know, the heir is still alive and in exile somewhere in or beyond the Savage Lands," he ended.

One of the men who had met Kander at the gate, Zardfin, lifted his hands out to the side. "So what do we do?" he asked.

"The heir must be found and returned," declared Jentrxn without hesitation. He turned to Kander. "You will lead the expedition to bring him back."

Kander's mouth dropped open. "Me?" he questioned. "Surely not me! I can't do anything right! It took me five years just to find out what happened to Patrexna. I was looking in the wrong places the whole time! And if it weren't for me, Thaxndar wouldn't . . ." His emotions choked him to an agonized silence.

"Kander, you're the only one who knows what Patrexna looks like." Jentrxn's voice was calm but firm. "And did not Thaxndar send you out to find the girl? And do you not now have some idea of where to look for her?" He paused briefly while his words sank in. "Can you say you have finished the task Thaxndar entrusted to you?"

Kander stared at the floor and shook his head.

Jentrxn leaned farther across the table and grasped Kander's arm. "Would you quit with your mission unfinished?"

"No, of course not." Kander set his jaw as he looked up and met Jentrxn's eyes. "I intend to find her if it takes me the rest of my life. But can't you put someone else in charge of the expedition? I don't know anything about that sort of thing."

The regent smiled and nodded. "Very well. We will find someone else to head the venture as long as you accept responsibility for finding the girl. In three days, the Resistance will be gathering at our stronghold in Tangle Wood. The leaders of the resistance will be planning a strategy for our struggle against Xvardris. We will decide then who will comprise the King's Company to bring back the heir."

Kander could feel the anxiety of the men as they waited for the night. Then, a few at a time, Jentrxn, his men, and Kander left for the stronghold in Tangle Wood.

As Kander made his way out of the city, the Pagyn priestess, Wazrxna, and the usurper king, Xvardris, met to lay plans for dealing with the resistance.

"What about this fellow, Jentrxn, who claims to be regent in exile?" asked the priestess. "I thought you were going to eliminate him weeks ago?"

"Well, yes." Xvardris face twisted into a grim scowl. "But before he can be eliminated, he must be found. I've had my people scouring the city." He met her eyes. "Jentrxn is a sly fox and seems to stay a step ahead of them."

Wazrxna's furrowed brow and scathing glare communicated her disapproval.

Xvardris smiled. "Don't worry. I have infiltrated their ranks and will soon have the information I need to take action against the rebels."

Wazrxna harrumphed in response. "Loose ends, Xvardris." She paced back and forth. "I do not like loose ends." She cast him another peevish look. "Somehow they have a way of unraveling."

"We will just have to make sure they don't unravel." Xvardris emanated confidence. "My mole has informed me that the leadership of the resistance is meeting in three days. Following that meeting, I will know who their leaders are and the location of their stronghold. Once I know that, dealing with them will be relatively simple."

The priestess' laugh mocked Xvardris' words.

"You don't trust me?" he carped.

"Humph! When it comes to these people, nothing is simple." She turned to leave, then glaring back over her shoulder, she added, "Actually, trust has no place with me, Xvardris. What I require is results." With that she walked out of the room.

Xzwendaria's standing army numbered about five thousand men. While Zandirxn was still living, he had purged the army of more than three hundred officers in order to put his own men, Pagyns brought in from Nefarious Reach, in command of the troops. Another thousand loyal Xzwendarians deserted after he usurped the throne. More than fifty deserters were caught, and Xvardris had them executed in front of their compatriots. "Those who are loyal to me will find themselves appropriately rewarded," he had announced to the troops, "but those who are not . . ." then he pointed to the pile of bodies.

After Xvardris took the throne, the displaced Xzwendarian officers marshaled the deserters and a throng of volunteers to form a resistance army. The Resistance numbered more than fifteen hundred men, who now manned the stronghold in Tangle Wood. Their commander, General Vandwert, had been second in command of the Xzwendarian army before Xvardris' rise to power. The first in command, General Elfradik, had formed an alliance with Xvardris during Zandirxn's reign. However, he disappeared the day after the king died and was replaced by General Bodrak, one of Xvardris' Pagyn transplants.

*T*angle Wood blanketed the foothills of the northwest reaches of the Viper Spur in the South Labyrinth Mountains. On the far side of that forest, with its back against the escarpment of the Viper Spur, stood an immense rock fortress more than a thousand years old, Havenholt—a remnant of an ancient kingdom that was antecedent to the Fairlander period. The granite bastion, because it was sculpted in the face of a cliff and hedged in by the jungle-like forest, defied direct assault.

Kander gazed in wonder at the powerful architecture, high walls, and archaic beauty of the fortress. As he rode up the steep, narrow grade toward the heights, he bent forward with his chin touching his horse's mane. A gated archway opened into a city-like stronghold. Rock-cobbled streets ran past buildings cut from rock and behind parapets manned by smiling, waving soldiers. The men of Kander's entourage waved back as they made their way to the stables.

Kander was glad to have his feet on solid ground again until he had to follow Jentrxn up what seemed an eternally long stairway that wound upward inside the mountain and came out at what Jentrxn called the Chamber of Council, a building chiseled in the rock face nearly at the apex of the escarpment. By the time they reached the top of the stairs, Kander's leg muscles burned and he gasped for breath.

Jentrxn had begun preparing a contingency plan for a government in exile the day after Xvardris became King Zandirxn's advisor. For more than four years, he had secretly refurbished the old fortress, stockpiled arms and food, and laid plans with key leaders.

One of those leaders, a man named Razrdris, had been captain of King Xzadrk's palace guard. He now was the commander of Havenholt, giving oversight to the general affairs of the fortress-city.

Major Targndel, another crucial partisan, had been King Xzadrk's information officer. He now coordinated intelligence gathering for the resistance.

Two women worked with Major Targndel. Xzwindra, previously a street orphan, served as the major's primary operative for intelligence gathering in Zwexdrof. Being a woman, she drew less suspicion as she wandered the streets of the city. Zedria, also a street orphan of sorts, was Xzwindra's primary informant. Her father, now a Pagyn official at the palace, refused to claim her. Her mother, a poor chambermaid to King Zandirxn's father, died giving Zedria birth. A friend of her mother's, who had too many mouths to feed, raised her until she was old enough to push out the door to fend for herself. For the last ten years, Zedria had made a living selling candles on street corners and door to door. She also plied her wares in the palace. And unbeknown to any of those present but Xzwindra, Zedria trafficked more than candles behind closed palace doors. She gathered valuable information from fluffy pillows and goose-down comforters—information to which no one else had access. Xzwindra knew Targndel would not approve, but to her Zedria was too valuable a source of intelligence to expose her secret.

Another important leader present at the meeting was Prior Forknedrn who acceded to the office of high priest after Thaxndar's assassination. And although there was no longer a temple, a large chamber within the fortress had been set aside as Sanctum Tempra, or the temporary sanctuary, where Prior Forknedrn built an altar upon which he continued the sacrifice.

Then there was Captain Favelthx. The others simply called him Captain Favel. He commanded the Regent's Guard, an elite troop directly responsible to Jentrxn. Captain Favel had not come over to the Resistance until after Xvardris had usurped the throne. Also at the meeting were three of Captain Favel's men, grim-faced Sergeant Tandrak, shifty-eyed Corporal Mifstern, and a happy-go-lucky private named Sedrnal. Of course, the commander of the Resistance Army, General Vandwert, was there. Ten men. Two women.

Five of the men, Jentrxn, General Vandwert, Commander Razrdris, Major Targndel, and Prior Forknedrn, formed the governing council of the Resistance. The others were invited to the council meeting because they were deemed essential to finding the heir to the throne of Xzwendaria and bringing him or her back from exile. However, not everyone at the meeting believed that the so-called heir actually existed.

"Tell me, Jentrxn," said Major Targndel, "How is it possible that in more than two years of intelligence gathering we have not uncovered the slightest rumor of an heir, while on the other hand, we have determined that King Zandirxn was in fact a eunuch. Castration does make it rather difficult to produce an heir, you know."

Several of those present snickered in response.

"In all my years in the palace, I have heard no rumors of Zandirxn fathering a child," added Zedria.

"If Thaxndar himself were standing here telling us that the king had produced an heir, maybe I could believe it," said General Vandwert. "But what we are dealing with here is secondhand information. And the reliability of the source of this information is suspect at best."

"Yes, and I worked closely with Thaxndar," broke in Prior Forknedrn. "I'm sure he would have told me about an heir to the throne, if indeed there was such an heir. He did not tell me. And I do not believe there is an heir. Didn't you say this event happened six or seven years ago, Jentrxn?"

The regent nodded and gave a simple yes in response. General Vandwert gestured toward Kanderxn. "I acknowledge that Kander has become a fine young man, but facts be known, he has not always been trustworthy. When Thaxndar took him off the streets, he was an urchin and a thief." He turned to Kander. "I mean no harm, young man, but truth must prevail." He gave Kander a sidelong glance. "Everything considered, I am afraid I cannot help but doubt your word."

"Gentlemen, before Thaxndar's death, he told me he had some extremely vital information to make public—after years of keeping it secret," interjected Jentrxn. "However, he also said that before he could make that information public, he had to confront the usurper face to face." Jentrxn paused and looked from one somber face to the next. "For myself," he continued, "I see no reason to doubt that what Kander has shared with us is true. I have known for some time that Thaxndar was searching for the girl Patrexna. Why was he so intensely interested in finding this girl? Why did he commission Kander to search the far reaches of the realm for her?"

"Thaxndar was a compassionate man," said the prior. "Her parents told him she was missing. No doubt they cried piteously, and he became their advocate in the matter. And I know for a fact he promised he would do all he could to find the girl. He told me so himself, but he never told me more. And why should he since there was no more to be told?"

"Patrexna confessed to Thaxndar in confidence," whispered Kander. "There is an heir. I have no reason to lie to you."

"There we are!" responded the prior, waving a hand at the young man. "And how did you come by this information? You say you eavesdropped on the high priest? That in itself calls your integrity into question."

"Good Prior, the young man's integrity is not the question we are dealing with," interrupted Commander Razrdris. "The question is what are we going to do about this report of an heir? It seems to me that if there is even the slightest possibility that an heir exists, we are obliged to conclusively prove the report either true or untrue, no matter the source."

Captain Favel listened. He never smiled. He never frowned. His face said nothing. On the other hand, Sergeant Tandrak's scowl spoke utter disbelief. Corporal Mifstern's face showed agreement one minute and disagreement the next. Private Sedrnal raised an eyebrow now and then while maintaining a continuous smile.

"Commander Razrdris touches the heart of the matter," said Jentrxn. He leaned on the table. "Dare we ignore this rumor that there might be an heir to the throne?" He looked around the room, taking in each grim face. "No. It is incumbent upon us to find this girl, Patrexna, and to determine whether Kander's tale is true or false. And we all do agree that the girl herself does exist. And if there is an heir, and frankly I pray there is, we must bring him or her to the throne."

"Heir or not, our first responsibility is to bring down the usurper king and remove the Pagyns from Xzwendarian soil!" declared General Vandwert. "If you want to chase a shadow, that's up to you. But my concern is not who shall sit on the throne tomorrow, but who is sitting on it today!"

"And I'm too busy gathering intelligence so we can stay a step ahead of Xvardris, to worry about pursuing, a story—a story I simply do not believe," declared Major Targndel, his tone acidic.

Prior Forknedrn came to his feet and shook a finger at the regent. "I for another will have no part of chasing your ghost, Jentrxn, not if Kander is going to be involved! As far as I'm concerned, the whole thing is simply the product of an overactive imagination and a warped desire for attention."

Jentrxn held up a restraining hand. "Your point is well-taken, Prior. But those of us who sit on the governing council cannot go looking for the heir anyway." Jentrxn remained unruffled by the unexpected opposition. "I intend to send Kander, Captain Favel, and these three men he has chosen." He gestured toward Sergeant Tandrak, Corporal Mifstern, and Private Sedrnal.

"Why all men?" piped up Zedria. She shook her head. "Always men, men, men! Why not a woman too? Why not me?"

"Being a man or woman has nothing to do with it. You and Xzwindra were asked to come to this meeting to provide information you might have picked up in Zwexdrof concerning rumors of an heir," said Jentrxn. "You are too important to our intelligence-gathering process to send on this mission."

"Especially you, Zedria," interjected Major Targndel. "You are our only inside contact at the palace. The information you gather is essential if the Resistance is to remain effective in countering Xvardris' efforts to gain full control of the realm."

"Then what about me?" asked Xzwindra. "Zedria can run things in Zwexdrof without me. After all, if they find this girl Kander speaks of, it might be helpful to have a woman along."

"I want to go!" Zedria flared. "I'm tired of the palace!"

"Zedria, the intelligence you gather at the palace is critical to our effort to stay a step ahead of Xvardris," grated Major Targndel. "For you to go on this mission would jeopardize the Resistance. You are needed here."

"Still, Xzwindra has a point," put in Captain Favel. "From a military perspective, having a woman along can create some interesting male-female problems. But in reality if we find the girl and her child, having a woman as a part of our company would be indispensable. I would like Xzwindra to be included."

So it was decided that Captain Favel, Sergeant Tandrak, Corporal Mifstern, Private Sedrnal, Xzwindra, and Kander would search for Patrexna and the heir to the throne of

Xzwendaria. Prior Forknedrn wagged his head and muttered, "They'll be wasting time chasing shadows!"

Chapter 12

"*I* warned you, Xvardris! And now your simple answer has proven to be anything but simple!" hissed the Pagyn priestess, as she turned toward the open window that looked out over the city. "You have found out where the Resistance is laired. That's good. But then you tell me their fortress is impregnable. That's bad. And although you assured me that absolutely no other person knew about the heir, out of nowhere comes this young man named Kander." She turned on him and glared. "Loose ends, Xvardris. Loose ends."

"As I told you, I sent five of the ten reapers, your darklings, to eliminate the girl and her child." Xvardris lifted his hands out to the side. "And I will dispatch Zanzxra to take care of Kander. Should the darklings somehow fail in their task, and even you have to admit that is unlikely, our spy will kill the heir should the Resistance find him. And, of course, there are the other five reapers. The heir will not come to the throne, my lady. I assure you, he is as good as dead."

Wazrxna shook her head. "Only dead is as good as dead, Xvardris. When the child is indeed dead, then and only then will I be satisfied that you have done your job. But if you should fail, Xvardris—if you should fail . . ." She left it for him to fill in the rest. She turned and faced Xvardris, her eyes burning like brands from the belly of hell. She spoke not another word.

Xvardris maintained his poise, casting her a grim smile.

Wazrxna brushed past him and whisked out of his chamber.

He had not previously noticed the beads of sweat on his brow. He summoned Zanzxra. While Xvardris awaited the Black Assassin's arrival, he paced back and forth. He was not happy with how things were going. Although his spy had filled him in on the details of the meeting in Tangle Wood, he had hoped that once he had located the Resistance, he could strike them unawares and crush them into nonexistence. However, his hopes were dashed against the massive walls of an ancient fortress. And then came the disconcerting report that the Resistance was aware of a possible heir to the throne living in exile beyond the eastern border of the realm. Xvardris smiled. "But not living for long," he muttered to himself. Although Xvardris was not facing the door, he perceived that Zanzxra had entered the room. He could feel the Black Assassin's malignant presence.

Zanzxra was the first slave Xvardris had acquired. He had bought him at a bargain price when he was but four years old. Zanzxra had been stolen from his mother's arms a year earlier in Avard. Xvardris was told that the woman had resisted the taking of her child and had paid with her life. But Zanzxra knew nothing of that, for Xvardris had woven a new past for him. He had told him that his parents had never loved him, that they had come to Athos from a far county and had sold him for a few pieces of silver because he was nothing to them but a nuisance. He told him his parents had not wanted a child to begin with. With such words, Xvardris had cultivated hatred in the child's heart. Further, unknown to Zanzxra, Xvardris had paid his nurse to abuse him verbally, physically, and more. Others were paid to abuse him as well. And once hatred was firmly implanted, Xvardris had groomed the boy to be a killer. He would give him a pet and then watch with pleasure as the boy would torture and kill the poor creature. Then when Zanzxra was thirteen, his resentment and hatred overflowed. With his bare hands, he killed his nurse. When Zanzxra turned fourteen Xvardris sent him to Netrag for formal training as an assassin. And over the years he had served Xvardris well.

Zanzxra stood before Xvardris awaiting his orders. The assassin was glad he was wearing a mask. It hid the dark circles around his eyes. He was not sleeping well these days, for he continued to see the priest in his dreams. And when he looked at his hands, they seemed to drip with blood. He washed them time and time again, but Thaxndar's blood remained.

Xvardris saw the dullness in Zanzxra's eyes and recognized it as boredom. He grinned and raised an eyebrow. "It's been awhile, hasn't it?" he chided. "Well, this should put the fire back in your eyes. A young man named Kander, so they tell me, is the priest's adopted son. Somehow he has found out about the heir. I don't know where he is now, but he will soon be going to Yeps. Find him and kill him. He will be with others, so make sure they cannot associate his death with you and in turn with me." Xvardris grimaced and waved a hand. "Make it look like an accident or a mugging, and if necessary kill the others as well."

"Even the spy?" asked Zanzxra.

"Yes." Xvardris turned his back on the assassin and walked over to the window and stared out at the city. "Should you have to kill the others, the spy would be of no further use—a detriment, actually." He turned again. "That is all."

Zanzxra bowed and left.

Alone, the usurper king stepped out on the balcony and let his eyes sweep the horizon. For a fleeting moment he imagined Zanzxra assassinating Wazrxna, the priestess, and saw himself as the ruler of all. The thought passed with a shudder as the picture in his mind changed to one of the evil priestess laughing at him, an image altogether too real. He looked over his shoulder. No one was there.

"Jentrxn, we were supposed to leave for Yeps yesterday," grumbled Kander as he paced from one side of the dank room to the other. "What if Xvardris gets to the heir before we do?"

"Since he's holding the heir in exile, he should have little difficulty getting to him first if this were a footrace," the regent responded. "But this isn't a footrace, Kander. Since Xvardris knows where the heir is, and we don't, the important factor in our quest is secrecy rather than speed. Captain Favel had business to take care of in Zwexdrof. The company will leave when he returns."

"Where are the others? I haven't seen any of them since our meeting." Lines of concern creased Kander's brow.

Jentrxn sat at a rustic-looking desk, holding a dried-out quill in his hand. Xzwindra also went to Zwexdrof with Zedria to let their operatives know that Zedria will be in charge while Xzwindra is away." Jentrxn's tone was patient. "Tandrak and the others requested a few days leave to see to personal business before heading out. I am told that Private Sedrnal got back sometime yesterday. Xzwindra, Tandrak, and Mifstern are due back today. Captain Favel understands the urgency of our quest. He will return as soon as possible—perhaps by tonight." He waved his quill at Kander. "Go get your things together, and be ready to leave first thing in the morning or as soon after Captain Favel returns. Until then . . .be patient." He dipped his quill in the inkwell again before looking up at Kander. "You have spent five years looking for the girl. A few hours more will not make much difference." Jentrxn turned his attention to the parchment on his desk.

Kander sighed, then slipped out the door. He had already packed for the trip so he passed the day wandering about the fortress. As the sun dipped toward the horizon, he became impatient and meandered down a cobbled street toward the main gate, anxious to know if the others had returned yet. He would ask the sergeant of the guard.

As he approached the gate, his step quickened. Captain Favel had returned from Zwexdrof. He was standing by his horse talking to one of the guards. Hopefully, the others had returned as well.

The guard turned aside to address another traveler, and Captain Favel, unaware of Kander's approach, prepared to mount his horse.

"Captain Favel," Kander called out.

Hand on the saddle horn, the captain looked over his shoulder.

Kander did not wait for a response. "What has taken you so long?"

Captain Favel put his foot to the stirrup and swung up into the saddle. "What has taken me is not your business." He turned his steed to the cobbled road. "Your business is to be ready to leave at first light tomorrow." Then he rode away.

A scowl creased Kander's brow as he watched Captain Favel disappear up the street. "A strange man," he muttered. He was not sure if he liked him.

"Rather curt, wasn't he?" Xzwindra's voice startled him. He swung about a smile splitting his face. Xzwindra nodded toward the departing captain. "He's a private sort of fellow but dependable. And since Jentrxn has confidence in him, so do I."

"Dependable?" There was scorn in Kander's voice. "He's been off doing whatever in Zwexdrof when we should be gone from here. I don't call that dependable."

Xzwindra laughed. "Kander, you will have to get used to the military." She shook her head. "Dependability is getting the job done, not bowing to a strict timetable. A timetable has its place, but it can also be a hindrance."

Kander let his eyes drift up the street. His face went to a grimace. "I guess I am being a bit prudish, aren't I?" He shrugged his shoulders. "After five years of looking for the girl, you'd think I would have developed some patience."

Xzwindra smiled. "Have you been up on the wall? You get quite a view of the forest from there." She began to move toward the steps that led up to the parapet. "The trees look so immense when you're walking beneath their shadowy canopy. However, when you look down on them from the wall, the perspective is different. Come on, I'll show you."

They mounted the wall, and as Kander looked out over the forest, he felt his spirit settle. "From up here, the world doesn't seem so small and confining." He turned and looked at the mountains behind. "They are majestic," he mused. "Baruch is an extraordinary artist, isn't he?"

"I suppose." Xzwindra stared off into space. "There is beauty here and there, but overall things are pretty ugly, if you ask me." She turned to Kander with raised eyebrows. "If humankind was supposed to be Baruch's greatest achievement, I would say he fell a bit short. I sometimes wonder if there really is a Majesty. When I look at our world, it seems random and absurd."

"I hear what you're saying, Xzwindra." Kander glanced down from the wall to the street of the fortress-city where two soldiers argued. "But tell me, is the ugliness we see Baruch's fault or ours? It seems to me that we are the ones who choose beauty or ugliness. And yes, too often we choose ugliness. " He shook his head. "No, I do not fault Baruch for the evil I see."

Xzwindra followed his gaze to the soldiers below. With angry gestures, the two men parted company. She turned back to Kander. "Each to their own," she said with a forced smile. "Let's find the others so we can make plans for tomorrow. Jentrxn wanted to meet with us once Captain Favel returned."

They left the wall and walked in silence back to the citadel. As soon as they arrived, they were directed to Jentrxn's quarters. The rest of the company was already there.

Sergeant Tandrak leaned against the wall with his arms crossed and a deep scowl darkening his face. Corporal Mifstern sat stiffly on a chair off to Tandrak's right, his eyes continually shifting from one person to the next. Sedrnal, wearing his seemingly perpetual smile, stood out on the balcony gazing at some distant scene. Jentrxn and Captain Favel were cloistered in a corner having what appeared to be an intense but quiet conversation.

No one acknowledged Kander and Xzwindra when they entered the room. Kander slipped to a corner separate from the others and sat down in an upholstered chair. Xzwindra joined Sedrnal on the balcony.

"And where did you spend your leave time?" Xzwindra asked, interrupting Sedrnal's thoughts.

Sedrnal gazed at her and shifted uncomfortably. His smile remained but lost its sparkle. He lifted a shoulder in answer to her question and said, "I think we're wanted inside." He walked past Xzwindra back into Jentrxn's chamber.

Xzwindra shook her head, twisted the corner of her mouth into a half smile, and followed.

Jentrxn and Captain Favel broke away from their private conversation and moved over to where the others were waiting.

Jentrxn stood in silence, his eyes measuring each member of the company, his demeanor grave. "I want you to know that I am absolutely convinced that the girl Patrexna does exist and that she bore Zandirxn's child." He took a deep breath. "Out there somewhere is a seven-year-old child who is heir to the throne of Xzwendaria. That child is our king or queen. And you, my friends, are the King's Company, charged with finding the child and returning with him or her. As regent of the realm, I charge you to find the child, protect the child with your lives if necessary, and return the child to the throne. The future of Xzwendaria rests in your hands."

He paused and looked from one person to the next. No one offered a response. He nodded as if acknowledging their tacit consent and then continued. "Captain Favel is officer-in-charge. He will lead the quest to bring back our king or queen. You will follow his orders explicitly. However, although Captain Favel is in charge of the expedition, Kander is ultimately responsible for finding the heir, so you will follow his lead in that regard. And again, it falls to each of you to see that the heir is returned once found." He again let his eyes shift from individual to individual. "I charge each of you to swear your allegiance to the heir!"

One by one they affirmed their fidelity. Captain Favel's face remained bland as he put his hand to his heart and swore. Sergeant Tandrak and Corporal Mifstern squirmed a bit and stumbled over the words. Private Sedrnal, smile firmly in place but lacking sparkle, pledged his vow. Xzwindra swore her oath with somberness as did Kander.

"You have sworn allegiance to the heir, and may Baruch hold you to your words," said Jentrxn. "Be ready to leave at first light. Now off with you." He rose to his feet. "Kander, I need to talk to you before you go."

After closing the chamber door behind the others, Jentrxn turned to Kander. He sat down on the edge of the table, his face grim. "I talked with Major Targndel about an hour ago," he said. "It appears that we have an informant in our midst. News of the meeting we had five days ago has already reached the ears of the usurper king. He knows about Havenholt, and I fear he knows much more. One of our own spies, a commander in Xvardris' army, told Targndel that he and the other commanders have been ordered to make plans to assault our fortress. Since our meeting, the only people to leave Havenholt other than Major Targndel himself are General Vandwert, Prior Forknedrn, Zedria, and the members of the King's Company. One of them is an operative for Xvardris—and I hope it is only one of them."

"And who do you suspect?" asked Kander.

"It is beyond me to suspect any of them." Jentrxn gave him a grim look. "I would trust any one of them with my life. It is difficult for me to believe that any of them would prove disloyal. There are only two of the eight that I do not know well, Xzwindra and Zedria. Targndel has worked closely with them both and assures me they can be trusted." A corner of his mouth twisted upward. "All our people can be trusted, yet one is a spy. What concerns me most is that the spy may well be a member of the King's Company. And if that proves true, your life might be in danger, Kander, so be wary."

"Who is privy to this information?" asked Kander. He was quite certain he knew the answer, and it was an answer he did not like.

"Major Targndel, his operative in Zwexdrof, and Captain Favel." Jentrxn looked into Kander's eyes, searching. He shook his head. "Do not worry, my friend. I trust Captain Favel even more than Major Targndel and the prior. Their integrity is beyond question."

"But as you say, sir, all are trustworthy—yet one is a spy. So, how can I trust any of them?" He sighed deeply. "Why not make a change? Surely you can assign others to this mission since the five you've chosen are all potential operatives for Xvardris. And I don't think I need to remind you that not only my life is in jeopardy. Once we find the heir, his or her life will be in jeopardy, as well."

"You are right, of course," said Jentrxn. His demeanor dimmed further. "I discussed that possibility with Captain Favel, and he recommended against making a change. He argues that if the spy is responsible to eliminate the heir, when he or she is found, then to make a change would cause Xvardris to panic. He believes that if Xvardris does not feel as if he is in control of the situation, he will send his assassin to kill the heir. And in that regard I am confident Captain Favel is right. I know Xvardris well. I too think it is best to play along with him. It will be up to you and Captain Favel to unsheathe the spy before you locate the king."

"You speak of the heir as he or she but also as king," said Kander. "What if the heir is, in fact, a girl?"

Jentrxn laughed. "Then we shall be ruled by a queen!"

"And what if the heir dies but Patrexna lives? Does that mean she will become the queen?"

"That is a question to be considered, Kander," said Jentrxn. "But at this point the heir lives, and I am confident you will return him or her to Xzwendaria."

"Can you really be so sure, Jentrxn?"

"We have the Majesty's word of honor," asserted the Regent. "Baruch promised Xtrakan long ago that he would always have an heir to sit on the throne of Xzwendaria. Baruch has kept his promise for six hundred years. Why would he break it now? The heir lives, and he or she will sit on the throne. How it will come about remains a question. That it will come about is not a point in question."

Kander nodded. Jentrxn's faith was much like Thaxndar's, a faith that tended to breed faith.

Kander pressed the issue further. "I know you don't believe it, but what if the spy is, in fact, Captain Favel?"

Jentrxn wagged his head emphatically. "I assure you he is not the spy! On that I will stake my life and reputation!"

"Well, in the end someone's reputation is going to be destroyed—and perhaps someone's life." Kander moved toward the door, stopped, and turned again to Jentrxn. "I certainly doubt that your reputation will be destroyed in the process. And sir, I trust you." He smiled wanly. "If your trust in

Captain Favel should prove ill-placed, your reputation will remain untarnished in my eyes. We all make errors in judgment now and again." He grimaced. "That I know altogether too well."

Kander did not immediately return to his quarters. Rather, he climbed up to the wall to look out over the forest and feel its calming effect—to watch the sun set and to prepare his mind for the quest that lay ahead. But as he gazed down from above the main gate, he saw a man steal through the shadows toward the forest where it appeared someone was waiting to meet him. The man was Captain Favel. Kander strained his eyes to see the other party through darkness and shadows. As he watched, the moon broke from behind a cloud. He grimaced. The person Captain Favel met appeared to be Zedria.

Chapter 13

Night swathed Havenholt in ominous shadows. In the darkness of his chamber, Kander tossed and turned, anxious for the morning. And as the night shades plodded slowly toward the dawn, dread of the coming day fostered more tossing and turning. "I'll be exhausted before the trip even begins!" he muttered angrily as he rolled over yet again.

At first light he pushed himself up from his bed and dressed. He had intended to seek out Jentrxn and tell him what he had seen from the wall, but as he stepped from his bedchamber into the cold, dank hall, a realization hit him. Going to Jentrxn will only delay our leaving, he thought. And besides, his mind is a closed book when it comes to Captain Favel. He will simply explain away the obvious, and we'll leave a day later. And the last thing I need is another sleepless night, though I'll likely have many more before this is over.

He gazed down the hall toward Jentrxn's chambers. A scowl crossed his face. He turned and headed toward the stable, thinking he would be there ahead of most of the others. However, when he arrived, he found that the horses were saddled and ready. The other members of the company milled about, making final preparations.

They were all there except Sergeant Tandrak, but just moments after Kander walked in the side entrance the crusty soldier came sauntering through the big double doors leading a packhorse. Obviously, Tandrak had been to the larder for supplies. He gave the reins of the packer to Private Sedrnal with a comment about rank having its privilege. The young soldier took the reins while maintaining a stolid demeanor. Kander couldn't help but smile at the military exchange—his first smile of the morning. He was glad he was not a soldier.

When the King's Company left the stable, Captain Favel did not take the road down toward the main gate. Rather, he led the company along a narrow, steep street toward the high wall. When they reached the upper level of the fortress, they went north to the base of the high wall, then followed it eastward to where it buttressed the mountain. There they dismounted before entering a cavern through which they advanced by torchlight.

"Why are we going this way?" Kander nervously scanned the shadows of the cavern.

"The main road in and out of Havenholt is watched. This egress from the fortress is little known and less conspicuous," Vexation edged Captain Favel's voice. "We are fairly sure Xvardris and his forces are unaware of our back door. Further, it comes out in the foothills along the eastern edge of Tangle Wood, which will help conceal our movements and is also a more direct route to Yeps." He looked at Kander, a scowl furrowing his brow. "Any more questions?"

Kander did have another question, but he held his tongue and followed on.

Xzwindra walked beside him. "A little touchy, isn't he?" she whispered. She cast him a comforting smile.

He smiled back and gave a slight nod in return but said nothing.

To Kander's senses it seemed they had twisted downward at least two miles when the cavern walls widened and the ceiling rose. They were in a large staging area. They mounted their horses and rode across the cavernous expanse toward a large iron gate. Guards opened the gate, and the King's Company rode out, Captain Favel in the lead and the others following two by two.

As he scanned his surroundings, Kander noticed that the gate was well-hidden in a deep cleft. A jagged brae rose to the left and the face of the mountain to the right. The defile opened into rolling foothills. As they left the protective womb of the mountain, Kander became uneasy. He scanned the ridge to his left and then to his right, half expecting an ambush. But the company rode forth without event.

Yeps lay two hundred miles around the spur and north of Havenholt, nearly ten days' journey, and Captain Favel feared that Xvardris' army might intercept them if they took the road that circled the Twin Spur Mountains to the west. So he informed them that they would be climbing to the pass that cut between the two mountains. "It will save time and keep us from the eyes of the enemy," he explained.

"I didn't know there was a pass between the Twins," commented Corporal Mifstern.

"There isn't," returned the captain dryly. "However, once we've made the crossover, there will be."

Eyebrows were raised, but not Kander's. At least in this, Captain Favel's doing something right, he muttered to himself as they clomped along the rocky trail.

The climb and crossing of the Twin Spurs took six days. Once beyond the gap between the mountains, they stopped in the upper foothills just south of Yeps and camped at the base of Pinnacle Peak.

"We can watch the entire Yeps Corridor from up there." Captain Favel pointed toward the top of the spire that stood like a sentinel above the surrounding hills. "Sedrnal, you'll take first watch. Stay to the south side as you climb. Be careful not to be seen. I'll be up to take a look around when we have finished setting up camp."

"Are we going to wait until dark before riding into Yeps?" asked Xzwindra. She was surprised they had stopped. After all, it was the middle of the day, and they were beyond the reach of Xvardris' army.

"Why don't we ride into Yeps and do whatever it is we need to do and be gone?" asked Private Sedrnal.

Captain Favel cast Kander a questioning glance, then turned back to Xzwindra and Private Sedrnal. "I'll make that decision when I know why we are here." He turned again to Kander. "Our friend here has been rather secretive about why we were are stopping at Yeps."

"And secretive I'll remain." Kander's tone indicated that the why of Yeps would not be discussed. "I'll be going into Yeps alone, at first light tomorrow."

"Boy plays hero!" spat Sergeant Tandrak. "And if something happens to you in Yeps, then what happens to our mission?"

"Don't worry. Nothing will happen to me in Yeps."

Captain Favel's eyes flashed like the blade of a sword, and he scowled. "My friend, if I were you, I would sleep with one eye open and never go anywhere alone. You know too much." Captain Favel held a dagger in his hand. He carefully ran his finger along its razor-sharp edge. His scowl shifted to a half smile. "Yes, I counsel caution. Xvardris has a long arm, and it would not be wise to compromise our mission because of one individual's imprudence."

Kander stared back at Captain Favel, wondering if there was more to his remarks than met the ear. The company waited silently, all eyes watching him.

After a few moments' thought, he slowly let out his breath. "All right, I will take Xzwindra with me. To hide my identity, I'll pose as a would-be prospector, and she will have to sham as my slave woman."

"As your what?" Xzwindra's face went livid. "As your slave woman? I'll not be a slave to anyone!"

Kander sighed and glanced upward. The others chuckled and he cast them a reproving glare. "Xzwindra, we have a mission to perform," he said, "and I need to gather vital information in Yeps for the pursuit of that mission. It's not like you'll actually be my slave woman. You will simply be posing. Besides, I wouldn't ask if it weren't necessary."

"Oh, so now you are actually asking me?" retorted Xzwindra, feigning a look of wonder. "For a moment, I thought you were telling me what I was going to do. How nice of you to ask! I don't like it, but I suppose for the mission, I'll go along with it."

Kander blushed. "I'm sorry," he said. "I should have asked you instead of just stating what I intended to do. You are justified in being upset with me, Xzwindra. Thank you for agreeing to go along with the plan."

Xzwindra shifted uncomfortably. Her eyes searched Kander's face for signs of hypocrisy, but she found none. She didn't know how to respond. She was not used to men treating her with respect. She shrugged it off and cast him a derisive grimace.

"I will be going into town as well," said Captain Favel.

Kander frowned as he cast the captain a questioning look.

"I want to be available should the need arise." The corner of his mouth twisted upward. "Don't worry. I won't be conspicuous about it."

"The garb of a soldier and not conspicuous?" jibed Kander. "And what if some of Xvardris' spies are watching the streets of Yeps? You are distinctly recognizable, Captain Favel."

"He's right, you know," broke in Sergeant Tandrak. "You'll need a disguise, Captain." He tilted his head toward Kander. "And I've been told our young guide is an expert at disguises."

Captain Favel nodded in agreement.

Kander frowned. He did not like the idea, but Captain Favel was in charge. However, Kander wondered if the captain might not have other reasons than his safety for following him into Yeps. "Know anything about mining?" asked Kander. He lifted a brown burlap bag from next to his saddle. He opened it and pulled out a crumpled, broad-brimmed miner's hat and a worn blue denim jacket.

"Not much, but I have been to the salt mine at White Mountain just south of Xzendr," responded the Captain. "I observed the basics."

"Good," said Kander. He handed the jacket and hat over to the captain. "The hat will help hide your face, which you should probably smudge up a bit with some ash once we have a fire going."

Captain Favel's brow wrinkled in disapproval.

"Your skin is too fair to pass for a miner. If you can think of a better way to alter your look, that's fine with me." Kander broke a smug grin. "You have come up from the Luxurd mine to spend a bit of yer' pay. And let's hope there aren't any other salt miners in town. That might make things a little too interesting for you. By the by, have you ever been to Luxurd?"

The captain's expression told him he had not.

"What kind of information are you after?" broke in Corporal Mifstern. He was in the midst of digging a fire pit.

"Can't say just yet," quipped Kander.

"What he's saying is that he doesn't trust us!" put in Sergeant Tandrak. He turned to Kander. "I'd like to know why you don't trust us, but I don't suppose you'd feel obliged to share that with us either, would you?"

"Let's just say that I'm not a very trusting person." He offered the sergeant a halfhearted smile.

"Well, it seems to me that if we can't trust one another, we're in a heap of trouble," said Corporal Mifstern. He peered up at Kander and Sergeant Tandrak and then shifted his gaze to the others. Their faces were grim, but no one responded. The only sound was the whisper of the slight breeze ruffling the leaves of a nearby tree.

Captain Favel broke the silence. "Well, I'm hiking up to take a look at the lay of things."

As dawn grappled with the passing shadows of night, Kander and Xzwindra set out for Yeps. Kander wore a tattered red shirt and pants held up with broad blue-and-yellow striped suspenders, and a small pick hung at his side.

Xzwindra's hair was ruffled into wild disarray, and she wore an old torn and soiled dress. She looked the part of a slave woman down to the defiance that burned in her eyes.

Kander had been told that the town had three inns. They went to the Twin Spur first. "Sit yourself over there in yon corner, and wait for me!" Kander gave Xzwindra a push in the direction he had indicated. Her eyes shot back fire, but she did as she was told. Laughter rolled after her from every corner of the room, and she came close to walking out on Kander's little scam. She took a deep, angry breath and flumped down in the chair he had indicated.

"She's a spunky wench!" someone piped up.

"Don't know as I would want to live with 'er," bellowed a deep raspy voice. Again the inn shook with raucous laughter.

"Is she for sale?" asked another. His tone sounded half joking and half serious.

"She's a top-quality woman!" growled Kander. "She's strong, a hard worker. She's a challenge ta' keep in line, but I manage. Still, despite her faults, she's company. The wilds can be pretty lonely."

Xzwindra glared at Kander, her face red with anger, but no one was looking.

"Ain't seen you in these parts afore?" quizzed a hoary-headed old-timer with a patch covering one eye. "Where ya' been landin' yer pick?"

"In the Coastals off ta' the west," answered Kander. Discouragement fringed his voice. "Nary a nugget in more than a year. Them mountains over there be dry as my dead mule's bones. But I've heard that beyond the Viper Run, out in the Savage Lands, there be jewels as thick as my slave woman's head!"

Laughter roared from wall to wall, and a defiant Xzwindra came up off her seat snarling.

"Sit down, woman!" bellowed Kander. More laughter.

Xzwindra dropped back into the chair, but inside rage churned like witches' brew.

"Ain't never been beyond Viper Run," Kander continued. "Any a' you men been out thata' way?"

"Ain't never been there, and ain't never goin'!" declared one of the men. He looked up from his drink and from beneath the broad brim of his hat. Captain Favel indeed looked the part of a pick-worn miner.

Laughter tickled at Kander's throat, but he held it back. Xzwindra was not as discreet.

"And jus' what are you laughin' at, woman?" Kander's brows were roiled, and his eyes lashed anger.

Xzwindra stopped laughing and turned away.

"That's better," he growled.

"That she tiger's got spunk, but the fella's got her under thumb, that's fer sure!" said Captain Favel. The place rolled with guffaws, and Xzwindra shifted angrily in her chair.

"Say, Pegran, you know the land beyond Viper Run, don't you?" one of the men asked the old-timer with one eye. "I been there, and if there are jewels out there, I sure ain't seen any of em," he rasped. With his good eye, he shot a piercing look at Kander, measuring him.

Kander couldn't believe his good fortune. Now he had to somehow get the old man off alone so he could talk to him. "And let me tell ya, boy, the Savage Lands is jus' that, savage! If I was you, I would plant my pick in more friendly rock than what ya got out there. Asides, it's no place fer a woman, not even a strong slave woman like that one of yours."

"Well, old-timer, why don't ya' join me an' my woman for a chat?" said Kander. "Ya can fill me in on that unfriendly place. Need to know all I can."

"Ain't interested," said Pegran.

"Well," Kander grinned and lifted a bottle, "ya' interested in a tip a berry-plumb ale?" The others chuckled as Pegran got up and sauntered over to join Kander and Xzwindra at the table in the corner, and then they went back to their normal swill and chatter.

Pegran had no more than sat down when the place echoed with the sound of the heavy boots of soldiers pounding along the outside wooden walkway. Moments later, several uniformed men entered. They wore the insignia of Xvardris' army. Their eyes scanned the room as if they were looking for someone in particular. One of the soldier's eyes brightened when he saw Xzwindra. "Say, woman, don't I know you from somewhere?" he barked.

"Don't ya be meddlin' wi' me slave woman!" spat Kander. Anger edged his voice. "Ain't you soldier fellas taught no manners?"

"I'm sure I know that woman, Captain," said the soldier to a man with gold bars on his shoulders.

Xzwindra spat at the soldier's boots.

Without a second thought, he responded by slapping her across the face.

"By pick and shovel, we'll have none a' that in our town!" shouted Captain Favel. He came to his feet, and instantly all the men in the room responded in kind. Fists flew, and a nasty brawl ensued.

While the others were brawling, Kander pulled Pegran off to one side away from flailing fists and broken bottles. "I'm with the Resistance," he whispered.

Pegran's face lit up.

Kander had taken a risk, but the old man's smile told him he had guessed right. "A number of years ago, you were hired to guide two Pagyns who were taking a pregnant girl somewhere to the east. We have to find the girl. We need your help, Pegran."

Pegran nodded while keeping his eye on the brawl.

"We're camped at the base of Pinnacle Peak," Kander whispered. "Meet us there after dark."

Pegran nodded again, gave a wink, and then joined the fray.

"What was that about?" asked Xzwindra. She had cautiously worked her way around the mass of boiling bodies to Kander's side. She had not overheard the conversation for all the noise.

"Time will tell." Kander cast her a sardonic smile, sucked in air, and added, "I guess I'd better join in if we're to make this look good."

When the dust settled, the soldier who had recognized Xzwindra was carried out unconscious, his jaw twisted and bleeding.

Captain Favel slipped his steel knuckles into his pocket and began helping the innkeeper put his place together again.

The commander of the offending soldiers apologized to the innkeeper, pulled his battered troops together, and left.

When it was over, Kander had a goose egg on his forehead and a tender midsection. Captain Favel came through the scuffle with a bruised left arm and a cut above his left eye. Despite the redness of her cheek from being slapped, Xzwindra smiled smugly as she looked at the two of them. They did not acknowledge each other, but went their separate ways.

*L*ater, Captain Favel joined Kander and Xzwindra outside of town. As they headed back to their camp, Xzwindra commented, "Slave woman, huh?" She looked from one to the other and added, "Revenge is sweet, and I didn't even have to lift a finger."

"Well, the ruse worked," said Kander as he felt the tender spot on his head.

"And did you get the information you were after?" asked Captain Favel.

Kander looked back over his shoulder toward Yeps. "We'll see," he answered.

Chapter 14

While the dying sun glinted off the top of Pinnacle Peak, Kander and Captain Favel sat in the shadows below licking their wounds. Xzwindra reveled in telling the story of their encounter with Xvardris' soldiers. She had just come to the part where Kander joined the fray in time to take two good hits while landing none of his own, when out of the darkness walked the one-eyed old-timer. Men came to their feet with weapons at the ready.

Kander lifted a hand as if to restrain. "It's okay," he said. "His name is Pegran. He's invited."

"No watch?" asked Pegran as he moseyed over to the fire.

Captain Favel glanced toward the hilltop. He shook his head and grinned at Pegran. "Do we we need one?"

"Not really, though I imagine ya' have one." He too glanced toward the peak above them. He let out a self-satisfied chuckle and nodded toward the fire. "Yer burnin' dry, an' yer well-hidden from pryin' eyes down in the valley. The winds carryin' yer smell southeast around the mountain." Pegran cast them a broad grin. "Guess you'll be okay."

"Thanks for coming," said Kander as he rose to greet him.

"Root brew?" asked Captain Favel. "It's hot and bitter."

"I'll take a draught then," said Pegran. "It's been a long time since I sat by a campfire an' had a good mug a' bitterroot." He took a seat on a large rock near the fire.

Sergeant Tandrak poured him a mug of the black, bitter brew.

"So, yer wi' the Resistance," said Pegran. He glanced about. "This all of ya?"

"We're just a contingent," said Captain Favel. "The Resistance is growing. We're well over a thousand strong, and that's not including the nonmilitary people who support us in whatever way they can."

They chatted about a number of things, Pegran probing, mulling. After a bit, Kander broached the subject that was uppermost on his mind. "Pegran, a fellow who used to work at Yeps Station for the horse train told me that seven years ago you accompanied two Pagyns and a pregnant girl at least as far as Luxurd and possibly beyond."

"That I did, lad. A beauty she was. Fine girl. Finest I 'er met," said Pegran. Then he paused and looked at Kander and each of the others with skepticism coloring his eye. "But what is that ta' you folk?"

"Were you with her when the child was born?" asked Captain Favel. His interest was growing. When they had arrived back at camp after the fracas in Yeps, Kander had taken him aside and told him the one-eyed man had the information needed to find the heir. He had been doubtful, but now he was listening.

"Well, not wi' her as such, if ya' know what I mean," said the old-timer indignantly. "The cook at the South Run Station, last one afore ya' get ta Zxendr Station, was wi' her. She gave birth ta' a boy, she did, an ugly little prune. But she thought he was Baruch's triumph. Cute, she called him. Humph! Cute!" He shook his head. "Held me tongue and didn't tell her what I thought."

"Pegran, did the girl say anything about the father?" asked Kander while leaning forward as if to impress upon Pegran the importance of his question.

"Crazy talk, that was all." Pegran waved his hand indicating that they really didn't want to hear it.

But Kander did want to hear it. He pressed the old-timer on the matter.

The wrinkle of Pegran's brow showed his cynicism. "Once when we were alone, which weren't often, she tol' me her son was a prince, the son a' King Zandirxn hi'self." Pegran laughed, but the others around the fire remained somber. He shrugged a shoulder. "That's what she told me! I tol' ya' it were crazy talk."

"No, Pegran, it wasn't crazy talk," said Kander. "She spoke true. Do you remember the girl's name?"

"Ya mean King Zandirxn really did rape the girl, jes' like she said?" The old man spoke through clenched teeth. "Wretched king got wa' he deserved then!" Pegran's face burned redder than the campfire's flames. "Her name? Patrexna. How could I forget it? Spent more n' half a year wi' those three . . . four. An' I saw to it that those Pagyn fellas treated her right too. Still, I was glad ta be rid a' em all. That baby 'bout drove me crazy wi' his cryin' an a whimperin'.

"Where did you take them, Pegran?" asked Captain Favel.

Kander raised a hand. "Wait, Pegran. Don't answer that question!"

"And why not?" asked Pegran.

"He's not the trusting sort!" put in Sergeant Tandrak in a mocking voice.

"Maybe he's got reason not to trust, and maybe he don't." Pegran eyed Kander carefully, and a grin slowly spread his face. "If I tell one a' ya where I took the girl, I tell ya all. Cause maybe I don't trust jes' tellin' one. But first, I wants ta know why you wants ta know."

Captain Favel swept a hand toward Kander as if to say, "It's up to you to tell him."

Kander explained their mission – the return of the king.

Pegran responded with a low whistle and raised eyebrows. "Well, ya' gots a long journey ahead a ya'. And a dangerous one too."

Ignoring Kander's plea not to tell the others where he had taken Patrexna and her child, he offered to them all, "Took em ta Eknard on the Savage Sea. From there I think the girl and the babe were taken over to Krok on Xziland. Thas' as far ta the east as any man ha' ever been. Will take ya six months ta a year ta get there. If'n ya gets there a'tall."

"We'll get there!" responded Captain Favel.

"Pegran, would you be willing to take us there?" asked Kander.

Captain Favel shot him a reproving glance.

Kander returned the glare. "Finding the girl and child are my responsibility, Captain! None of us have been beyond Luxurd, let alone clear across the Savage Lands. We need a guide, and I already know that there is none better than this man sitting here by our campfire!"

Pegran sat up straight and smiled proudly. "Why thankee for the compliment, lad! I'd be glad ta show ya the way, if the good Cap'n doesn't mind."

So it was that with a nod from Captain Favel, Pegran became the seventh member of the King's Company. An hour later, he slipped back out into the night.

At first light, Pegran came riding back into camp on an old sway-backed horse. "Name's Dusty," he said. He had his few necessities strapped behind his saddle. He looked around at the camp. "Well, we'd better be headin' out if'n ya' can get things put in order here." he added with a grin.

Sedrnal buried their fire pit. The company mounted up and followed Pegran south. "Viper Run be a dangerous place," Pegran commented over his shoulder.

Chapter 15

Zanzxra drifted into Yeps no more than an hour after Pegran joined the King's Company at their campfire behind Pinnacle Peak. The assassin made his way about the streets and alleys of the city searching, watching, and listening. When people saw the seven-foot tall behemoth with hulking shoulders and bulging, powerful arms, they shied away. Clad in black, his head covered with a black silk mask showing only his eyes and mouth downward, he struck fear even in the stout of heart.

The only buildings the black assassin entered were the inns where he drank ale, watched, and kept an ear to the nearby tables. At the Wind Blown, he overheard a conversation describing the brawl down the way at the Twin Spur. He wondered. Slipping out into the night, he made his way to the Twin Spur. There he drew the innkeeper aside. The hosteller broke a sweat, his voice trembled, and he wrung his apron as he told Zanzxra all he could remember.

"The young prospector and his slave woman were the center of the whole affair," he explained. "Strangers from the Coastals off to the west. They were headed east to look for jewels. No, they didn't take a room for the night. Honest, I have no idea where they stayed the night. After the brawl, they skedaddled out of here."

Zanzxra tossed a gold coin to the man's trembling hand. Once the giant was out the door, the innkeeper wiped his brow, took a deep breath and went back to work.

Two miners who sat at the table nearest to where the conversation had taken place got up and left minutes after the black assassin.

Zanzxra inquired at the other inns. None of the hostellers remembered a young prospector with a slave woman in tow though they had heard about the brawl. The black assassin looked out toward the foothills. A grim smile twisted the corners of his mouth.

Zanzxra generally slept during daylight hours since murky shadows and darkness suited his purposes better than light. So the morning found him out in the foothills seeking a dark hole and sleep. He found a cleft at the base of a bluff and squeezed into it. But sleep did not come readily, for when he closed his eyes he saw flames and Thaxndar's lifeless face grinning at him. When he finally did fall asleep, the dead priest haunted his dreams.

Pegran recommended taking the horse train to Luxurd Station. "T'will save the horses," he said.

But Captain Favel refused to return to Yeps. "We'd be sure to draw attention," he argued. "We'll catch the train at Three Trees Station. It's a hundred miles south and farther away from the prying eyes of Xvardris' spies."

A string of five wagons, one attached to the next, drawn by a team of twenty draft horses, formed the Viper Run Horse Train. Three wagons were enclosed, and two were open cargo wagons. The enclosed wagon farthest back carried stock while the two forward carried passengers. One of the passenger cars was a diner where meals were prepared and served. The other passenger car was divided into eight compartments that comfortably seated four passengers and uncomfortably seated six. A shifting, rickety boardwalk provided for movement between wagons.

The horse-train road, made of hammer-crushed rock laid over with slabs of slate, rose twenty feet above the hardpan, forming a snakelike mound that twisted its way from Yeps to Luxurd. The draft horses pulled the train at a speed of four to five miles an hour. A train leaving Yeps Station at midday, traveling nonstop, would arrive at Three Trees Station at noon the next day. There they would stop long enough to change teams and take on passengers should there be any.

Yeps was station one and Luxurd station fifteen. Each station lay approximately one hundred miles from the next.

The Viper Run Train Company maintained six trains on the run, so that a train passed through each station every five days barring a breakdown. And each station maintained a herd of about one hundred head of horses. Going south the train's cargo was primarily grain for the herds, while the return cargo was ores from the mines—salt, gypsum, copper, silver, gold, and more.

Pegran led the King's Company into Three Trees Station an hour before the train arrived. They had spent two days camped in the hills west of Three Trees while they waited for the train. Sergeant Tandrak had spotted the train twisting its way toward Three Trees Station on his watch. Their horses already saddled, they mounted up and rode down to meet it. While the train master changed teams, the King's Company boarded their horses and found two empty passenger compartments across from each other.

Upon inquiry they found that five passengers had boarded the train at Yeps, all miners returning from their yearly holiday away from the mines, two of whom they were to discover had taken part in the brawl at the Twin Spur Inn.

"Pegran!" The greeting came from a lanky, bright-eyed fellow in pants held up by over-the-shoulder button straps. "Headin' back out inta the Savage Lands, are ya? See ya' took up wi' the young prospector and hi' slave woman. Guess we showed them soldiers, din't we!"

"Aye, we showed em', Pegle." Pegran cast the man a conspiratorial grin. "But that black eye would seem ta indicate that it weren't entirely a one-sided show."

"Ya' got me on that one, Pegran." Pegle's eyes sparkled with laughter.

Kander, who was with Pegran at the time, was glad he had adopted his prospector guise for the duration. He shook his head and chuckled to himself as he listened to their banter.

"Pegran, ya might know this," Pegle's demeanor turned serious. "The night afore I left Yeps, there were a big man dressed in black, stood a full head taller than yer prospector friend here, wore a black mask o'er the top half a' his head, an' were askin' about yer friend and the slave woman. Real interested in 'em, he were. An' the feller weren't the friendly sort, if'n ya' know what I'm sayin'."

Pegran cast Kander a questioning glance and saw that Pegle's words were not good news. He turned back to the miner. "An' what did the man in black find out?" he inquired.

"What there were ta' find out, I s'pose," responded Pegle. "The line that were given at the Twin Spur were that the young prospector an' his slave woman were strangers from the Coastals and that they were askin' if'n Pegran were available ta guide them ta look fer jewels out in the Savage Lands." He jacked an eyebrow at Pegran. "That feller din't appear ta b'lieve the line any more than I b'lieved it. Ya' can bet he'll be follerin' at yer heels."

"Pegle, ya got too much intee'lect ta be a pick-swingin' miner," gibed Pegran. "We're obliged to ya, friend."

"Anytime, Pegran." Pegle eyed the old prospector thoughtfully then lifted a finger in warning. "Be careful. What-ever 'tis yer up to seems ta be stirrin' a cauldron a trouble. If'n ya need me an my partner here, ya know where ta find us."

Pegle's partner, a brutish looking fellow with a thick, bushy beard and rock-hard gaze, nodded.

Pegran tipped the brim of his hat and smiled. "If'n we need you and Norgran, we'll holler fer sure." He turned to leave but continued speaking over his shoulder. "An' we couldn't call on two better fellers, either."

When they joined Xzwindra and Captain Favel in their tray, as the compartments were called, Pegran pressed Kander for an explanation. "Who is this hulkin' feller in black that's a follerin' us?"

Xzwindra and Captain Favel were both familiar with the Black Assassin and were not pleased to hear that he was pursuing them. The corners of Captain Favel's mouth drew down, and he commented to Kander, "Well, I told you to sleep with one eye open, didn't I?"

"Indeed, you did." Kander stared hard at the captain. "But tell me, Captain Favel, how did you know the Black Assassin would be sent to eliminate me? Did you know when he was sent to eliminate Thaxndar?"

Captain Favel smiled sardonically. "You still do not trust me, do you?" He shook his head. "I see no reason to respond to your questions."

"Ya know, I've noticed there be a bit a' bad blood 'tween you two," said Pegran. He looked from one to the other. "I don't like it! Not a bit. If we can't trust each other, we be in a heap a' trouble, and that fer sure. Ya've pulled me inta this deadly mess, clear up ta' me neck, so ya' can tell me right now 'zackly what be the problem 'tween you two."

Captain Favel laughed and Kander gave him a fixed stare.

"I'll tell you what the problem is, Pegran." Captain Favel's laughter died, and he became cold sober. "Someone within the Resistance is a spy, and it is quite possibly one of our company, excluding Kander, so our young friend here trusts none of us. And I believe I happen to be his number-one suspect in that regard. And I'll grant, it could just as easily be me as any of the others, but it is not me. However, if you were to ask any of the others if they are the spy, they would no doubt deny it as well. Is a traitor going to admit to being a traitor? Of course not! And there lies our dilemma. No matter what I say or do I remain a suspect." He smiled and raised his hands. "So, Pegran, the answer to the quandary?"

"The answer is simple," said Pegran. He turned and faced Kander. "Ya'll have ta' trus' yer enemy, an' that's that. If the spy were out fer blood, he would already ha' spilt it. Never would a' let ya get this far. Second, once we be out in the Savage Lands, if'n not so already, the spy has no way a' communicatin' wi' any a' his contacts. So, until we find the king, ya' trus' yer enemy, even wi' yer life, or we're never gunna get ta' the king." He raised an eyebrow and peered at Kander. "Ya' hear me, lad? Cause the Savage Lands be jes' that, savage, an' we go through em' hand in hand, so ta speak, or we don't go at all!"

Captain Favel cast Kander a questioning look.

Kander glanced from Pegran to Captain Favel and then back to Pegran. He nodded. "You're right, Pegran." He took a deep breath. "It won't be easy, but hand in hand it will be." He extended hand and arm and Captain Favel responded in kind. They grasped wrist to wrist, and squeezed, acknowledging agreement.

"There! It be settled. An' I'll sleep a lot easier now," said Pegran. He turned to Xzwindra who had acknowledged surprise at hearing about there being a spy. "What about you, slave woman?"

She scowled in response.

Pegran laughed. "No offense, but yer name be more than me lips can spit," said Pegran apologetically.

"Men!" she grated, but her caustic scowl eased to a smirk; not quite a smile.

"How 'bout if'n I call ya Windy? Tha's not quite such a mouthful. Can't quite handle those X's an' Z's."

"Pegran, you're a tease!" Xzwindra's smirk shifted to a half laugh. "Yes, you can call me Windy, but no wise cracks with it."

"Wise cracks? Me?" responded Pegran.

They all laughed.

"And I'm getting fed up with this slave woman bit!" added Xzwindra. She cast a reproving glance in Kander's direction.

"I truly am sorry, Xzwindra," said Kander. He lifted his hands in a gesture of helplessness. "However, we'll have to maintain the charade until we get beyond Luxurd Station. And you're doing great. So far you've been pretty convincing. Must be the fire in your eyes." The fire rekindled. "Yes, that's the look!" he teased.

"Ya' live dangerously, lad!" said Pegran. He shook his head in disbelief. "Some people jes' ain't got the sense Baruch gave a mule."

"Look at that monster of a snake!" broke in Captain Favel. He pointed out the window to a place beyond the slope of the mounded road that the train rattled along the top of. "It must be as long as I am tall and fat as my upper arm!"

The window was an oblong opening without a pane. A wooden cover hung below the window on heavy hinges, and above the window were wooden blocks that turned to hold it in place when closed. Four heads pressed together to hang out the window to get a good look at the red-eyed viper, so named because its eyes were brilliant red. They contrasted with the snake's dull grayish-brown body. The serpent's hooded head stood high, and it appeared to watch them as the train passed.

"Thas' why they ha' blinders on the horses," said Pegran. "If'n the horses saw that little specmin a' sand flesh, they'd spook sure."

"What if it comes up on the road bed?" Repulsion edged Xzwindra's voice.

"Won't happen." said Pegran. He dropped back down in his seat. "The mound the train rides on is made with blue purgipsom mixed in with the rock grit. The vipers keep their distance from purgipsom. Can't say why, but they'll come ta' the edge a' the mound but no farther. An' sure as hot sand, won't cross it."

"And you actually camp out there with those vipers slinking about?" Kander stared back toward where they had seen the snake. "Aren't they dangerous?"

"Their bite be instant death, lad," Pegran leaned back in his seat and crossed his legs out in front of him. "An' they can sense warm flesh a mile away. Did ya' see how they watched as we passed? If'n yer out on the hardpan an' they gets the scent a' ya, they'll stalk ya for a hundred miles if need be."

"And you sleep out there?" asked Xzwindra her eyes wide and questioning. "Aren't you afraid they will come bite you during the night, or don't they come out at night?"

"Oh, they come out at night, all right," said Pegran with a broad story-tell grin. "They're mainly creatures a' the night. Tha's why they got those shiny red eyes. An' they'll bite ya' as soon in the dark as in the day. But ol' Pegran don't fear no critter a' the wild." He waited for Xzwindra's amazement to register. Once satisfied that she was in awe, he winked at her and continued. "I carry a bag a powdered purgipsom wi' me. At night I sprinkle the blue powder in a circle around my camp, an' I sleep like a baby. Why I've woked up in the mornin' ta a' crowd a' those critters settin' outside the circle google-eyein' me wi' gray salivy a drippin' from their long, pointy fangs."

"You couldn't stay inside your circle until they lost interest," said Captain Favel, who was as engrossed in the old man's story as Xzwindra. "So what did you do next?"

"Well, I keep a long sword handy when I be campin' in the Run." He sat up straight and pretending to have a sword in his hand, and howled, "Swish! Swish! Swish!" The oldtimer smiled broadly and shook a finger in the air. "An' ya know, even wi' out their heads, those wretched critters wiggle an' squirm the whole day long. Don't stop till after dark—so I'm told. Course, I don't wait around ta see."

Captain Favel gave the old man a "you can't be serious" look, while Xzwindra's smile oozed with skepticism.

Kander grinned and shook his head. "You tell a good story, Pegran!" he said with a laugh. "You almost had me believing you there for a moment."

A hurt puppy look came into Pegran's eye. "Ya' doen' believe me? Where be yer trus', boy? He reached inside his shirt and showed them a leather necklace from which hung at least thirty two-to-three-inch long viper fangs.

Kander examined them closely. They were solid, except for a thread-thin hollow running end to end.

"If'n ya doen' believe my story, then how da' ya explain these? Ya think I jes' walked up on the little critters while they was a sleeping, plucked their fangs, an' ran? Would that make a better story, lad?"

"Wow!" Kander's voice echoed with awe. "You are an amazing fellow, Pegran. I didn't mean to, you know . . ."

Pegran broke out in ribald laughter. "I wouldn't believe it if I din't see it either, lad! An' those two din't believe me any more then you did! But the story be true. True as any story I ever tol'."

As Pegran spoke, the west wind picked up, swirling sand in the window. They closed the cover and withdrew into silence. Lost in thought, Captain Favel leaned his head back and stared off into space. Pegran leaned into the corner, closed his eyes, and snored. Xzwindra practiced tying knots with a piece of leather cord Pegran had given her. Kander sat studying his companions, wondering how they had come to be who they were. Interesting people! he thought. And despite myself, I'm even beginning to like Captain Favel.

The horse train rattled on.

Chapter 16

Xvardris sat with chin in hand gazing out a nearby window at the seemingly endless green sea of trees that stretched out toward the mountains and Havenholt.

General Bodrak walked in. "My scouts have returned," he said. He waited, but Xvardris did not turn to look at him. He grimaced and continued his report. "There is no way to assault the Resistance stronghold. War machines are essential, and the fortress is inaccessible to such contrivances. The forest is too thick and the walls too high. Could we attempt the walls, hundreds, if not thousands, would die in the effort."

"Humm. So, two hundred miles of trees stand between us and the Resistance stronghold," mused Xvardris.

General Bodrak did not respond. He waited stone-faced and patient, though his eyes did shift toward the window.

Xvardris finally turned and faced the general, his gaze icy. "The price of taking the stronghold is inconsequential. The Resistance must be crushed!" He walked over to the window and, leaning both hands on the sill, thoughtfully stared out across Tangle Wood. After a time, he turned again to General Bodrak. The corner of his mouth slowly curled upward. "When we have destroyed Havenholt, we will have decimated the enemy, heart and soul. Clear a staging area in the forest fifty miles back from Havenholt. We will build the war machines as we clear the forest. Once the war machines are built, we will clear more forest and as we clear the forest we will advance toward the stronghold."

Following his meeting with General Bodrak, Xvardris ordered more than a thousand slaves shipped in from Athos. He also conscripted nine hundred men of Xzwendaria to forced labor. Camps were established in Tangle Wood, and with whips cracking the slaves set to clearing the forest.

Jentrxn's spies informed the Resistance council of Xvardris' plans. The Resistance allowed the camps to be built and the clearing to begin. They lulled Xvardris into thinking that his plan would not meet with any direct resistance.

But once Xvardris became smugly confident, General Vandwert and his men struck with storm-like fury. They swarmed from the surrounding forest, overpowering the soldiers who drove the slave laborers. Some slaves fled into the forest in hopes of gaining freedom, but most joined themselves to the Resistance. Almost to a man, all the Xzwendarians who had been conscripted to forced labor returned to Havenholt to become Resistance fighters. In one day the Resistance army grew by nearly a thousand men, and the weapon forges of Havenholt burned hot and the hammers rang.

General Bodrak had warned Xvardris of just such a possibility, but in his pride he had not listened. "They do not have the strength or the courage!" he had declared. "They are holed up in their safe little den quaking with fear!"

But quaking with fear they were not. The men of the Resistance were willing to pay the price that fighting for freedom extracted.

"One victory does not win a war!" raged Xvardris.

Within a week, word came to Havenholt from Major Targndel that troops were pouring in from Nefarious Reach with more slaves. Major Targndel was convinced Xvardris had a new plan, but he had not yet found out what that plan entailed.

General Bodrak came before Xvardris and bowed slightly. "Sir, the troops are in position, and the slaves can be put to task on a day's notice." He hesitated momentarily as if contemplating whether he should say more or not. "May I ask," he ventured, "the nature of your plan?"

Xvardris leached a smile. "We will burn the forest!" he declared. His face spoke triumph. "It is the season of the Ardent Zephyrs. The forest is dry, and smoke will blow toward the mountains, engulfing Havenholt. If we're lucky, we will suffocate the Resistance. At the least, we will make their wretched lives miserable while opening a way of attack."

"But sir, you are talking about nearly three hundred square miles of forest." A hint of protest edged General Bodrak's voice.

Xvardris' mood went frigid. "General, if you don't have the stomach to carry out my orders, I'm sure I can find someone who does."

"My lord," General Bodrak gave an acquiescing nod, "I only meant that it would take a long time to burn the entire forest and then clear a two-hundred-mile path for our war machines."

"You have finished building the machines?" Xvardris' tone remained harsh.

"They are ready, my lord," said the General.

"Then once the forest starts burning, you can begin clearing, and I don't care how long it takes, as long as the job gets done!" Xvardris' words cracked like a slave-driver's whip. "Have I made myself clear, General?"

"Yes, my lord." General Bodrak bowed submissively.

Xvardris' smile returned. Controlling others pleased him. "Set the forest on fire along the western edge," he instructed in a calm, steady voice, "but also at the northern and southern ends. And should the Resistance try to escape between the mountains and the burning forest, you will have your armies waiting, ready to crush them."

"As you say, my lord," responded General Bodrak.

Xvardris waved him away, and the officer hurriedly left the room.

That night Zedria saw to it that General Bodrak drank more than a general should drink. And as a result, the general's tongue became looser than a general's tongue should become. The next morning, the general was sick, and the conversation of the previous night troubled him, but he could not bring it back out of the black fog that enveloped his mind.

Major Targndel told the council what he had learned from Zedria.

General Vandwert shook his head, a look of amazement sheeting his face. "How does she get her information?" he asked.

"I don't know. I don't ask. And frankly, I don't care," returned the major. "Her job is to get information, and that is what she does. The question is, what are we going to do with the information?"

"With the Ardent Zephyrs blowing smoke and fire down our throats, this place will quickly become unlivable," offered the general. "We had best begin evacuating the fortress immediately. If we leave now, we will not have to deal with the heat and smoke, and Xvardris will not expect us to fly the coop so soon. We'll catch them by surprise."

"And just where do we fly to?" injected Razrdris. He stood off to one side, arms folded, a scowl creasing his brow.

"Into the mountains north of Pristine Wood," responded the General curtly.

"Too close to Nefarious Reach's front door," put in Major Targndel. "We'd be walking right into the enemies' jaws. South through Fetter Wood seems a better option, if you ask me. Still, either choice leaves us unprotected and hinders our ability to gather information."

Jentrxn shook his head. "Bivouacking several thousand men somewhere out in the foothills would be a logistical nightmare, and Major Targndel is right. We would have no defenses." Jentrxn took a deep breath and smiled wryly. "Legend has it that a massive stronghold stands in the middle of the Murkwold."

Waving a mocking hand, Prior Forknedrn laughed. "The Murkwold is a place said to be haunted by demons and is feared by men everywhere." He looked around the room from one leader to the next. "Even if there is a deserted fortress in the Murkwold, would our people follow us there? I fear not."

"It seems to me," said Razrdris, "that to leave Havenholt would be absolute folly. We will be playing right into Xvardris' hands no matter what direction we go. We must stay where we are and face whatever we must face."

"And when this place is thick with smoke, and our people are dying because they cannot breathe, what then, Razrdris?" scoffed General Vandwert.

"We trust Baruch. He will not let us down." The fortress commander ignored the skeptical glances. "We continue to talk about what we must do, but we have not sought Baruch's face in these matters. I say, let us seek his face and know what he would have us do."

Prior Forknedrn's face went red as the others looked to him for a response. He shrugged his shoulders. The others waited in silence. "Of course, Razrdris is right," he said at last. "We would do well to seek Baruch's face before we make any decision. I will prepare the sacrifice, and we will wait upon Baruch for his decision."

The smoke of the sacrifice rose to the heavens, while the five leaders waited with faces bent to the earth. The sun smiled on them from above the western horizon. They waited in silence as darkness whelmed the fortress. When they looked up, they saw a pillar of fire burning above the altar. The sacrifice and wood were utterly consumed. The five men remained prostrate through the night while the fire burned on. When the day dawned, the pillar of fire turned to smoke, rose from the altar and vanished. The leaders of the Resistance rose. They spoke not a word. The decision was made. They would remain at Havenholt.

Razrdris took several of his guardsmen and entered the bowels of the fortress to determine how many people could be housed in the caverns behind the fortress once the city was engulfed in smoke. To his delight, he found that a cold wind blew outward from one of the tunnels that reached back into the darkness.

"Where does this tunnel lead?" Razrdris asked his master of chambers.

"To regions unexplored," responded Bndel. "I know this stronghold inside and out, but even I do not know where this tunnel leads. We call it the Black Cavern, for its darkness is deep."

"Well, then, let's do some exploring!" Razrdris urged.

"That will be difficult," said Bndel. "The reason the Black Cavern has remained a mystery is because the wind that blows through the tunnel is so strong that our torches will not stay lit. And when we shield the torches, they do not provide sufficient light to pierce the great darkness."

"Humm," mused Razrdris. He gazed about the chamber. "Where does the wind that comes from the cavern go? It is not felt in other parts of these lower chambers."

"We keep that great door shut." Bndel pointed across the chamber to a big wooden door. "You probably noticed when we entered that we passed through a small side door into a short passageway, then through another small door into this chamber. We call that passageway the Buffer. Because we never have both doors open at the same time, the wind is diverted from the fortress and forced out those vent ducts over there."

Razrdris looked to where Bndel was now pointing. Two very narrow cuts about twenty feet apart pierced the rock wall and extended out the side of the mountain to somewhere. The holes were about three feet in diameter. Razrdris smiled and set his fists to his hips. "Wonderful!" he said with a laugh. "Close off the vents, and open the big wooden door."

"Sir, that will create a wind of immense force, and it will blow right through the fortress stables," said Bndel. "Are you sure that's what you want us to do?"

"The force of the Black Cavern wind is so great that if you are out on the mountainside, you can't even get near the opening of the vent holes," piped one of Bndel's men. "The way we have things set up right now, the force is controlled. If we open the main door . . ."

Razrdris interrupted. "I want you to have Vandwen move the stables up to the next level. Then close off whatever apertures are necessary to direct the force of the wind out and up the face of the fortress proper."

Bndel and his men immediately set to work directing the wind so that by the time the black smoke of the burning forest reached Havenholt, the breath of the Black Cavern would blow out from the base of the stronghold and carry the rancid smoke up and over the escarpment.

Chapter 17

A day after leaving Three Trees, the slow-moving horse train pulled into Dry Lakes Station. Just east of the station, seven large, sandy hollows that once held water beckoned the living toward death. In contrast, Warm Lake lay west of the horse-train station at the foot of Shadeless Bluff, and Rush Creek tumbled over the bluff, providing Warm Lake with a continuous supply of fresh water. However, although Rush Creek flowed into Warm Lake, it did not flow out again. The sun's fiery evaporating powers and the watering of the horse herd used up every gallon of water that Rush Creek dumped into the lake.

Kander noticed that the eastern shoreline of the lake and a stretch of land reaching down to and circling the way station was colored light blue. Purgipsom he presumed.

"What about horses, Pegran?" asked Kander as they exited the train. "Do the vipers attack horses?"

"Men, desert antelope, rabbits, and the like, but not horses, though the horses be petrified of em." Pegran scowled and waggled his head. "I don't know what it is, but there is somethin' about horses those slitherin' vermin don't much like—probably the smell. Do have an odor all their own, ya' know."

Shortly after they pulled into Dry Lakes Station, the northbound horse train arrived, heavy with ore and carrying miners headed to Yeps for their turn at holiday. Captain Favel noticed a heavyset fellow leave the southbound train to converse with three miners who had just exited the northbound train. The big man looked this way and that and over his shoulder as if he was telling some dark secret. The others responded with raised eyebrows, nods, and scowls.

And they talk about women gossiping! Captain Favel muttered to himself. So now the news travels north, and the Black Assassin will soon be traveling south. Men!

In the shade of the way station, he also noticed Pegle and Norgran in close conversation with another miner from the northbound train. Pegran joined them. Captain Favel watched Pegran's brow crease and his countenance grow grim. Finally, Pegran broke away from the miners, caught Captain Favel's eye, then nonchalantly sauntered out toward Warm Lake.

A few moments later, Captain Favel followed.

"There be a troop a' soldiers a waitin' at the next station," said Pegran once they were out of earshot. "They don't seem ta be goin' anyplace, an' they be checkin' ever'one who passes through from the north. Apparently, they be lookin' fer members a' the Resistance that might be headed south ta recruit miners to their cause. Xvardris realizes that if the miners were ta' strike it would tie knots in his purse strings. He wouldn't be able ta' pay the army he's amassing. But whatever his reason fer the soldiers, it puts us in a bad way, cap'n."

"How many soldiers are we talking about?" Captain Favel's gaze rested on the waterfalls across the lake.

"There be all a' thirty." Pegran looked over his shoulder to make sure no one had followed them out to the lake. "But they be on foot. No horses. Now, if we could get the train master ta' cooperate, we could get off the train afore Thirty-five Pines Station, camp in Vipers' Den Holler in the foothills ta the west, then meet the train south a' the station later in the day an' be on our way again."

"It's worth a try, but I hope you have plenty of that blue purgipsom." Captain Favel cast Pegran a hopeful smile.

"I'll pick up another bag here at Dry Lakes," said Pegran as they headed back to catch the train. "An' we'll need the purgipsom. Vipers' Den Holler be a breeding ground fer the critters."

"Then why camp there?"

Pegran laughed but offered no explanation.

The trainmaster, aware of Pegran's reputation, took great pleasure in having him aboard—fodder for a tale or two when he got back to Yeps. So when Pegran approached him with his curious request, the good trainmaster was happy to oblige him with a "breakdown" north of Thirty-five Pines.

"What you do after the train breaks down – well, what can I do if you decide to go on by horseback?" The trainmaster's smile almost crackled. Fodder for a story indeed!

Ten miles north of Thirty-five Pines, the southbound Viper Run Horse Train came to an unexpected halt. While the miners hurried to the front of the train to see "what in the mother load" was up, the King's Company hoofed it back to the stock car. They lowered the ramp, removed their horses, raised the ramp again, saddled up, and headed west across the desert toward the foothills.

The surprised miners and train crew broke into a cacophony of hoots and hollers. "Vipers galore out there!" someone shouted.

"Hey!" yelled the trainmaster feigning anger. "You can't leave my train! This is an unscheduled stop! Fools! It's dangerous out there!" He threw down his broad-brimmed hat. "The devil with ya' all!" he shouted. "Ya' won't ride my train again!"

A viper lay sunning itself on a rock beyond the mounded train run. It slipped from its resting place and slithered after the horsemen.

The crew and three of the miners laughed, made mocking gestures, and shouted, "You'll think again when a viper's tooth sticks ya!"

Pegle and Norgran allowed a brief smirk as they watched the trainmaster repair the "broken" strap, then returned to their tray. And with a jolt, the horse train continued its run to Thirty-five Pines Station.

Soldiers surrounded the train as it pulled up to the station. The officer in charge commanded everyone to stay put and demanded to see the train's passenger list and manifest.

Miners' credentials were checked against the passenger list and the cargo inspected. Seven passengers and nine horses were missing. The trainmaster explained that there had been a breakdown and that while he was making repairs, the impatient fools had removed their horses from the stock wagon and lit out across the desert. "Claimed to be prospectors," he told them. "The female? A slave woman."

The other passengers were questioned. They confirmed the trainmaster's story. However, one questioned whether the seven really were who they claimed to be. "Never seen that many prospectors traveling in company," he said. "Prospectors are loners. Too greedy to work with anybody, seppin' maybe a guide. I'd be suspicious a' that lot if I was you, captain. I'll bet they're up ta' no good a' some kind."

"Did they have a leader?" asked the officer.

"Pegran was their guide. An' if Pegran's their guide, then Pegran's their leader," said the miner. "But a fella' called Favel seemed ta' be the leader a' the other six. A tall fella' with dark hair—somber sort a' fella'. Not unfriendly, mind ya', but the serious kind."

"Favel? The name sounds familiar." The officer stroked his blond, pointed beard. Then a knowing smile broke across his face. "Captain Favel? Surely not."

"Yes, that's what they called him when they thought no one was listenin'," chimed in one of the horse train crew members.

"Well, well." The officer's eyes sparkled. "I served under Captain Favel's command before he went over to the Resistance. So he is the one they have sent to foment discontent among the miners. Which way did the renegades go after they left the train?"

The horse-train crew member bit his lip. He wished he had kept his big mouth shut. If he had only known! The miner who fingered Captain Favel and the others to begin with, gave the officer the information he wanted.

The officer turned to the trainmaster. "Horse train stopping out on the run? Unheard of!" scoffed the officer. "Perhaps you are sympathetic to the cause of the Resistance?"

"No, the trainmaster was not in cahoots with those varmints," interjected the miner. "Strap broke that held the lead horse in her harness, and it had to be repaired. But those two . . ." He nodded toward Pegle and Norgran, "Those two may ha' been conspirators with them. They spent a lot a' time jaw flappin' with Pegran."

"That be true," said Pegle. He shot his fellow miner an angry eye. "That ol' sand flea an' I been friends fer nigh unto a millennia. But talkin' ta' a friend ain't bein' a conspirator, 'cause there weren't nothin' to conspire about! Fer that matter, Gorlon, seems I saw you and Fendrik speakin' with Pegran back at Three Trees. Smilin' big, backslappin' an all. Maybe yer a conspirator yerself!"

"Everyone knows Pegran!" defended Fendrick. "Course Gorlon and I had a word with him. Nothin' wrong with that, Pegle!"

"My point exactly!" said Pegle.

"Enough! Enough!" groused the officer. "We've got business to tend to."

He turned to the trainmaster again. "To prove your innocence in this matter, you'll lend me and my men the other ten horses you're carrying." He grinned broadly and gave the trainmaster a good-natured slap on the back, then turned away. "Lurndrin, get the horses off the stock wagon!"

"There's a whole herd beyond that stand of trees over there, Lieutenant Wndark. Enough horseflesh for all of us to have mounts," piped up one of the soldiers.

The lieutenant looked at the young soldier and shook his head. "We aren't spreading our legs over the back of those monstrous draft horses!" he jibed. "Besides, they aren't broke for riding. Have you ever ridden a horse that's not been broke? No! So keep your fool tongue in your mouth."

Lurndrin and three fellow soldiers soon returned with the ten horses from the stock wagon, saddled and ready to ride.

Lieutenant Wndark picked out nine men, including Lurndrin, and told them to mount up.

"What about me?" protested the unfortunate soldier who had suggested riding the draft horses. "I have rank over Lurndrin and Grandx!"

"So you do." The lieutenant steadied his mount and lifted himself into the saddle. "That's why I'm putting you in charge of leading the rest of the company on foot. Just follow our dust."

"Sir, I wouldn't go chasin' out across the desert, if I were you." The young way-station attendant who kept the herd stepped forward. He wiped his brow. "There are as many vipers out there as cactus. Those fools who left the train have fled into the jaws of death."

"Son, if I had wanted your advice, I would have asked for it!" snapped Lieutenant Wndark. He turned his horse and rode away. The others rode after him.

With the young attendant's words ringing in their ears and a sudden burst of sweat on their brows, the foot soldiers followed.

The young way-station attendant tipped his hat back and shook his head. "Poor fools," he mumbled.

Chapter 18

Vipers appeared as if suddenly conjured from the desert dust.

Pegran paid little attention to the snakes as he led Kander and the King's Company across the sandy hardpan toward Viper's Den Hollow. The horses were skittish despite the blinders Pegran had made for them, and Xzwindra turned white and put a death grip on her saddle horn every time she saw one of the slithery dust devils. A tingle of dread crawled up Kander's spine whenever a specter of death rose from the dust. Corporal Mifstern kept his hand on the hilt of his sword, his eyes shifting to one side and then the other. Private Sedrnal's smile waned. And although Sergeant Tandrak showed no emotion, his eyes constantly shifted from side to side as well.

Their one-eyed guide led them into a broad canyon. When they were well into the middle of the canyon, he lifted a bag of purgipsom from his packhorse. He rode in a wide circle, spreading a line of blue powder around them and an outcrop of rocks. "There be a viper behind that near rock over there!" he called over his shoulder as he continued his work. "Kill it an' search the inside a' the circle fer others. We don't want no surprises while we wait."

Kander was closest to the rock in question, but he wasn't about to get off his horse to kill the deadly snake. Captain Favel gave Sergeant Tandrak a nod. The grim-faced sergeant slid from his horse, drew his sword, and disappeared behind the rock. A moment later, a viper's body whipped through the air and landed outside the blue circle of life. "Well, the beginning of a viper-tooth necklace!" Sergeant Tandrak declared as he emerged with the viper's head in hand. Kander shivered visibly. Xzwindra eased her horse to the far side of the group.

"All right, off your horses!" ordered Captain Favel. "Search the area carefully. We'll make our stand here if those soldiers figure out that we left the train and are fool enough to come looking, and it's likely they will."

Kander and Xzwindra reluctantly joined the others in the search. Private Sedrnal killed a second viper up in the rock pile and smiling proudly, held up its severed head for all to see.

"Those snakes put off a wretched odor! Get rid of that thing." Captain Favel turned his face away.

After breaking off the teeth, Private Sedrnal gave the viper's head a toss and then the viper itself. No other vipers were found.

"We'll set up our defense among the rocks, and we'll set our watch on top of that large boulder. That will give us a panoramic view of the Hollow." Captain Favel's eyes swept the horizon. "When you pull watch, keep an eye on the eastern horizon, but be sure to scan the entire spectrum now and then. If the soldiers come, they could approach from any direction. But you're most likely to see them first off to the east."

"Will they be mounted?" asked Corporal Mifstern.

"As far as we know, they do not have mounts of their own. But that doesn't mean they won't be mounted," said Captain Favel. "They may have horses available that we don't know about. They could confiscate the other horses on the train. And although it's not very likely, they could try the draft horses."

"Well, they be fools if'n they come out here without mounts!" declared Pegran. "Dead fools! And, fact is, they ain't too bright if they come with mounts!"

"I'll take first watch." Kander took a deep breath of the hot desert air and wiped his brow. "I want to pull my weight along with everyone else."

"No, Kander." Captain Favel did not even give Kander's request a moment's thought. "As much as I would like to have you carry your share of that burden, I can't allow it. If the enemy attacks suddenly, the watch will be their first target.

You're one of the two who have seen Patrexna, and you are primarily responsible for finding her and the heir. We can't afford to have you stretched out on a rock with an arrow sticking out your back or chest."

"Then I'll take first watch," volunteered Xzwindra.

Captain Favel started to protest, but when he saw the look in her eyes, he changed his mind. He gave her an affirming gesture, and she headed for the tall boulder.

"She just wants to be up where the vipers can't get at her!" muttered Kander. "Speakin' a' snakes," said Pegran, "take a look."

They followed his finger to two gigantic vipers that lay just outside the circle of purgipsom, their amber eyes seeming to sparkle with desire.

"Whew!" whistled Private Sedrnal. He pointed off to the right. "Another one. And look, two more over there."

"So tell me, lad," Pegran laid his hand on Kander's shoulder, "what da ya' think a' me tall tale now?"

"Are you going to kill them?" Kander shivered as he spoke.

"Not for the time bein'." A grin spread the old man's face. "Fer now those varmints be ta our advantage should those soldier fellas trot on out here."

The rock formation within Pegran's circle was large and provided ample shelter for the King's Company and their horses. Suppertime came. They ate it cold.

When he finished eating, Sergeant Tandrak climbed the rock. "My watch. You can go grab a bite." He emphasized the word "bite."

Xzwindra made a face, then reluctantly worked her way down to where the others lounged in the late afternoon shade. Her eyes searched the ground.

Kander smiled. He understood how she felt.

"Do you know how many of those slithering vipers have gathered outside our camp?" she said as she sat down next to Pegran. She didn't wait for him to answer. "I counted seventeen."

Pegran just grunted and continued to pick his teeth with his knife, which looked much too large for the purpose but seemed to suit him just fine.

"I'm surprised you don't cut your lip." Kander shuddered at the thought of it.

Private Sedrnal chuckled.

Pegran picked up a small twig left behind by a tumbleweed. He effortlessly split the twig end to end. Kander shook his head.

"Captain Favel!" The call came from up on the boulder, and the urgency in Sergeant Tandrak's voice drew everyone's attention.

Captain Favel leaped to his feet and scrambled up the rock.

Sergeant Tandrak lay on his belly looking toward the east. "Horsemen on the horizon," he said. Captain Favel crawled over and lay down beside him. The sergeant pointed out a silhouette of riders. "Looks like they picked up our trail, Captain. They're less than a half hour away."

Captain Favel nodded. He patted the sergeant's shoulder approvingly and then scurried down to where the others were anxiously awaiting the news.

They strapped on their swords and readied their bows. Xzwindra and Kander had been shown how to use the crossbow at Havenholt, but they were far from proficient. Sergeant Tandrak and Private Sedrnal also used crossbows. Captain Favel and Corporal Mifstern used longbows. Pegran used what he called a flexbow. It was shorter than a longbow and its curves more dramatic. The shank was thick and its pull stiff. The arrows Pegran used were shorter and not as big around, though he claimed his bow would shoot any arrow made. And despite its shortness and strange shape, he boasted, "It'll outshoot any longbow that's ever been crafted!"

Sergeant Tandrak slipped down from the rock.

"Five horsemen circled north and five south," he rasped in a half whisper. "They know we're here. Must have seen me before I flattened out."

"Haaa! Yaaa!" The shout rang across the basin. Then the thunder of horse's hooves beating the hardpan came to their ears.

"Make ready for battle!" shouted Captain Favel. Each member of the King's Company moved to his assigned position.

Five riders came pounding in from the south. But as they approached the line of blue pergipsom, they suddenly became aware of the vipers. The riders' blinderless horses spooked, reared, and twisted violently. A well-placed arrow from Captain Favel's longbow sent one rider to the ground. A second rider took an arrow in his shoulder but kept his saddle. The other three riders fought to control their horses and to pull away form the vipers.

The horsemen who thundered in from the north happened on a less-infested position. Only two vipers lay in their path. One horse reared.

Kander loosed an arrow. It missed its mark but caused the rider to lose his balance. As the soldier fell, his foot caught in the stirrup. Before he hit the ground, one of the vipers struck, and the horse bolted.

Kander's stomach rolled. The thought of killing another human being set his hands to shaking. He was glad the snake had gotten the soldier instead of his arrow.

At the same moment that the unfortunate rider fell, Lieutenant Wndark bolted across the protective line, sword flashing overhead. Before Kander could set another arrow, the leader of the enemy was upon him. Kander fell back between two rocks, avoiding sword and horse. A bowstring twanged. Kander could see Pegran hurriedly setting another quarrel. He looked up. Panic filled the lieutenant's eyes as he pulled his steed aside and rode away. Kander shuddered. The head of Pegran's arrow projected from the retreating soldier's back. Kander turned and emptied his stomach.

Another soldier entered the circle from behind Sergeant Tandrak, who turned and loosed his quarrel, seemingly at the last moment. It lifted the unfortunate soldier out of his saddle. His horse fled out into the desert.

The remaining two horsemen who had attacked from the north turned and pounded hoof after their leader, and three of the soldiers who had come in from the south joined them.

As the soldiers caught up with their leader, he turned on them with anger. "Attack!" he gurgled. "Attack you fools! Ohhh!" He slumped farther, grasping the mane of his horse, his breathing labored.

The soldiers ignored his command. They took the reins of his steed and turned back toward the way station.

As the defeated riders came up out of the hollow, they met the rest of their company. The foot soldiers had fought their battle too. More than half their number had fallen prey to the deadly vipers. The remaining foot soldiers retreated with the horsemen. Thirty men had gone out on the run. Only fourteen returned. Actually, thirteen; Lieutenant Wndark died before they got back to the station. A young sergeant, previously second in command, was now the leader of the ragtag band. He gave no more thought to attacking the fools camped out in Viper's Den Hollow. "The vipers will take care of them," he assured the others.

"*T*he train should be on its way south," said Captain Favel as he cinched his saddle. He looked off toward the horizon. The sun lit a distant mountain peak. "We'd better get moving if we are going to catch up with it before dark."

Kander looked over at Xzwindra and smiled. She too was glad to be sitting astride her horse once again and leaving Viper's Den Hollow.

Pegran led them from the safety of the blue circle at a gallop. They passed the vipers and headed toward the southwest, leaving Viper's Den Hollow behind. They galloped up through the foothills and out onto the Run. Ahead of them, the horse train trundled along its snakelike mound.

"In less than the blink of a horse's eye, we'll be a sittin' in our trays again," laughed Pegran.

"And none too soon, either," called out Captain Favel. "Daylight's about gone."

Vipers watched longingly as the small company thundered across the hardpan. The last rays of the sun slipped behind the distant mountains as they reached the train. Captain Favel spurred his horse up the mound and blocked the road.

"Whoa! Whoa!" The trainmaster braced both feet and pulled back on the reins. With a smile and a wink, he cursed and howled. Passengers' heads stuck out the windows watching and listening. The King's Company loaded their horses while the trainmaster protested vehemently. Once they were aboard, the train lurched forward, and they were on their way to the next station.

The three men who had caused problems for the King's Company at Thirty-five Pines came striding to Captain Favel's tray in a confrontational mood. The surly miners were focused with intent and did not notice that they were followed.

Gorlon, Fendrick, and Juflek blocked off the doorway to the tray. They stood shoulder to shoulder with their chests puffed out and demanded to know what was going on.

"If ya' think yer gunna' get the miners ta' strike, think again!" Fendrick's words were backed up by a gush of bad breath. "The miners are for the miners. We don't care who rules in Zwexdrof as long as we get our pay."

"We know you're wi' the Resistance!" growled Gorlon with an air of pride, as if that information gave him power over Captain Favel and the others.

"Yer gettin' off the train at the nex' station!" Juflek caressed the club he held in his hand. "Ya' can head right back where ya come from. We don't need the likes a' you snoopin' around the mines. The mines be dangerous, . . if ya get me drift."

"That be mighty big talk, Juflek." Pegran stepped between Captain Favel and the three miners. "How do ya plan ta back it up since the three a' ya be slightly outnumbered?"

Gorlon, Fendrick, and Jufleck's eyes went wide, and they glanced about anxiously. Pegle and Norgran blocked the way from which they had come. And Sergeant Tandrak, Corporal Mifstern, and Private Sedrnal filled the hallway opposite. The three miners nervously turned back to face Pegran, Captain Favel, Kander, and Xzwindra.

Pegran cleared his throat, then spoke in a calm steady voice. "I tell ya' what, boys, our business ain't a miner's strike, but at the same time what our business is ain't yer business!" He smiled broadly. "So yer gunna tend ta yer own business from here on out. The three a' ya are gunna forget that ya ever saw the likes a' us. Ya got that?"

"An' when ya get back ta the mines," interjected Pegle, "yer goin' ta continue to keep yer mouths shut. Cause Norgran, meself, an our frien's will be keepin' an eye on ya."

"Far as I'm concerned, we might jes as well feed 'em ta those vipers right now, Pegle." Norgran spread a toothy smile. "Now that would be some fun. Did ya notice how those soldiers bloated when they was bitten? Instant it were, an I ain't never seen such terror in a man's eyes when death were hauntin' his soul!"

Simultaneously, the three miners swallowed hard and forced ridiculous grins. They knew they were bested. "Hey, we didn't mean no harm, fellas!" Fendrick offered a helpless smirk. "Did we, Gorlon? We was jes' wonderin' what's up. Strange things bin happnin'. Can't blame us fer wonderin'!"

"But hey, who cares what's up?" Juflek twiddled his fingers against the side of his club. "I mean yer business is yer business, Pegran. As far as I'm concerned, I ain't seen ya in months, since last time ya hit Luxurd." He laughed uncomfortably.

"See, ya doen' have ta get nasty wi' us, Pegran!" added Gorlon. "We doen' want no trouble. An we woen' make no trouble either. We'll jes head on back ta our tray an' forget this lil' incident ever happened. What da ya say, fellas?"

Pegle and Norgran stepped aside, and the three miners clambered over each other to get back to the safety of their cubicle. Their door slammed shut behind them.

"A little hard on them, weren't you?" said Captain Favel as he looked down the narrow corridor toward where they had disappeared.

"I used ta have a mule," responded Pegran. "He had a bent ta do things his own way. I was convinced by a frien' that a gentle han' would tame the critter. An' I was gentle as a woman with a child." He sighed and looked about from face to face.

"Well, what happened?" demanded Private Sedrnal.

"I was a makin' my way through Brackenwild Reach when I happened on a war party a' ogremen. That ol' mule an' I hid in a stand a' bracken. The war party passed us by. But they were no more than a stone's throw away when that ol' mule started brayin'. I tried ta hush the mule with kin' gentle words, but he jes brayed the louder. The ogremen scrambled after me. I jumped on that ol' mule's back, drove my heels in his flanks. The wretched creature wouldn't budge. He jes stood there a hollerin', 'Come an' get ol' Pegran, you ogremen. Here he be!' Well, I jumped from his back ta make a break for it, but me feet no more n' hit the groun' when that dad-burn mule turned and put both hind feet ta me moon. Bam! I be flat on me face in the bracken, a stalk a' which gouged out me eye." He stopped. The only sound was the squeak of wheels. Everyone stared at Pegran expectantly, waiting for more.

Even Gorlon, Fendrick, and Juflek had opened their door again and stuck their heads out, one on top of the other. They gawked and listened. Jufleck became impatient. "Well, what happened then, Pegran?" he hollered from the other tray.

With his good eye, Pegran gave the three miners a reproving glance. "I got ta' me feet an' foun' meself face ta face with more 'n twenty wild ogremen who were threatenin' me life with club and spear." Pegran's voice rose to create an atmosphere of intensity. "But those wild ogremen stopped dead in their tracks! They suddenly let out a dreadful howl! 'HEYAAAA!' they shouted. Then they turned and ran crackety-wham through the bracken ta who knows where." Pegran paused for effect.

Kander felt like he could almost hear the ogremen crashing through the brush. "Well, why did they run?" he asked.

"Guess they never seen one a' Baruch's creatures with an eyeball a danglin' on his cheek." Pegran rasped out the words slowly, with relish.

"That's terrible!" Xzwindra wrinkled her nose in repulsion. "Enough to make a person sick!"

"Well, I s'pose ya be right, lass. That be jes about what it did." Pegran whipped out his knife and sliced it across in front of his face. "Anyway, I cut what was holdin' the eyeball ta me head, an' since it were of no particular use ta me anymore, I tossed it at the ogremen, which resulted in another 'HEYAAA!' Never saw those wild men again. An' in deference ta those who would have the unpleasantry a' lookin' at me empty eye socket, I fashioned me this patch an been wearin' it ever since."

"And what about the mule?" asked Sergeant Tandrak.

Pegran glanced to see if Gorlon, Fendrick, and Juflek were still listening. He nodded congenially in their direction. And as if the three heads were one, they nodded back. "Ya, what about the mule?" called out Fendrick.

"Well, boys, a mule with no sense don't make no sense, if'n ya know what I means." Pegran ran his finger along the edge of the blade in his hand and gave the three miners a broad grin. "So when I got back ta Yeps, I took the ol' mule ta the butcher. Tell me, boys, ya ever et mule jerky?" The three wide-eyed miners shook their heads. "Well, I lived on that ol' mule fer more 'n a year, an' ya know he nary again crossed me. Ya see, boys, sometimes a gentle han' jes don't work. An' I tell ya what, a miner with no sense don't make no sense ta' me either." Then he turned to Captain Favel. "Captain, ya ever et miner meat? Wonder how long t'would take ta get tired a' miner meat? Imagine t'would make fer some pretty chewy jerky."

"You wouldn't!" Gorlon's voice cracked as he gulped out the words.

Pegran ran his finger along the blade of his knife again and laughed like a mad man. "Rumor has it that I'm half crazy!" he howled. "An' ta live in the Savage Lands, one has ta be half crazy. An' a crazy man will sometimes do a crazy thing. An' if ya want ta see jes how crazy I am, you fellas jes open yer mouths one time—jes one! An you'll see how crazy ol' Pegran is!" And again he broke out in a fit of mad laughter, and Gorlon, Fendrick and Juflek instantly disappeared back inside their tray.

The next day the attitude of the three miners had changed considerably. They warmed up to their fellow travelers and became downright cordial. However, they kept their distance from ol' Pegran.

Chapter 19

The horse train ran from Yeps to Luxurd and back again, and for the trainmasters the journey was long and wearing. The only rest they got while on the road was a catnap now and then while an assistant took the reins. However, upon reaching Luxurd, the trainmasters were given five days off before being assigned to another train headed back to Yeps.

The fourth day of his holiday, the trainmaster who had brought the King's Company to Luxurd hurried down to the station to meet his good friend, the driver of the incoming train. When the train arrived, the waiting trainmaster's attention was drawn to an extraordinary man who stepped from one of the trays out onto the platform. The man stood more than a head taller than those around him. He was dressed in black and had broad shoulders and bulging muscles. A grim visage gazed about from behind a hoodlike mask that draped the upper half of his face.

I sure wouldn't want to have a run-in with that fellow! the trainmaster mumbled to himself.

The trainmaster who had just finished his run came tramping along the boardwalk. The two friends greeted each other with small talk about how the run had gone, commented about the strange man, and then headed into town.

That night the two trainmasters sat at a round table in the shadows at The Run End Inn, an establishment mostly frequented by horse-train workers. Miners generally preferred The Pick and Shovel or The Deep Shaft Inn.

The trainmasters had just finished their meal and ordered a tankard of ale when the Black Assassin came striding through the swinging doors. Thwak. Thwak. Thwak. The doors seemed to mock the sudden silence that swept the room. Zanzxra stopped, looked around, and then went to the bar. He talked briefly with the innkeeper, whose previously dry brow suddenly beaded with sweat. After a moment, the innkeeper pointed a shaky finger toward the two trainmasters.

Zanzxra walked over and sat down without asking if he was welcome to or not, but the trainmasters offered no protest. "You're Drandk?" he addressed the trainmaster who had brought Pegran and the King's Company down the Run. The trainmaster nodded his assent. "A fellow named Kander boarded your train at Yeps, and I understand that in spite of a little trouble along the way, he exited your train here at Luxurd. Where can I find him?"

"Kander? Let me see, . .Do I remember a fellow named Kander?" Drandk tried to act like he didn't recognize the name.

"Don't play stupid!" growled the assassin. His hand flexed as if squeezing the life out of something.

Drandk gulped in response.

"Playing games is dangerous," said the giant of a man. "You know exactly who I am talking about. He's traveling with Pegran, and you know who Pegran is . . . and you know who Kander is. Where will I find him?"

"Well, yes, yes. . ." stumbled the trainmaster nervously. "Kander? Oh, yes, of course! Fine fellow, he. Very likable." He shrugged his shoulders. "Like everyone else, he got off here at the station, and that's the last I saw of 'em."

Drandk didn't see where it came from, but suddenly the man in black held a terrible-looking dagger in his hand. And he wasn't merely toying with it.

"I'm telling the truth!" Drandk's legs flexed, and his chair shot back about six inches. "They got off at the station," he gushed, "and I haven't seen em' since. All I know is that they were headed out into the Savage Lands. That's all I know!"

The assassin's dagger flashed. A moment before he felt the pain, Drandk felt hot blood dripping down his cheek.

"As I said, playing games is dangerous!" Reaching over to the other wide-eyed, trembling trainmaster, the assassin smirked and wiped the blood from his dagger on the man's shirt. He turned back to Drandk. "If I find you've lied to me, I'll be back."

The dagger disappeared. Zanzxra rose and moved over to where the innkeeper stood transfixed. As the assassin approached him, the innkeeper stumbled back against the wall. Zanzxra asked a question, and the answer came tumbling forth. "They. . .they stayed one night," stuttered the innkeeper. "Th. . .they're f. . .four days ahead of you!"

Zanzxra turned on his heels. Thwak. Thwak. Thwak. Once he was gone, the inn sighed in relief. The trainmasters stared at the swinging doors while praying the man would not return.

*T*he assassin headed east toward the South Labyrinth Narrow, the gateway to the Savage Lands. Zanzxra walked through the night, but when the sun began to fill the morning sky, he sought shelter and rest. He curled up in a deep crevice beneath a large rock. As the assassin tried to sleep, his thoughts took him back to Zwexdrof and the temple. Again, when he closed his eyes, Thaxndar's pallid face came into view, and the priest's glazed eyes gaped at him. The assassin grimaced and turned on his hard bed, angrily wiping a tear from his cheek.

Chapter 20

Before the King's Company stretched a massive wilderness of hardpan and rock called the Stakz—so named for the unusual rock formations that jutted up from the desert floor. Looking out over the immense flat desert, its surface more clay than sand, Kander shook his head. The stakz of rock seemed out of place. "Some of the stakz appear to be rippled masses of lava. It's as if the earth below the desert overheated and bubbled up through the hardpan," he commented to Xzwindra.

She nodded. "They do form strange-looking shapes and figures."

Pegran pointed out across the desert. "Some formations be small an' others large. An' there be caves in most of the large stakz. Some a' the caves look ta me like air bubbles rose ta the surface, then burst and cooled. But in other caves there be long, twistin' tunnels that may ha' formed when the outer crust cooled an' the inner hot stuff ebbed back downward. I calls those lava caves." He raised the eyebrow over his good eye. "But there also be caves that seem to be the result a' molten rock foldin', ripplin', and dippin' as it cooled. And there be yet other tunnels that appear to ha' been dug by some people that ain't around no more. Those tunnels usually be connected ta the natural tunnels."

"An ancient civilization of some sort?" questioned Xzwindra.

Pegran nodded. "Spose so. Even find pictures, some etched and some painted, on the walls a' some a' the caves."

Kander wiped his brow. "Well, at least the caves will provide some shelter from the sun."

"We'll need shelter from more than the sun," grated Pegran.

"How so?" asked Captain Favel.

"The Stakz be different from all other parts of the Savage Lands." Pegran grimaced as he looked from one to the other of the company. "Don't know if it be the sweltering heat, the terrible dryness a the place, or somethin' in the rocks, 'cause at times ya can hear a crackling sound when you come near the Stakz, and at night ya can actually see sparks dancing on the taller rocks, but whatever it be, soon after a violent storm be comin'—a storm like nothin' you ever seen, I calls em power storms."

"From the sounds of it," said Captain Favel, "there could be some kind of magnetic deposits in the Stakz. Perhaps the dry air collects energy, and when the conditions get just right, boom! you have one of your power storms."

Pegran shrugged. "Yea, or mayhap it be a spill a' anger from those people who died off years gone by."

At that moment, a power storm exploded out over the basin floor that lay before them. The desert came alive with blue bolts of lightning flaring up into the air, dancing across the hardpan, and exploding from stakz to stakz.

"Wow!" Corporal Mifstern's gaze shifted from one stakz to another. "Yer right, Pegran. Never seen anything like it!"

"We can't go hiking out across there!" exclaimed Xzwindra.

"Oh, the Stakz be dangerous all right. But that be where we have ta go ta get ta where we be goin'." Pegran grinned. "When a storm comes, ya head fer the rocks an' hopefully a cave. But even inside a grotto or tunnel, the air be alive, an' yer skin will feel like little bugs a crawlin' all over, an' yer hair 'ill stand on end." He shook his head. "Why, sometimes the cave walls crackle with little dancin' threads a' blue fire."

"Why anyone would want ta live out here is beyond me!" complained Sergeant Tandrak. "No wonder the people who made the pictures ain't there no more."

They watched from the hillside until the storm died away.

"Well, the power storm be passed," said Pegran. "We had best be at it."

Dusty whinnied as if in agreement.

Pegran led the King's Company out onto the desert floor and headed for the nearest stakz. Within the outcrop of rocks, they found a cave with a number of interesting wall carvings. But Pegran didn't give them much of a break. He pushed them on to the next stakz and then the next.

"Why are we hurrying from one stakz to another?" Kander wiped his brow but found it dry. Sweat was there, and yet it wasn't. He was glad he was riding. "Walking would be the pits!" he muttered.

Suddenly, Pegran shouted, "Head fer that stakz!" He pointed off to their right. Blue sparks danced on the higher rocks. "The ancients be dead and gone, and we may join em ifn we don't fine' a cave, an' quick."

They set their heels to the flanks of their already skittish horses.

"And what do we do if we get caught out here on the hardpan?" shouted Xzwindra as she spurred her horse alongside Pegran's.

"Flatten yerself on the ground, an' hope fer the best," he responded. "Most a' the action be between the upper parts a' the stakz, but anything higher than the hardpan itself be vulnerable."

"The horses?"

"Have ta lay them on their sides as well."

They made the stakz before the storm broke but barely.

"And how long are we going to be out here?" asked Kander. He had not liked Viper Run, but he liked this place even less.

"Couple a weeks or so, I spose," returned Pegran. "Jes' depends on how things go."

"I've been out here as long as I care to be already," snarled Xzwindra.

"Keep yer patience, Windy, me girl, cause we'll be out here longer than any of us wants ta be."

The storm passed, and they headed back out onto the hardpan.

Pegran kept Dusty trotting at a steady pace while keeping his eyes on the stakz ahead. "An' another thing," he called out to the company. "Ye will want ta watch out fer decrodiles!"

"Decrodiles?" Kander rode up alongside Pegran. "What's a decrodile?"

"Decrodiles be lizardlike varmints," answered Pegran. "Got ten stubby legs, but in spite a' their short legs, those critters be quicker than scat. And they got long, powerful snouts that be filled with lines a' razor-sharp teeth. Most be six to seven feet long. But I've seen with me own eye a dek that were all a' ten feet long."

"Wonderful!" responded Xzwindra from behind their one-eyed guide. Her frown drooped yet further.

"And what are our chances of running into one of these decrodiles, Pegran?" asked Captain Favel. "Do I guess right that if they are to be found, it will be in the caves?"

Pegran looked over at Captain Favel and smiled. "Now that be our biggest problem, Capn. Deks generly be out an' about at night. Come the heat a' day, they seek the cool a' the lava caves, so we'll have ta keep an eye fer em."

Sergeant Tandrak rode at Captain Favel's other side. He leaned forward and looked across at Pegran. "And what does it take to kill one of these decrodiles?" he asked.

"Well, now, that be yet another problem." Holding the reins with his right hand, Pegran ran the fingers of his left hand through his unkempt hair. "The deks have armorlike hide that be thicker than a soldier's shield, an' hard as the hilt a' yer sword. Still, there be a soft spot each side a' the critter's head, where ya'd spec ta fine ears. An' a'course the wretched creatures do have eye sockets. Other than ear flesh and eye sockets, the only vulnerable area be the underside a' their throat, which be a little hard ta get at, if'n ya know what I mean." Pegran momentarily looked back across Captain Favel at Sergeant Tandrak. "But I spose the bes' way ta kill a dek be ta stick sumpin' in its mouth, cause once a dek locks its jaws, it won't let loose fer nothin'. But whatever ya stick in a dek's mouth bes' be strong enough that the critter's teeth won't bust it ta smithers. An' once the dek's jaw be locked, ya fine a soft spot an drive yer sword ta the brain. But watch the varmint's tail! That be as deadly a weapon as the critter's jaws."

Corporal Mifstern's eyes shifted this way and that, scanning the reaches of the hardpan. "And what do the decrodiles find to eat out in this desolate place?" he called out from behind Pegran.

"Oh, there be other varmints that live out here in the Stakz," answered Pegran. "But, like the decrodiles, ya won't see em durin' the heat a' the day. Maybe ya'll see a critter at dusk or perhaps at dawn. There be stakz hares, sandfur foxes, dust dogs, which be a small rodent that digs in the hardpan, ifn ya can believe that. But the dek's favorite meal be stakalopz or wild burros. Both be a' the smallish variety but make a tasty meal fer a decrodile."

Suddenly, Dusty skittered, and Pegran noticed the mane between her ears rose. "Head fer it!" he shouted as he dug in his heels and galloped toward the nearest stakz. The others spurred their horses after.

Kander looked up as he raced toward the stakz and saw blue fire dancing on its pinnacle. "Looks like we're in for it again!" he mumbled.

Pegran led them up a wide ridge toward a dark crevice, the entrance to a cave. In spite of all his talking, he had apparently had his eye on the spot for some time.

The company swung down from their horses in a flurry of commotion. They pulled and tugged them back under an overhang outside the cave. The horses danced and skittered. "Whoa! Whoa!" several voices assured.

The dry desert air felt alive with energy. Kander noticed that the hair on his arms no longer lay flat, and it felt like bugs were crawling up his back. His horse nervously clattered its hooves on the rocky ground outside the cave. Kander looked out at the desert. The air had a blue cast to it.

"Torch!" shouted Pegran.

A moment later, Captain Favel stood beside him with torch in hand, Private Sedrnal having taken the reins of both men's horses.

Pegran and Captain Favel entered the cave, the torch sputtering sparks and its light dancing on the walls. A small burro, its slender legs quaking with fear, stood in the shadows at the back of the cave.

"They don't seem to like power storms either," commented Captain Favel.

Pegran nodded. "They can sense what's coming. But the little fella standing there a shakin' afore the storm means no decrodiles about. So tell em ta get those horses inside."

At that moment, the storm broke. Blue lightning flashed across the sky, thunder rolled, and the earth quaked. Blue fire crackled on the walls of the cave. The horses trembled and skittered their hooves on the rock floor as they entered the cave, and the people shuddered at the magnificent display of violent energy that sheeted the desert. And although the basin was alive with blue fire, a strange darkness engulfed the Stakz.

"Eerie!" said Xzwindra.

"Did you check the back reaches of the cave for decrodiles?" asked Kander, although he already knew they hadn't.

"No need," said Pegran.

"No need?" responded Kander. Disbelief edged his voice.

Pegran laughed. "A burro would never seek shelter in a cave where a dek be lyin' in wait. They fear the jaws a' death more than the desert storm. An' desert critters like burros and stakalopzes can tell ifn a decrodile be present."

Kander cast him a skeptical look.

Pegran grinned. "They be able ta smell em."

"How does a decrodile catch a stakalopz or a burro then?" asked Private Sedrnal.

"Deks have a keen sense a' smell themselves. They find a cave that a stakalopz or a burro already took shelter in, an' in they go fer supper." Pegran looked around the chamber, hoisted his eyebrow knowingly, and continued, "Or sometimes a critter 'ill get struck by lightnin' while trying ta escape a power storm, an' there ya go, the dek be served up a nice hot meal."

"You've got a wretched sense of humor, Pegran!" Xzwindra slowly approached the frightened burro and extended a trembling hand. Pegran quietly chuckled in response. The burro cringed but otherwise did not move. When her hand touched its coarse hair, she found it was standing on edge. She could feel little sparks of energy as her hand ran down the burro's back.

The power storm battered the desert for nearly an hour. Then, its energy spent, the storm ended as suddenly as it had begun.

The company left the cave and headed north toward the next stakz. The burro followed at a distance but eventually wandered off in another direction and disappeared.

Xzwindra thought it strange how an animal could just disappear in the desert. She felt disappointed that the amiable creature was no longer following them and wondered what would become of it. Would it live only to become food for a decrodile?

That night they found shelter in a lava tube. "The most likely place ta fine' water," said Pegran with keenness in his voice. Their supply had run low. "Condensation forms pools in the deeper parts of the tunnel," he explained. "Got the taste a' dirt an' rock, but 'ill keep ya' alive."

They struck flint to their torches and checked the cave for critters. The horses had a wild look in their eyes and resisted entering the cave.

Pegran fully expected to find a decrodile, probably in the deeper recesses of the fissure. "If there be water, that be where we'll fine' the critters," he warned.

They slowly worked their way deeper into the cave, torches held high, eyes examining every shadow and crevice. Pegran and Corporal Mifstern bore the torches while Captain Favel carried a long spear in one hand and his sword in the other. Sergeant Tandrak clutched his crossbow—cranked and ready. The other members of the company waited with the horses near the entrance of the long lava tube.

As they worked their way deeper into the stakz, the cave air grew damp, and drips of water fell from the ceiling and ran down the walls. They turned a corner, and the tunnel opened into a broad chamber. The torchlight revealed a large pool of water in the middle of the chamber. Stalactites hung from the ceiling, and stalagmites jutted up from the floor. With a point of his finger, Pegran silently drew their attention to a long pointed tail that protruded from behind one of the stalagmites.

The dek slowly backed away from the pool and turned to see who had intruded into his world. The long, rough-skinned creature's eyes stared dull and listless, but his white teeth shone in the torchlight. The dek's jaws hung agape. Without warning it charged.

"Quick with that spear!" shouted Pegran.

The dek covered the distance between them more swiftly than Captain Favel had imagined possible. His heart leapt to his throat as he sidestepped the jaws of death and stuck the broad blade of his spear in the angry creature's mouth. The massive jaws closed on the elongated spearhead, straining to tear through the metal. Attempting to control the movement of the huge dek, Captain Favel dropped his sword and grasped the handle of the spear with both hands. The decrodile whipped its great head sideways and threw Captain Favel to the floor.

Instantly, Sergeant Tandrak stepped forward, and with a singular fluid motion, he avoided the butt of the spear, stuck his crossbow to the side of the decrodile's head, pulled the trigger, and leapt out of the way. The giant dek convulsed wildly, jaws flailing. The spear clattered on the cave floor. The creature's tail shuddered and then went still. Its dark eyes stared into nothingness.

"That thing's a monster! Got to be at least twelve feet long!" declared Captain Favel. He had rolled, come to his feet, and moved back out of Sergeant Tandrak's way. "Could live without encountering one of those things again! It wouldn't have a mate hanging around, would it?"

"Not the season. Loners this time a year." Pegran stepped off the length of the dek. "Ya were close, Captain. A tad more than eleven feet long."

"Say, what's that over there?" Corporal Mifstern pointed to the shadows beyond the subterranean pool. The still form of what appeared to be a man sat at the base of a stalagmite, its head lulled to one side.

The thing Corporal Mifstern had spotted was mannish but not a man. The mannish creature appeared to have scales. Its hands were slightly webbed, with clawlike fingers. Its face was rather manlike, but its neck was hooded. It had a low forehead, a snakelike nose, and fangs like a viper. One leg was missing, bitten off just below the knee.

Sergeant Tandrak shook his head. "Looks like the dek had lunch."

"Question be, what exactly did it have for lunch? Never seen a thing like it." Pegran scratched his head and then knelt down and examined the creature carefully. "Well, since the dek only took one bite, must not a found the feller ta be very tasty."

"The clothes are Pagyn," said Captain Favel. The peculiar creature wore a pullover leather vest and leather breeches. "But the dark scaly skin . . . and the serpentlike head . . ."

"Reminds me of a statue I saw one time—the Pagyn god they call Bayl," interjected Corporal Mifstern.

"Yes, the creature does rather look Baylish. Except that Bayl has no legs or arms." Captain Favel sat crouched beside Pegran, studying the dead creature, looking for clues as to where it might have come from. "A foul looking thing isn't it? No pockets. No emblems. There is nothing by which to identify it except the thing itself."

Pegran gave the creature a push with the end of his torch. It sizzled against the dead thing's shoulder. The creature toppled to the side.

"Why, look there! The critters got a tail stickin' out the back a' its pants!" Pegran stood to his feet. "Now swingin' a stalk like that behine ya would be a trick, wouldn' it?"

The others laughed uncomfortably.

As Captain Favel stood, he noticed a glint of metal off to the side. He walked over and picked up what he presumed was the creature's discarded weapon. It had nearly escaped his notice because the long wavy blade was as dark as the floor of the cave.

"Feel how light this is." He tossed the unusual sword to Sergeant Tandrak. He hefted it and lifted an eyebrow, and then handed it to Corporal Mifstern, who gave a low whistle.

Pegran waved it off when it was offered to him. "I got no need ta be puttin' me hand ta metal held by some kina demon creature."

Captain Favel carried the sword back to where the others were waiting at the mouth of the cave. When they were told about the demon, as Pegran persisted in calling the creature, they went to see the thing. After examining it, they felt uneasy, but still they had little choice but to spend the night in the cave.

In the morning, they renewed their water supply and continued on across the Stakz. Kander was glad to leave the demon creature behind. He had the strange feeling that the creature's presence had something to do with them and their mission. The creature seemed a harbinger of ill.

Chapter 21

*T*angle Wood, an immense forest, burned with intensity. The smoke rode the winds toward the mountains, and the acrid smell permeated the air for miles, even out to the plains west of Zwexdrof.

One division of Xvardris' army bivouacked in a smoky encampment north of Tangle Wood, and a second division camped south of the forest. Xvardris expected the Resistance to come charging out of the smoke from one direction or the other—or both. And when the Resistance came forth, Xvardris intended to crush them beneath his heel. His forces waited with bated anticipation, but the Resistance did not exit.

*I*nside Havenholt, the opaque, pungent air made its way into a chamber here and there, but for the most part, the wind coming up from the Black Caverns kept the air fresh and invigorating. The airstream was cold, but the group endured it with added clothing.

"The forest has been burning for more than a week now." General Vandwert looked about at the other council members, a grim lot. "That means Targndel has been gone a week as well. I am concerned as to what might have become of him."

The day the forest had been set ablaze, Major Targndel had slipped out of Havenholt to make contact with his operatives. It was essential that the Resistance remain informed of Xvardris' plans: After the fire, then what? Targndel had been determined to find out. Now it was two days past when he said he would return.

"He'll show up," said Jentrxn. "He's a survivor, General. But the forest is dry and is burning more rapidly than expected. He may be having a time of it finding a way through the burning."

"And if he doesn't make it back?" asked the general.

"Well, we already have a pretty good idea as to what's coming after the inferno dies and the smoldering dissipates," said Razrdris. "The question is, how long before they can begin their move, and how long will it take them to get their war machinery in place?"

"And will our defenses be ready?" asked Prior Forknedrn.

"They'll be ready!" said the general. Defensiveness edged his voice. "And the sooner we get to it the better! I'm sick of being confined to this dank old fortress. Give me the open field, my charger, pounding hooves, clanging steel! At the least, a good battle would warm my blood again. This place is cold!"

"What about Captain Favel and Kander and the King's Company?" asked Razrdris, ignoring the general's complaint. "Any word concerning them?"

"We're waiting on Targndel for that too." Jentrxn tapped his fingers on the table. "Says he's pretty sure he knows who the spy is, but he didn't give any hints."

"What if he is the spy?" The creases across General Vandwert's brow ran deep. His mood remained foul. "Maybe that's why he hasn't showed up. Don't look at me that way! It's possible!"

"Don't be so skeptical, General," responded Jentrxn. He laughed half-heartedly in an attempt to lighten the air. "Targndel is not the spy. If he were the spy, we wouldn't be here. We would be enjoying Xvardris' dungeon or worse. The spy is with Captain Favel. Of that I am convinced."

"And who do you think it is?" asked Prior Forknedrn.

Jentrxn would not commit himself. "We'll see what Targndel has to say."

"Well, I think the spy is right here in this room!" continued General Vandwert. "And if it isn't Targndel, it could be our good prior."

Prior Forknedrn's jaw dropped open in disbelief. "How dare you!" he cried. "If anybody is a spy, it's Razrdris, not me. He's the one who always has a different idea, who resists everything we try to do!"

Razrdris laughed. "At this rate, the mere rumor of a spy in our midst will be sufficient to destroy us." He spoke calmly. "We have stood together for the restoration of Xzwendaria, so let's not stand alone now, or there will be no restoration. If we cannot trust each other, we're doomed."

"See what I mean?" jibed the prior with an air of self-justification.

"Razrdris is right." Jentrxn caught General Vandwert's eye and held it. "United we will defeat this enemy. Divided we will fail. Despite the rumors of a spy, we must keep trust with one another. It is the only way."

General Vandwert let out his breath and nodded his assent.

Prior Forknedrn said, "Humph! I suppose so!"

Although they all acknowledged they must stand united, an element of tension remained as they awaited Major Targndel's return.

Chapter 22

*T*wo days and another power storm after leaving the cave where they had encountered the decrodile, the King's Company sought shelter for the night in a large stakz. They had seen the maw of the large bubble cavern from a distance and set their course accordingly. Inside the cave, they found a number of the strange pictographs and a man-made tunnel leading deeper into the stakz. The tunnel connected with a lava tube that led down to numerous conjoining caverns.

"Humph! Impossible ta inspect em' all!" spat Pegran after they had returned from exploring only part of the cave's depth.

"Maybe we should move on to a different stakz and a smaller cave," suggested Captain Favel. "I'd rest easier. This place gives me the creeps."

"Too late in the day," growled Pegran. He was not happy about the situation, either. He uncinched Dusty's saddle. "We'll jes have ta take our chances."

They made camp in the outer bubble cavern. The pictographs fascinated Kander. After seeing to the needs of his horse, he examined the strange array of figures cut into the walls. Dusk shadowed the cave. Kander was thinking about lighting a torch when he noticed blue fire starting to dance on the walls. He scowled. "Looks like we're about to get another power storm," he called over his shoulder. He gazed at the wasteland outside the cavern and saw blue light crackling on the tops of distant stakz.

Then the power storm broke with a vengeance. A moment later, two wide-eyed stakalopz came darting into the cave. They did not care that the cave was already occupied. Minutes later, a ten-foot-long decrodile came ambling out of the desert.

The dek stopped just inside the mouth of the cave, apparently confused by the realization that others were present besides the stakalopz. It swung its head from side to side as if trying to decide which morsel would make the best meal.

Everyone stood motionless as if frozen in time. The decrodile, taking advantage of the moment, charged Xzwindra, the chosen prey. She commanded her feet to run, but they did not respond.

Captain Favel grabbed for his spear. Sergeant Tandrak scrambled for his crossbow. But there was no time.

Pegran was old but not slow. He lunged between Xzwindra and the decrodile. And the dek's jaws closed on flesh. The bones in Pegran's left leg popped in unison with a flash of blue light and a nerve-shattering peal of thunder. The dek's razor-sharp teeth severed the limb just below the knee. The monster swallowed, and Pegran's leg disappeared. Before Pegran's body hit the floor of the cave, the dek's mouth opened again ready to take more. But before the creature could strike, Captain Favel's spear stabbed flesh behind the dek's lower row of teeth. The brute's maw crashed shut on the broad steel blade, and as the dek's jaws snapped shut, Sergeant Tandrak's bowstring twanged. The arrow pierced the dek's right eye and sank to the monster's brain. The dek' convulsed wildly, shuddered twice, and then lay still on the cave floor. However, the damage was done. Pegran's left leg was gone, his wound bleeding profusely.

Corporal Mifstern, trained in medical procedures, grabbed a piece of rope and tied a tourniquet to stop the bleeding. It was for this kind of eventuality that Captain Favel had included the young corporal as one of the King's Company. Pegran remained conscious but grimaced in pain. Corporal Mifstern ordered a fire. Kander and the others gathered bits and pieces of desert shrubs and grass they found scattered about the cave. A short time later, a small fire crackled in harmony with the cave walls.

After heating the blade of his knife over the fire, Corporal Mifstern applied it to the stump of Pegran's leg to cauterize the arteries and seal the wound.

Xzwindra sat with Pegran's head in her lap, tears falling from her cheek to his.

"Quit blubberin,' girl! Yer gunna' drown me!" Pegran's eye was closed, his face wrinkled in pain. "Don't be feelin' sorry fer me. Suppose ya think I did that jes' fer you, don't ya? Well, I didn't. I did it cause I needed a new story ta tell. The one about my eyeball be gettin' kina old." Pegran opened his eye. Despite the anguish, it sparkled with laughter. "An' this 'ill make a story, let me tell ya! Old one-eyed Pegran loses his leg savin' a pretty young damsel. I like it, I tell ya! I like it well! What do you think, girl?"

Xzwindra tried to smile. The tears continued to trickle down her cheeks. She bent down and kissed Pegran on his leathery, wrinkled forehead.

"Now that makes the story even better!" The old man's voice purred with pleasure. The smell of burnt flesh hung heavy on the air. "Yes, sir, had ta lose me bes' leg ta get a kiss from a pretty woman!" He shook his head and tried to smile. "Why, I was so ugly when I was a wee lad that me own mama refused ta kiss me. Yer some uncommon girl!"

"Oh, Pegran!" Xzwindra wiped the tears from her cheek and then his. "You're a very special old man. Thank you, Pegran."

He managed a smile and then winced as Corporal Mifstern seared the wound again.

"The bite a' that dad-burn dek' was a snap compared to what the good corporal be doin' ta me!" Pegran ground his teeth. "Why, I didn't even feel the critter's blades cut through the bone, but I tell ya, sonny, ya sure be makin' up fer it!"

The young corporal looked up at the old man and smiled. "And for that very reason, you'll live to tell your story," he responded. "But your walking days are over."

"Well, put me on ol' Dusty, and let's be on our way! We got a long trek ahead of us."

The power storm crackled in the background, laughing as if mocking his brave words.

"Sorry, old man, but you're not going any farther on this journey. Private Sedrnal will stay with you and see you back to Luxurd Station," said Captain Favel. Torchlight revealed that creases of concern etched in his face.

Outside the lava cave, the power storm raged, and inside blue fire frolicked on the walls. But that was nothing compared to the fire that exploded in Pegran's eyes and the rage that danced on his face. "I'm the one who knows the way!" He came up off Xzwindra's lap as if he planned to stand nose to nose with Captain Favel, but instantly he fell back again. "An' I'm the one who knows the wild. Ya can't go on without me! I got ta show ya how ta get ta where ya be goin'. Understand? So, back off, Cap'n, 'cause I be goin' with ya, an' that be that!"

"No, Pegran, you're not going." Captain Favel spoke gently but firmly. He knelt down and put his hand on the old man's shoulder. "There are two reasons you're not going, Pegran. One, you need further medical attention that we can't give you. You'd die on us before we ever got to where we are going. And second, you'd slow us down. We simply cannot afford the time to play nursemaid. Our business is urgent. Time is of the essence, and it's going to take us long enough as it is. So draw us a map, and tell us what you can about the country we'll be passing through. But hear me, Pegran, for your own welfare and ours, you are returning to Luxurd."

"Now that be some expression a' appreciation!" Pegran thundered. The power storm gave his words emphasis. "I should oughta' get up on me one good leg and whip yer impudent hide!"

"He's right, Pegran." Xzwindra ran gentle fingers across the old man's forehead.

Captain Favel stood to his feet again.

"So yer turnin' against me too!" He looked up into Xzwindra's blue eyes and feigned hurt feelings. But deep inside he knew Captain Favel was right, but being the stubborn old man that he was, he couldn't let it pass without resisting. "Ah, ye ha' hurt me feelins,' girl!"

Xzwindra brushed the hair back and kissed his forehead again. Pegran looked at Captain Favel and winked, his smile warm again, and his eyes sparkling with delight. He looked up at Xzwindra and searched her eyes. "Ya know, if'n I had a daughter, I'd want her ta be jes' like you, girl!" he said. She smiled wanly and gently brushed his forehead with her lips.

Pegran drew a map and told Captain Favel and Kander what he could about the Savage Lands. Then Corporal Mifstern insisted that he rest awhile.

Private Sedrnal took Captain Favel aside and protested his not being able to continue the quest. But in truth he was pleased with being trusted with the responsibility of caring for the old guide and of getting him safely back to Luxurd.

Captain Favel told him to meet them at Yeps when they returned—however many months away that might be. "Gather what information you can," the captain instructed the young private. "At Luxurd look up Pegran's friends, Pegle and Norgran. They'll take care of Pegran, and I imagine they will help you out any way they can. Once you've entrusted Pegran to their care, dress as a miner and head back up to Yeps. Take a holiday. Make contact there with Targndel's operatives. Let them know what we are up to, and find out what you can about what's going on with the Resistance. We'll need to know when we return. We'll inquire for you at the Twin Spur. Go by the name Wndel Blakhl."

So the next morning, Captain Favel led the King's Company northward out across the Stakz while Private Sedrnal and Pegran headed south toward Luxurd. Most men would not have been able to travel so soon, but Pegran was too ornery to sit still or to let the shock of losing his leg hold him down.

"I'm going to miss that old man," said Kander as he looked back to where the two lone riders plodded away over the hardpan. "He's crusty, but there's something about him that makes a person smile and mean it. You know what I mean, Xzwindra?"

"Yes, I know what you mean." Her mood was pensive. "He doesn't play games. With Pegran, what you see is what you get, and what you get is what you see. He's real in his own way. That's refreshing."

"Yup, that's it!" Kander gave Xzwindra an appreciative nod. "You put the spear through the ring on that one. Would that we were all that real!"

"Still worried about the spy thing?" She gave him a teasing, sidelong glance. "Captain Favel still under your skin?"

"No, he's not exactly under my skin. I just wish I knew," said Kander thoughtfully. "Actually, I'm beginning to like Captain Favel. But that worries me too. Once you start liking someone, the truth is harder to see."

"Well, just remember what Pegran told you back at Yeps, Kander. Like it or not, out here trust is essential to survival. And Captain Favel is essential to our survival and to finding the heir. Personally, I don't believe he is the spy. And as far as I'm concerned, if I have to trust anyone, it's going to be him. On the other hand, if there is someone I don't trust, it's Sergeant Tandrak. But out here I'm even going to trust him. That's just the way it is. So hang in there, Kander. We've got a long way to go yet."

"You're right, Xzwindra. It's all cast aside for now. I'll worry about it when we get to Eknard. Until then the watchword is survival."

"And speaking of survival." Lines of concern creased Xzwindra's brow. "What about the big man dressed in black? Do you think he's still following us?"

"The Black Assassin?" Kander chuckled and shook his head. "He may have followed as far as Luxurd Station. But follow us out here? I doubt it. But if he is fool enough to follow us out here, then I'm certainly not going to worry about him. A man out all alone doesn't have much of a chance—unless, of course, it's Pegran. No, I'm not worried about the Black Assassin."

Chapter 23

*T*he firestorm startled the Black Assassin to wakefulness. Reverberating thunder brought him to his feet with the image of Thaxndar's sad eyes blurring his vision. Then sheets of blue lightning swept away the dread image of the priest, and a second crackle of thunder shook him to the bone, causing him to shudder. The blue light dancing on the walls of the small cave in which he had taken shelter for the day intrigued him. Outside lightning flashed from stakz to stakz, across the ground, and up into the heated late-afternoon atmosphere. Zanzxra moved to the mouth of the cave and gazed awestruck at the explosive dance of blue fire.

"Baruch is indeed powerful!" he muttered, and then he laughed to himself. It was the first time in his life that he had admitted Baruch even existed. "Just an expression," he said aloud, excusing his words. Zanzxra set his jaw. He refused to believe in Baruch, and he did not believe in the Pagyn Bayl either, at least not as a god. He knew full well that Bayl was demonic in nature. And although he served the Pagyn cause, he did not bow to their god. He simply lived to avenge the grievances of his childhood.

"I have wreaked vengeance and death, seeking to satisfy the rage that burns so violently within me," he whispered aloud as he watched the power storm. He allowed a sigh. Vengeance and death did not satisfy. They only made the void he felt within that much deeper. But his course was set. It is impossible to undo what I have done, he mused. I'm a wretched man—a wretched man! He wept bitterly.

Zanzxra lifted his head, took a deep breath, and closed his eyes. "Thaxndar!" he cried. The visage of the priest shook him. Their tears momentarily mingled. With effort he wrenched his eyes open and ran from the cave out into the storm.

"Strike me dead! Kill me! I deserve no better! Take my life! Please take my life!" he shouted. He fell to his knees, his eyes looking toward the heavens, his hands and arms spread wide. Lightning danced all around him, yet he remained untouched. The storm ended, and he lingered on his knees, his shoulders slumped in disappointment. Tears continued to trickle down his checks. He wanted to close his eyes to the world, but he dared not.

A half hour later, he rose and continued his quest, somber, grim, discontented. He followed the marks left by the horses' hooves. "They plod slowly on," he mumbled. A joyless smile spread his face. He moved swiftly across the hardpan in pursuit. When the sun set and the waning moon rose, his pace quickened. He had excellent night vision. His eyes shifted side to side, carefully scanning the desert before him and the shadows around him for any sign of his prey.

He had been traveling for some time when he approached a large stakz. A sand hare shot out from its shadows as if spooked by some demon. Zanzxra drew his dagger. His pace became more measured and deliberate. The giant assassin flinched when the fifteen-foot decrodile came tearing out of the darkness.

The dek stopped in its tracks when it became aware of Zanzxra's presence, the rabbit seemingly forgotten. The monster flexed its legs and raised its neck and head. Its eyes were set, and its jaw gaped, saliva dripping from between its teeth.

The creature appeared ready to charge its prey when its prey charged it. The decrodile instinctively rose on its two hind sets of feet, digging in its nails to meet the charge. Zanzxra stopped just short of the dek's huge jaws that reached out to meet him. The monster's razor-sharp teeth slammed together just short of ripping Zanzxra's belly. In the same instant, the assassin's left hand went out and wrapped around the tip of the creature's snout as his right hand brought his long dagger up under the fleshy part of the decrodile's throat and drove upward to where he presumed it would find the creature's brain. Zanzxra twisted the blade, then pulled it out and leapt away. The dek's tail came flying around to inflict a crushing blow, but Zanzxra leapt again. The tail passed beneath his feet. He landed out of the dying monster's range, turned away, and continued his trek northward.

Zanzxra caught up with his quarry the night Pegran lost his leg. The assassin cautiously made his way to the stakz where his prey had sought shelter. The power storm had passed, and they were all busy taking care of Pegran. He listened and watched from the shadows outside the cave's entrance. He smiled then headed north, studying the layout of the various stakz. One of the stakz far in the distance was much larger than the others. He had measured the pace at which the King's Company traveled. So when he reached the stakz the middle of the next day, he knew they would arrive there that evening.

Within the stakz stretched a labyrinth of caverns. Zanzxra had studied the caves the King's Company had stayed in previously. He knew they would do a fairly thorough job of searching for the ten-legged monsters. He checked out every inch of the cave and its various side tunnels. With his night eyes, he did not need the light of a torch. At the back of the main cavern, he found a narrow rise of rounded rock. Behind the rock the wall angled upward to a shelf where he found a cleft that reached back into the lava. Zanzxra twisted his face into a sneer, slipped into the hole, and went to sleep.

Darkness came to the stakz. Zanzxra, tossing in his sleep, suddenly came awake. The clatter of hooves came to his ears. He soundlessly crawled out of his hole and looked over the edge of the shelf. Three burros had clopped into the cave seeking shelter. The tension he had felt eased away, for it seemed to him that Baruch's frailer creatures would not enter where the ten- legged monsters dwelt. With the burros present, his own prey would not hesitate to enter either.

Zanzxra watched the burros. They nuzzled and touched noses. Then they began to play, scuffling, kicking, chasing in circles. Zanzxra smiled. It was a wonderful scene, such as he had never really taken time to watch before. However, when he realized he was smiling, he forced a frown and crawled back into the shadows. He did not close his eyes or try to sleep again. He was glad the burros had awakened him from his dreams.

Before long the sound of horses' hooves and the chatter and laughter of the King's Company came to the assassin's ears. A scowl sculpted itself in Zanzxra's face. They will not be laughing when the sun rises and they find Kander lying in a pool of his own blood, he mused to himself. Or perhaps I should kill them all.

Zanzxra watched as Captain Favel and Sergeant Tandrak searched the cave and disappeared back in the dark tunnels. It was apparent the presence of the burros had set their minds at ease. They seemed relaxed and unaware of danger. The assassin grinned into the darkness as he watched and listened.

Most of the conversation he overheard was about the body of a second serpentine creature found out on the hardpan during the day. "Just like the one by the pool," commented one of the company. "Probably fried by a bolt of blue lightning," said another. Zanzxra had passed the body of the dead creature the night before but had thought nothing of it. Wazrxna's children did not concern him.

He continued to watch as the five travelers finished their meal and laid out their bedrolls. The burros skittered past them and wandered out into the night. Zanzxra's eyes followed Kander's every move, and he noted that Kander was bedding down nearest the entrance of the cave. Zanzxra patiently waited, listening to each person's rhythmic breathing and watching their breasts rise and fall. Two hours passed. Then, very carefully, without making the slightest sound, he worked his way down to the cave floor. Slowly, quietly, he passed by the sleepers and approached Kander, dagger in hand, his lips quivering with the lust of anticipation. With measured carefulness he reached his razor-edged blade toward Kander's throat. And as was his blood-lust habit, the assassin looked into his victim's face to watch death come.

Zanzxra shuddered. His hand began to tremble. Tears rose to his eyes for he found himself looking into the glazed eyes of the priest. "Thaxndar," he whispered.

"Vengeance and death have no meaning," the priest seemed to say in return, though the specter's lips did not move. "The void will only grow deeper. Death will not satisfy, Zanzxra."

Zanzxra wept, and his tears fell on Kander's cheeks. His prey awoke and stared up at him but did not move. The Black Assassin's blade rested ever so slightly against his prey's throat. Zanzxra grimaced momentarily and then removed the cold steel from Kander's neck and stood to his feet. "No more!" he mumbled, "No more!"

The Black Assassin pulled away from Kander just as Sergeant Tandrak raised his crossbow. Zanzxra still seeing the priest's face heard a shout of, "No!" Then he heard the twang of a bowstring. He looked up, eyes wide, as the quarrel drove into his chest. He stumbled backward, shaking his head. He smiled slightly. The apparition had left him. He saw Kander staring up at him. He wavered and then fell to his knees. He still held the dagger in his hand but had no desire to use it.

Kander rose and came to him. Why does he come to me? he wondered. Kander took Zanzxra in his arms as he drooped farther toward the cold stone floor. The assassin felt the knife slip from his fingers. He forced a smile, a true smile, in spite of the awful pain deep in his chest. It felt strange to smile and yet wonderful. He grasped Kander's arm. "It's my just dessert." The words rattled from between drawn lips. "Remember me, friend. Someone must remember. My true name is Deth." He coughed up blood, breathed heavily, and then continued. "Though I am a dead man, yet in my death I confess faith in Baruch. Will he receive me?" He coughed once again violently and grasped at his chest. Blood dripped from the corner of his mouth. "I go to make peace with your priest. I have never ceased to see his face since the day I murdered him. Even as he died, I knew he forgave me."

Again he coughed and then fought for breath. "My misery is over at las.. . . ." He slumped in Kander's arms.

Kander gently turned the Black Assassin and laid him on the floor, and there in the dark lava cave, he wept over the man who had killed his adopted father and had intended to kill him.

Sergeant Tandrak looked on disgusted and confused. Captain Favel understood. Corporal Mifstern had no real idea what was going on. Xzwindra felt pity. They watched and waited patiently.

Finally, Xzwindra crept over to Kander's side, and laid her arm on his heaving shoulders. Her touch brought comfort, but it did not dry his tears. Later, Kander buried Zanzxra where he lay, under a cairn of rocks. He refused any help. He laid every rock with his own hand. He took Zanzxra's dagger and placed it in his saddlebag. He dried his tears, mounted up, and they continued their journey. But Kander would not soon forget Zanzxra, the Black Assassin, his friend for the briefest of moments.

Chapter 24

"*H*e could have killed me had he wanted," explained Kander as they rode north beneath the intensifying rays of the morning sun. It was going to be another hot day.

"I know," said Sergeant Tandrak, grim-faced and subdued, "But I didn't know it when I loosed my arrow. He was standing over you with a dagger in his hand. I had to do what I had to do. And even though he chose not to slit your throat, he was an assassin sent to do just that. I find it hard to understand how you can pity a man who has blood dripping from his hands, including the blood of Thaxndar. He was a brutal man—a cold-blooded killer."

"Yes, he was." Kander watched the distant stakz and wiped the sweat from his brow. "Yet, when he pulled his dagger back from my throat, when his tears fell on my cheek, he was no longer a brutal killer. He was a changed man. It is that man for whom I felt pity."

Tandrak frowned and nodded. "Then you were right to pity him." He tipped the broad- brimmed hat back on his head. "But I cannot say that I was wrong to kill him. I had no choice."

Kander smiled understandingly. "I know, sergeant. I know. And I do not hold it against you. Any one of us would have done the same. You are not the cause of my sadness. He is the cause of that."

They rode on in silence until suddenly Kander rose in his saddle. "Blue fire!" he shouted.

Captain Favel gave a command and drove his heels to his horse's flanks, lighting out for the nearest stakz. The others followed hard at his heels.

The small stakz offered no cave, only a large fold reaching out to offer slight shelter. They dismounted and pulled the horses in under the bluff. They pressed against the wall and waited. Suddenly, the storm broke with a terrible fury. Blue fire exploded all around them. They watched with fear and awe, and as the storm continued, their fear abated and their awe heightened.

Captain Favel saw him first, a horseman coming toward them, slowly, majestically, riding through the midst of the tumult of blue fire. The man rode a stunning gray charger. The shaggy skull of a gray wolf covered the rider's head. The wolf's yellow eyes seemed to sparkle. The creature's cured carcass draped the man's shoulders and extended down his back. Gray paint slashed the man's right cheek like a bolt of lightning. Another slash cut across his nose and down his left cheek, passing through a gray circle that seemed to either represent the sun or the moon. His chest and arms were sun-browned and brawny. He wore gray leather britches and gray moccasins. At his side hung a sword, across his back a longbow, and in his hand he held a scepter-like wooden pole with a strange blue-colored rock strapped to the upper end.

Lightning flashed. Blue bolts struck at the intruder, and yet he rode on unharmed. The deadly bolts of blue fire, instead of striking the man, appeared to be drawn to the strange scepter and absorbed into the blue rock. Although fire exploded all around the curious man, he passed through the raging storm like an apparition riding through the midst of armies engaged in pitched battle. The man could not help but be aware of the small company huddled beneath the wall of the stakz, yet he appeared determined to continue east without word or acknowledgment.

Sergeant Tandrak and Corporal Mifstern drew their weapons.

However, the rider ignored them and continued on.

Captain Favel signaled for them to put their weapons aside. The power storm had diminished. "Hail, friend!" called the captain as the man passed by.

The great gray charger stopped, turned, and the strange man faced them. His eyes—dark, deep, piercing—met Captain Favel's eyes and searched them. He did not speak.

"Would you stop and share our food?" asked Captain Favel.

The man neither smiled nor frowned, rather his eyes moved from individual to individual, weighing, searching—seemingly, knowing. He looked into Xzwindra's eyes and gazed long.

Finally, she could bear no more and turned away.

He shifted his eyes to the desert and watched as the power storm died away. He turned again and with a nod acknowledged Captain Favel as the leader of the company, but then addressed Kander. "Why have you come to the plain of Blue Fire?" He asked, as if Kander alone had the authority to answer his question.

"We are on a journey to the east in search of a mother and her child," rejoined Kander. He did not want to say too much, and although his inner instincts told him the man could be trusted, he was not sure. Besides, their quest was not this man's business.

"You speak truth." The man on the gray steed searched Kander's eyes.

Kander felt uncomfortable but did not turn away.

The rider raised an eyebrow. "Yes, you speak truth, but you do not tell all," he said. "Sometimes that is wise. I know of the woman and her child. She is as beautiful as Baruch's fire."

Kander's mouth dropped open. Momentarily stunned, he stuttered, "How . . . . how do you know about them?"

"They passed over the Plain of Blue Fire many seasons back," he answered. "Few pass this way, for as you have discovered, this is not an easy land."

Kander looked puzzled. How did the strange man know what they had discovered?

The man responded to his puzzled look. "It is impossible to travel so far in this land without experiencing its severity," he said. "But even more, your eyes speak to me. They tell me that you have suffered a painful loss."

"Well, yes. Two of our company had to return to Luxurd," replied Kander. "One of them lost his leg to a decrodile. But he is a rugged old man. He'll live through it. He was our guide."

"Few make it as far as you have without a guide. But I am sorry for Pegran. But you are right. He will live," said the strange man.

"How did you know who our guide was?" responded Kander, amazed at the stranger's perception.

"Pegran was with the princess you seek when she passed this way long ago," said the strange man. "And Pegran is the only rugged old man who knows this land and would be so bold as to lead such a company through it. But Pegran was not your only loss, for I read death in your eyes."

Kander grimaced, for Deth was a painful subject. "Yes, but it is a story I do not revel in telling." He looked away from the man toward the distant stakz.

"Very well," responded the stranger. He turned to Captain Favel. "I will share your table."

The man slid from his horse.

Captain Favel introduced himself and each of the others.

"And I am Grey Wolf." The name fit.

"You don't actually live out here, do you?" asked Captain Favel as they sat down to share a cold meal.

"I live where I please," responded Grey Wolf. "But, yes, the Plain of Blue Fire is my home. Here my heart is at peace."

"This is a violent place to be at peace in," declared Sergeant Tandrak. "The power storms and those wretched iron-jawed monsters are not my idea of peace."

"As I said, it is not an easy land," said Grey Wolf between bites of dried desert hare. "But it is not the land that is at peace. It is my heart that is at peace when I am in this land. Here I feel the presence of Baruch."

"Tell me, Grey Wolf, are you the last remnant of the ancient people who used to dwell in this land, the people who etched the pictographs in the cave walls?" asked Captain Favel.

"The cave dwellers are my people." Grey Wolf ran his finger along the bolt of lightning on his cheek. "I have read their pictures. You might say that in me their civilization is reborn. Yet, with me it will die."

"What became of the cave dwellers?" asked Corporal Mifstern.

"The pictures do not tell all." Sorrow edged Grey Wolf's powerful voice. "But the pictures speak of a strong people who worshipped Baruch. Yet in time, because of their strength, they became self-aware, self-trusting. They turned their backs on Baruch. They forsook the sacrifice." A scowl crossed his face, and he nodded his head. "Yes, they were strong and thought that they no longer needed Baruch. It was then that he sent the blue fire. But they discovered the fire stone." He motioned toward the stone strapped to the pole he had carried when he came to them through the storm. "The people refused to forsake their pride. The pictures show laughter on the face of Baruch and defiance on the faces of the people. It was then that the death lizards appeared, and the pictures indicate that strife arose between the fathers of the clans. They blamed each other for the deathbane. A terrible war ensued. Brother killed brother. The pictures tell no more. The story is over but without an end. Did the people die? Did they leave the land of the deathbane? Only Baruch knows."

Grey Wolf's words filled Kander's mind with questions. "Did your mother and father still live in this place when you were born, Grey Wolf?" he asked.

A deep sadness came into Grey Wolf's eyes. He sighed. A tear rose to his eyelid and trickled down his cheek. "A golden coin gave me birth. And my father's name was Unfaith. The man who called himself my father made himself fat by breeding his mare and selling her offspring into service. I brought the breeder a good price. But by the power of Baruch, I burst forth from that womb of darkness, and he brought me to this land where he showed me the pictures. Here Grey Wolf was born."

"You speak in riddles!" said Xzwindra with a hint of irritation in her voice. "You have told us a fine story, but you have told us nothing about who you really are. If you ask me, you're hiding something behind a veil of mystery."

"You say I have told you nothing, but in fact I have told you all. That is my story. If it is a riddle, then it is a riddle," said Grey Wolf. His demeanor remained unperturbed. "But then, you too are a riddle, my lady. I speak riddles with my lips. You speak riddles with your eyes. You refuse to hear and understand the words I speak. But I hear what your eyes speak, and I understand."

Xzwindra's neck went red, and she turned her eyes away. She tried to hide both her anger and the pain. She did not like this stranger who had so suddenly ridden into their lives.

Kander saw the pain expressed in Xzwindra's eyes and wondered what its cause might be. And as for Grey Wolf, it seemed to him that the desert rider had perhaps had a bad childhood. The man obviously did not have a high regard for his mother, whoever she might have been, and did not seem to have a high regard for women in general. But then, Grey Wolf did not seem to have much esteem for the men in his life either. Little wonder he was a loner!

"The fire stone of which you speak," Captain Favel motioned toward the strange scepter, "protects you from the lightning. What is the source of its magic?"

"Magic?" Grey Wolf shook his head. "There is no magic. All things are what Baruch made them to be. What people call magic is nothing more than a power given by Baruch that one person comprehends and uses, while another person does not understand the power, yet wonders at its effects. So, as long as I understand the power of the fire stone, and you do not, it is magic to you."

"Riddles!" mumbled Xzwindra. Kander was the only one close enough to hear her words. He smiled. Grey Wolf glanced in her direction but said nothing.

"Where does the fire stone come from?" asked Corporal Mifstern. "Magic or not, we could use one of those to help get us through this land of yours."

"Such stones are rare." Grey Wolf maintained his somber mood. "The pictures told me where to find the ancient firespar. It belonged to one of the clan chieftains and has come to me by the hand of Baruch. I'm afraid you will have to make your way across the Plain of Blue Fire without its help."

"Maybe so," said Captain Favel thoughtfully. "But what about your help? Would you guide us across the Plain of Blue Fire to the entrance of the Deathreach?

Xzwindra shot Captain Favel a disapproving glance. She had seen all she wanted to of the stranger and wished only for him to be gone.

Captain Favel ignored her glance. His concern was to see them all safely to their destination.

Grey Wolf seemed to ponder Captain Favel's request. Finally, he nodded and said, "I will show you the way . . . for the present. But should I decide to go my way, I shall, for my soul is in bondage to no one but Baruch himself."

"That figures!" Xzwindra leaned back against the wall and stared out at the desert.

"Because your own soul is in bondage, do you resent the freedom of another?" Grey Wolf's tone was not cutting, but his words were.

Xzwindra offered no answer. She finished her meal in silence.

The others chatted amicably. Then the horses were readied, and with Grey Wolf leading, they continued their journey across the desolate hardpan.

Chapter 25

*T*he King's Company spent the night in a large cavern where a spring bubbled with fresh water. It flowed into a pool from a rent in the cave wall, then ran out the mouth of the cave toward the thirsty hardpan. By day the desert sun lapped up the cool water before it reached the waiting earth. At night the dry earth drank briefly but to no avail. Its eternal thirst remained unquenched.

In the recesses of the cave, Captain Favel and Sergeant Tandrak found the remains of yet another Bayl creature.

"Grey Wolf, come take a look!" shouted Captain Favel.

The desert warrior looked down on the Bayl creature and then up at Captain Favel and Sergeant Tandrak. "Five such creatures came to the Plain of Blue Fire," he said. "Only two passed through to the Deathreach, as you call it. One of those two died out on the Plain of Endless Earth. The other traversed the Parchwood and continued on to the Plain of Sticks."

"Brackenwild Reach, I presume," said Captain Favel to no one in particular.

"That is what Pegran calls it." Grey Wolf acknowledged the Captain's comment. "But the pictures of the ancient people name it the Plain of Sticks."

"Where are these creatures from?" asked Sergeant Tandrak, drawing Grey Wolf's attention back to the remains of the serpentlike man.

"They came out of the west, and I followed them here in my land," said Grey Wolf. "They appeared to be creatures of the dark, for they traveled only at night and hid in the dark recesses of these lava caves during the time of the sun. Beyond that I do not know, for they do not appear in the pictures."

Suddenly, Captain Favel stiffened. There was movement in the shadows beyond the light of their torch. He readied his spear, and Sergeant Tandrak cranked his bow and set an arrow.

Grey Wolf motioned for them to wait. The decrodile charged out of the darkness. Grey Wolf stepped forward unarmed, save for the sword that hung in its scabbard at his side. The creature stopped and raised itself up on its hind feet to meet the challenge. Grey Wolf's brilliant gray eyes met the death lizard's dull-brown eyes. The creature backed slowly away, seeming to cringe in fear. It dropped to its feet and retreated into the shadows once again.

"I'll be!" declared Sergeant Tandrak. "How did you do that?"

Grey Wolf turned to him. "The death lizard preys on fear. If it is not able to strike fear in its prey, it will turn away. It is actually a cowardly creature. In fact, I am forever safe from that particular lizard. It will remember my scent and refuse to come near me in the future."

"And what if one of the creatures comes upon you while you sleep?" The corner of Sergeant Tandrak's mouth turned up in a half smile.

"When I sleep, I trust Baruch to protect me," said the desert warrior. "Thus, I sleep without fear. And since I sleep without fear, I presume the creatures avoid me then as well."

"You learned that from the pictures?" inquired Captain Favel.

"The ancients teach many things through their pictures but not that," said Grey Wolf. "The ancients never learned how to deal with two curses. The first was their pride. The second was the death lizards.

"I learned the death lizards' secret by watching them—how they relate to each other," he continued. "Death lizards confront each other fearlessly, then after gazing into each others' eyes, they slink away, each to its lonely existence. But if the same two lizards meet again, they merely sniff the air, then avoid each other."

"And what about Pegran?" asked Sergeant Tandrak. "Was he afraid?"

"Did the death lizard attack him?" asked Grey Wolf. "One can be very courageous and still have fear in the heart. Pegran is courageous, but even Pegran is afraid of the death lizards."

"I was afraid of the death lizard you just faced down," said Captain Favel, as they headed back to where the rest of the company waited. "Why did the decrodile not turn aside and attack me?"

"Because you were with me. And as I said, the death lizards are cowardly creatures." Grey Wolf studied Captain Favel's face. The desert warrior had met few men who would admit to their fears.

As they walked through the long lava tube back to the main cavern, Captain Favel thought about Grey Wolf's words. They made sense to him, for he had seen many men who were not unlike the decrodiles, men who preyed on others' fears. If they could intimidate and strike fear, they would do so again and again. But when the person being preyed on would take a fearless stand, the attacker, in turn, would prove himself a coward.

Both Captain Favel and Sergeant Tandrak slept easier that night because of Grey Wolf's presence.

*C*aptain Favel found Grey Wolf mystifying. The desert warrior was different from any man he had ever met, not just his strange attire, but because he exuded extreme confidence without arrogance. On the other hand, Grey Wolf struck Sergeant Tandrak as being smart but perhaps a bit naive. Corporal Mifstern found Grey Wolf interesting, but he felt uncomfortable in his presence. Kander both liked and disliked the strange rider of the wild. He envied Grey Wolf's confidence and seemingly natural instincts but felt uncomfortable with his forthrightness. And he did not like it that Grey Wolf made Xzwindra feel anxious. And obviously, Xzwindra did not like Grey Wolf at all, though as the days passed she learned to tolerate him. Still, she avoided him when possible. And Grey Wolf made no effort to appease her.

With Grey Wolf serving as their guide, the King's Company passed through the stakz and came to the Deathreach, where they camped beneath a fold of lava in the last of the stakz. And from the lava fold, they looked out on the utterly barren-looking Plain of Endless Earth.

"Going from Hades into Hades!" complained Sergeant Tandrak.

That night Grey Wolf mounted his charger without speaking a word to anyone and rode off toward the west.

For the first time in days, Xzwindra smiled. At last she was rid of the strange self-appointed sage. But to her great consternation, when she awoke in the morning, Grey Wolf had returned but without the firespar. No one asked him where he had taken the ancient scepter.

"What about water?" asked Captain Favel as they turned their horses toward the vast, flat wasteland.

"Oases are scattered across the Plain of Endless Earth." Grey Wolf motioned toward the great dust bowl before them. "They are far spread, but Sterling Gray knows his way to the places of water. Still, I must speak words of warning. You will experience great thirst on the journey, but I assure you that you will not die for want of water, for the Endless Earth knows other secrets of life as well as the oases."

"Why not head over to the mountains and make our way through the foothills?" asked Corporal Mifstern. "Wouldn't that be easier?"

"There are no creatures of death out on the Plain of Endless Earth." Grey Wolf looked over his shoulder at the young soldier. "Out here our only enemy is the sun. In the foothills, creatures of death are plentiful, from the mountain-pit viper to the vicious humpback bear." He turned and looked at the young soldier. "And there are hellcats with teeth that tear like daggers. The Plain of Endless Earth can be a terrible place, but it is a safe place if you know its secrets."

"Sounds good to me," commented Sergeant Tandrak as he tied a white cloth around his head and let it drape loosely over his back and shoulders. He nodded to the others.

"You've all been given cappas. Pull 'em out, and do the same."

"This is crazy!" groused Kander as he worked at tying the knot. "I feel like stripping naked, not putting on more!"

"Strip naked, and the sun will fry you like an egg on a skillet." Sergeant Tandrak rubbed grease on his face as he spoke. "You'd be dead before we reached the first oasis. The cappa may seem uncomfortable, but it will keep you alive. And don't neglect the grease."

Kander grudgingly complied. The congealed animal fat was nasty, but he found that the headpiece was not nearly as uncomfortable as he had thought it would be. And although he hated to admit it, the cappa did provide a welcome shade from the burning rays of the sun.

Although the broad, flat surface of the Deathreach was sandy, it was not a loose sand. The horse's hooves made a dull clomping noise as they struck the sun-baked crust. Heat rose off the desert in eerie waves. Here and there huge cacti rose from the desert floor, wrinkled and crusty but green. Their needles were terrible looking things, eight to ten inches long, sticking out in nests of five, evenly placed up and down the huge trunks. Some of the trunks were nearly three feet in diameter and rose upward to as much as thirty feet. Most were fifteen to twenty feet tall. There were few small cacti, but then, the cacti were few and far between in general. The company might ride for miles and see only one or two, while at other times they might see ten or twelve in the span of a day. Once they came upon a stand of seven all within a few feet of each other. Grey Wolf called it the Place of Seven Cacti.

Sergeant Tandrak pulled a face and shook his head. "I wouldn't call seven cacti and desert dust much of a place."

Corporal Mifstern laughed and said mockingly, "Come on over to my place, you know that wonderful resort called Seven Cacti."

Grey Wolf cast them a blank glance but otherwise ignored them.

The second day out, they stopped to rest and feed the horses. The horses were allowed a small scoop of grain each day. Each horse carried its own supply, and the packhorse carried extra.

While feeding his horse, Kander heard an unexpected sound, a chirp followed by a melodic trill. He looked about and in the upper reaches of a cactus, perched on a needle next to a hole it had apparently pecked in the desert tree, he spotted a sandy-colored bird topped with a brilliant yellow crown.

"A desert suntop," said Grey Wolf. "Its song cheers my heart when I travel the Endless Land. It is one of the secrets of the desert. Be still and listen to its song, and you will have the heart to continue on. Learn its ways, and live in a barren waste."

Kander stared at the songster of the wild, then shook his head. "It does seem cheerful enough for living in such an insufferable place," he agreed.

Suddenly, the desert suntop quit singing, cocked its head sideways, dove from its perch, fluttered its wings, and picked something off the side of the cactus.

"Food," said Grey Wolf. "Sand beetle. Appealing to birds but not to men. Still, when the need is great, they are edible. And see those yellow clumps that grow at the base of the needles? Fungus. Those too are edible."

"I think I'd rather eat the bird!" commented Kander.

The desert suntop fluttered back up to its perch. Out the corner of his eye, Kander saw Grey Wolf cast a stern glance in his direction. Kander laughed. It was the first time he had seen Grey Wolf show emotion. "I'm just kidding, Grey Wolf. How could I kill a bird that sings such a beautiful song?"

Kander was surprised to see the desert warrior break a smile. "Now you are beginning to learn the ways of the Endless Earth," said Grey Wolf. He spread a hand toward the desert. "But there is much more to learn."

"Oh, bother," mumbled Xzwindra. She mounted her horse. It was time to move on. "As far as I'm concerned, there is nothing of value in this desert, and nothing to be learned except how to be rid of the place."

Grey Wolf stared at her momentarily but said nothing in response.

Before nightfall the weary riders came to their first oasis, or so Grey Wolf called it. The others had imagined trees and grass and a clear pool of cool water. What they found was a dampness that seemed to barely reach the surface of the desert floor. They found more cacti than usual, and a variety of kinds. The only grass the oasis offered was clumps of sword grass that sprouted up here and there.

"You call this an oasis?" groused Corporal Mifstern.

"Grey Wolf's folly!" muttered Xzwindra.

"Well, yes, I was expecting something more," added Sergeant Tandrak.

"Can the horses eat that stuff?" Captain Favel gestured toward the sword grass. He wondered both if the grass was edible—nonpoisonous—and if eaten, would it grow back again.

"They can eat it," said Grey Wolf. "They can also eat the cactus flowers. The flowers are especially nutritious—for people too."

To get water they had to dig a hole and wait. Slowly, brown, murky water seeped from the earth and filled the hole. Once the horses satisfied their thirst, the company waited for the hole to fill up again, and then Grey Wolf dipped water into a long leather bag, hung it on a cactus, and let the water leach through the leather and drip down into a more thin and supple second water skin that held the water without seeping.

"Removes grit and other impurities," he said. They filled the rest of their water skins, and although the tepid liquid tasted earthy, it was life-sustaining and refreshed them in body and spirit.

The next morning as they prepared to leave the oasis, Grey Wolf warned Captain Favel, "It is far to the next oasis. This is one of several difficult stretches where water will be scarce. We must drink only at need."

Captain Favel passed the word on to the others.

Travel was slow and the sun hot. And in spite of Grey Wolf's warning, after three days their water was gone, and their strength waned. Grey Wolf watched the company with careful eyes.

Xzwindra faded most quickly. When she began to mumble incoherently and speak of things that were not real, he stopped the company.

Captain Favel watched as Grey Wolf dismounted, but the captain said nothing. He was too weary.

Grey Wolf approached a medium-size cactus. He grimaced. "Once destroyed these plants will not grow again, but our need is great." He took out his knife and sliced a thumb-size hole in the outer skin of the cactus. He broke off a long needle and stuck it into the soft inner fleshy part of the plant. A white milky substance ran down the needle and dripped into the water skin he had hung below it. Slowly he drained the cactus of its life.

While the milky water dripped into the skin, Captain Favel helped Xzwindra from her horse. He set her down where the cactus cast its shadow.

Once he had obtained enough of the life-giving milk, Grey Wolf gave it to the captain to give to Xzwindra. While she regained her strength, he filled the other skins.

After the skins were filled, Grey Wolf took out his sword, stood on the back of his horse, and sliced the top off the desert plant. Then he cut the meat out and stuffed it in the long leather skin he had used to strain the murky water back at the oasis. Once the skin was full, he gave each of the King's Company a large piece of flesh and told them to eat it. "It will restore your fluids and provide sustenance," he encouraged.

An hour or so later, they were back in the saddle. Though still feeling weary, Xzwindra was able to continue on. The others' felt their strength renewed as well. And so day after day they mounted their seemingly tireless steeds and rode on out across the seemingly endless earth. The ancient name for the place was certainly appropriate. They rode. They walked the horses. They rode. They walked. They slept. On and on they went for twenty some days. In their weariness they had lost count. But finally they came to Parchwood.

Parchwood was a strange-looking forest that appeared to have died in some era now long past, a forest of trees without leaves, a forest floor without flowers, grass, fungi, or brush, and a forest with no animals—a place without life.

As they entered the forest, Kander gestured toward the trees. "With this dry air and insufferable heat, I'm surprised that Parchwood hasn't caught fire and burned itself into the parched earth!"

"Parchwood will not burn," responded Grey Wolf. "The wood of these trees is as hard as the blade of your sword. In fact, strike a branch with your blade, and your blade will be the worse for it. Even with an ax, you cannot chop the trees of Parchwood."

The others laughed. Surely Grey Wolf was exaggerating. But when the hot desert wind picked up, although it nearly whipped their cappas from their heads, the tree branches did not sway at all. Even the smallest branches remained stiff and still. And when the astonished company moved close enough to touch the trees, they found that they were as hard and brittle as rock, seemingly harder. They had never seen anything like it. Grey Wolf had not exaggerated at all. And so the King's Company passed by the Stone Forest, as Kander tagged it, and came to what Pegran's map called Draw Gulch, a huge split in the earth, a gaping canyon some fifty miles wide that snaked east for more than 1,500 miles carrying the Savage River out to the Savage Sea.

"What is it like down there?" Captain Favel leaned on his saddle horn and let his eyes scan the vast expanse below. "Would we be better off traveling east up here on the rim or down in the canyon by the river?"

"The river is a hard way, but there is water," said Grey Wolf. "There are trees for shade and grass for the horses to feed on. However, in some places the water is deep and great escarpments bar the way. One must either swim around the barriers or climb over them, a difficult way for a man, let alone his horse. But Sterling Gray has passed that way before."

"And if we stay up here?" Captain Favel ran the back of his arm across his brow.

"We must pass through Parchwood and cross the mountains," said Grey Wolf. "That too is a hard way. Trees without life. Creatures of death. No natural food for the horses and little to no water."

"Cactus?" asked Kander.

"None," returned Grey Wolf.

"And what about the canyon?" asked Captain Favel. "What dangers lurk down in its shadows?"

"Snakes with clattery rattles on their tails – and hellcats," said Grey Wolf. "The snakes will bother us little. They are neither large nor aggressive like the vipers. They are dangerous only if directly disturbed. And as for the hellcats, they are vicious, but they are few and far between. The greatest dangers are climbing the rocks and the river itself."

"Well, we are out of grain for the horses, and water is essential," responded Captain Favel, "so, I guess our way is chosen by our circumstances."

Grey Wolf nodded in acknowledgement, turned his horse aside, and led the King's Company to a narrow path that twisted down the side of the canyon wall into Draw Gulch.

From far below, keen eyes observed their descent.

Chapter 26

*T*he King's Company took most of the day to traverse the narrow ledge that led down to the canyon floor. Trees with their leaves fluttering in a gentle evening breeze, lush green grass, and cool, rippling blue water were a welcome sight.

The group brought their horses to the river, watered them, and cooled and cleaned them off with a good rinsing. The horses freshened, they tethered them in sight of the river where they could graze on the verdant foliage. Once camp was made, the sweltered travelers headed for the river themselves. They were ready to cool off and be rid of the gritty desert dust both from body and clothes. Even Grey Wolf took the plunge.

With the distinctive gray markings washed from his face, Grey Wolf looked much like any other man. But immediately upon leaving the water, he took out a gray powder, mixed it with a small amount of liquid, and reapplied the markings just as they had appeared before.

That evening Captain Favel allowed a fire. The King's Company ate their first hot meal in days—rabbit stew. Together they reveled in every sip of broth and in every bite of meat and root.

"We haven't had a really decent meal since Havenholt," remarked a sparkle-eyed Corporal Mifstern.

They slept comfortably that night and rose refreshed with the dawn. The drudgery of crossing the desert lands had been washed away in the cool waters of the Savage River and chased into the recesses of memory by their night dreams. Morning smiles broke through the weariness that had sculpted itself into most of their faces. Even Captain Favel was smiling.

On the other hand, Sergeant Tandrak, though having a fresher look about him, maintained his normal dour air. Although Grey Wolf remained stoic as ever, his eyes seemed more vibrant with life. And as the new day dawned, they broke camp oblivious to the eyes that followed their every move.

Grey Wolf led the King's Company eastward along the rippling, winding Savage River. Although there was no path, the way was not difficult the first two days. Then they came to a rock wall that wanted to deny them passage. However, the shallow water allowed them to skirt the wall's extremity with more inconvenience than trouble. But on the fourth day, they came to a high wall with a deep swirling pool at its base. Here Grey Wolf led them away from the river and up and over the back of the barrier. The climb was slow, difficult, and dangerous.

As the company came to the saddle of the high wall, Captain Favel noticed a change in Grey Wolf's demeanor. He sat higher in his saddle, and his eyes scanned every crook and cranny. The group stopped just beyond the crest.

Captain Favel pulled up beside Grey Wolf. "What is it?" he asked.

"I sense an unfamiliar presence." Grey Wolf continued to search the shadows on the hillside to the right. "An evil thing lurks somewhere near at hand."

"Man or beast?" Captain Favel followed Grey Wolf's eyes up to a shadow-shrouded ledge.

"Mostly beast," said Grey Wolf.

"Mostly beast?" Captain Favel raised his eyebrows, "A servant of Bayl? One of those mannish-looking serpent creatures?"

"No." Grey Wolf turned and faced Captain Favel. "I have felt the presence of the snakemen before. The presence I sense now out in the shadows is evil but a different evil. It is more man than the snakemen and yet more beast."

"Is the creature stalking us?" asked Captain Favel.

The others all listened intently to the conversation. A shiver ran down Xzwindra's spine.

Kander's thoughts immediately went to Deth. Maybe Xvardris had sent out more than one such assassin.

"The evil is watching," said Grey Wolf. It is probably sizing us up, deciding whether to chance an encounter when there are so many of us. But a beastly mind does not always reason logically. It would be foolish for it to attack us, but one never knows what evil might do."

"Well, let's get on with it." Captain Favel put his heels to his horse's flanks while his eyes swept the hillside and then down toward the river. "We'll soon find out if it is going to follow us or not. There is rough terrain ahead." He pressed Sterling Gray forward. "The day is pretty well spent. By the time we get down this side of the high wall, we will only have an hour or so before we'll need to find a place to camp."

Traversing the east side of the wall required dismounting and walking the horses for a considerable distance. Sergeant Tandrak brought up the rear, his watchful eyes scanning the south wall of the canyon.

"The presence continues to follow us," said Grey Wolf when they were ready to make camp.

Captain Favel examined the hillside and shrugged his shoulders. "Well, we'd better set a watch tonight."

When Xzwindra relieved Corporal Mifstern, the moon was high and full and the canyon had taken on an extraordinary aura. Xzwindra stood atop a boulder that shadowed their camp to the south, a vantage point that gave a sweeping view of the canyon wall as well as the extraordinary moonscape. She watched wispy clouds pass over the face of the moon. Lost in thoughts of bygone days, she did not notice movement among the rocks that stretched between her perch and the high wall.

Suddenly, an unexplainable chill ran down Xzwindra's spine. She turned and saw fiery green eyes flying at her out of the shadows. She brought up her crossbow and pulled the trigger all in one fluid motion. The hellcat screamed as the arrow drove home. The sleek creature of the night fell at her feet. The snarling cat gazed up at her and then fell silent as the light in its eyes died.

When the hellcat let out its blood-curdling scream, the camp below came to life. Men scrambled for their weapons, while up on the rock Xzwindra exhaled a sigh of relief. She let down her guard and laughed in relief.

Then a second creature lunged out from the shadows, a savage, mannish creature. It came swiftly and silently. Xzwindra was unaware of its outstretched arms, wolfish eyes, lithe naked body, or its daggerlike teeth. Too suddenly for her to respond with her bow, the creature's terrible hands enveloped her. A gurgling growl wretched from the evil thing's throat as its teeth ripped into her shoulder.

Xzwindra's screams filled the night, echoing from the canyon walls.

Grey Wolf sprang up the rock to Xzwindra's aid ahead of the others. He ripped the snarling, naked thing from her back. The evil turned on the desert warrior like an animal caught in a trap. However, the naked brute was no match for Grey Wolf. He twisted the evil thing about so that its teeth gnashed air, and he thrust its face downward on the ground.

Sergeant Tandrak grabbed a strand of rope, and while Grey Wolf held the fiend, Tandrak bound its wrists behind its back and then its ankles.

Meanwhile, Captain Favel and Kander helped Corporal Mifstern with Xzwindra, fetching water and other necessities.

Xzwindra's shoulders, back, and neck were deeply lacerated. Mifstern cleansed the wounds then applied his yellow salve. Kander could see terror in Xzwindra's eyes. He touched her arm. "The creature is no longer a threat, Xzwindra," comforted Kander, "Grey Wolf has seen to that."

Xzwindra offered a faint smile. However, the terror that sheeted her face clearly indicated she was not convinced.

The creature firmly tethered, Grey Wolf rolled it over onto its back. Wild, rage-filled blue eyes lashed out at him and the others. The creature's hair was long, thick, and tangled like a rat's nest. Its demeanor was much like that of a rat. It squirmed, snarled, and gnashed its teeth.

"The brute is filthy and fetid!" Sergeant Tandrak turned his face away and sucked fresh air. "What do we do with it now?"

Captain Favel walked over, knelt, and examined the helpless miscreant. It growled and tried to bite him. The captain stood and turned his nose away. "From the looks of him, he must be about sixty years old." Captain Favel shook his head. "I suppose he was once a man, but you could hardly call him one now."

"I've heard rumors of such a man as this," said Grey Wolf. "Villagers call him Wild Man from the North. Others call him Snarl."

"Fitting, if you ask me. The latter, that is," put in Corporal Mifstern. His back was to them as he continued to dress Xzwindra's wounds.

Grey Wolf nodded in agreement. "It is said that he has wandered the Savage Lands for years. However, this is the first time I have encountered him. He's a pitiful thing, is he not?"

"Pitiful? I'd call it wretched!" grated Mifstern over his shoulder. "Look at what the thing did to Xzwindra. He was trying to eat her alive. The brute is a cannibal!"

"Captain Favel, you still haven't answered Sergeant Tandrak's question," pressed Kander. "What are you going to do with the wretched creature?"

"Well, we certainly can't release him to the wild again." Captain Favel gestured toward the poor creature that lay with panic-filled eyes shining in the moonlight. The brute did not seem to comprehend what was going on around him. "Nor can we just leave him here bound and at the mercy of the elements."

"Well, we could cut its miserable throat and feed it to the hellcats!" Sergeant Tandrak felt no pity for the Wild Man. To him Snarl was the equivalent of a hellcat or a viper—a deadly menace to be dealt with appropriately.

"No, his life is not ours to take." Captain Favel looked Sergeant Tandrak in the eye. "Wastrel that he is, this poor creature is still of our own flesh, a reminder of what could have been had any one of us taken a different path in life. We have no choice but to take him with us."

"Take him with us!" protested Kander. "You've got to be kidding!"

Captain Favel turned to face him and smiled. "Kander, you allow room for compassion toward an assassin who has probably murdered a hundred or more people in cold blood, and yet you feel no compassion for this poor creature?"

Kander shrugged. A look of confusion creased his brow. "It's not that I feel hatred for the creature, but he is evil, and I do not see the wisdom of taking him with us. To say the least, the vile creature is dangerous, and beyond that, caring for his needs will hinder our progress." He stopped and his shoulders sagged. "Besides, having him with us would subject Xzwindra to continued anguish."

"Then, tell me, Kander, what shall we do with Snarl?" asked Captain Favel. He motioned to where the wild man lay bound in his fetters on the rock.

Kander looked at the poor creature and shook his head. Grim-faced, he turned and walked over to where Corporal Mifstern was lifting Xzwindra to her feet.

"Wrap a cloth about the creature's mouth, and haul him down to the camp, Sergeant Tandrak." Captain Favel turned his attention to the hellcat. "I'll see to this critter."

Corporal Mifstern and Kander helped Xzwindra down the backside of the rock. "I'm freezing cold," she complained. Yet sweat beaded her brow. Corporal Mifstern's face turned grim with concern. When they got Xzwindra down to camp, he tucked her into her bedroll. "I'm so cold," she whispered as she pulled the blanket tightly about her neck. Her hands trembled, yet perspiration continued to drip down her temples.

"We've got problems," Corporal Mifstern whispered to Captain Favel when he returned to camp. "Xzwindra is burning with fever, and I've got nothing with which to treat it."

Standing nearby, Grey Wolf heard the corporal's comment. He went to Xzwindra, knelt, and laid his leathered hand on her forehead. For a second time, he showed emotion. Grim lines of concern etched themselves into his seemingly impervious brow. He strode to his saddlebag (a bag he carried draped at the back of his riding blanket). From within the skin bag, he withdrew a small leather pouch. "Hot water," he demanded.

Immediately, Corporal Mifstern complied. The coals were still hot from earlier that night. He handed Grey Wolf a steaming cup.

Grey Wolf sprinkled a mixture of herbs into the water and offered the brew to Xzwindra. She resisted. Gently, Grey Wolf made her drink the elixir.

"Parendara. It will help, but it will not heal," said Grey Wolf in response to their questioning glances. "It will keep the fever from destroying her mind, but it will not make the fever go away."

"What we need is an elixir of reactive fennel and aperients of tarragon." interjected Corporal Mifstern. The others looked at him with raised eyebrows. "They are rare medicinal herbs that grow in hot, damp areas where there is little sunlight. But unfortunately, even if the herbs were growing right under my nose, I would not recognize them. I've used fennel and tarragon, but I've never actually seen the herbs before they were dried and crushed. However, I do know that their properties tend to heal infections and kill the bane that causes fever."

Corporal Mifstern looked at Grey Wolf as if to ask whether he was aware of the herbs he had mentioned.

The desert warrior shook his head. "I learned what I know about herbs by reading the pictures of the ancients. And the ancients' names for the herbs were different from the names you use. If you could describe the plants—but you cannot, so . . . "He lifted his eyebrows and grimaced.

"Well, if Grey Wolf's herbs keep Xzwindra's brain from frying, she at least has a chance," said Mifstern. He nodded toward Snarl. "But be careful when you're near that vile creature. His bite appears to be venomous."

"How long before we can expect her fever to break so she'll be able to ride?" asked Captain Favel. "Any idea?"

Corporal Mifstern looked over at Xzwindra, then back at the captain. "When the fever breaks, if it does, it will leave her as weak as an old rag. It'll be at least a week before she can ride and that if we're lucky—much more if we're not." He gave Captain Favel a grim stare. "What we really need to do is get her to a healer."

Captain Favel turned to Grey Wolf with a questioning look.

"There is probably a healer at Ograf." Grey Wolf motioned toward the east. "But Ograf is not a safe village. And it is far."

Captain Favel laid his map out in the moonlight. He and Sergeant Tandrak examined and calculated. "More than five hundred miles," declared Tandrak, and then added a low whistle. "It will take weeks to get there."

"Well, we don't have much choice," said Captain Favel. "Once she's able to travel, we will have to take her to Ograf no matter how long it takes or how unsafe the village might be."

Kander sat with Xzwindra through the rest of the night, cooling her forehead with a damp rag, holding her shivering hand, and watching. Part of the night she slept. Part of the night she seemed delirious. She stared into the night but did not appear to see, and off and on she babbled unintelligibly. Kander whispered words of comfort, but Xzwindra did not seem to hear them.

Before dawn Grey Wolf rose, built up the fire, heated water, and gave Xzwindra another draught of his herbal brew. He examined her at various times throughout the day. Her condition did not change. The brew controlled her fever but did not break it.

After a second day of waiting and with no change in Xzwindra's condition, Captain Favel gave orders to cut a number of trees near the river. "We will make a raft and float down to Ograf."

Grey Wolf opposed the idea. He did not like cutting down trees. "There are so few in the Savage Lands," he complained.

"I don't like it either," responded Captain Favel. "However, in this instance it is a matter of life and death."

They cut the trees and began building the raft. The work proved difficult. For tools, they had two axes, a hatchet, their swords, spearheads, and knives. They secured one log to another with wooden pegs driven into overlapping notches. It took ten days to build the raft, and during that time Xzwindra's condition remained unchanged.

While they worked on the raft, they kept Snarl tethered to a tree by means of a rope tied around his neck. His hands remained tied behind him, and a leather gag was in his mouth. He had eaten through the cloth gags. Grey Wolf had tied the creature's tether so that when he fought the rope, the neck piece pulled tighter and tighter. This arrangement tended to diminish the wild man's rage. But what concerned Grey Wolf most was that Snarl refused to eat the food set before him.

Four days on the rope without food left Snarl withdrawn and placid until approached. Then he would butt, kick, and try to bite them through the leather gag.

By the fifth day, the King's Company, busy working on the raft, paid little attention to Snarl for the greater part of the day. It was not until they stopped work to take their evening meal that they realized Snarl had escaped. Apparently, the wild man had eaten through the leather gag and the tether.

"He ran up into the hills," said Grey Wolf. "The last I saw him, he was scrambling along the base of the canyon wall with three feet of rope hanging from his neck and with his hands still tied behind his back."

"You mean you saw him escape and did nothing?" Kander could not believe his ears. "What if Snarl had attacked Xzwindra again? You put her and all of us at risk!"

"If the wretched creature had attacked anyone, I would have killed him." Grey Wolf showed no emotion.

"What if he returns?" asked Corporal Mifstern.

"He'll not come back," said Grey Wolf. "He will find a way to free his hands and then will return to his wild ways. He will not soon forget what he has endured so he'll keep his distance."

"I hope you're right," said Captain Favel. "But with Snarl on the loose, we will once again need to maintain a watch."

"Snarl will not return," repeated Grey Wolf. "Whoever stays up with the woman will be watch enough."

"Very well." Captain Favel nodded. "But whoever is watching Xzwindra had best keep his crossbow handy."

Snarl may have watched the King's Company from a distance, but he did not bother them again. After another five days, they finished the raft. The next morning, they prepared to break camp and continue their journey.

"Well, it's time to see how this pile of logs navigates the river." Captain Favel addressed his words to Grey Wolf. "You and Sergeant Tandrak take the horses by way of land."

"A great red rock stands in the middle of the river, perhaps a day's journey from here." Grey Wolf motioned toward the east. "There is a stand of pines at the river's edge off to the right of the red rock—a good place to make camp. We will meet you there."

Grey Wolf had skinned the hellcat and tanned its hide while the others were building the raft. Captain Favel made a bed of pine boughs over which he spread the hide. Kander carried Xzwindra aboard the raft and carefully laid her on the soft berth. Corporal Mifstern kept an eye on her while Captain Favel and Kander poled the raft out into the swift current of the Savage River.

Grey Wolf and Sergeant Tandrak headed up into the rocks, leading the horses, and carrying most of the supplies. "The journey to Ograf will be long and dangerous," commented Grey Wolf as he gazed down at the bobbing raft. He turned away, and they rode on.

Sergeant Tandrak scanned the rocks for any sign of Snarl. He shook his head and muttered, "Should have killed the wretched creature."

Chapter 27

*T*angle Wood was little more than a smoldering stand of black stumps. Wisps of smoke rose here and there, but the destruction of the forest was complete. Xvardris' slaves were busy clearing charred tree trunks and moving the war machines closer to Havenholt.

A frustrated Major Targndel found himself trapped in Zwexdrof. Somehow Xvardris had found out that he was in the city, and now guards manned every gate and checked all who passed. Xvardris' soldiers were searching shops and houses, turning every stone, and Major Targndel barely stayed a step ahead of them.

When Zedria returned from her clandestine meeting with Captain Favel, Xvardris' men arrested her at the city gate.

Major Targndel had watched from a distance, and he had not seen Zedria or any of his operatives since.

In the garb of a beggar, he worked his way toward the busy western gate. From an alley, he watched to see how well the guards were checking passersby. A beggar friend named Haltrin hobbled to the gate ahead of Targndel. The guards tore off his robe, pulled back his hair, and had a local identify him. Then, after roughing him up a bit, they ran him out of the city.

Targndel slipped deep into the shadows. He shuffled his way to the other side of the city to check out the eastern gate. Again, he had no chance of getting past the guards so he made his way to the southern gate. Milling with marketers, he watched the gate from a distance. Soldiers were everywhere.

As he turned to leave, he heard the rumble of wheels on flagstone. A caravan of wagons and stumbling slaves came down the street toward the gate. They were, no doubt, being taken out to the work in Tangle Wood. The caravan slowly trudged past the market.

Hmm, mused Major Targndel, soldiers, wagons, carts, and masses of slaves. At an opportune moment, he slipped out from the market and in among the slaves.

The slaves cast him wary eyes but kept shuffling along without drawing attention to him. Major Targndel moved with stealth through their ranks, stooping, slipping under their chains, and then stealing up into the back of a wagon. It was filled with whorls of rope for pulling war machines. He squirmed deep under the coils and out of sight. The slave driving the wagon had seen him climb aboard, but he had simply given him a wink and then paid him no mind. Targndel had chanced that the slaves would assume he was someone trying to escape the city and would be sympathetic. It was his only hope.

At the gate Xvardris' guardsmen thoroughly checked wagons, carts, and the masses of slaves. When they came to the wagon filled with rigging, a soldier climbed in among the heavy whorls of rope, looked about, and then told the driver to pass on.

Having finally escaped the city, the caravan took Major Targndel toward his intended destination, Havenholt. But it also trundled him right into the midst of the camp of Xvardris' main army.

Officers barked orders, and slaves began unloading the rigging. Targndel knew that soon he would be found out. His every muscle tensed, ready to spring into action. His heart pounded as he saw calloused hands wrap around the coil of rope to lift it away. Targndel found himself looking into the eyes of a slave. With one hand, the slave signaled for him to remain still, and then he tossed the coil out the back of the wagon and then another and another, until the wagon was empty except for Major Targndel lying up against the front rail of the wagon.

"Boger, toss me those bags a' trash!" cried the slave. Boger, another slave, obliged and Targndel was soon buried under a heap of trash and brush.

"Hey you!" Targndel heard one of the soldiers shout. "That's not a trash wagon. Get that stuff out of there. It goes in that old dogcart over there!"

"Why didn't ya say so sooner!" griped the slave. "But, hey, since it's filled, why not jes' take this one out an' dump it? Same difference in the long run!"

"Cause I said ta put it in the other one! An' that's all the reason ya need. So get it done, Findr!"

"Boger!" hollered Findr. "Bring that ol' dogcart over here!"

Boger jumped aboard and backed horse and cart up to the wagon they had just filled with trash. BUMP. "Whoa!" shouted the carter.

The two slaves transferred the brush and garbage from wagon to cart. At Findr's beckoning, Major Targndel crawled out of the wagon between the two slaves' legs and onto the dogcart. Soon Findr and Boger once again had Targndel out of sight under a mound of trash and branches.

"Now get that stinkin' stuff outa' here!" shouted the soldier.

Findr sat himself on the back edge of the cart, and Boger shook the horse's reins. Off they lumbered through the midst of the camp and the still smoldering forest to the refuse dump.

"There are sentries beyond the dump, so keep your head low," said Findr once Targndel had crawled out of the cart. "They're a lazy bunch, so you should be able ta snake yer way past without much trouble."

"Best to ya," put in Boger.

Targndel took an offered hand from each of the men before stealing off toward Havenholt. He was filthy, hungry, and tired by the time he reached the gates of the fortress.

Major Targndel knocked on the gatehouse door, knowing that his progress toward the fortress had been watched. The small barred window in the door swung open, and dark angry eyes peered out at him. "No place for beggars here," spat the gatekeeper. "Be off with you!"

"I am Major Targndel, and I must see Jentrxn immediately."

The gatekeeper raised a bushy eyebrow. "Yer not the Major Targndel I am familiar with!"

"I am Major Targndel."

"We'll see," said the gatekeeper, and he slammed the window shut.

Targndel leaned heavy against the wall and grated his teeth. He knew fortress procedures. The gatekeeper would send for someone higher up.

When the window in the door swung open again, Razrdris, the fortress commander, looked out at him. He frowned and shook his head. "Great disguise, Targndel. You not only look like a beggar, but you smell like one too." He turned to the guard. "Let him in."

Major Targndel stumbled through the gate.

Razrdris caught him by the arm. "Bring a horse cart!" he called to one of his aides. "He'll need a ride up to the citadel." The aide hurried off to the stable. Razrdris turned to Targndel. "Sit over here, Major." He helped him to the stairway that led up to the wall.

Targndel gladly sat down. He felt as if his legs could not carry him a step farther.

"You're a mess, Major. What happened?"

"Later." Targndel waved him off. "What I need right now is water and food. I'm famished!"

"What you need is a bath!" said Razrdris after calling for a goblet of water. Targndel drank deeply. The horse cart arrived. "You'll have to wait for food until we get to the citadel. Here, I'll help you climb up."

Targndel tried to stand, but he could not raise himself from the step on which he sat. Razrdris and one of his men, heads turned to the side, lifted him from the step and helped him up into the cart.

Razrdris reluctantly crawled up beside him. "To the citadel," he told the driver, and with a snap of the driver's whip, they were off.

Targndel leaned on one side rail while Razrdris leaned out over the opposite rail to avoid the stench. Once at the citadel,

Razrdris took Targndel straight to the bath. Targndel protested. He wanted to eat first.

But his protest went unheeded. "You would contaminate your food before it ever got to your mouth," chided Razrdris. "Take off those louse-infested clothes and into the water with you! We'll bring your meal to you in here."

Moments later, clothes tossed in a heap to the side, Razrdris eased Targndel down into the bath. "Make sure you wash thoroughly from head to foot. Hard to tell what might be crawling on you," laughed Razrdris, then he called an attendant and told him to burn the pile of clothes and to bring others. Not long after that, a waiter arrived, tray in hand. Major Targndel bathed and then ate in the comfort of his bath.

Soon Jentrxn, General Vandwert, and Prior Forknedrn arrived. Targndel protested the lack of privacy. "You guys are like vultures!" he complained. "Can't a man have a few moments of peace before you start picking away at his brain?"

"You were supposed to be here weeks ago!" General Vandwert ignored Targndel's plea. "Where in the love of swords and daggers have you been?"

Targndel set aside his meal and slipped under the water as if shutting the intruders out. A moment later, he popped back up, shook the water from his hair, and looked around the small bathing room. "You still here?" he said with mock surprise.

General Vandwert rolled his eyes toward the ceiling. "You're as impertinent as a jackass!" he barked.

"We've been more than a little concerned for your safety, Major," said Jentrxn more calmly. "And it appears our concern was justified. Do you want to tell us about it?"

"Now that's better," said Targndel with a reproving glance toward General Vandwert. The general's neck went red, and Targndel laughed. The general frowned and remained stoic.

"I have been a hunted man." Major Targndel turned serious again. "In fact, if it hadn't been for a couple of kindhearted slaves, I never would have escaped." Then he told them his story.

"Have you learned what Xvardris' plan of attack will be?" asked the Prior. "Surely as long as you were away, you have learned something of value."

"I have learned very little." Targndel pushed the wet hair back from his face. "Xvardris' lackeys arrested Zedria as soon she returned to the city. And my other operatives? They too may have been arrested." A scowl crossed his face. "That or they dared not show their faces, especially to me. To do so would likely have cost them their lives and mine as well. But I can tell you what I saw. Xvardris' slaves are clearing a path through what used to be Tangle Wood Forest from Zwexdrof to Havenholt and are moving their war machines forward. As I see it, they will arrive outside the walls in less than six months. And I presume they think they have us penned in, so time is not a factor to them. After all, we can't do much damage to their cause immobilized behind stone walls."

"Humph! I told you we should have left Havenholt when they set Tangle Wood on fire," protested General Vandwert. He gave Jentrxn a biting glance. "Now we will be forced to fight them on their terms and on their timetable."

"They may have burned the forest, but it is still a large place. The blackened trees and stumps and the swales in the land will easily hide both foot soldier and horseman," said Jentrxn. "We can still fight them on our terms, and I have a plan for doing just that."

Jentrxn went on to outline his plan, and even General Vandwert was impressed. But then, Vandwert was anxious for battle.

"What about the King's Company?" asked Prior Forknedrn, turning his attention back to Major Targndel. "Any word concerning them?"

"Nothing official." Targndel then asked for a towel, covered himself with it, and climbed out of the bath. "The only thing I know for sure is that Xvardris' assassin was sent after them with the express assignment of eliminating Kander." He looked about the room, his eyes alive with hope. "And that means the heir does exist!"

"Any word on who the spy might be?" asked Razrdris.

"No. Nothing along that line." Targndel slipped into his clothes. "But I wonder about Zedria. You would think a spy would have let Xvardris know about Zedria much sooner than this because of her contacts in the palace. And when they arrested her, why at the gate and not the palace? Was it to make a public show? I wonder if there is more than one spy? Was Zedria working hand in hand with one of our people? How was she able to learn so much by selling candles at the palace? Many questions terrorize my mind but no answers."

"No answers?" put in General Vandwert. "Try this for an answer. Leftrip was at the gate the night before the King's Company left Havenholt. Captain Favel was seen slipping past the gatekeeper, who happened to be a friend of his. Leftrip hurried up to the wall and watched Captain Favel meet with Zedria at the edge of the forest. They talked briefly and then the captain returned, looking this one way and that, as if he did not want to be seen."

"That's Leftrip's story," said Jentrxn with some irritation. He did not want to believe that Captain Favel could possibly be a spy.

"Leftrip was not the only one who witnessed Captain Favel's clandestine meeting with Zedria," continued the general. "Kander was on the wall as well. Leftrip said the young lad seemed deeply concerned. He did not even seem to notice Leftrip coming and going."

Jentrxn's countenance turned grim. He refused to believe that Captain Favel could be a spy because, unknown to the others, Captain Favel was Jentrxn's younger brother.

After the meeting broke up, Jentrxn went to the north wall. He stood on the wall in silence looking out over the vast plain of blackened trees. But his mind was not on the burned forest. He had chosen his brother to lead the King's Company because he knew if there was anyone he could trust with such an important mission it was he. Tears trickled down Jentrxn's cheeks. "It cannot be true! It cannot be true!" he mumbled to himself. He did not notice that Razrdris had joined him.

Razrdris put a hand on his friend's shoulder. Jentrxn acknowledged his presence with a forced smile. "It will all turn out for the good, my friend," said Razrdris gently. "Baruch has promised so."

"I have believed so until now, Razrdris." Jentrxn gazed out over the charred forest. "Time will tell." He turned and slowly walked away.

Chapter 28

*F*or three days, the Savage River surged along at a pace they could handle, but on the fourth day the rafters encountered a series of rapids that threatened to tear their makeshift craft apart. Straining themselves to exhaustion, Captain Favel and Kander avoided disaster. And once past the white water, they collapsed to the floor of the raft. They looked at each other appreciatively but said nothing.

After a brief rest, the two men returned to their poles, and with shaky arms, they pushed the raft to the river's edge and tied it to a tree hanging out over the bank. They climbed ashore, drew a rope around a second tree, and secured the raft in close. Then they sprawled out on their backs on the lush green grass.

Corporal Mifstern carried Xzwindra ashore, her forehead wet with fever. He placed her in the shade of a tree and then dropped onto the grass next to Captain Favel and Kander, casting them an approving smile. "Good work," he commented.

"How is she doing?" asked Kander.

Corporal Mifstern shrugged. "No change."

Kander simply nodded in response, and the three of them fell silent.

Captain Favel lay with the back of his head cupped in his hands. He was first to break the quiet. "Well, Kander, you have not trusted me from the start of this adventure," he said. "So, tell me, where do we stand now?"

"I don't know," responded Kander. He sat up and leaned his elbows on his knees. "I want to trust you. I want to think that you are not the spy. In fact, I find that I am actually beginning to like you. And that makes it harder not to trust you. But I must admit, I still wonder. After all, one among you is a spy."

"Humph!" broke in Corporal Mifstern. "You couldn't convince me that one of us is a spy. As far as I'm concerned, if there is a spy, he's back at Havenholt."

"Time will tell," said Captain Favel. "Time will tell."

"That's what they say, but it ain't always true." The raspy voice startled the three men to their feet. Captain Favel reached for his sword. "Hold yer hand, fella. Ya don't need no weapon. What do ya spec' me ta do, whip ya wi' me red handkerchief?"

In one hand the bushy-bearded man held a red kerchief with which he was wiping his brow and in the other hand the reins to his donkeys. The two beasts of burden were well-laden with supplies, and they both suddenly brayed loudly as if expressing emphasis to their master's words. The man himself was fairly short, wide of bottom, large of foot, and had a humped-up back that made him look like his shoulders were bent forward. He appeared to be late middle-aged, perhaps in his early fifties.

"Name's Steknr. Some folk call me Maggot, Maggot the Dirt Delver. Others call me Maggot the Diamond Digger. An' a few simply refer to me as Humpy." A congenial grin split his face. "But I only endure people I like a callin' me by that name. An' so far, I like you people, so ya can jes' call me Humpy—lessin' I change my mind, a course."

"Isn't that a rather derogatory name?" asked Kander. He was uncomfortable referring to a man by his deformity.

"Pooh-shah, boy, I am what I am, an' I am what Baruch made me ta be." The prospector wiped his brow again and looked Kander in the eye. "I don't mind me hump, da you?"

"No, of course not." Kander found himself taken aback by the prospector's answer.

"Well then, if there be nothin' wrong wi' me hump, then what in the digs is wrong wi' callin' me Humpy? Course, if ya do it ta make fun, thas sumpin' else, but if ya call me Humpy cause ya 'preciate me, well thas all right . . . see? So, if I likes ya all right, an' you likes me all right, then there ain't no kinda problem wi' callin' me Humpy."

"Humpy it is then!" laughed Kander. "And I'm Kander. This is Captain Favel. That's Corporal Mifstern. And she is Xzwindra."

Humpy's countenance changed. A grimace creased his brow, and he seemed suddenly tenser. "Soldiers, huh? Ya ain't out lookin' fer a miner who be falsely wanted fer stealin' gems back at Xzendr are ya? Cause if ya are, I ain't seen the feller, an' besides, ya can tell that Xvardris feller that the miner didn't steal no gems in the firs' place!"

"No, Humpy, we're not looking for a miner," said Captain Favel, for that was who Humpy had addressed his comment to. "We do not work for Xvardris, the usurper. We are on an urgent mission for the Resistance, those who are opposed to the usurper."

"Well, deep diggins, I'm wi' ya all the way!" he declared as he slapped his knee. His gaze shifted to Xzwindra and he turned somber. "What's ailin' yer woman? Snake bit?"

"Worse," said Corporal Mifstern. "Have you heard of the wild man called Snarl?" Humpy's face went to a scowl, and he nodded. "Well, she was attacked and bitten by him about two weeks ago."

"Humph! Strike me a mother lode!" declared Humpy. "An' she's still alive? Been bitten' by him meself, an' if I hadn't had the herbs, I'd never ha' made it. Fix a fire! Les' take care a that girl!"

"You mean you have reactive fennel and aperients of tarragon?" asked Corporal Mifstern. He pushed his hat back, shook his head, and smiled.

"Ya live out here alone, ya better carry the fever mix wi' ya," said Humpy as he began rummaging through his supplies. "Dorinalac too. Makes a powerful brew!"

Soon they were tipping Humpy's medicinal brew to Xzwindra's lips. She resisted, but they got it down.

"Stuff tastes dreadful," said Humpy with a laugh. "But it'll do the trick. Her fever 'il break wi' in the hour. How ya kep' her alive so long?"

"Grey Wolf gave her an herbal mix that held her fever in check, but it wasn't powerful enough to break it," said Corporal Mifstern.

"Grey Wolf, huh?" said Humpy as he looked around.

"He will be here in awhile," said Kander. "He and Sergeant Tandrak are bringing the horses by land. Xzwindra was in no condition to ride, so we brought her down river on a raft." He nodded toward their makeshift craft.

"I'll keep me feet on solid groun', thanky!" said Humpy, as he followed Kander's gaze toward the river. "Where ya be goin'? Ain't headed ta' Ograf, are ya?"

"We're on our way to Eknard, but we were going to go through Ograf to try to find a healer for Xzwindra," answered Captain Favel. He pulled out his map and spread it on a large rock. "Besides, it looks to me like going through Ograf is the shortest route to Eknard from here. Why?"

"Ograf ain't a safe place," said Humpy. He wrinkled his face to a grimace. "I sneaked in there jes' over a week ago. For some reason, the place be crawlin' wi' Pagyn soldiers. You mentionin' captains and corporals and all, I thought ya might be with em. Anyway, they seemed ta be a lookin' fer somebody." He raised an eyebrow. "Could be you."

"Impossible!" Captain Favel looked from Humpy to Kander, then back again. "They would have to have left Zwexdrof long before we did. No, they couldn't be looking for us."

"So ya say. But there be a northern supply route from Nefarious Reach across the mountains ta Ograf." Humpy gave Captain Favel a toothy grin. "Now by my reckonin' I'd say they coulda' lef after ya an' arrived in Ograf before ya." He shook his head. "It be not impossible. An' if yer mission be what ya say it be, then ya can bet a seam a' pure silver that thas exactly why they be there. Why else would Pagyn troops be blockin' off the only passage east?"

"The only passage?" said Kander. "Can't we cross the mountains on the south side of Draw Gulch?"

Humpy shook his head. "That section a' rock ain't called the Eastern Wall fer nothing,' boy. The only way pas' the wall be by way a' Ograf." He hesitated momentarily and his scowl deepened. "Or down ta the south through the Pass a' Phantazia. Ograf be guarded by Pagyn soldiers . . . an' the pass be guarded by Pagyn spirits, so they say."

Captain Favel looked at his map. "The Pass of Phantazia is too far out of our way. We'll simply have to try to get past the soldiers at Ograf."

Humpy laughed and shook his head. "T'will never happen! The pass east a' Ograf be a narrow one. A hundred good men couldn't fight their way pas' the soldiers that be camped there." He shook his head. "No, sir, not even a slim chance, Cap'n! If ya plan ta continue east, ya will ha' ta go south. But if I was you, I'd jes' turn me rear end aroun' an' go back the way I come. Find some hole ta hide in elsewhere."

"We have no choice but to go east," said Captain Favel. "If we have to go south to go east, then south it will be."

"Then while we slurp gruel at yer fire tonight, I had bes' tell ya 'bout the Shades a' Phantazia." Humpy gave Captain Favel and Kander a serious squint-eyed look and a wink. "Tis bes' ya know what you'll be facin'."

The prospector finished his say to the sound of horses' hooves. Grey Wolf and Sergeant Tandrak came riding through the dark, down the rocky trail, and into camp.

Humpy's donkeys began braying again. To quiet the burros, Humpy gave them some special sticks to chew on.

Grey Wolf and Sergeant Tandrak reined in their horses. A moment of silence followed as the riders took in the newcomer and he them.

Humpy nodded as did Grey Wolf. The hush was broken by a groan.

"Hey!" cried Corporal Mifstern. "Xzwindra's fever has broken!"

"Tol' ya that fever brew a mine be a powerful potion." Humpy's eyes twinkled as he spoke. The others' smiles were expressions of relief. Even Grey Wolf's eyes brightened.

Xzwindra did not open her eyes or converse, but for the first time in days, she slept peacefully.

Chapter 29

Wazrxna, priestess of Bayl, returned to Athos from Zwexdrof. She had ordered King Werfhx of the so-called Realm of Amity to send troops to Ograf to ensure that those who had been sent to bring back the heir would be cut off and captured if possible or killed if necessary. The priestess now entered the Temple Tenebrous. The five remaining darklings stood at the foot of the altar. Sadness showed on their serpentine faces.

"What is it?" asked Wazrxna. She knew they could not answer, for the darklings did not speak. They looked at the priestess, showing deep anguish through their eyes. "Something troubles you, my pets. We shall soon find out the cause of your sorrow. Your father will tell me."

A misty smoke rose about the altar. The red haze gave off an unnatural sense of heat. Wazrxna mounted the stairs and went to the apex of the high altar some thirty feet above the temple floor. Red smoke swirled about her feet as if moved by a fit of anger. Above the throne, partially coiled about a bar suspended from the ceiling, hung a huge greenish-brown serpent. The creature, two feet in diameter and twenty feet long, looked down on the priestess through dull-yellow eyes with black bars slicing through them. The viper gazed intently at the priestess. Its tongue slithered in and out of its mouth as if testing the air above the altar.

Wazrxna stood atop the altar but did not seem to notice the serpent. She raised her arms and began to chant Pagyn words of praise to Bayl. She begged his presence, for the darklings, his children, were troubled, and she would know the cause of their anguish.

"Sss-I am here,"hissed the serpent, its eyes now alive and fiery. "Sss-our children have good reassson to be sssorrowful. Xvardrisss sssent their brothersss forth in sssearch of the heir to the throne of Xzssswendria, but they have all died in the Sssavage Landsss. Hisss asssassin is dead asss well. The sssearchersss have foiled usss. The heir ssstill livesss. The man named Kander ssstill livesss asss well. He mussst be ssstopped, my love...Ssss."

"Yes, Lord Bayl!" declared the priestess with her hands and face raised toward the face of the viper. "Troops have been sent to intercept those who seek the heir. Should they somehow get by the troops, we have our spy in their midst who will kill the heir. Should something happen to the spy, I am sure the remaining darklings would be delighted to avenge their brothers, Lord Bayl."

"Ssss – how do you know the ssspy can be trusssted, my love...Ssss?" responded Bayl, the demon lord who used the great serpent for presence.

"The spy, though of Xzwendarian blood, is of my own womb." Wazrxna's face shone with pride. "The spy will not fail."

"Isss thisss known in Xzsssswendria?" asked the viper. "Hasss your ssspy been uncovered? Rumor among the ssspiritsss sssaysss yesss."

"The spirits are wrong!" retorted Wazrxna, her tone defiant. "No one knows the truth of the spy's birthing. The spy is considered to be a most loyal subject and true to the Resistance. Even the spy's father does not know that I am the mother. He thinks the mother is a woman he met on the streets of Zwexdrof, a woman who supposedly died after giving the child birth. I am confident the truth remains a secret, Lord Bayl."

"The truth of the ssspyss's birthing remainsss a sssecret," said the great serpent. "But the ssspy isss sssuspected, my love. I think it would be wisesss to sssend the darklingsss. The heir mussst not return to Xzssswendria...Ssss."

"Yes, Lord Bayl." Wazrxna bowed.

"When thisss isss over and the Resissstance isss crussshed, we will deal with Xsssvardrisss." The serpent's yellow orbs seemed alight with anger. The conversation continued briefly, and then Bayl dismissed Wazrxna and curled his head up onto his back and laid it there as if to rest.

A moment later, its eyes once again became the dull eyes of a serpent.

Wazrxna left the temple and strode to the palace. She gave instructions to Werfhx. Then she left for Zwexdrof, where she could more closely monitor Xvardris. She would be glad when the Resistance was crushed and her puppet would no longer be needed, for she could see ambition behind his pretended submission to her will.

Chapter 30

Xvardris paced anxiously. His war machine was progressing slowly—too slowly for his liking. But removing stumps and clearing space for the forward movement of the war engines was a time-consuming business, especially with slave labor. Xvardris' lieutenants drove the slaves hard, pushed them with tongue and lash, but the slaves did not have a will to work.

Actually, for the most part, the slaves were supportive of the Resistance and surreptitiously did what they could to slow the progress of Xvardris' army.

Findr and Boger appeared to be hardworking slaves who were supportive of Xvardris' efforts. Verbally, they castigated the Resistance, and they worked much harder than the other slaves, though they were seen as being somewhat witless.

"You two try hard, but I swear you can't do anything right!" the slave drivers would complain.

Boger would wink at Findr and then wipe at his nose and cry like a baby. Findr would sniffle and huff as if he simply could not handle having his feelings hurt.

The guards pitied the two buffoons and paid them as little attention as possible. They had more important things to do than to play nursemaids to a couple of feeble-minded hacks.

In reality Findr and Boger were the organizers of support for the Resistance within the ranks of the slaves. They were the brains behind the work slowdown and the acts of sabotage to wagons, harnesses, and the engines of war equipment—frayed ropes, ungreased moving parts, and loose wheels.

Most problems were attributed to lazy, careless slaves and inattentive slave drivers. As a result, Xvardris' rage trickled down through the ranks, creating a general air of tension that further undermined the project.

The slowdown allowed the Resistance to further prepare for their defense. They left their fortress at night to dig holes beneath stumps where soldiers could hide and also prepared two horse camps, both at a distance from the path Xvardris was cutting through the forest—for purposes of ambush and counterattack. And with the extra time given by the slaves, they were able to dig trenches in the ravaged forest that would further hinder the movement of Xvardris' war engines once they drew near the fortress.

But of primary concern to the leaders of the Resistance was the King's Company. Would they succeed in finding and returning the heir?

Although he was determined to crush the Resistance into the rocks at Havenholt, the fate of the heir lay heavy on Xvardris' mind as well. He was fully aware that his own survival, let alone his plans for becoming the supreme ruler, depended on successfully solving that problem.

Chapter 31

The last thing Xzwindra remembered was some vile creature wrapping its coarse arms around her body and ripping at her shoulders and neck with its teeth. From that point on, her memory faded into a world of ghastly dreams.

She remembered Grey Wolf bending over her, his face twisted in a sneer, a cup of poison in his hand. But as the feared brew crossed her lips, she had immediately felt a sense of well-being. For days she saw shadowy ghouls moving about her. Various vile faces came and went: Corporal Mifstern's face angry and demanding; Kander's face sheeted with mockery and laughter; Captain Favel's face leering and contemptuous. She wanted to cry out for help, but although she opened her mouth, no words came forth. She remembered too a strange stubble-haired demon sneering, snickering, reaching for her soul. He too offered her a brew that would end her suffering – a brew of death. She resisted but the demon forced the poison down her throat. In vain she tried to scream. Yet, as the potion reached into her being, she felt its powers of life rather than death. She gave in and drank more freely. Slowly, the haze of the shadow land began to lift. Light overcame the darkness that enveloped her soul. She opened her eyes and found herself surrounded by those she had seen in her dreams, except that now they were all deeply concerned, caring, reaching out to her with compassion. But who was this stubble-haired man? Was he the demon of her dreams? She had never seen him before. He was not one of their company.

"Well, it looks like you'll live!" Humpy gave Xzwindra a toothy smile. "Tol' them it were powerful stuff. Tis the dorinalac. Activates the other herbs an' makes em work faster." Then Humpy conversed with Grey Wolf about herbs and their effects. As Humpy explained what the plants looked like, a light flickered in Grey Wolf's eyes.

"Hefdel, lanseed and pendlweed," he declared. "Apparently, the ancients did not know the extent of their medicinal value when mixed together. They used them individually as soothing balms, though not the pendlweed. That was used to activate other herbal curatives." Grey Wolf gave Humpy an appreciative nod. "I have learned much today. Thank you, friend Humpy."

"I'd a tol' ya long ago if I had know'd ya had a hankering ta know," responded Humpy. He and Grey Wolf had often crossed paths as they wandered the Savage Lands.

"Grey Wolf," Captain Favel broke in, "apparently Pagyn soldiers are waiting for us at Ograf. They have cut off the road to Eknard. Humpy tells us we will have to go south through the Pass of Phantazia. Do you know of any other way that Humpy might not be familiar with?"

"There are no other ways past the Eastern Wall," said Grey Wolf. His eyebrows raised slightly. "The pictures tell of the Shades of Phantazia. I have long wanted to pass that way and hear the voices that ride the winds that blow through the pass." He stopped and his face twisted to a scowl. "But you must know, the pass is fraught with danger."

"Tell us more," returned Captain Favel. "What are the Shades of Phantazia? Why are they so dangerous?"

"They are spirits who have been cast down from a higher realm. They are grotesque—demonic—yet their voices are sweet and compelling, and their eyes are beautiful," explained Grey Wolf. "It is said that the Shades of Phantazia whisper softly so that only you can hear. They verbalize your fantasies, reveal the secrets of your heart and mind, and beckon you to look into their eyes."

"And if you do look them in the eye?" asked Xzwindra anxiously. She did not like the sound of this strange place.

"If you look in their eyes, you will see their grotesque forms. Although repulsed, you will not be able to withdraw your eyes," continued Grey Wolf. "The pictures say that what you see in the shades' eyes will drive you to madness and ultimately cast your soul into utter darkness. What happens then is not known, except those souls do not return."

"That is quite a story, Grey Wolf." Kander gave the desert warrior a disbelieving look. "But it seems to me that if what you say is true, there would be no one to tell about it."

"Ah, that is why I long to pass that way." Grey Wolf's eyes sparkled with excitement. "Long ago a beautiful young maiden named Llprinda went the way of the pass. She heard the voices and wondered at their sweetness. She looked into the eyes of the terrible shades and beheld their beauty. The darkness beckoned her but to no avail, for Llprinda was so innocent that the vile shades found in her soul only sincere remorse for her sins and a pure desire to be all that Baruch had made her to be. It is said that she had such light in her soul from the presence of Baruch that the darkness had no effect on her. The light of Baruch within her dispelled the darkness. The shades, distraught and cast into fits of anguish, bid her pass unharmed."

"And what became of Llprinda?" Kander leaned forward, chin on hands. Though he did not believe a word of it, Grey Wolf's story was interesting.

"Where she came from and where she went to after she crossed the mountains is not revealed in the pictures," said Grey Wolf. Sadness crossed his face. "But as far as I can tell by her name and what is revealed in her story, she was one of the ancients and was looking for her brother, Ddlandr, who had traversed the pass a year before and had never returned. The pictures suppose that he was taken by the shades and was devoured by the darkness, for he was a rebellious lad. He did not have the innocence of Llprinda."

"For myself, I think I would rather face a legion of Pagyn soldiers than pass the way Grey Wolf speaks of," blustered Sergeant Tandrak. "Let us go on to Ograf and fight our way through or die in the effort. But by all means let us avoid the Shades of Phantazia."

The others agreed—except Captain Favel. "If we die fighting Pagyn soldiers because we fear what lies within, then what of the heir?" he chided. "We will pass the way of the Shades of Phantazia, and we will return to tell about it."

"And you think we are all so innocent or strong that we can pass such demonic allurements unaffected?" Sergeant Tandrak stood with his arms crossed and a scowl cutting deep lines in his face.

Captain Favel's eyes met Sergeant Tandrak's. "I am not that naïve, sergeant, but we will find a way. However, we must first reach the pass. And from the look of this map, that will be a challenge in itself. Grey Wolf, what is the Brackenwild Reach like?"

"The ancients called it the Plain of Sticks," answered Grey Wolf in his calm, grave manner. "For the most part, it is a desolate land of dust and dry brush, sometimes so dense and tangled that it is impassable. On the other hand, a number of large depressions, called wolds, lie scattered across the Reach. The pictures indicate that in the distant past they were vast lakes. Now green grass, stubble trees, and pockets of water fill them."

"Sounds better than that awful desert we just crossed!" Corporal Mifstern looked over his shoulder, as if he could see the desert off in the distance. "By the sound of it, these oases are real and not just puddles of mud and a scattering of cacti."

Humpy snorted. The others turned to him with questioning looks on their faces. He shrugged his shoulders and shifted the focus back to Grey Wolf. The Savage Land wanderer, the desert warrior, or rogue as they had begun to call him smiled in response.

"What didn't you tell us?" asked Captain Favel. "More decrodiles? More vipers? More hellcats?"

"Indeed, there is more to tell. Primitive tribal people live in many of the wolds." Grey Wolf looked from one listener to the next. "The pictures do not mention these people." He shrugged a shoulder. "I once thought it possible that they might be descendants of the ancients. However, they are not a friendly people, so I doubt it. They seem to be some kind of farmers, though what they farm I don't know, but I do know that they are very protective of their land."

"These days they be called the ogremen of Brackenwild," put in Humpy. "An' since there ain't no gems out there, I keep me distance. Went out that away jes' once. They chased me fer two days, an' I ain't been back since."

"If they're farmers, what kind of weapons do they use?" asked Xzwindra.

"A few use rather poorly crafted bows, spears, and knives," said Grey Wolf. "But most ogremen use clubs, slings, and stone hatchets. They do not speak our language, and when they feel intruded upon, they act without asking questions."

Kander grimaced. "Sounds exciting," He jibed.

"These be the Savage Lands," Humpy reminded him. "As they say back in Xzendr, if ya don't wanna' dance ta the music, don't get out on the dance floor."

"What about you, Humpy? Are you going with us?" asked Captain Favel.

"Do I look like a fool jes' out from the city?" responded the prospector. He waved a defiant finger in the air. "Like I said, there be no jewels out there. An' where there be no jewels, there be no good reason fer me ta go. So I think I'll jes' keep pokin' aroun' down here in the Gulch."

The next day Grey Wolf and the King's Company parted ways with Humpy. They had pulled the raft ashore. Humpy figured he would use the logs to build a wayhouse for use as he wandered up and down the draw.

Xzwindra, though still weak, mounted her horse and along with the others headed up out of Draw Gulch.

After two days of tedious riding, they reached the rim. From a slight rise beyond the edge of the gulch, they looked out on the vast, brushy plain they would have to traverse. Gloom shadowed their faces. With the trek across Deathreach still fresh on their minds, none of them looked forward to what lay before them. Only Grey Wolf seemed unaffected by the prospect of crossing Brackenwild Reach.

Breathing a collective sigh of dread, the company set out, wary of the peril that awaited them.

Chapter 32

The ground of Brackenwild Reach was not sandy like Deathreach but rather a fine, powdery dirt. Every time a horse's hoof landed on the hardpan, a cloud of dust mushroomed upward. The fine, lung-clogging dust rode the air in whatever direction the waterless breeze blew. When there was no breeze, it hung in the air like a low-lying cloud. The intense heat caused their sweat to grab the dust, caking, drying, cracking.

"This is the most unpleasant place we've been so far," complained Kander, his voice muffled by the cloth that covered his nose and mouth. "What has it been, three months since we left Havenholt? Will we ever get to where we're going?"

"All of three months," said Captain Favel. He was riding beside Kander. "And, Baruch willing, we will eventually get to Eknard. But from the looks of the map, it could take us another three months."

"And then back again!" Gloom edged Kander's voice. "And the farther we go, the more dreadful it gets!"

Grey Wolf led the way as they twisted through the tangles of dried bracken. Captain Favel and Kander followed behind and after them Xzwindra and Corporal Mifstern with Sergeant Tandrak bringing up the rear. With deliberate slowness they snaked through the snarled boscage, the Plain of Sticks.

Grey Wolf's eyes tracked the waste before them. While he winnowed through the labyrinth of tangles, he scanned the horizon above the brush, watching for rising dust—signs of movement out on the reach.

"Grey Wolf, why are you constantly searching the horizon?" Kander felt the rogue's tension. "Trouble?"

"When the clans are out on the prowl, they pay no attention to their dust," explained Grey Wolf. "They just pad along, raising a dust cloud as they go with no apparent understanding that the dust could warn others of their presence."

"You mean if they see dust rising, they have no idea that something or someone is causing it?" asked Corporal Mifstern as he moved aside his cloth and spit brown phlegm.

"Apparently, that is true," said Grey Wolf. "It would seem that when they see dust, they simply see dust and no more. It is hard to imagine, but in truth they are a simple people."

Suddenly, Grey Wolf raised his hand and reined in Sterling Grey. The others drew their horses to a stop. They all followed Grey Wolf's gaze. A mile or more ahead of them, a small cloud of dust rose above the brown-gray bracken and came toward them.

Grey Wolf watched the movement of the dust with a calculating eye. "There's a ravine back to our right." Grey Wolf turned Sterling Grey and led the company to the ravine and then into the brush. They dismounted and tethered their horses to brambles in the lowest part of the depression. Then they crawled to the lip of the shallow draw and gazed out through the bracken that lined its perimeter.

Nearly three-quarters of an hour later, the ogremen passed by.

Captain Favel grimaced in concern when the ogremen walked over the tracks they had left behind.

Grey Wolf gave him a look that said, "Don't worry."

The tribesmen paused, looked at the tracks, pointed. It was as if they were saying, "Oh, look, aren't these strange tracks?" They appeared to laugh with a strange chattery sound, and then they padded on. Twenty-three ogremen passed by. They were long-legged, tall, and skinny. Their only clothing was what Grey Wolf called a loin flap of fur. They also wore gaudy necklaces made from animal teeth and colorful rocks. Leather bands about their upper left arms had various markings, while their ankle bands were all the same. Grey Wolf later explained that the ankle bands bore the symbol of the clan, while the arm bands identified the individuals, like person's names.

Although most clan members hefted clubs, two wielded spears, and three carried small bows. "A raiding party," said Grey Wolf after the ogremen had passed toward the north.

"But what would they be raiding?" asked Sergeant Tandrak. "We've not yet come to one of the wolds you spoke of."

"They run slightly toward the west." Grey Wolf watched the dissipating dust cloud. "They are probably circling a wold that lies over by the mountains. I avoided that wold because it's inhabited by a clan. No need to purposely go where we are not welcome."

They mounted their horses and headed south again. At first, everyone sat high in the saddle, watching the horizon in every direction. But after an hour or so, they relaxed again.

Grey Wolf and Sergeant Tandrak continued to keep vigil, but there were no signs of tribesmen the rest of that day.

When night came, they found a rocky draw and made camp. They preferred the rocky ground to the dusty dirt where every movement raised a cloud of grime. And Grey Wolf, much to everyone's surprise, built a fire. "The clans are not nocturnal," he explained. "And it seems a fire out on the plain is no different to them than dust. They may see, but they do not understand. A fire is just a fire."

"Ahhhhhh!" Xzwindra startled everyone with a scream of terror. Her trembling hand brushed a living creature from the top of her head. A huge, hairy spider tumbled over the rocks, regained its legs, and scurried off into the brush. The spider had apparently jumped from an overhanging branch. And Xzwindra was not fond of even the smallest spider. Despite her frantic antics, no one laughed at her. She was surprised. Apparently, she was not the only one who did not like spiders.

"Fuzzy jumper," said Grey Wolf with a shrug. "Creepy looking things but harmless. The pictures seem to indicate that they are quite intelligent for being spiders, and they get as big as a man's hand."

Xzwindra caught her breath and shuddered. The spider she had brushed from her hair was large but not that large.

On the other hand, Kander found the fuzzy jumpers fascinating and decided to catch one. He searched the brush where the spider disappeared but did not find that spider or any other. However, that night a spider found him. And it was larger than the fuzzy jumper Xzwindra had brushed from her hair. Kander stretched out on top of his bedroll (it was too hot to climb inside) and was just about to fall asleep when he felt something crawling up his leg. In spite of the heat, a chill ran up his spine. He was instantly wide awake. He thought to slap whatever it was away but restrained himself. Slowly, he lifted his head, and the moonlight revealed a huge Fuzzy Jumper.

"Now don't run away, spider," he urged softly. He slowly reached out his hand and stroked the fuzzy critter across its rounded back. The spider stood still and let Kander stroke it again. It seemed to instinctively know that Kander intended it no harm. It crawled away, stopped, then returned and stood by Kander's hand. He petted the spider several times before it crawled off into the night. Kander fell asleep. But when he woke up in the morning, he found the fuzzy jumper cuddled against the nape of his neck. The creature's body was neither warm nor cold, though its softness gave a sense of warmth.

"You can't tell head from hind end," commented Kander as he picked up the hand-size ball of fuzz. "Unless it's walking, of course. It sure is a friendly fellow."

"Well, keep the friendly fellow to yourself!" adjured Xzwindra. She was not at all impressed that Kander was able to handle the creature. "He may be your friend, but he is not mine!"

"You had best leave Mr. Fuzzy Jumper in his natural environment." Corporal Mifstern motioned toward the stand of brush. "Spiders are not the kind of creatures one makes pets of."

"I suppose you're right." Kander set the spider aside and picked up his saddle. Mr. Fuzzy Jumper leaped up on the cantle. "But Fuzzy Jumpers are certainly not normal for spiders. I've never seen a wild creature act so friendly and petlike."

He lifted the saddle to his horse. The spider crawled about the top of the saddle and skittered back onto the horse's rump. The horse's skin rippled at the feel of the spider but otherwise paid no attention to the creature. When everything was packed, and they were ready to leave, Kander picked up the fuzzy jumper and put him on a nearby branch of bracken brush. He swung up into the saddle, turned his horse to leave, then felt something hit his pant leg. He looked down to watch the spider scurry up his leg and settle into a niche on his bedroll.

"I guess Fuzzy Jumper will leave when he's good and ready," said Kander with a shrug. The others laughed, except Xzwindra, and so it was that they took to the trail again, if trail there was! The spider stayed with Kander throughout the morning. However, as the sun rose and the heat of the day intensified, Kander looked back and saw with disappointment that the Fuzzy Jumper was gone from its niche.

As the sun drooped behind distant bracken, the King's Company camped at the edge of a wold in a stand of stubble trees. Although the ogremen were not nocturnal, the King's Company kept a quiet camp and set a watch. They slept with their weapons near at hand. No ogremen materialized. By dawn they were riding south again.

That day the dust rose above the bracken a mile or so to the east, but that was as close as the ogremen came. When evening settled on the Brackenwild, the company camped in a stand of thick brush, then once again, with the rising of the sun, continued on their way. That afternoon they came to another wold. This time they breached the rim. And while they grazed their horses at the outer extremity of the wold, Grey Wolf scouted for water and checked the wold for inhabitants. He returned an hour later.

"Apparently, the clans share this wold as they pass by on their way to other places," said Grey Wolf. "They come. They go. They camp. But none of the clans live here, even though there is a good water supply. And since there are no ogremen about at the moment, we can fill our water skins and water the horses. But let us be quick about it. Never know when a clan might show."

They mounted and Grey Wolf led them down into the depths of the wold to three ponds. They watered the horses, filled their water skins, and took quick baths.

Grey Wolf's countenance remained grim throughout. "Hurry along!" he urged. "The ponds are places of danger."

To the east beyond the ponds, the wold rose steeply, leveled off for perhaps a half mile, and then rose steeply again. The small flat between the two rises grew thick with brush and stubble trees. Once they finished bathing, Grey Wolf led them up onto the flat, where they set up camp in a small but well-covered clearing. No one complained. They trusted Grey Wolf's judgment.

In fact, they had not finished tethering the horses when a mutter of strange voices reached their ears. They crawled through the trees to the edge of the rise where they could look down on the ponds. A tribal clan of some thirty men came padding along from the west, chattering like a family of squirrels. Their voices were high-pitched and clattery. The ogremen stopped at the ponds where they drank, dipping water with what looked to be hollowed-out gourds that hung on leather thongs around their necks. When they finished drinking, they began gathering firewood. It appeared they were planning to spend the night.

"So much for a comfortable night's rest," complained Kander. He turned to Grey Wolf. "Are we safe up here?"

Grey Wolf shook his head. "The ogremen will not find us unless we somehow draw attention to ourselves."

"Look!" Captain Favel nodded toward a path that approached the ponds from the south, where a second clan of ogremen cautiously made their way toward the unsuspecting clan already at the ponds. "This should be interesting."

"Twenty-seven in that clan." Sergeant Tandrak pointed toward the approaching tribe. "Thirty-one ogremen camped by the ponds."

Suddenly, the attacking clan burst into a fit of high-pitched howls and stormed the other clan, who responded with similar howls, grabbed their archaic weapons, and met the enemy. Both clans continued to chatter wildly as they engaged in battle.

Interestingly, the ogremen did not seem to have any inclination to draw blood. Spears were used like staves to beat and pound but not to stab. And while they waggled their clubs with dangerous fury, their bows seemed tempered.

"If one clan were intruding on the other's wold, they would fight to the death," explained Grey Wolf. "But they are on common ground. Their purpose is to drive the opposing clan away from the ponds, to dominate but not to take life. That is the way of the tribes of the Brackenwild Reach."

"It is a strange way." Sergeant Tandrak frowned and shook his head.

"Maybe the ogremen are more intelligent than I thought," whispered Corporal Mifstern. "They may be primitive, but in their own way they are civilized. Perhaps they are more civilized than we are."

"It does raise an interesting question for us," interjected Kander. He rested his chin in his hands as he watched the strange battle.

"Yes, it does." Captain Favel tipped his hat back on his head. "If we are attacked by a clan, do we fight according to their rules or ours? Will the ogremen apply the same rules of engagement to fighting with us as with another clan?"

"How can we fight by their rules with our weapons?" A note of irritation edged Sergeant Tandrak's voice. "Swords are for drawing blood. I'm afraid I prefer being uncivilized as to having my head beaten in with one of their cudgels."

The battle raged on below them, but the King's Company couldn't tell which clan was winning. In fact, they couldn't tell which clan was which, since they were too far away to identify one from the other by their ankle bands. All the ogremen looked much the same. They were just a mass of ogremen flailing away at each other, until finally a shrieking high-pitched cry pierced the air from the leader of one of the clans.

Instantly, the fighting stopped, and one clan bowed on its knees before the other. The victors raised their hands and chattered a victory chant. The other ogremen then got to their feet, picked up their fallen, and slinked to the far side of the ponds to dress their wounds and set up camp away from the water.

The clansmen who had first arrived at the ponds were the victors. Of their thirty-one tribesmen, apparently only four had been knocked senseless. Of the twenty-seven attackers, nine had to be dragged or carried away. Two of their company appeared to have suffered broken arms or legs.

Corporal Mifstern wanted to go down and dress their wounds and set their broken bones, but Captain Favel restrained him.

The two clans stayed the night. They seemed to ignore each other's presence once the battle was done. And when morning came, they went their separate ways.

Once the ogremen were gone, Grey Wolf and the King's Company broke camp, went down to the ponds, topped off their water skins, let the horses drink, then returned to the dusty hardpan and labyrinth of bracken brush.

Three days later, they had their first face-to-face encounter with the ogremen of the Brackenwild Reach. A clan approached them out on the plain from the east. The King's Company sat on their horses in a draw, expecting the clan to pass by without taking notice of them. But as the ogremen came near, they turned in their direction. When the clan saw the King's Company down in the draw, they stopped and stared. The ogremen looked from one to the other and then raised a howl that sounded like a pack of wolves preparing for a kill. They rushed the King's Company, clubs at the ready.

As the ogremen skirted a stand of bracken to drop into the draw, not wanting to engage the roving clan, Captain Favel shouted, "Let's get out of here!"

Grey Wolf nodded, and the King's Company went thundering over the dirt, throwing up a cloud of dust between themselves and the ogremen. The clan did not chase them for long. After about half an hour of twisting through the brush, the King's Company heard the ogremen let out with a loud chatter and chant.

"They have won the victory," said Grey Wolf. He held up a hand and brought the company to a halt. The ogremen's noisy cloud of dust was now moving off toward the west. "They have humiliated their enemy. They have made us turn like scared desert rabbits and run away from them."

Sergeant Tandrak waggled his head and laughed. "So, the victors continue on their way, having routed their enemy. Strange people these."

The others laughed with relief. They were glad they had not been forced to engage the ogremen in battle, for they had no desire to spill the ogremens' blood.

They set out once again, aware that they were not yet free of Brackenwild Reach and its dangers.

Chapter 33

While Kander and the King's Company trekked the Brackenwild Reach, Xzwendarian blood was being spilled back in Zwexdrof. Xvardris ordered the arrest of everyone suspected of collaborating with the Resistance. The usurper cast them into the palace dungeon, one hundred and seventeen loyal citizens in all. Then, each day at noon, he had one of the traitors decapitated publicly in the palace courtyard. And so, with an executioner's ax, the Pagyn usurper subjugated the people of Xzwendaria.

The first blood shed was that of the palace mole. Xvardris had Zedria brought before him prior to her execution. She stood in the presence of the usurper, hands chained behind her back, but with her head held high. Defiance sculpted her brow.

"You are a fool, Zedria." Xvardris offered her a mocking smile. "Our spy should not have confided in you concerning our plans, and you, my dear, should have kept your tongue, as well. We trusted you here in the palace. We do not take well to the treachery of trust-breach. What do you have to say for yourself?"

Zedria glared at Xvardris, but answered not a word.

He shook his head. "It is a pity that one so young and pretty should die by the executioner's ax," he stated with feigned concern. Then with a flip of his hand, "Take her away."

The people of Zwexdrof were forced to turn out to watch the execution. Men, women, and children wept for Zedria. They were outraged but helpless. The usurper's soldiers were everywhere. The people had seen the young woman on the streets selling candles. They wondered why one so innocent was being executed. And they wondered as the other innocents followed – each day blood, tears, and a deepening anger.

Chapter 34

Grey Wolf and the King's Company passed through Brackenwild Reach without encountering any more ogremen clans, but the harsh conditions of the Reach itself had taken a toll on them. Their dirt-caked skin was dried out and in places, blistered. Their eyes were red and sore, their hair gritty, and their lips cracked.

"Wretched place!" jibed Kander as he looked back on the Reach.

As they passed beyond the last wold, they looked out across fifty miles of flat, lifeless hardpan to a break between two mountain ranges.

"Windy Gap," observed Grey Wolf. "Scorching winds blow through the gap from the south." He spread a hand toward where they were going. "Desolation," he stated without emotion.

Kander grimaced as he turned to face the new challenge. He noted that the hot wind carried a fine grit that bit at the skin. He shrugged. "Thankfully there is no dust – at least not like the dust of the Brackenwild," he muttered.

The King's Company headed out across the desolate stretch of hardpan that lay between them and Windy Gap. The horses' hooves beating the hard ground sounded like rumbling thunder, a sound muffled by the wind that seemed to increase in intensity the closer they got to the gap. And they all grimaced against the insufferable heat that rode the wind.

When they left Brackenwild Reach, the day was fading. As the sun slipped behind distant mountains, Grey Wolf turned on his horse. "We will travel on through the night," he said. "The winds that blow during the daytime are too strong and torrid to face. They would blister the skin yet further."

No one objected.

The rogue led them toward a spur of the mountains that jutted out from the west. They rode at a gallop. Grey Wolf did not want to be out on the plain come daylight. "We'll camp in the rocks near the foothills," he called out over his shoulder.

"Why not take to the mountains and skirt Windy Gap?" asked Captain Favel above the wind and pounding hooves.

"Because Windy Gap is like an immense gorge!" shouted Grey Wolf. "Once we round the horn we will be hemmed in by massive escarpments both north and south. The mountains themselves are impassable. We have no choice but to conquer Windy Gap."

They made the horn as the dawn broke behind them. Grey Wolf knew exactly where he was going. He had obviously traveled this way before. He led them into the protective shelter of three enormous boulders. The King's Company was surprised to find unscorched scrub grass growing in their shade.

"How long will it take us to get through Windy Gap?" asked Kander as he dismounted. "And what about water and food for the horses?"

"A canyon reaches back into the mountain wall two nights' journey from here," said Grey Wolf. "There we will find water and grass for grazing our horses. From there it is four nights' journey to Rest Mere."

They tethered the horses and set up camp in the lee of the boulders. The wind howled through cracks and crevices, but only a light breeze reached them. The fiery sun rose in the sky. The rocks provided shade from the white orb's hellish grin but not from the searing heat. The day would be long and miserable.

"Does the wind never stop blowing?" Corporal Mifstern's words were a complaint more than a question.

But Grey Wolf answered his question anyway, indicating that the wind did, in fact, continuously howl through the gorge but less so at night.

"Where does the wind come from?" Xzwindra let a handful of gritty dirt sift through her fingers. "And does it never rain in this awful wasteland?"

"The Forever Wind comes from Witherdeep." Grey Wolf motioned toward Windy Gap and the south. "And I do not know if it rains in this place. But I think not."

"What is Witherdeep like?" Kander leaned hands behind his head against the boulder, his eyes closed. "It does not sound like a very pleasant place. Not that any place in the Savage Lands could be described as pleasant."

"Actually, Witherdeep may prove to be our greatest challenge yet." Grey Wolf made no attempt to lift Kander's falling spirits. "I have traveled to the crater's edge. However, I have never entered the Witherdeep. But I can tell you that heat rises from the bowels of that immense hole like steam from a pot of stew."

"So the winds that rage through Windy Gap are created by the heat of the Witherdeep?" Captain Favel ran a wetted cloth over his brow. "That would mean there is no wind in Witherdeep itself."

"Yes, the Forever Wind comes from Witherdeep. And you are right. It leaves no wind behind. I do not understand this thing, but it is so." Grey Wolf shook his head as if to emphasize his lack of comprehension. "While sending forth the Forever Wind, Witherdeep itself seems to be forever still. Yet, there is life within Witherdeep."

"How could anything live in a place as arid as what you just described?" Corporal Mifstern gave the desert warrior a disbelieving glance.

"In the pictures, the ancients speak of terrifying creatures called witherworms," said Grey Wolf. He raised an eyebrow and went on. "You might call them slithering dirt dragons. The best I can tell from the pictures they are ten to fifteen feet long, and they crawl just below the surface of the ground, causing it to hump, crumble, and then collapse in a cloud of dust behind them. The worms have stingers. And it is said that whatever, or whomever, they sting withers and turns to dust. Once their victims have turned to dust, the witherworms process the nourishing remains much like earthworms process dirt."

"And I suppose we have no choice but to pass through the dreadful place?" Sergeant Tandrak looked up at Grey Wolf, momentarily hesitating in the process of working the blade of his sword on a whetstone.

Sergeant Tandrak read Grey Wolf's answer in his face. The conversation turned to other things, and so passed the day.

When the sun slipped behind the mountains to the west, the King's Company mounted their horses and galloped into Windy Gap. The powerful air current tried its best to push them back, but they pressed on through what proved to be a long, hard night. And the shelter they found the next morning was not as adequate as that of the previous day. The scorching wind whipped around the rocks, biting at them and blowing about a coarse brown dirt. Further, the rocks were situated so that where they best provided shelter from the wind they provided little shelter from the sun. The sun and wind grated on everyone's nerves—everyone except Grey Wolf who remained as stoic as ever.

When shades of darkness settled upon the gorge and the wind lessened in intensity, the weary company gladly mounted up and moved on. The night was long, tedious, and sapped the King's Company of energy and spirit. As dawn crept into the gorge, they turned aside into the shelter of the box canyon Grey Wolf had spoken of earlier. There they found relief from the wind, and at the far end of the canyon, they came to a true oasis with green grass and shade trees. A spring flowed from a rock, providing life-giving water. At the base of the rock, the water pooled then seeped out to water the oasis but flowed no farther than the roots beneath the layer of green.

The King's Company breathed a collective sigh of relief at the sight of the oasis. "Looks like we might actually catch some sleep today," commented Sergeant Tandrak.

They made camp near the water pool. Kander opened one of his saddle bags to put away his head cover, and as he did, the Fuzzy Jumper leaped out onto the rump of his horse. "Hey, look here!" shouted Kander as he broke into laughter.

Even Xzwindra found the huge spider's unexpected presence humorous. From the horse's rump, the creature jumped over to Kander's shoulder and settled there until Kander put his bedroll on the ground, then the Fuzzy Jumper sprang down onto the bedroll.

The Fuzzy Jumper had a habit of reaching its right foreleg over and laying it across its left foreleg and rubbing it back and forth. The spider rather looked like it was playing a violin. So Kander cast aside the name of Mr. Fuzzy Jumper. "Not creative enough," he told the others. "I think I'll call him Fiddler."

Kander never forced Fiddler to continue the journey. In fact, his only encouragement was to momentarily rein in his horse, look at Fiddler, and give him opportunity to hop aboard if he so desired. So it was that Fiddler, the Fuzzy Jumper, chose to be Kander's pet and to continue to travel with him. Fiddler would run off at night to hunt for food but would be tucked in the nape of Kander's neck when he woke each morning. And Fiddler kept his distance from Xzwindra. It was as if the spider sensed her fear and chose to leave her alone.

After another night of pushing their way through Windy Gap, Grey Wolf led the parched, weary travelers past the western high wall of the mountains and up a narrow breach into the foothills to Rest Mere, a large blue-hued lake that lay in the fold of a lush, beautiful valley—a truly pleasant place in the midst of the Savage Lands. There they took the luxury of three days' respite for themselves and their horses before continuing on.

The day before they left Rest Mere, Grey Wolf mounted Sterling Grey and headed up into the mountains. He took the packhorse with him. The others watched and wondered. He had given no explanation.

"What if he doesn't return?" asked Kander.

Captain Favel shrugged. "We leave in the morning with or without him."

Late in the day, the desert warrior returned. The grain bags that had been empty for more than four days were now bulging.

"So in what mountain meadow did you find a harvest of grain plucked and ready to fill all those bags?" muttered Corporal Mifstern.

Grey Wolf shook his head. "Not all of it is grain," he said. "The pictures tell where the ancients maintained stores in a cave. They set the stores aside for use when they were forced to travel in these parts. But unfortunately they do not tell why they came to this part of the Savage Lands," explained Grey Wolf. "I have continued to maintain stores in the cave, for at times I travel this way. When I do, I stay in the Cave of the Ancients. But that cave is a hideaway that I reveal to no one."

They accepted Grey Wolf's explanation without further questioning and were grateful for the grain. It would help sustain the horses. From what the desert warrior had told them, the journey ahead promised to be as difficult as that which lay behind.

"It would appear that there is no water in Witherdeep," commented Grey Wolf as he took a bulging gunnysack from the packhorse. He tossed the sack into the lake. It was attached to a leather cord, which he in turn tied to a small tree near the shore. The gunnysack floated for a brief time, gurgled, and sank.

Captain Favel watched the desert warrior with curiosity. "What are you up to, Grey Wolf?"

"Water for the horses." Grey Wolf motioned toward where the gunnysack had disappeared. "Water and extra nourishment. The bag is filled with cubes of dried cactus. They are extremely porous and will soak up water and, despite the heat, will hold the water for days. When the horses chew on the fibrous cubes, they will get both water and nourishment necessary for their survival and ours."

"I suppose you learned that from the ancients too." Captain Favel smiled and shook his head. "They were certainly intelligent people."

"Their pictures teach many things." Grey Wolf rubbed the packhorse's neck. "But the ancients did not have horses. They were introduced to this area much later. The cactus cubes are my own discovery. I had to come up with a way of caring for Sterling Grey's needs when traversing these desert lands."

Captain Favel was impressed. Not that that meant anything to Grey Wolf. He shrugged off personal praise. "We all learn things," he said.

At first light, Grey Wolf hauled the gunnysack to shore, tied it to the packhorse, and covered it with the skin of the hellcat to keep the sun from drying it out. The company broke camp. Fiddler crawled into Kander's saddlebag, now nearly full of grain for his horse. The grim faced company followed Grey Wolf across the sweltering, windswept desolation toward Witherdeep.

The tedious, daunting trek took them the entire day. That night they made camp at the rim of the vaporous hole. The King's Company stoically gazed into the abyss where searing heat rose in ethereal streamers to blur their vision of what lay below.

"Wretchedly hot!" declared Kander.

"Yeah, I feel like we're about to walk into a pot of boiling water." Corporal Mifstern wiped at his brow. He turned to Grey Wolf. "Are you sure there is no other way?"

The desert warrior loosed the saddle from his horse. "There is no other way," he declared without emotion.

"I've been thinking," said Xzwindra. "I don't imagine that many creatures wander down into this dreadful hole during the heat of the day, so if the witherworms feed on animals then perhaps they are nocturnal creatures and it will be safe to travel the Witherdeep during the day. Dreadfully hot but safe."

"Hopefully you are right about the worms being nocturnal." Captain Favel rested a hand on his hip, jacked an eyebrow and shifted his gaze to Grey Wolf. "What worries me is how we will protect ourselves and the horses while we sleep. We will be spending nights down there."

Grey Wolf, busy about making camp, made no effort to respond.

"I suppose that will depend on what the floor of the pit is like," said Sergeant Tandrak. "Hopefully there will be some rocky areas where the worms can't dig."

"Grey Wolf, there must be some way to avoid the witherworms." Kander addressed the desert warrior directly. "What do the ancients have to say?"

"They passed through Witherdeep and lived to tell of it," responded Grey Wolf. "If they had not passed through, the pictures would not speak. But how they passed through is not told." He lifted a shoulder. "That we will have to discover for ourselves."

The night was sultry, uncomfortable, and the King's Company got little sleep. They rose early, wiped the sweat of the night from their brows, and headed down into the great crater. The ground at the rim was hard as brick, but the steep slope going down into Witherdeep was loose rock and sand. They made the descent on foot, leading their jittery horses. And so both man and beast slipped and slid down into the dreadful pit.

"And how will we ever get back up to the rim, especially with the horses?" jibed Kander.

Grey Wolf cast him an impassive look. "We will find a way."

The drop into Witherdeep was all of five hundred feet. The floor of the crater proved to be mostly hard sand that was so hot that in spite of their leather footwear, it felt as if they were walking barefoot across hot coals.

"Look. Trails of loose sand two or three feet wide," observed Corporal Mifstern. "I guess the witherworms are not just legend."

"Well, at least some large rocks are scattered here and there," commented Xzwindra. "Not that they will do much good for the horses."

"No signs of life," said Kander.

Captain Favel nodded. "A dead land," he added. He took a deep breath. "Well, let's cross to the other side."

Grey Wolf calmed Sterling Grey and then mounted up. The others followed his lead, but their horses snuffled and pranced skittishly and with great reluctance headed out across the hard sand.

Chapter 35

*T*he desert-weary travelers were no more anxious to head out across the Witherdeep than their steeds.

Kander looked up through the waves of heat rising from the sand. "Can't even see the rim of the crater," he muttered. He shook his head. "I've had enough of this heat!"

The others simply pulled a look of having eaten sour grapes in response.

The weary company plodded along hour upon hour. Everything remained the same, hot sand, outcrops of rock—utter desolation. And as the day lengthened, they wondered how they would avoid the worms come evening. They saw nothing that would provide refuge from the dread creatures, whose trails crisscrossed the sandy floor of the crater.

Xzwindra's eyes flashed fear. "What will we do?"

No one had an answer for her question. Not even Grey Wolf, though he seemed unworried.

Before darkness fell, they saw their first sign of the dread worms. Captain Favel extended a hand, and every eye shifted to where his finger pointed. The earth was moving, bubbling like water tumbling down a mountainside after a hard rain.

The worm moved toward them from the north. Captain Favel broke from the group as if to meet the creature. As it drew near, a round, eyeless, extremity lifted out of the sand. A great stinger suddenly thrust forth from a depression in its tawny end to protrude like the horn of a unicorn. The worm moved forward with the forepart of its body coiled back and upward as if to strike. Captain Favel loosed his spear just as the worm lunged in his direction. The spear drove into the worm's head just below the deadly stinger. The creature's strike instantly turned to recoil. The force of the worm's reaction jerked its entire body up out of the sand. It writhed about on the floor of the desert, trying to get back beneath the sand, but seemed to have no means of doing so.

Captain Favel's spear did not inflict a mortal wound. The worm dislodged the lance as it thrashed about on the sand. It also drew in its stinger as it fought to survive.

"How do you like that! If you get the worm out from beneath the sand, it's helpless." Sergeant Tandrak's voice echoed with hope. "I wonder how deep the worms go. If we circle our camp with a barrier of large rocks, perhaps they will hold the witherworms at bay."

"Sounds worth trying." Corporal Mifstern nervously scanned the desert floor. "Don't you think so, Captain? I mean, what are our options?"

Captain Favel agreed, and they immediately set about using the packhorse and ropes to drag in large rocks to make a circle just wide enough to hold them and their horses.

The circle was not half done when a second worm came boiling through the sand. Once again Captain Favel galloped out to meet the worm, but this time his spear did not produce the same result. The witherworm recoiled but did not throw itself out of its track. The creature cast the spear aside and struck. However, Captain Favel escaped beyond its range. The worm backed its length into the sand once again, roiled closer, and then with a fluid motion jutted itself half out of the ground, extended its stinger, struck, and then repeated the motion. It had no apparent eye sockets and gave the impression of choosing its victims either by sound or scent.

However, in the midst of pressing Captain Favel, the beast abruptly turned aside and attacked Kander, who, taken by surprise, stumbled backward, barely avoided the worm's spike. Kander scrambled to his feet and staggered farther away, but the creature, ignoring those closer, attacked him again. Kander fell. The witherworm aimed its stinger and struck.

At that same moment, Sergeant Tandrak lunged up under the worm's body and drove his sword into its midsection, rolled to the side, and leapt away. The sand dragon recoiled, turned, and lashed out with its horn at its assailant. The stinger barely missed Sergeant Tandrak's shoulder.

As the creature struck at Sergeant Tandrak, Grey Wolf plunged his sword into the worm's hind section still buried beneath the rippled earth. He drove the sword inward and then ripped upward. The worm's other end shot high into the air, sending the desert warrior rolling across the dusty ground. The creature writhed side to side and then slammed itself hard on the ground, tearing loose from the sand. It thrashed about, shuddered for a long moment, and died. The first worm lay on the sand some hundred yards away still squirming.

"So, its vital organs are in its hind section," observed Captain Favel with an air of elation as he helped Grey Wolf to his feet. "We have learned much tonight!" Then over his shoulder, "Corporal Mifstern, perhaps you can break off the worm's stinger. We may find a use for it. But you will need to be careful not to touch the poisonous end of the thing."

The stinger that protruded from the dead worm's extremity was the only thing about the apparent head end that was different from the hind end. Kander suggested that the witherworms might actually move backward through the sand. Perhaps their stingers were part of their hind-sections, and that what they presumed were the tail ends, were the dragons' heads since that was where the vital organs were located.

"Hard to say," commented Captain Favel. He glanced at the dead animal. "Really no way of telling."

Corporal Mifstern chopped at the base of the stinger with an ax. His seventh blow fractured the spike's root. His eighth whack dropped the barb to the sand. He picked it up, and handling it with care, he and the others examined it end to end. The point of the stinger had a tiny opening through which the worm emitted its poison. Interestingly, they found no opening at the base end. They determined that the poison was created within the stinger and probably leached out on contact. The spikelike horn measured just over four feet long and had the balance of a javelin.

Captain Favel handed the stinger to Sergeant Tandrak. "You're the one who risked your life to kill the worm," he commented, then lifted an eyebrow and added, "You know, you might try using the spike on the next worm that happens along. Might be that a dose of its own poison will do the job better than sword or spear."

They finished the stone barrier. Night came, bringing some relief from the torrid heat, but no one slept. The barrier was untested. They tethered the horses in the center of their compound, and by the light of a blurry moon, they watched the desert floor beyond their circle of rocks. It was not long before one of the worms found them. It came tearing the hardpan, and when the witherworm reached the line of rocks, it lifted its head (or tail) from the sand and tried to strike at the desert travelers over the top of the barrier.

Sergeant Tandrak hurried forward, launching the stinger they had removed from the previous worm. It sailed through the air javelin-like and struck the witherworm, piercing its flesh. The wounded creature lashed backward, lifted its striking end high in the air, hesitated momentarily, then collapsed on the sand.

Corporal Mifstern sharpened his ax, climbed over the rocks, and removed the worm's stinger. Not long after he returned to the safety of the barrier, the worm, having died by its own poison, shriveled up and decomposed to dust.

Later, when another worm came boiling through the sand, it stopped short, went to the withered dust of its kin, stopped again, and then moved slowly through the other worm's dust before turning and heading back out into the desert.

"Wonder what that was all about?" quipped Corporal Mifstern.

While the rest of the King's Company tried to sleep, Sergeant Tandrak kept watch. He had not been watching long when a worm came pushing through the sand. He shouted a warning to the company and then shouted a more frantic warning when the sand dragon sank down and passed under the rock barrier. It came up near the horses. Sergeant Tandrak hurled one of the stingers, but not before the worm had driven its spike into Xzwindra's horse. Both horse and worm died, shriveled, and became dust.

"Well, so much for a protective barrier," complained Captain Favel as he stood studying the situation. He rubbed his chin thoughtfully. "To keep the worms from passing under the rocks, it appears we will have to meet them near the edge."

The plan worked. Eight worms attacked during the night, and they were able to kill all eight outside the barrier. The King's Company lost only Xzwindra's horse, that and another night's rest.

With the light of day, the King's Company prepared to leave their ineffective shelter. Wiping their brows and grumbling about their lack of sleep and the intensifying heat, they mounted up. Xzwindra rode with Corporal Mifstern. Kander had offered to have her ride with him, but Xzwindra had raised an eyebrow, smiled, and glanced at his saddlebag.

The only one who seemed unaffected by the heat and loss of sleep was Grey Wolf. He sat tall in the saddle, his eyes alive and alert. The rest of the company sat droop-shouldered in their saddles, faces grim and eyes dull. The ethereal heat waves rose before them like dancers in a dream, and by midday they were slumped in their saddles, fighting to stay awake. They pressed on by strength of will that came from their desire to be done with the Witherdeep.

As the horses beneath them dawdled wearily onward, the sound of their hooves drumming the hardpan altered. Kander found himself imagining he was plodding along the cobbled streets of Zwexdrof. Unthinking, he lifted his head from where it rested against his horse's mane. He fully expecting to see the walls of the city, but his eyes looked on ever-present waves of heat rising from the desert floor, a floor that appeared to be rock instead of hard dirt. Clatter. Clatter. Clatter. The horses' hooves echoed in his ears, slowly waking him from his dreams. He stared out through the undulating heat to where far in the distance the bedrock of the desert floor seemed to rise and form a massive dome. Kander shook his head trying to clear his mind of the illusion, but it remained. The others became aware of the change as well. Still, they clattered on but sitting taller, watching, wondering.

Evening finally overtook them, and the intensity of the heat dissipated. Kander, Xzwindra, Captain Favel, Sergeant Tandrak, and Corporal Mifstern slid from their horses and crumpled on the hard surface of the Witherdeep. Visions of the dread witherworms crossed their minds. Sand? Rock? They felt the ground but were unsure of reality. The desert floor felt like a rock surface, but perhaps it was just an illusion. What did it matter?

Grey Wolf fed the horses a bit of grain and some of the watersoaked cactus meat. By the time he finished, the rest of the company had forgotten their fears and were carelessly sprawled on the ground fast asleep. The rock surface was unyielding, but the heat vapors were less intense.

In the dimming light, Grey Wolf looked out on a desert floor that now gently rose toward the dome they had observed throughout the day. He shrugged a shoulder, ground tethered the horses (there was no place for them to wander off to), and joined the others in sleep.

With the morning came aching bodies but clearer heads. The surface beneath them was indeed rock. In fact, Xzwindra thought it had the appearance of being a massive rock ball buried beneath the desert floor with its rounded top left protruding above the surface. The group, after stretching out their stiff muscles, saddled up and proceeded toward the ball's apex.

In spite of being stiff and sore, the company was a cheerier lot than the previous day. The night's sleep had not only cleared their minds, but it had also restored a measure of energy. Still, the day was dreadfully hot. The rock surface seemed to absorb and then radiate the heat back toward the sun. But in spite of the heat, they did not falter in the saddle as they had the previous day. Upward they plodded, fascinated by the strange world called Witherdeep and thankful that for now they did not have to worry about the witherworms.

At midday Grey Wolf pointed toward the apex of the rock dome they were climbing.

"What is it?" asked Xzwindra.

Corporal Mifstern pursed his lips. "Appears to be some kind of rock formation," he quipped.

"Could it be an ancient city?" questioned Kander.

No one offered an answer. They just plodded onward.

By evening they could tell that what had occupied their vision throughout the day was indeed a massive rock formation, but with design. Still, it did not appear to be a city.

"Strange structure," commented Captain Favel. He turned to Grey Wolf. "What do you think?"

Grey Wolf gazed at the monument that appeared to be yet a half-day's journey away. Captain Favel's eyebrows went up in a gesture of surprise. Grey Wolf was smiling. "And what in the desert sands could bring a smile to your face, Grey Wolf? Is the sun getting to you?"

"The pictures tell of a place one might refer to as paradise," said Grey Wolf. "I always thought it was the ancients' vision of what heaven would be like. The pictures show death, then a curved surface with wavy lines rising toward the sun. At the crest of the curved surface is the rock monument at which we stare. In the pictures a line of people are walking toward the monument. I thought they were the ancients who had died and in turn were passing through some kind of gate into eternity. I presumed the death depicted in the pictures was the stretch of desert inhabited by the witherworms. But seeing this, I wonder if perhaps the ancients were making a pilgrimage of sort to this monument."

"But how was such a monument ever constructed out here in this heat and desolation?" Captain Favel wiped his brow. He looked at Grey Wolf, but the desert warrior gave no answer.

The entire company was eager for the next day to dawn so they would continue their journey toward the strange edifice that lay before them. However, their anticipation did not keep them awake that night. They slept well, but it did make the following day more endurable. Still, the heat was so intense during the early part of the day that they could barely make out the monument through the rising vapors.

As the day wore on and they drew closer to the rock structure, they could see that it was, indeed a massive stone edifice built by men. They could not imagine where the stones might have been cut from or how anyone might have moved them into place.

"It looks like an altar the size of a small mountain!" Kander's eyes were wide and his voice spoke wonder.

The base of the monument was the breadth and width of a large city. Stone upon stone it rose, wedging its way upward. "Must be four-hundred-feet tall!" Sergeant Tandrak gave a slight whistle. The apex was smaller than the base by about half. And the foundation appeared to be perhaps a halfday's journey from corner to corner.

"Wow! The thing's more massive than I first imagined!" said Corporal Mifstern.

"But what is it?" Xzwindra shook her head. "What purpose does it serve? Why was it built and by whom?"

When they arrived at the base of the monument, they found that a first level of blocks rose some thirty feet above the domed surface of the desert. The tightly fitted blocks had the appearance of being a city wall. However, they saw no gates, windows, or crenelations. The edifice puzzled them. Xzwindra continued asking why? But no one had an answer.

"Could be some kind of ancient tomb." Kander let his eyes scan the upper reaches of the edifice. "Or perhaps a temple."

"I can't imagine building a tomb the size of a city." Captain Favel trotted along beside Kander. "And why build a temple in such an inaccessible place as this?"

They spent the rest of the day riding along the wall, if wall it was. After the sun set, they made camp at the base of the monument. "It will provide shade come morning," said Grey Wolf, nodding toward where the scorching orb had disappeared.

"Maybe when we circle the edifice, we will find a stairway leading to the top," said Xzwindra. "Kander might be right. It could be an old Pagyn temple. The Ancients may even have made sacrifices to the sun at its summit."

Kander thought Xzwindra's idea plausible. Grey Wolf and Captain Favel did not. Sergeant Tandrak and Corporal Mifstern expressed no opinion on the matter. "We'll see tomorrow" was all they would say.

The next morning, shaded by the massive structure, the King's Company rode north. Grey Wolf's eyes continually scanned the face of the strange edifice. Kander watched the desert warrior, and wondered what he was looking for. It was not yet midday when they turned the northwestern corner and once again headed east along the northern wall. In the early afternoon, when they had trekked somewhere near half the distance of the massive structure's width, Grey Wolf raised his hand, and reined in Sterling Grey. He pointed toward the wall. The others looked but saw nothing different about that section of the wall than any other of the miles of stark, stone facing they had passed.

"See how this smaller block is actually set within the larger block." Grey Wolf continued to let his eyes rove over the face of the monument. "Perhaps it means nothing. But it could be the way into the structure—a doorway of sorts."

There were raised eyebrows, but no one argued against the possibility. The block set within the large foundation stone was about ten feet high and five feet wide. Grey Wolf dismounted and examined the inset rock more closely. The face of the smaller rock felt the same as that of the larger rock. In fact, the grain of the smaller rock indicated that it had been cut from the larger piece. But interestingly, Grey Wolf noted that the seam was not as tight as the seams between all the other foundation stones. He stepped back and looked at the block thoughtfully. The others waited in wondering silence. Then Grey Wolf stepped forward again, put both hands against the inset stone, and pushed.

The company's silence turned to muffled laughter. However, the laughter stopped when the block moved.

Grey Wolf maintained steady pressure. The block slowly slid back into the wall to a depth of about ten feet before it clunked to a stop. Grey Wolf looked back to the others, who, having alighted from their horses, now stood at the entrance with their mouths agape.

The removal of the inset revealed dark passageways five to six feet inside the opening that reached back into the wall both to the right and the left.

"Let's take a look." Captain Favel joined Grey Wolf inside the recess. "The rest of you wait out here. I'm sure we won't be long, since we don't have any torches or lanterns."

The two men entered the passageway to the left of the movable block. The tunnellike opening went several feet then turned sharply to the right. When they felt their way another twenty to twenty-five feet, they came to a wall that again turned right. They judged they were now at the inside end of the block. It was refreshingly cool inside the edifice, but that was to be expected. Conversely, they also found the unexpected. The inside of the monument was well lit. And what their eyes beheld there struck wonder. Captain Favel hurried back out to where the others were waiting.

"You've got to see this!" Captain Favel wore an ear-to-ear grin. "But I tell you, you won't believe your eyes. Bring the horses."

The tunnel was just large enough for the horses to be led through single file. Their hooves echoed on the stone floor. The cool air seemed to enliven the equines' spirits. Anticipation of what lay ahead enlivened the company's spirits as well. And indeed, once inside, their anticipation was rewarded with awe.

The structure rose to form an immense pyramid-like dome. But whereas most pyramids were rock surrounded by air, this one was just the opposite. It was a huge man-made cave. Shafts strategically located at various levels, reaching up through the ceiling to the outside, provided both light and air. The dome hovered over a canyonlike hollow, several hundred feet deep, from where the rocks of the giant edifice had apparently been cut. And down in the great gulf, the entranced company beheld a magnificent city.

"How in the world?" Kander whispered in awe.

"Impossible!" muttered Xzwindra.

"This is unreal!" Corporal Mifstern scratched the side of his head.

The foundation wall, through which they had entered, was at least thirty to forty feet thick, and a concourse about twenty feet wide extended around the entire inside circumference of the structure. Before them a wide marble stairway descended to the city far below. "Wow!" they mused nearly in unison.

"Do you suppose anyone still lives down there?" Xzwindra spoke quietly, as if she feared her words might be overheard. "You don't think this could be the place where the ancients disappeared to, do you?"

No one answered her question, but it was a thought Grey Wolf had already entertained. "I will go down to the great city," he announced perfunctorily.

"What about the horses?" Sergeant Tandrak gazed down the steep stairway, then looked back over his shoulder. "Are we going to take them with us? And what about the door? Are we just going to leave it open?"

Grey Wolf and Captain Favel returned to the entrance and examined the block that served as a sliding door. They slid the block forward. "Ingenious!" Captain Favel pointed to a metal hook inset in the back side of the block, and then a second hook inset in the back wall. A frayed and rotting piece of rope hung from the hook in the block. Grey Wolf gave it a light tug. It crumbled to the floor. Captain Favel got a rope from the packhorse, pushed the door forward another two feet, attached the rope to the metal hook, and ran it through the second hook. He stepped aside and pulled on the rope. The door easily drew back toward the rear wall. The men conferred briefly, then pushed the block to its closed position.

Kander watched Grey Wolf and Captain Favel from within the side corridor. When the door clunked shut, a shudder ran up his spine. "I feel like I've just been sealed in a great tomb," he mumbled nervously.

When they returned to the stairway, Kander watched Captain Favel check the load on the packhorse before heading downward. "This place is eerie," he jibed. "You'd think our voices would echo, but they just die on the air." Then he tried to put the best face on it. "Well, at least it's cool in here."

"It looks like there are trees growing down there." Xzwindra pointed down toward the city. "And are those lights?"

They all took a second look. It had appeared dark down in the hole previously, but now that their eyes had adjusted to the lighting provided by the holes in the dome, they saw that Xzwindra was right. They did see trees, patches of grass, and yes, even lights. At first, they had thought they were seeing reflections from sunbeams reaching through the shafts above, but no.

"Yes, Xzwindra, I do believe what you see are lights," said Captain Favel.

Taking care with the horses, the King's Company descended the marble stairway.

Chapter 36

Unable to function any longer and fearing for their lives, all but a few of Targndel's spies fled Zwexdrof. They made their way through the ashes of Tangle Wood to Havenholt to join with the rest of the Resistance and to report what was happening in the city.

Targndel grieved when he learned that Zedria had been beheaded. Outrage boiled his blood when he heard that Xvardris was carrying out daily executions in order to intimidate the people of Zwexdrof. He brought his concern to the council.

"It will be at least three more months before Xvardris' war machines arrive," he began. "That means he will have slaughtered nearly a hundred men, women, and children by the time we are able to confront him on the field of battle. Something must be done to stop his atrocities."

"Well and good, Major," began General Vandwert, "but what do you suggest we do— march on Zwexdrof and bring death and carnage to the entire city as well as to our limited forces?"

"Obviously not, General." Targndel flashed the general an angry look. "However, we must do something. We cannot just sit here and watch while innocent people are murdered."

"What Xvardris is doing is unconscionable," agreed Prior Forknedrn, "but it would not do to act foolishly and spend even more lives. Acting now could destroy our chances for ultimate victory."

"Sadly, the prior is right." As regent, Jentrxn was responsible for the final decision. "I do not like it, but there is nothing we can do until we have defeated Xvardris' army here at the gates of Havenholt. Here the battle will be fought on our terms, and we will have the advantage. We do not have the men or arms to face them on their terms."

"What about a small strike force?" asked Commander Razrdris. "They could ride into the city by night like a flying arrow, totally unexpected, free the prisoners, and retreat back to Havenholt."

"Never! It would never work!" General Vandwert shook his head. "Even if such a force were able to penetrate the citadel in order to free those who have been imprisoned, the strike force would not be able to get the refugees from the dungeons, through the city, beyond the walls, and then across the burn and back here to Havenholt swiftly enough to avoid Xvardris' army."

General Vandwert shook his head. "Besides, even if we were to free the people Xvardris presently holds in his prison, we would play right into his hand," said Jentrxn. "Xvardris would simply round up others and spill more blood in order to coerce the Resistance into further action. No. Any attempt to save the prisoners would cost even more innocent lives in the long of it."

"The only way I see of stopping the executions is to eliminate Xvardris!" Prior Forknedrn crossed his arms and sat back in his chair. "It is painful—entirely unacceptable— but we will simply have to wait."

"You are right, prior." Major Targndel leaned forward, his hands flat on the table. Surprise that the major agreed with him registered on Forknedrn's face.

"Then it is agreed," said Jentrxn. "We shall wait."

"No. That was not what I meant," returned Major Targndel. "What I meant was that Xvardris must be eliminated. I will return to Zwexdrof and do just that!"

"Here! Here!" declared the wide-eyed prior. His voice rang with piety and pomp. "I'll not be a party to assassination! Not on your life! That's out of the question!"

"You'll not be a party to assassination?" Major Targndel's eyes flashed with anger. "So far Xvardris has beheaded Zedria, an old man who is not even a part of our movement, two old women guilty of nothing more than gossip, a fourteen-year-old girl who had been seen buying a candle from Zedria, and who knows how many others. That, my good Prior, is assassination! And if we sit back and do nothing, we are a party to it." Targndel took a deep breath and then continued. "Granted, assassination runs against the grain. It is a hard choice, but frankly, in this situation we have no just options."

The prior grunted angrily.

"You see, Prior, it's like this. You do not kill dogs just to kill dogs. However, if a dog goes mad and ravages through the city to devour children, then you kill the dog. Xvardris is a mad dog who is devouring our children. And if we as a ruling council condemn the wild dog to die, then I will not hesitate to carry out that judgment by whatever means I must!"

The prior shrugged his shoulders and settled back into his chair. "Well, since you put it that way. . ," he grumbled.

The council in turn declared Xvardris to be a manslayer and thus a criminal of the Realm of Xzwendaria and that he was wanted by the council either alive or dead. Further, they gave Targndel a certificate of authority to pursue the matter as he saw fit. Still, they encouraged him to find someone else to carry out the order, since he was a ruling council member.

He shook his head. "I am the only one who has any chance of getting anywhere near Xvardris. I have knowledge of the city and access to the secrets of the citadel that others do not have," he responded. "If I die carrying out the operation, so be it. You will be able to carry on just fine without me. Razrdris is capable of running the underground in my absence, and others are capable of commanding the fortress in his place, if need be. But I must do what I must do. I could not live with myself otherwise. I will leave tonight for Zwexdrof."

There was no further argument. That night Major Targndel rode out of Havenholt and headed south to Aynek. From there he would make his way back to Zwexdrof in disguise.

Chapter 37

"And what purpose does killing a bunch of common folk serve, Xvardris?" asked Wazrxna. She had been keeping pretty much to herself at the Black Chancel in the middle of Zwexdrof. But after the slaughter of several children, she came to the palace and confronted Xvardris.

He laughed at her question. She showed no amusement. His laughter turned to a grim scowl.

"They are all children of people who are sympathetic to the Resistance," he declared. "Some of their parents are spies. Others have harbored spies. It sends a message to the people that aiding the Resistance will not be tolerated. And it just might provide sufficient leverage to pry the Resistance army out into the open where we can crush it."

"You expect people to believe that mere children took part in aiding the enemy?" shot back the priestess. Her eyes flashed dark and menacing. Xvardris turned away from their glare. "All killing children will do is enrage the entire populous," she continued. "We have slowly won many over to our cause." She grimaced, breathed heavily, and shook her head. "Xzwendarian children mean nothing to me, but executing them does not benefit our cause. It must stop at once, Xvardris."

"My lady, I understand your concern," he answered, his tone almost pleading. "But I have thought my actions through quite thoroughly. This spilling of blood will cause the Resistance to respond just as you have. They will do whatever they must to stop the executions. Then we will have them in our grip. Please, my lady, give me at least four more weeks. I promise, you will not regret it if you do."

The silence hung heavy as Xvardris awaited her response. His heart pounded anxiously in his chest. He was risking much by pressing Wazrxna on this matter, but he was confident his plan would work.

"Very well," grated Wazrxna. "But this is one promise you had better come through on. Your continued inability to tie up loose ends causes me great concern, Xvardris. There are others who desire the throne of Xzwendaria. But I have always considered you to be my most capable liege." She paused for effect, her eyes still fiery. "I must admit, I am beginning to wonder."

"I will not fail you, my lady," pressed Xvardris. He bowed slightly. "Rest assured, I will not fail you in this."

"You had better not fail me," she said with cold intensity. "And tell me, what of the heir?"

Xvardris' frown deepened. The heir was a subject he loathed to discuss, for he had received no communications from the darklings or his assassin. He had nothing to report himself. However, he felt confident that even if the darklings and his assassin should fail, his spy certainly would not fail him.

"Xziland is a long way off," he said, effecting a careless air, as if to imply that all was going as planned. "I expect news of the heir's death to arrive any day. The darklings should soon return to the Black Chancel, and you will thus be the first to receive the good news, my lady. In fact, when you came to the palace, I thought that perhaps you were bringing news of the same."

"Your eyes belie you, Xvardris," Wazrxna took on an almost gloating air. "You are concerned that the darklings and your beloved assassin have failed. And your concern is well founded. Bayl has come to me in the temple. The five darklings are dead, as is your assassin. But the heir still lives, Xvardris."

Shock sheeted Xvardris' face, and his eyes shouted a silent no. He cared not about the darklings (good riddance), but Zanzxra?

He started to speak but she lifted a hand palm outward. "No, I do not know how the darklings or your assassin died. But the fact is they are dead."

"Then the fate of the heir rests in the hands of our spy." Xvardris' turned away, unwilling to meet Wazrxna's eyes.

"Yes, there is your spy. But if somehow your spy should be found out or should fail, as unlikely as you may think that is, did you not think it unlikely that the darklings or your assassin would fail? Something must be done. I shall send out the other darklings on my return to the chancel." Wazrxna turned to leave, took two steps, stopped, and turned back again. She reached a long pointy finger toward the usurper king who now faced her. "Hear this, Xvardris: If the heir should return to Xzwendaria, you will have failed, and Bayl does not tolerate failure."

Xvardris raised an angry fist in the air and declared, "If the heir should somehow return to Xzwendaria, I will kill him myself!"

In response, Wazrxana laughed a scornful, deep laugh. She left the palace and returned to the Black Chancel.

When the hated priestess was gone from his chamber, Xvardris called his aide and gave the order for another child to die.

Chapter 38

Once the King's Company reached the bottom of the long stairway, Grey Wolf stopped to examine a wall that stretched along the street leading toward the stone city. The wall was etched with pictures like the ones in the caves out on the Stakz.

"The stone city is called City of the Sun, and this is a memorial wall," said Grey Wolf. He read further. His face turned grim. "The ancients did inhabit the city for a time. When they found the city, it appeared as if it had never been lived in, and they decided it was paradise, prepared for them by Baruch. The trees, green grass, and strange fire lamps, which they called forever flames, were already here when they arrived. The pictures explain a variety of mundane details about living in the city. Then, the pictures say, 'We found death, although at first we did not know that the god dwelling in the midst of the city was death. We found the god in a great hall below the earth. The god glowed like a living stone. We forsook Baruch to worship the Sun Stone. But the god of the City of the Sun brought death to our people."

"That's a strange tale," said Captain Favel thoughtfully as his eyes perused the pictures. "What do you make of it, Grey Wolf?"

Grey Wolf looked toward the city. It stood somber and silent, no indications of life except for windows here and there that danced with light. The desert warrior shook his head, turned to the pictures again and continued to read in silence.

Time passed. The others waited patiently. Finally, Grey Wolf turned to the others. "The pictures tell a sad story." Grey Wolf grimaced. "But at last I know what became of the ancients. It is not the wonderful history of my imagination. The pictures indicate that once the ancients bowed before the living stone, they could no longer walk beneath the rays of Baruch's sun. When the sun shined on them, their skin rotted away before their eyes but less quickly if they stayed within the protection of the city." He stopped for a moment, shook his head sadly, and then went on. "The pictures tell the story of the slow, painful death of the ancients. And the picture maker closes by saying, 'Only ten of our people remain, and all have the sickness of death upon them.' The picture maker's name was Teldrinda, which means, 'I have never seen the sun.'"

A tear trickled down Grey Wolf's cheek. The others waited silently. It was a solemn moment. Each of the King's Company felt touched, for Grey Wolf had never shown such deep emotion.

"Now I have lost two families to the Pagyns." Great pain edged Grey Wolf's voice. The others did not press the matter, but he chose to tell more. "I was one of twelve children. My father prostituted my mother to any man who would pay his asking price. My father, as he was called, was not my father. My real father could have been any of a number of men, men no better than the man who called himself my father—the man who sold me into slavery when I turned fourteen.

"He sold me to a slave trader in Athos, who in turn sold me to another trader who took me to Xzwendaria. At Belem I was sold for a third time to a man named Egrnal, a vile and abusive man. When opportunity presented itself, I ran away with his favorite horse, a yearling."

He glanced at Sterling Grey, and a faint smile creased his lips. Then he continued his story. "I fled to the Savage Lands, where I lived among the stakz. I learned the language of the pictures and adopted the ancients as my people, since I had no people I could call my own. My name was Trevr, but now it is Grey Wolf." He sighed deeply. "And now my heart is broken by this tale of death."

"Maybe Baruch sent you to the Savage Lands for a new beginning," encouraged Xzwindra.

"Would that it might be so." Sadness echoed deep in Grey Wolf's voice. "But when I was sold into slavery, I was made a eunuch. Thus, I am the last, not the first."

"I am sorry, Grey Wolf." Kander laid his hand gently on the desert warrior's shoulder. Grey Wolf turned and met Kander's gaze. It seemed to Kander that even the eyes of the wolf that the man wore as a headdress looked sad. Kander continued, "In the end, my friend, all that really matters is that you become the man Baruch made you to be. Every man stands before his Maker, and although a man may stand alone, if he stands true, it is enough. My story is much like your own, Grey Wolf. I grew up without mother or father. And in my youth, while living on the streets as a thief, a priest of Baruch took an interest in me, took me in, and adopted me. His name was Thaxndar. He was assassinated by the Pagyns. So at least to some degree, I understand your sense of loss."

Grey Wolf wrapped his powerful arms around Kander, and Kander returned the embrace. The hardened desert warrior and the adopted son of the priest wept. And others wept as well.

Even Sergeant Tandrak felt the unusual warmth of wetness upon his cheek. And those shared tears became a force that bonded them all in a deeper friendship.

Grey Wolf, living alone in the Savage Lands, had never had a true friend. "Friend," he said quietly to Kander as he grasped his arm, hand to wrist. "Friends all," he said turning to the others. He slowly looked each in the eye. When his glance found Xzwindra's eyes, she blushed. Grey Wolf turned his gaze toward the stone city. "I would see this City of the Sun, the place were the ancients spent their last days." Grey Wolf's tears were gone, his stoic face back in place. "Then we must leave this place and continue our journey."

"What about the living stone?" Corporal Mifstern's question belied his fascination with the apparent marvel that lay somewhere within the stone city. "I wonder if there really is a living stone in some chamber in the bowels of this place. Shall we look for ourselves to see if there really is such a stone?"

"No!" Grey Wolf's voice grated with finality. "The Sun Stone is a Pagyn thing. To look upon it does not honor Baruch. To look upon it is death. The living stone is forbidden!"

"Just because we look doesn't mean we have to worship," defended Corporal Mifstern. "The Sun Stone is probably just a myth anyway. But I would sure like to see whatever it was that they construed to be a living stone. I mean that some bright, shining stone killing them off is absurd. The ancients probably died of some plague they brought here with them and blamed it on the stone. After all, stones are just stones."

"The Sun Stone is forbidden," repeated Grey Wolf firmly. Then he mounted Sterling Grey and continued on toward the city proper.

The streets of the City of the Sun were narrow, probably intended for milling people rather than horses or carts. The King's Company rode two abreast with their feet almost scraping the walls – walls that seemed to shelter emptiness. They came to a stairway that led up to what appeared to be a stone house. Grey Wolf pointed to a large iron ring that hung from the wall. They dismounted and tethered their horses. They had no idea as to the original use of the iron ring, but it served their present purpose well. Grey Wolf led the way up the stairs to explore the house. The door was plain, made of some kind of rock-hard wood and squeaked eerily when he pushed it open. To everyone's amazement, the chamber within was furnished. The furnishings were old and fragile. But what most caught their attention was a metal lamp that stood on a rock pedestal in the middle of the floor. The furnishings more or less surrounded the pedestal. There appeared to be no oil pot for the lamp, no wax, wick, or pitch. Nevertheless, a blue flame rose above the elaborately wrought bronze pole.

In an adjoining room, they found a large bed with ornate head-and-foot boards. A skull and long black hair lay on the pillow. Captain Favel carefully pulled back the covers and found bones and dust. Across the room a lamp, similar to the one in the living chamber, burned brightly.

"But who lights the flame?" Grey Wolf asked the question of no one in particular. Then he turned to Captain Favel. "Someone must yet live in this city."

They returned to the living chamber. Grey Wolf went to the lamp and snuffed out the bright blue flame, engulfing the room in partial darkness. Some light did make its way in from the adjoining room. Grey Wolf stepped up on the pedestal and examined the pole. "Humm. It is hollow and smells funny." He turned to the others and shrugged his shoulders. "The flame does not return."

"Let's leave this parlor of death and explore other parts of the city," said Xzwindra. She shuddered visibly. "This place is morbid."

"I do not understand the forever flame," said Grey Wolf. He was the last to leave the house. "It dances on the metal pole and burns nothing. No oil. No pitch."

"Perhaps the City of the Sun is a magical city." Corporal Mifstern laughed, but the tone of his laughter indicated that he thought it might be.

Grey Wolf pulled the door shut. As he did, the inside of the house erupted like a volcano whose moment had come. The heavy wooden door ripped away from its hinges, slamming Grey Wolf in the back and pitching him to the walkway. The explosion sent the others tumbling down the stairs. Fire shot out the windows. The noise of the explosion was deafening. The horses whinnied wildly and strained at their tethers.

Grey Wolf pushed the smoldering door aside, got to his feet, and cautiously returned to the house. The furnishings were in shambles, but what caught his attention was the metal lamp. It stood intact, and to his amazement, a blue flame danced above the pole once again. He shook his head in wonder.

"This is a strange place," he mused as he joined the others. "The forever flame has returned to its place above the lamp."

They were all amazed with him.

Scraped and bruised, Kander crawled back up the stairs to see the strange sight. "Wow!" was all he could say.

They left the house and explored other parts of the city. Everywhere they found death and no signs of human life. As evening settled on the city, they set up camp in a large parklike square in the middle of the city. Trees, bushes, grass, and even flowers grew here and there. But what astonished them was an absence of weeds. They decided it must be due to the restricted environment. On the other hand, Corporal Mifstern seemed convinced there was magic in the air.

Xzwindra took care of picketing the horses where they could graze on the gardenlike flora. Corporal Mifstern dressed cuts, scratches, and slivers inflicted by the explosion. But no one had any serious wounds. They considered themselves fortunate that the blast had taken place after the door was shut. They laid out their bedrolls and ate their evening meal. The conversation turned again to the forever flame.

"It is a great wonder," said Grey Wolf.

"This whole domed complex is a great wonder," said Captain Favel. "Did any of the pictures tell how it was built?"

"Yeah, how did they lift all those massive rocks to the surface and then place them one on top of the other to build the outer facade?" Kander swept his hand toward the great stone sky above them. "It is simply beyond grasping."

Corporal Mifstern got up and stretched. "It is a fascinating place." He stood with his hands on his hips and let his eyes scan the city. "All those lights burning, yet not a living soul to be found anywhere." He turned to Xzwindra. "I believe I'll take a walk. Want to come along?"

She shook her head. "Sorry. I've seen all that I want to see of this city." She cast him a wan smile. "This place gives me the creeps."

"Your loss," he muttered as he turned away.

"Don't get lost in the big city," teased Captain Favel. Corporal Mifstern's lips smiled in response but his eyes didn't, as he headed across the park, hands in his pockets.

The others laughed, except for Grey Wolf. He lay quietly on his bedroll gazing at the lights of the city.

Corporal Mifstern reached the edge of the park and sauntered down one of the streets they had previously explored. He had seen a doorway ornately engraved, with picture writing across the lintel. Grey Wolf had read the pictures but had refused to tell them what the pictures said. However, Corporal Mifstern had studied the pictures over Grey Wolf's shoulder. There were people walking through a door and down a long stairway and others bowing before a rock that appeared to be emanating light. As he walked down the desolate street, Corporal Mifstern smiled to himself. He would return to the door and take a quick peek at the Sun Stone—if there were such a thing.

"The forever flames were real enough," he mumbled to himself as he looked for the door. "Perhaps this Sun Stone is yet another wonder of this strange world. Forbidden or not, I would see this living stone for myself."

Corporal Mifstern felt a surge of excitement when he saw the door. He cast a glance over his shoulder to be sure that no one had followed him. He pulled on the huge ring that hung from the middle of the door. The door creaked open. Again, he looked over his shoulder, and then he slipped inside and pulled the door shut.

A forever flame lit the small chamber in which he stood. Across from the door the chamber opened into a long hallway, also lit by forever flames. He hurried down the long hall. He felt like he was being watched, yet knew he was not. At the end of the hall, a stairway led downward. Again, forever flames danced at the ends of metal flame holders that stuck out from the walls. Corporal Mifstern hurried down the stairs. He was anxious to see the stone and return to the city streets without Grey Wolf finding out about his escapade. The stairs descended perhaps fifteen feet, turned, descended again, and turned yet again, and so on. He had no idea that the chamber would be so far below the city. At the end of the stairs, he came to another long hallway and at the end of the hallway another ornately carved wooden door. Corporal Mifstern's hands trembled as he pulled it open. With tense excitement, he poked his head inside.

"I'll be!" Awe sheeted his face. No forever flames were in the large chamber, yet it was filled with a compelling, yet soft, light. With a broad grin expressing his self-satisfaction, Corporal Mifstern slipped into the chamber of the Sun Stone.

He let out a low whistle. "Wow!" he muttered. The stone sat in the center of the great hall. It was uncut and had no discernible form. In fact, its glow undulated so that the shape seemed almost fluid. For several moments he stood, hands hanging at his sides, gawking at the stone, and then he reverently approached the monolith.

"This is indeed a living stone." Corporal Mifstern's eyes gaped at the pulsating light, surrounding or coming from the stone. He could not tell which. "I see why the ancients were so taken by it. I have never seen such a wonder in all my life!"

He drew near, extending a hand with its palm toward the wondrous stone. The monolith did not emit heat. In fact, he felt a sensation of coolness. He cautiously stepped closer, feeling awe but not any sense of peril. The light from the monolith was bright but not blinding. With a trembling hand, he touched the stone. The light engulfed his hand so that he could not see his fingers. The surface of the stone felt cool to the touch as he ran his hand across its face. The monolith was smooth, but its surface was not flat. "Extraordinary!" he whispered. He was glad he had come.

He frowned and muttered aloud, "Should I tell the others, or keep it to myself? Grey Wolf will probably be angry. But I wish they all could see this."

He did not know how long he had spent basking in the light of the Sun Stone before he finally pulled himself away and headed back up to the city. The street was empty. He breathed a sigh of relief. For some reason, as he climbed the stairs up to the street he had expected to come face to face with Grey Wolf upon opening the door that led out to the city. Thankfully, Grey Wolf was nowhere to be seen. His secret was safe. A mischievous grin crossed his face. He had gotten away with looking at the forbidden stone. His grin turned to silent laughter.

When he slipped back into camp, the others appeared to be asleep. He quietly made his way over to his bedroll.

Captain Favel rolled over, opened his eyes and looked up at Corporal Mifstern, who smiled and nodded in return. But the look that crossed Captain Favel's face alarmed him. "What's wrong?" muttered Corporal Mifstern.

Captain Favel stared intently.

"What is it?" Corporal Mifstern repeated.

"Your face—your whole body—glows!" said Captain Favel.

Corporal Mifstern held up his hand. It looked normal to him! The others were now awake and staring with the same wide-eyed look as Captain Favel.

"I don't know what you're so excited about." Corporal Mifstern's tone was defensive. "I've just been for a walk, and I see nothing extraordinary about my appearance."

"You have looked on the forbidden stone." Grey Wolf stood in the shadows beyond Captain Favel. "Its brightness has touched you."

"I don't know what you're talking about!" Panic edged Corporal Mifstern's voice.

"You have indeed stood in the presence of the Sun Stone!" pressed Grey Wolf.

Anger colored Corporal Mifstern's neck. His jaw squared. Silence.

Grey Wolf pressed him further. "You entered the Pagyn hall of worship, didn't you?" They all waited with bated breath for his response.

He looked from one to the other, seeking a sympathetic eye, but all he found were questioning stares.

"Okay, so I looked at the Sun Stone." He broke the silence. "I even touched it. The stone is a great wonder. You all must see it before we leave this place. It is wonderful! It pulsates with light and is smooth to the touch. It truly is alive. It is little wonder the ancients were so affected by it. Come, I will show you!"

"No!" Dismay edged Grey Wolf's voice. "The stone has touched you with its light, but the pictures indicate that its light is death. You have seen a great wonder, my friend, yet I fear that your looking at it will prove to be a terrible folly."

"The Sun Stone is harmless!" Corporal Mifstern laughed uncomfortably. "You're making much of nothing, Grey Wolf. The living stone did not kill the ancients. It was probably some plague they brought with them from the outside. They were superstitious and attributed some unknown disease to the Sun Stone. You really must see it for yourselves, all of you. You can make your own judgment."

"I would like to see the stone. What can it hurt?" Xzwindra glanced fleetingly toward the desert warrior. "As far as I'm concerned, Grey Wolf is being unreasonable. Let's look for ourselves."

"I will not look upon this Pagyn idol." Grey Wolf showed no change of emotion. "If you choose to look on the Sun Stone, then here we part company. I will ride with you no farther. To look upon the living stone does not honor Baruch and will bring death."

Corporal Mifstern laughed mockingly. "I did not worship the stone. I merely observed it like I might observe any extraordinary sight. Don't be so priggish, Grey Wolf."

"I have spoken," was the desert warrior's only response.

The others looked to Captain Favel.

"Our mission is to find the heir and return him to Xzwendaria." A scowl creased his face. "Anything that has the slightest potential of hindering our mission must be avoided. Grey Wolf is necessary to our mission. If any of you desire to go against his wishes and look at the stone, you have one of two choices. Return here to look at it after our mission is finished or look now and part company."

Corporal Mifstern shook his head in disgust. The others agreed that seeing the stone was not that important. Sergeant Tandrak did not care if he saw it or not. Kander thought it would be interesting but could live without seeing it. Xzwindra, not thinking about the crossing of the desert, expressed disappointment and her intent to return to see the Sun Stone at another time.

They slept uneasily that night. The bond of friendship they had finally come to share before entering the city now seemed tenuous. An air of tension hung over them. To

Xzwindra and Kander, it seemed like Grey Wolf did not care that his determination not to have anything to do with the Pagyn stone was causing a rift in the company. But Captain Favel fretted the most. He did not like having disunity within the ranks.

When morning came, the unhappy company silently made their way up to the concourse that circled the city. They pulled the door to and leaving the City of the Sun, they returned to the terrible heat of Witherdeep.

"The City of the Sun is indeed paradise compared to this!" groaned Xzwindra.

"Well, I for one will return someday," said Corporal Mifstern emphatically. "And I will bring others with me. We shall start a new civilization in this grand paradise."

Grey Wolf cast Corporal Mifstern a doleful scowl but said nothing.

Xzwindra laughed and said she would consider returning with him, but she didn't know that she would want to spend the rest of her life in what seemed to her to be more a crypt than a city. However, she did want to see the strange stone. "But there is the desert," she groused.

"And the worms," added Kander.

Heat rose from the rock surface. The sun beat down relentlessly. Toward the end of the day, Corporal Mifstern began to experience discomfort, a feeling of nausea, and then of panic. "This heat is terrible. I can hardly breathe!" he complained. And by the time they stopped for the night, he was sucking air in great gasps.

They made camp, but Corporal Mifstern slept very little. In the middle of the night he rose and prepared an elixir of herbs. It didn't help. He felt weak as he lifted himself into the saddle the next morning. He looked at his hands. They were covered with red blotches that looked and felt like burns. His face felt hot. He reached up and touched his cheek. He winced in pain. As the day progressed, the others noticed the growing blotches and that he rode slumped in his saddle in front of Xzwindra.

"It is the Sun Stone," said Grey Wolf. "It is just as the pictures said. Once the ancients looked upon the stone, they could never again walk beneath the sun."

At that Corporal Mifstern became alarmed but refused to admit that Grey Wolf was right. "It is just the wretched heat of Witherdeep!" He shot Grey Wolf an incensed sidelong glance.

By the next day, Corporal Mifstern's eyes were dull and glazed, his hair began falling out, his skin appeared to be melting on his body, and he exuded such a wretched odor that Xzwindra could hardly stomach it. She had to turn her head aside to breathe. And by the time night came to the Witherdeep, Corporal Mifstern no longer had the strength to ride. Although Xzwindra tried, she could no longer hold him in his saddle nor could she endure the awful stench. They laid the dying corporal on his bedroll. He could no longer see and could barely talk. "Grey Wolf!" he called hoarsely.

Grey Wolf knelt beside him and laid a gentle hand on Mifstern's shoulder. The desert warrior ignored the stench. "Looking on that stone was indeed my folly," whispered Corporal Mifstern. He reached up and took hold of Grey Wolf's arm. "Forgive me, Grey Wolf. I did not realize—the Sun Stone is indeed death. Forgive. . ."

As the word forgive passed from Corporal Mifstern's lips, his arm fell limp. Death claimed its own. The others stood watching, stunned by the turn of events.

Grey Wolf stood up. Tears trickled down his cheek. "Why does the Sun Stone bring death?" he wondered aloud.

That was the last time any of them spoke of the Sun Stone. They left Corporal Mifstern lying on his bed, hands on his chest, glazed eyes looking up at the sun. There was nothing more they could do. Reluctantly, they continued on their way. Xzwindra shuddered as she mounted Corporal Mifstern's horse. It all seemed unreal to her.

As they came down to where the sloping rock met the sand, the sun was setting once again in the west. They made camp, and few words passed between them. They each mourned their friend in silence. When dawn broke, they mounted and prepared to ride forth.

"So once again we face the witherworms," commented Sergeant Tandrak.

"We will ride hard today," said Grey Wolf. "We will push our steeds and ourselves to the limit of our endurance." He looked out over the worm-infested hardpan and pointed. "See through the vapors? This stretch may not be as wide as where we entered Witherdeep. Perhaps we can be gone from here before the worms awake this evening."

They thundered across the hardpan, pressing their reluctant horses to a gallop. The sun-beaten horses' flanks lathered as they ran, their nostrils flared, but on and on they went, as if they too feared the worms. Then, near midday, Grey Wolf raised a hand, and they reined in their weary steeds. The horses were fed and given water by way of the cactus meat, then wiped down with dirt. Then they were off again. Later in the day, they stopped, cared for the horses' needs, and their own before galloping on. And as the sun dipped below the horizon behind them, they could see the high banks of the outer edge of the Witherdeep in the distance. But off to their right the ground stirred. It rippled toward them. Grey Wolf dug in his heels. Sterling Grey responded instantly. The others dug in their heels as well. Another worm came from the left. The horses seemed to sense the danger. They drove toward safety with every muscle flexed to its limit. And when they arrived at the bank that led up and out of Witherdeep, they did not hold back. Riders and beasts leaned forward and drove up toward the rim.

They had expected loose rock and sand, but the east bank was hard clay. When they were well beyond the reach of the witherworms, they slowed to a laborious climb. And once on the rim of Witherdeep, they stopped, sighed with relief, and nearly fell from their horses. Before them, scattered trees stretched up toward rugged, daunting mountains and the Pass of Phantazia, the next leg of their journey.

The King's Company's hearts weighed heavy, for behind them, out in the Witherdeep, lay the body of their compatriot and friend and before them another challenge. They made camp in a copse of trees. The horses grazed on dry grass. Again the company ate in silence.

As he stretched out on his bedroll, Kander looked off toward the dark mountains. "The Pass of Phantazia." His voice trembled as he whispered the words. He scowled, laid his head down, and slept a sleep haunted by what lay behind and by what lay ahead.

Chapter 39

When he arrived at Aynek, Major Targndel looked up one of his spies, a man named Jelknerd. He passed himself off as an uppity merchant who cooperated with the Pagyns. As a result, he was hated by the town folk who were unaware of his activities on behalf of the Resistance. Targndel came to him under cover of darkness. The byways of Aynek were not as closely watched as the streets of Zwexdrof.

Jelknerd was a bulbous, round-cheeked fellow, bold and always smiling. He was delighted to see Targndel and to hear news of what was happening with the Resistance.

"I am glad you escaped the purge in Zwexdrof." He smiled broadly and wagged his head. "News has been scarce the last couple of weeks. Is it true that Xvardris has been executing a spy a day?"

"It is true that he is killing an innocent person each day. Few of the executed have been spies. Many have been women and children. That is why I am here. I need to find a way to get back inside the walls of Zwexdrof."

"You're a fool, Targndel!" Jelknerd's smile turned to an expansive frown. "Do you not value your life, man? There's a price on your head! If I were to turn you in, I would receive a handsome sum in return."

"Jelknerd, as far as I'm concerned, my life is not worth the price of even one of our children so vilely laid out on Xvardris' chopping block!" Targndel met Jelknerd eye to eye. "The killing of our women and children must stop!"

"And just how do you propose to stop it?" Jelknerd motioned toward a table. The two men sat down. Jelknerd set a mug of brew before his friend and then after swigging from his own mug, he shook his head and leaned heavily against the back of his chair. "Don't know how it can be done. Zwexdrof is crawling with Pagyns. And anyone who helps you will do so at the risk of his or her life and the lives of their family. Go back to Havenholt and wait it out, my friend." He shook his head again. "There is nothing you can do. Besides, you are too important to our cause to be throwing your life away needlessly."

"Do not try to deter me, Jelknerd." Targndel, his brow deeply creased, leaned over the table with his mug grasped between his hands. "My course is set. If something should happen to me, Razrdris will take my place. It will be up to you to pass the word on to our operatives. But hopefully it won't come to that."

Jelknerd shook his head yet again. "This is madness!"

Targndel ignored his friend's comment. "I need a disguise," he said.

Jelknerd stared long and hard and then slowly let his breath out. "I'll provide you with a false identity. But you'll have to work for me for a couple days to establish credibility for the ruse to work."

The next day Targndel went to work in Jelknerd's store. But first the merchant remade the major's person. Using a chemical that Targndel was unfamiliar with, Jelknerd turned the major's hair white and coarse. He combed it straight back instead of off to the side. With special putty Jelknerd had developed for such purposes, he created boil-like lumps all over Targndel's face, and he molded his ears so that they were slightly pointed on top. He coated the putty and skin with a clear gluelike substance. He also added a shaggy white mustache and a few white chin whiskers. A bent back and a hump on one shoulder added further character to Targndel's new identity. Shoes, one having a slightly raised heel and sole, added a limp. A twisted cane and white hair on the back of his hands provided the final touch.

"Cousin Fidrdink!" declared Jelknerd. "My dear cousin Fidrdink!"

The next two days "Cousin Fidrdink" limped about the store, stocking shelves, sweeping, and dusting. Late the second day, three Pagyn soldiers came tramping into the store. They looked at Targndel, pointed, and laughed.

"Who is the gnarled old man you have workin' for ya?" asked the captain. Suspicion edged his voice.

"Him? He's my cousin, Fidrdink, from down Noved way," answered Jelknerd. He gestured toward the street. "Can't get the townsfolk ta help out around here any more. His old lady kicked him out a' the house, so he came beggin' at my door. Felt sorry for the poor worm. Besides, I needed the help – what help he is. He spent his life a wagon driver. A bit clumsy around the store, but he'll learn, he will, if I have ta' kick em' in the seat a thousand times."

The soldiers laughed then forgot about Cousin Fidrdink. Slowly, he continued to push dirt from one place to another with his broom while watching the soldiers out the corner of his eye.

"We need another shipment a' flour hauled up ta Zwexdrof. Xvardris' larder is runnin' low." The head soldier laid his hand on a stack of flour sacks. "My boys will be here first thing in the mornin' to accompany yer wagon. We don't want the Resistance gettin' their hands on this stuff."

"It'll be ready," assured Jelknerd.

When the soldiers returned in the morning, the wagon was only half loaded. The leader scolded Jelknerd for his negligence.

"Couldn't find anyone willing ta drive! Couldn't find anyone ta help load, 'cept my slow pated cousin." Jelknerd waved his hands this way and that in a display of anger. "Had to go to the stable and get the wagon myself, and here we are a fat man an' a cripple loadin' fifty pound sacks a' flour." Jelknerd wiped his drippy brow. "An' I hate ta tell ya, but one a' yer men will hafta drive the wagon." He shook his head. "As I said, I can't find a soul willin' ta go up ta Zwexdrof fer any price—considerin' what's been goin' on up there and all."

Jelknerd knew that the Pagyn soldiers would never stoop to perform such a menial duty as driving a wagon. Their wagons were all driven by slaves (and the slaves were all working on Xvardris' war machine).

"Well, then you'll have to drive the wagon," said the captain.

"An' close my store for more than a week?" he spat. "An' who will provide yer garrison with supplies while I'm gone?"

"You can leave the store in your good cousin's hands," laughed the captain.

"Posh! He can push a broom across a dirty floor, but he doesn't have brain one fer runnin' a store!" shot back Jelknerd angrily. "You'll have ta find yer own driver, I tell ya!"

The captain cast Jelknerd a grim scowl. "Didn't ya say yer cousin used ta drive wagons fer a livin'?"

Jelknerd looked at Cousin Fidrdink with a blank "I never thought of that!" stare. Then his broad-jowled smile returned. "Humm. That I did, and I'll be glad ta have 'em out a' my hair fer awhile." Then, in a whisper, he urged, "When ya get ta Zwexdrof, if ya can find the poor fellow a bit a' work, it would be a favor to me."

The soldier shot Jelknerd an angry glance and sneered, "They'll send him straight home when the job's done! Not my boys' business ta find employ for the unemployable!"

Jelknerd and Cousin Fidrdink finished loading the flour. Poor cousin Fidrdink clumsily climbed up into the seat of the wagon, gave a raffish wave and was off for Zwexdrof with the soldiers tailing behind.

Chapter 40

"It will take most of the day to cross through the Pass of Phantazia," explained Grey Wolf. They had already spent one day twisting up into the mountains after leaving Witherdeep. Now they fussed at tethering the horses to a lead line. "With your eyes blindfolded, you will not be able to look into the eyes of the Shades of Phantazia. You will hear their voices. They will beckon to you. And to keep you from ripping off your blindfolds, your hands will be tied behind your backs."

Sergeant Tandrak started to protest, but Grey Wolf held up his hand. "Trust me, Sergeant, it is the only way."

"How do we know that you will not be drawn into darkness by the shades' eyes?" Captain Favel asked the question that was on everyone's mind. "And if you are led astray, then you will in turn take all of us with you. We will be entirely at your mercy."

"And that is the reason I will be able to resist." There was no emotion in Grey Wolf's voice, only an air of confidence. "As a boy, I was at the mercy of my father and mother. They sold me into slavery. I have been at the mercy of others, and they have always failed me. I was cast into slavery and darkness. I vowed by the strength of Baruch never to do the same. Baruch will not fail me, Captain. And I will not fail any of you. I trust Baruch, and I ask you to trust me."

"You ask for a lot!" Sergeant Tandrak jerked at the tether line to test the knot. "As for me, I have always trusted myself. Frankly, I'm not used to trusting anybody that far."

"The choice is yours, Sergeant. It is not for me to force anyone to trust me." Grey Wolf turned and faced Sergeant Tandrak eye to eye. "But tell me, friend, will you be able to resist what the shades offer? They may test your mettle by offering fame, strength, success, or some coveted position or rank. They may tempt you with women, riches—or a thing as simple as a bottle of whiskey. The shades know what you desire, Sergeant. They know what you covet deep in your heart. They are aware of your most secret fantasies. No, I would not force you to trust me. However, I do ask you to place your trust in me."

"Well, putting it that way, and all, I guess I don't have much choice, 'cause you're right. I dare not trust myself." Sergeant Tandrak's mood had become almost pensive.

The others readily agreed. They did not hesitate to put themselves in Grey Wolf's hands. They mounted their horses. Grey Wolf blindfolded them and tied their hands behind their backs. Then, with the horses tethered one to the other, he led them into the first stretches of the Pass of Phantazia.

A hot breeze sucked up the narrow canyon from the Witherdeep. At first the wind was like a gentle sigh, but the farther they went, the harsher the blast. They were glad it came from behind them. Eventually, the narrowing trail led into a long corridor-like gorge that passed between two high, rugged walls. The canyon was replete with pinnacles, crevices, and caves. And the wind seemed to push the angst-ridden company toward the unusual canyon that only Grey Wolf could actually see. As they entered the divide, the wind's natural whisper changed. Its sigh became voices calling from some distant place, but at first they could not tell what the voices were saying. However, the farther the King's Company went, the clearer the voices became.

Sergeant Tandrak's face turned red. He began to sweat. Saliva filled his mouth. He licked his lips. He had never felt such intense desire in his life. He longed to remove the blindfold, to look, to indulge. Surely, such wonderful voices would not deceive.

Captain Favel grimaced. He swallowed hard. Beads of sweat broke out on his neck. He had not expected to be tempted with that! In spite of the blindfold, he fought the desire to look into the eyes of the Shades. However, he quickly realized that but for the blinder he would look. He wept bitterly. Driving desire and disappointment with himself tore at his heart.

Xzwindra turned white. Her skin became cold and clammy. She had been certain of what the Shades would reveal but knowing did not make it easier. She gritted her teeth and squirmed in her saddle. From the start, she had experienced no sense of delusion. She had feared the Path of Llprinda, and her fears were well-founded. Desire and terror ripped at her soul.

Kander focused his mind on Baruch. He talked to him. He cried out to him. And, in fact, his cries distracted the others from the intensity of their desires. But eventually the persistent voices of the Shades got to him. They revealed his deepest desires. Lust filled his heart. Again he cried out to Baruch. He wept for shame, knowing that were it not for the blindfold, he could not resist looking into the eyes of the Shades and pursuing his contemptible fantasies to his own detriment.

Grey Wolf too heard the voices. With his jaw set and his eyes on the path before him, he pressed on, intent on being faithful. He must not fail! But suddenly the color drained from his face. His stoic demeanor broke. Emotion gripped him as never before in his life. The Shades whispered words he had not expected. The voices did not test him with lust, riches, or fame. Rather, they touched an area of his heart he had long ago sealed off for reasons of self-preservation.

"Your father waits in the darkness, Trevr," whispered a shade.

"It is your real father, Trevr," whispered another. "Do you not long to know who your father is?"

"He has been looking for you for years. He longs to see you, Trevr," added a sweet gentle voice.

"He loves you, Trevr," whispered yet another voice. "Your father weeps for you. His heart is broken. He needs you, Trevr."

"Come, Trevr, we will take you to him," urged the gentle voices in unison. "Look in our eyes. See your father's face. You long to see him, Trevr. He longs to see you. He is waiting for you to acknowledge him. He weeps. Do you not care, Trevr? Do you not love him, Trevr?"

Grey Wolf wept like a child starved for its mother's milk. He pressed his legs to Sterling Grey's sides as if trying to hold back. Tears blurred his vision. He could no longer see the trail. His father was waiting. Oh, how deeply he longed for his father. Yes, he would look! He must see who. . . At that moment, Kander cried out to Baruch. Grey Wolf instinctively echoed the cry. "Help me, Majesty! Help me!" And as he cried out he realized how arrogant he had been! How wrong he had been! He had thought he could ride through the pass unaffected by the shades. He had never before formulated it into words or thoughts, but now he realized that he felt superior to others, since he did not share their vices. He saw himself as pure and strong. But as he listened to the voices here in the Pass of Phantazia, he discovered that in reality he was vulnerable and weak.

The desert warrior shook with fear. He feared he would fail his friends—that he would look into the Shades' eyes and the entire company would vanish into darkness. "Desire has won the battle," he muttered. Yes, he desired to see his father—to know his real father. The consequences of looking seemed suddenly irrelevant. He had no choice but to look! He had to know! He could hear his father's tears! His father! He must see his father! Grey Wolf broke his pact with the trail and looked up. He sought the demon eyes. But his own eyes, still blurred by his tears, could not find the eyes of the Shades of Phantazia. In that same instant that he broke covenant, a terrible explosion of guilt ripped at his heart.

"What have I done?" cried the wounded warrior. "I have betrayed my friends! I have sold them into slavery! Forgive me, Baruch! Forgive me!"

A great fear fell on Captain Favel, Kander, Xzwindra, and Sergeant Tandrak. What had Grey Wolf done? Their chests shrank into tightness. Their throats turned dry. Words failed their lips. Blood pounding in their heads left them dazed.

At the moment Grey Wolf cried out to Baruch, the Shades' hold on his emotions broke. Awareness of Baruch's forgiveness swept over him. He wiped away the tears that clouded his vision and again made pledge with the pathway before him.

Then the King's Company passed beyond the high walls of the terrible divide and out into a broad rocky canyon scattered with scrub pines and wind-beaten thickets.

The wind howled viciously, pushing at the weary travelers' backs, but the dread voices of the Shades of Phantazia had fallen silent. The five riders wept like little children waking from garish dreams. Grey Wolf pressed on to a meadow somewhat protected from the blustery wind, a stretch of green grass that lay at the base of a rocky bluff. In the middle of the grassy meadow stood a singular tree with branches that spread outward, beckoning them to come and rest in its shade. Grey Wolf led the King's Company to the tree, stopped, untied their hands, and one by one they removed their damp blindfolds.

The tears continued to flow as each rider dismounted and sank to his or her knees in the grass, relief overwhelming them. And although the temporary terror passed, a deep inner anguish remained. Grey Wolf alone would later speak of the trial endured as they passed the Shades of Phantazia.

Chapter 41

Fidrdink rode into Zwexdrof accompanied by the Pagyn soldiers. The streets, usually bustling with people, were nearly barren. The faces of those who did venture out were drawn and somber. Dread hung on the air. Major Targndel hid his growing anger behind his own somber disguise.

The soldiers led Fidrdink and his wagon of supplies to the rear of the palace where the scullery door opened onto a raised loading dock. Targndel pulled the wagon alongside the ramp and brought it to a halt. "Whose gunna unload this thing?" he rasped.

The soldiers laughed and jeered. "You are, old man!" they said, almost as one.

Fidrdink protested, but in the end he had no choice but to do as the soldiers told him. Slowly, tediously, he stacked the bags of flour on the dock. The soldiers finally gave up on him and left a burly kitchen worker standing by to oversee his work.

"I s'pose I'll need ta stack these inside somewhere," growled Fidrdink as he dragged a sack across the dock.

"We got slaves ta do that." The kitchener waved him off. "Jes' get it unloaded, an be off with ya, old man!"

"Well, I could get it unloaded a bit faster if it would please ya ta ha' one or two a' them slaves ta gi' me a hand!" urged Fidrdink.

"You brought it! Yer responsible ta unload it!" spat the kitchener. "I wouldn't ask me slaves ta do another man's labor. Now hurry along, old-timer, 'cause I ain't got all day!"

Major Targndel had hoped to get inside the palace while someone else unloaded the wagon. Wouldn't happen! Not with this kitchener in charge! He swallowed his disappointment and kept working.

A half hour later, he set the last bag of flour down on the loading dock. Fidrdink wiped his brow and begged a drink of the kitchener, again hoping to get inside the palace.

The kitchener laughed in his face. "Off with you, you gnarly faced old man!" he snarled. "You've taken up enough a' my time! If ya nee' ta wet yer whistle, ya can do it a' one a the inns! Now, be on yer way!"

"Drat!" Targndel muttered as he gave the horses rein. "Now what do I do?"

Not far from the palace, an inn called the Inn of the Shadow hunkered between an empty warehouse and a rundown mercantile. Targndel took his horse and wagon to a nearby stable and hobbled over to the inn. He ate his evening meal alone, sitting in a corner. He rented a room for the night—on the third floor. He had asked for a room on the first floor, but the innkeeper just looked at him blankly, handed him a key and said, "Third floor, end a' the hall." The innkeeper returned to his work and ignored Targndel's presence.

Targndel stood there a moment looking at the hosteller, then shrugged his shoulders and limped off to the stairway leading up to his room. "It doesn't do to be old or ugly," he mused. "A sad commentary on our social order—a telling betrayal of humanity's baser side."

Once in his room, he locked the door and went to the window. The pane, thick with filth, hid what lay without from the eyes of those within. It took some doing to get the window open. Mold appeared to have sealed it shut. The room itself smelled musty. "Saved just for people like me." Targndel smiled as he stuck his head out the window to see if there was any way to get down to the ground. "Nothing seems to be going right," he grumbled. The drop was sheer.

He went over to the bed and pulled back the covers. Bedbugs scurried into the wrinkles. A shudder ran up Targndel's spine. He looked around the room. It was bare except for a small table and a rickety chair. On the table an oil lamp and flint promised light, but no oil was in the lamp! He looked up at the ceiling where a square opening covered by a board dripped paint peelings. His eyes lit up. An entrance to the crawl space between rooms and roof! he mused. He returned to the window, stuck his head out, and looked upward. He grinned and muttered, "Yes, if I can get to the roof!"

Once darkness fell, Targndel climbed from a rickety chair, to the table, and to the crawl space. He carefully replaced the cover. At the back of the crawl space, a square vent faced the backside of a building that stood slightly higher than the inn. The space between the two buildings was claustrophobic. "Just right!" whispered Targndel. He removed the vent, crawled out, and pressing his back to one building and his feet and hands to the other he tediously inched his way up to the roof. Having replaced his uneven shoes with soft moccasins he crept carefully and quietly along the edge of the roof to the warehouse. He easily jumped the four feet from the inn roof to the warehouse roof.

Targndel had often used such byways to move about the city undetected. Thus, he knew that the building behind the warehouse was only two stories and that a ladder reached down the back side of the warehouse, giving him access to the lower building. He worked his way along the building tops, down to a one-story unit where he climbed into the branches of a tree and climbed down to the ground within a hundred feet of the palace wall. He eased across the deserted street and into the shadow of the dark stone wall. He cautiously worked his way along until he found a tree high enough and near enough to the wall to provide access. Once over the wall, he found himself in the palace garden.

The palace, a beautiful old building decorated with greenery, presented the greatest challenge. Vines grew from the ground clear to the upper parapets. Would they hold his weight? Targndel stole his way to a dark corner and began the dangerous climb. Being familiar with the layout of the palace and Zedria having previously told him that Xvardris had taken over the king's quarters, which was no great surprise, he edged his way up to the second level. He climbed ever so slowly. A sudden movement might catch a guard's attention. Once at the second level he inched cautiously from vine to vine across the face of the castle to the chamber adjacent to Xvardris' apartment, the queen's quarters. Being there was no queen about the palace, he presumed and desperately hoped that the quarters were not occupied.

Light shined from the king's window. However, the embrasure adjacent remained darkened. Targndel made his way to the thick stone sill, hid in the shadows, and listened. He heard nothing. He gently tried the window's doorlike frame. It swung inward on near silent hinges. Slowly and carefully, he made his way across the dark room to the drapelike door that connected the two apartments. He put his ear to the thick curtain and heard moans and giggles. He waited. Suddenly, he was aware of a man's voice and women answering. Laughter—a door opening—a door closing—a moment of silence—heavy footsteps approaching the curtained doorway. Just as rays of light shot into the room, Targndel reached the door leading to Xvardris' apartment. He took a deep breath, turned the handle, and quietly slipped into the adjoining room.

Xvardris, having finished with the girls he had brought to the queen's quarters and having sent them away, returned to his own quarters by way of the same door Targndel had just escaped through.

Xvardris sauntered over to his bed, laughed a self-satisfied laugh, and declared, "Ah, the wonderful privileges of royalty!" He carelessly threw back his covers and was about to climb into bed when he heard a noise behind him. He whirled about and stood face to face with a strange, ugly old man.

"How did you get in here, old man?" Xvardris' mood turned peevish. The cold sweat that fear brings had wet his brow. The old man just stared at him. "Who are you, and what do you want?" His question was met with silence. Xvardris swept a hand toward the door. "Get out of my chamber before I call the guards!" he threatened, though he knew that none were near at hand to hear his call.

"Usurper, you have killed our women and children," rasped Targndel accusingly.

"Bah! They only got what they deserved, and you'll get the same if you do not leave my chamber immediately, old man!"

"But I am not an old man." Targndel dropped Fidrdink's vocal tone.

Xvardris' mouth dropped open, but the only sound that came out was a guttural whimper.

"I believe you have been looking for me, Xvardris. I am Major Targndel of the Resistance." Xvardris' eyes widened. Targndel continued, "You have carried things too far. You should not have killed our children."

"You'll never get away with this!" Xvardris found his voice, though throaty and filled with fear.

Too late he saw the flash of steel. His eyes went yet wider and a snivel escaped his lips as he crumpled to the floor.

Targndel left a note lying on Xvardris' body that simply read, "The Resistance." Grim-faced he turned and left by the way he had come.

Xvardris' corpse was not found until late the next morning.

*T*argndel trundled south along the edge of the ravages of Tangle Wood toward Aynek. Dour lines creasing his knotty brow, for he had not enjoyed the vile deed the usurper had forced on him. He had done it for the children,women, and innocent old men. That provided the only consolation of soul for killing a man in cold blood.

When Wazrxna arrived at the palace after hearing of Xvardris' death, laughter danced in her eyes. She looked down on Xvardris' cold body, now lying on his bed, and shook her head. "I told you the loose ends would cost you your life." She stared momentarily out the window. "Humm. The work of Major Targndel, I presume," she mumbled to herself. "Well, Major, you have saved me the bother of this messy business."

Wazrxna circulated word that she and General Bodrak had ordered Xvardris' execution because of his barbarous deeds. And she ordered the release of all of the prisoners still being held in the palace dungeon. The city breathed a tearful sigh of relief. And although Wazrxna purposed to win the hearts of the people by her magnanimous gesture, she failed, for the servant, who had found Xvardris' body had seen the note left by Targndel, and soon the whole city knew the truth. The Resistance had avenged the children.

Nefarious Reach, at Wazrxna's directive, placed General Bodrak on the throne of Xzwendaria in place of Xvardris. King Bodrak, as he called himself, determined to win the affection of the people, ruled Zwexdrof with a relatively gentle hand, while the Pagyn war machine pressed on toward Havenholt.

Major Targndel returned to Aynek, worked for Jelknerd for several days longer, and then one day he was gone. "Decided the work was too hard," explained Jelknerd to the soldiers who came in for their supplies. They laughed. "A wretchedly ugly fellow!" mocked their captain.

Major Targndel, shed of the uncomfortable disguise, made his way back to Havenholt and vowed never to forget his days as a gnarly faced old man. It was an experience that forever changed his attitude toward the unfortunates of society.

Chapter 42

Marshwood Forest was like no forest that any of the weary travelers had ever seen. The trees were tall with heavy, broad leaves. They hung with stringy moss and crawled with strange looking vines. The forest floor cultured a variety of short grass, tall grass, and ferns. Small ferns with narrow leaves. Very tall ferns with broad leaves. Also, fungi of one kind and another seemed to grow everywhere. And there were other plants such as no one in the King's Company had seen before. The forest floor, soft and damp, squished beneath their feet. Sink holes and bogs barred their way, and strikingly colorful, large birds with long, ponderous beaks, fearlessly scolded them for intruding into their domain.

"The birds I can handle." Xzwindra scowled as she looked about nervously. "But the snakes. . . ."

There were small snakes, large snakes, green snakes, brown snakes, and multicolored snakes. Some snakes crawled on the ground, and others hung from tree branches. They had counted seventeen snakes already, and that made the prospect of camping in the forest altogether uncomfortable, not only for Xzwindra, but for all the King's Company.

"How long will it take us to get through this loathsome forest?" Xzwindra continued to press the matter.

"A week." Captain Favel turned to follow Grey Wolf around a wide morass. "Maybe more if we keep having to skirt these miserable bogs."

"The farther we go, the more I regret having come on this trip." Resentment rang in Xzwindra's voice.

No one reminded her that she had come of her own choice, because deep inside they all felt what she alone dared to express, except perhaps for Grey Wolf. The trip had not been pleasant for any of them. And the fact was, none of the others liked snakes any better than she did, though Grey Wolf made no display of how he felt about them.

That night they camped on a slight rise where the ground was fairly dry. Kander gathered dry wood from trees that had died but were still standing and built a fire. Sergeant Tandrak cooked a savory stew, the smell of which wafted on the air creating anticipation. They had not had a hot meal since leaving the Draw Gulch. However, they were not the only ones enticed by the appetizing odor.

"We've got company." Kander looked beyond the others to where a young woman crouched beside a fern, staring at their cooking pot with longing eyes. When the others turned to look, she scurried into the protection of the darkening forest.

"Woman of the forest, you are welcome at our campfire." Grey Wolf spoke gently. "You will not be harmed. The stew is about ready. Come join us. Do not be afraid."

There was no response. The woman remained a shadow among the trees and ferns. She did not come any closer, but neither did she leave. Sergeant Tandrak dished up the stew, and as they ate, the girl slowly crept in toward the fire.

"Don't be afraid," encouraged Sergeant Tandrak. He held out the steaming ladle. "We mean you no harm. Here, let me dish you a bowl of stew."

Suspicion flashed in the girl's eyes. She looked from Sergeant Tandrak to the others. They could see her fear. Strangely, when her eyes came to Xzwindra, the girl's fear seemed to intensify, and she immediately retreated into the shadows. Grey Wolf took the bowl of stew from Sergeant Tandrak and set the libation on the ground. The girl crept forward to where she could reach the bowl. She grabbed it and retreated only a short distance before she wolfed the stew down ravenously. It seemed she had not had a meal in days.

"What is your name?" asked Grey Wolf. She just looked at him blankly and continued slurping at the stew bowl. He told her his name and introduced each of the others. "Do you live here in the forest?" His question was met with silence.

"Do you understand our words?" asked Captain Favel. She nodded. He smiled. "Do you have a name?" She nodded. "Is it a pretty name?"

"Lrondie," she said. Her voice was sweet and mellow.

"That is indeed a pretty name," responded Captain Favel. "Don't be afraid, Lrondie. We will not hurt you."

"Face!" she said, pointing at Grey Wolf. Captain Favel laughed. She was apparently afraid of the paint and the wolf head that draped over Grey Wolf's own.

"Grey Wolf is harmless," assured Captain Favel. "He looks a bit strange, but he will not hurt you."

She pointed at Xzwindra. "Hag!" she said angrily.

"Hag?" questioned Xzwindra. "What does she mean by that?"

"What is a hag?" Captain Favel lifted his shoulders questioningly.

"Heather Hags – evil!" said the girl. "I will not return!"

"Of course not," agreed Captain Favel. "But Xzwindra is not a hag. She is not evil, Lrondie. Xzwindra is good."

Lrondie looked at him skeptically and then looked long and hard at Xzwindra. Finally, she nodded. "Different," she said, and she cautiously scooted closer. Her livid brown eyes sparkled, her waist-length black hair shone, despite being dirty. Though dressed in rags, her delicate features pleased the eye.

"They will come," she said, and her eyes again danced with fear. "You must leave. You must flee from this place."

"Who will come? Why must we flee?" asked Captain Favel.

"The Heather Hags will come. They will imprison you. They will make you their slaves!" Urgency edged her voice.

"Slaves?" Grey Wolf's tone beckoned her to tell more.

So Lrondie told her story. "I am the daughter of Tundruli, the Hag of Hags. Though born and raised a hag, I refused to participate in their perversions. The Heather Hags make love woman to woman. However, they keep man slaves for breeding purposes. The hags treat their slaves like animals." She hesitated. A tear sat on her eyelid. "The hags kill the weak, the sick, and those no longer useful for breeding. And when a male child is born to one of the hags, he is left out in the forest as a sacrifice to Bayl, the great serpent who rules the forest. Bayl comes and swallows the child whole. This I have seen with my own eyes. And because I would not practice the hags' perversions, my mother disowned me and sent me out into the forest to be judged by Bayl. And Bayl has condemned me to live alone in the forest these ten years."

"How could a mother do such a thing? And how in history have you survived in the wild for ten years?" Compassion and anger stirred in Captain Favel's voice. "What do you eat? Where do you sleep?"

"I eat what I find." Londie stuck out her bowl for more of Sergeant Tandrak's stew before continuing. "I forage for roots, fungi and eat leaves and snails when I have to. And I sleep beneath the trees. And the one who made the trees protects me. I do not fear Bayl. The one who made the forest is greater than the one who rules the forest."

"Have your people always lived in these woods?" asked Kander. Londie's story fascinated him.

"No." Londie shook her head. "The Heather Hags came to Marshwood Forest not fifty years ago. They came to establish paradise, a realm where they would be free to do as they pleased. Back then they called themselves Wood Queens. But not long after they came, they were struck with a plague. They claim it was brought on by the heather leaves from which they made tea. The disease caused deformities. They no longer stood tall and stately like queens. They became bent and twisted like the heather bushes. Thus, they became the Heather Hags." She hesitated and then pointed to herself. "See." Londie stood up. Her back was humped, and her shoulders curved forward and were crooked so that she leaned a bit to one side. Her upper left arm twisted outward so that when her hand hung at her side, the palm faced forward. And her right calf also had an unsightly twist to it. Her foot stuck outward, and she limped when she walked.

"And now a new disease affects the Heather Hags," continued Londie. "The new disease brings death. Those who get the disease waste away. They age before their time.

And their children are born old and die young. Their slaves are affected as well. And if you are enslaved by the Heather Hags, you too will grow old too quickly. That is why I tell you that you must flee this place."

"It doesn't sound like it would take much to defend ourselves against the bent old women you describe," said Sergeant Tandrak.

Londie smiled mischievously. She waved a crooked finger in the air. "You will not see the hags, but their darts will find you, and you will sleep the sleep until they have you safely locked away in a cage." Lrondie laughed a crackly sort of laugh. "The hags watch the way through the wood. They will find you. Yes, they will find you. And they will enslave you. You must flee this place at once!"

"Will you go with us, Lrondie?" asked Grey Wolf. "It may be Baruch of the Trees has sent us this way to deliver you from this place of death."

Lrondie's eyes lit up. She had never thought of anyone actually caring about what happened or did not happen to her. She gazed at Grey Wolf in stunned silence.

"Yes, Lrondie," added Captain Favel, "we would like you to come with us. We are your friends. We do not worship Bayl. We bow only to Baruch."

Lrondie covered her eyes and wept.

Grey Wolf slipped off into the forest early the next morning to scout the way. He returned with a frown creasing his brow. "Lrondie spoke truth," said the desert warrior. "The Heather Hags are aware of our presence. They wait in ambush. To avoid them, we will have to circle to the south.

Lrondie chose to go with the King's Company, though she had no idea where they were going. Grey Wolf gave her his hand and pulled her up to ride behind him on Sterling Grey. As Lrondie and Grey Wolf rode, they talked and an affinity grew between them. They both understood the awfulness of slavery. They had both lived alone in the wild. Both were rejected by their mothers, and neither knew who their father was. The others of the King's Company pitied Lrondie because of her disfigurements, but Grey Wolf took no note of the deformities.

Led by the desert warrior, the King's Company rode south and then attempted to go east again, but thick foliage and impassable bog pressed them farther and farther south, until they came to a small stream that flowed east. The stream itself was not deep, but the marshy bed over which it flowed made it impossible to cross. They worked their way eastward along the stream until they came to where a large tree lay fallen across the creek. They cut the tree flat and then carefully led the horses across the precarious bridge to where high ground stretched south and east.

Captain Favel tied a rope to the bridge and to his horse and pulled it away from the far bank. As he loosed the rope, the end of the tree drifted downstream and over to the close bank. The company cheered. They all felt more at ease with the stream between them and the Heather Hags.

They followed the small stream, which eventually joined a much larger stream flowing out of the northwest. They continued along the river traveling eastward. After more than a week of trekking about the unusual forest, avoiding snakes, and watching extraordinary birds, the river led them to the eastern edge of Marshwood. There they looked out over an expansive morass called the Bog of Marshmoor.

The Bayl River, as their map named it, blocked their way to the north, and the great bog denied them further passage to the east. They had no business to the south and had no desire to return the way they had come, so they made camp on an island of dry ground at the edge of the forest. Grey Wolf slipped off on foot to see if the Heather Hags had made any attempt to follow them. Captain Favel and Sergeant Tandrak examined Pegran's map to get a better idea of where they were and how they might best get to where they were going.

"We either go back and take our chances with the Heather Hags, or we raft our way through the Bog of Marshmoor," said Captain Favel.

"Well, I certainly prefer poling a raft to the idea of having to trek through that awful forest again!" Sergeant Tandrak cast a baleful eye toward Marshwood. "And those miserable snakes, whether poisonous or nonpoisonous, provide as much incentive to raft the bog as the hags do!"

Indeed, on several occasions, they had encountered large and small snakes. If it had not been for Grey Wolf's quick thinking, a thirty-foot Bayl would have crushed Sergeant Tandrak, as Lrondie called it. The Bayl had dropped half its body from a tree branch and instantly wrapped Sergeant Tandrak in its coils.

Captain Favel drove his spear through the creature's head, while Grey Wolf tied a rope around the snake's tail and cinched it to the tree branch from which it hung. Writhing in pain, the wounded Bayl released Sergeant Tandrak and attacked the branch that pinched its tail, curling, twisting, and even sinking its fangs into the bark. They left the snake to its own survival without looking back – the worst of numerous encounters.

Captain Favel, Sergeant Tandrak, Kander, and Xzwindra cut trees, felling them into the river, stripping, strapping, and constructing a raft that would carry them and their horses. They had been working on the raft for two days when Grey Wolf finally returned. Lrondie had feared that the hags might have taken the desert warrior, so when she saw him walk out of the forest, her eyes sparkled with delight.

"The hags are about a day's journey behind us," Grey Wolf explained. "They obviously know that there is no passage to the east, so they wait near where we camped last night ready to ambush us when we return."

"Well, if they wait back there for two days, it will take them another day's travel to get here, and we will be gone – poling our way through the Bog of Marshmoor," said Captain Favel as he directed Grey Wolf's attention toward the river. "Hopefully, they will wait that long." He nodded toward where the others were working. "The raft won't be as fancy as our last one, but it will do the job."

Two-and-a-half days later, they prepared to board the horses. They attempted to lead them aboard, but the wary beasts resisted. They did not take to the idea of rafting through the bog. However, speaking calmly and coaxing gently, including someone pushing from behind, the company finally got the nervous equines on board. They loaded their supplies, glanced toward the forest, and were ready to go.

The raft, made of logs two to four feet in diameter, stretched more than twenty feet side to side and thirty feet end to end. Small logs cut with a flat surface lined the dips between the larger logs. The chinks were pitched with mud and grass. Two poles were infixed in the middle of the raft with a tether line for the horses between. They poled the raft away from shore and drifted out into the bog.

Grey Wolf had left for a time and rejoined them just before they pushed off. He had slipped away to check on the hags. "None too soon!" he said as he tethered Sterling Grey and pointed back toward the forest. The others looked but saw nothing. Lrondie hid behind Grey Wolf, trembling with fright. Kander and Sergeant Tandrak leaned into the long poles.

"There!" Captain Favel pointed toward a large willow tree at the edge of the forest. The Heather Hags stood looking out from between the willow's drooping branches, their eyes flashing with anger as their quarry slipped away into the bog.

Chapter 43

*T*he Bog of Marshmoor was a vast expanse of floating marsh grass, reeds, and water willow trees, interspersed by tangles of thick swamp brush. At times the bog seemed almost unnavigable as the swamp travelers attempted to maneuver their large craft around the water willow trees that stood above the morass on roots that looked like twisted stilts. The reeds and swamp brush with roots that reached down into the muck below the surface of the water also hindered their progress. And root systems that held the large mats of swamp grass in place, keeping them from floating hither and thither over the bog, kept the raft from moving freely over the bog as well. In the middle of the Bog of Marshmoor, Pegran's map showed a large lake named the Murkmere. They intended to cross the lake.

The King's Company found the Bog of Marshmoor delightful but frightening. It was delightful because of the vast variety of extraordinary birds that made their home in the swamp. Their songs filled the air and lifted hearts. And their colorful plumage captivated the eye. The thunder of a hundred large birds taking to wing as one caused them to momentarily cease their activities and stand in awe. Small birds peeped, and large birds squawked. Birds with long legs waded, while birds with short legs hopped and flitted from bush to reed. Birds with webbed feet paddled aimlessly from here to there, while birds with long narrow toes walked unhindered across the beds of grass with their heads oscillating back and forth. Short-billed bug-and-seed eaters mingled with long-billed fish eaters. Some of the birds sported pointed bills, and others displayed flat bills. All the birds competed for the title of most colorful. "Not a plain bird in the Bog," commented Kander.

But the Bog of Marshmoor also vaunted its frightful features. Currish-looking, long, black eel-like fish, with rippled gills, mottled blotches, and googlish eyes, slithered beneath the surface of the water. And the large-headed, mud-brown gazing fish, as Kander called it, four to six feet long, sported a strange looking antler-like horn on top of its head. The gazing fish would suddenly poke its head out of the water and stare at the passersby with seemingly ravenous, iridescent yellow eyes. And there were snakes: mottled green, black, brown. Some were as small as a foot in length, while others were more than ten feet long and a foot in diameter. Sometimes the snakes swam beneath the water like eels, and at other times they lay coiled on the swamp grass or lazily draped about tree branches. Interestingly, none of the snakes ever attempted to board the raft.

Xzwindra suspected that the swamp dragons, as she called them, did not like the smell of the horses. And for that matter, she did not like the smell, either.

Captain Favel tried to keep the raft cleaned off, but still, the smell went with them.

The journey from Marshwood through the bog to the Murkmere, took three-and-a-half days. The river moved slowly, while the morass did all it could to hinder their progress. At times they had to pole their way around trees and islands of grass, but at other times they were able to simply let the raft float with the current until at last they reached the lake.

Once on the Murkmere, the now weary rafters faced a headwind blowing out of the northeast. And out on the lake they discovered another interesting peculiarity of the Marshmoor, small islands of swamp grass, unanchored roots dangling beneath, pushed by prevailing currents and winds, floated freely across the surface of the Murkmere. And they found themselves pushed in among the islands of swamp grass and away from the current of the river, which they were counting on to get them across the lake to the outlet since the lake was too deep to pole. They tried paddling the heavy raft but to no avail.

"Round poles don't make very effective paddles," commented Sergeant Tandrak.

"Perhaps we can rig some kind of sail." Captain Favel never seemed to panic, even in the worst of circumstances. "Then we could use the wind to scud the raft back into the current."

Rigging a sail appeared to be their only hope. So they set to work stitching together a patchwork sail out of whatever they could afford to use for that purpose, an extra jerkin, a pair of pants, or a blanket. But after rigging a pole near the front of the raft and attaching the A-shaped sail to the top of the pole and the sides of their craft, the wind died—total calm. And it was only then that they noticed an unusual, large blanket of thick swamp grass floating in the middle of the lake. The island of matted grass captivated their interest in that unlike other blankets that lay flat and grassy, this bed of swamp grass appeared to have haystack-like clumps of something growing on its surface. But the island floated at too great a distance to be able to clearly identify the true makeup of the strange clumps.

The lull lasted three days. Then as suddenly as the winds had died, they came to life again. But much to the anxious rafters' disappointment, a strong northeaster pushed them even farther from the current that flowed across the middle of the lake. They hurriedly lowered the makeshift sail.

"Drat!" cried Kander. He pointed toward the distant island. "That mass of swamp grass is blowing our way. And if this wretched wind doesn't shift, it will pin us against the swampy shore and make sailing impossible. Then we'll be stuck out here until a southwest wind kicks up. And who knows when that might be?"

As the bed of swamp grass approached, what had looked like clumps of brush took on the appearance of beaver huts made of sticks—small willowy branches and leaves, mud-caked, and dried to a gray-brown hue by the wind. And some kind of animal appeared to be moving about on the face of the grassy island. The rafters readied their weapons just in case the creatures should prove aggressive or edible. They had not been able to bring themselves to kill any of the birds, and although they had tried to spear some fish, their efforts had proved fruitless.

However, the creatures that inhabited the floating island proved neither hostile nor edible. In fact, the swamp creatures looked almost human and yet not.

As the massive mesh of swamp grass pushed up against the raft and pinned it to the shore, the inhabitants of the grass island grouped to stare at the people who had intruded into their world. The King's Company stared back at them.

The strange, almost human creatures, on closer examination looked froglike in appearance. They stood upright with a slight stoop to their backs and bend to their knees. The creatures gamboled about on large webbed feet and gestured freely with their larger than normal hands, also slightly webbed. They wore no clothes. The unusual creatures didn't seem to have any aspects that needed covering. Their broad protruding mouths gave the appearance of perpetual smiles, and their eyes, sitting like two bubbles on top of their heads, sparkled with life. They had no apparent noses or ears. But mossy-looking hair sprouted in a disheveled feather-duster look on top of their heads between and behind their eyes, hair that came in a variety of colors—green, greenish-yellow, brownish-yellow, and shades of brown. And the creatures all gawked and smiled at the rafters.

"Be careful," whispered Captain Favel as the grass island encompassed the raft. "The creatures may be more dangerous than they look."

The inhabitants of the floating island looked at each other questioningly and then looked back at the intruders. The frog people continued to smile. As the raft and the mass of swamp grass settled against the not exactly stable shoreline, one of the frog people stepped forward as if to greet them.

Captain Favel and the others instinctively took a step backward.

"Howdy! Howdy! Howdy!" it declared. "We ain't had no visitors to the marshmoor in more than three hundred years. Sure is nice to see some human folk. How'd ya ever bring those big animals across the swamp? By the Bog, they look heavy enough ta sink an island. Course, yer island's made a' different stuff than ours. That's as it appears, sure 'nough."

Captain Favel and the others breathed a sigh of relief. The creature's demeanor utterly disarmed them of fear. "We came down from Marshwood forest by raft – trees that float," said Captain Favel. But the creature didn't seem to understand. "Anyway, once we got to the Murkmere, the wind blew us off course, and we haven't been able to get back out into the current so we can get across the lake to the outlet. And now, to complicate our situation even further, we are trapped by your island."

"Marsh mud and grass rats – think nothing of it." The apparent leader of the strange clan waved his hand rather too wildly above his head. "When Baruch's ready, he'll send a backwind, and away we'll all go, back ta the other side. Might be a day. Might be a week. Might be a month. But in Baruch's time, the wind 'il blow. Everything in Baruch's time. Yes sir, in Baruch's time. No hurry out here in the Bog. No, sir, there's no hurry, by muck and by mud! No, sir, no reason ta be in a hurry out here. Yer not in a hurry, are ya?"

"We are, but we aren't." Captain Favel couldn't help smiling. He stepped to the edge of the raft and extended his hand. "I'm Captain Favel," he said. The creature looked at the extended hand and seemed dumbfounded as to what it meant. Captain Favel withdrew his hand and gesturing to each of the others on the raft, introduced them by name. Each of the frog people bowed slightly as each name was mentioned.

"We are from Xzwendaria and are passing through on our way to a village called Eknard." Kander sounded in a hurry, and the leader of the clan gave him a wide-eyed look.

"By sail birds and eel fish, that's interesting." The leader swung his hands wildly again. "Didn't know such places existed. But hey, didn't know you existed till we squashed up along side ya here. No, sir, by muck and by mud, had no such idea. But don't be in a hurry. All in Baruch's time. Yes sir, in Baruch's time."

Kander frowned because he was indeed in a hurry, and being stuck out in the bog irritated him immensely.

One of the other frog people, a creature with leafy-looking yellow hair stepped up and whispered in the leader's ear, then stepped back to join the others. The leader's eyes rolled in a circular motion, and he slapped the side of his head. Then he grimaced and rubbed away the pain.

"By the bog, I do forget my manners," he declared apologetically. "I'm Freddie Bogfrogl, this is Fendrick Bogfrogl, and that is Freda Bogfrogl, and Falin Bogfrogl, there's Felisa Bogfrogl, over there, Fenela Bogfrogl, and he's Frinkie Bogfrogl, and that's Frankie Bogfrogl, and Frannie Bogfrogl, Fedula Bogfrogl, Farin Bogfrogl, behind him little Fusha Bogfrogl, and that little guy is Fister Bogfrogl, the baby is Finkie Bogfrogl, and her mom is Frukie Bogfrogl, that's Faddy Bogfrogl, and next to her Filbert Bogfrogl." Then with just a hint of disgust flashing in his eyes, he turned to the fellow with the leafy yellow hair. "And this is my grandson, Fiffle Bogfrogl. But he prefers to be called F. F. Bog Frog. Anyway, by muck and by mud, that's us the whole lot of us, every F Bogfrogl in the bog! "

"You have quite a family, Mr. Bogfrogl," responded Captain Favel, and he offered a slight bow. "Do other creatures like yourselves dwell in the bog, or are you the only ones of your kind?"

"By muck and by mud, you're a smart one!" declared Freddie Bogfrogl. "But Bogfrogl is not our name. Bogfrogl is what we are. We are five families of F Bogfrogls. We're just one of four clans of Bogfrogls. There are also the B Bogfrogls, the L Bogfrogls, and the G Bogfrogls – Twenty-five Bogfrogl families in all. And last we bumped into each other, there were thirty-two B Bogfrogls, twenty-one L Bogfrogls, and forty-seven G Bogfrogls. That means there are one hundred eighteen of us in all, by fen and by fern." He stopped and tilted his head toward the yellow-haired fellow. "Now, if F. F. Bog Frog would ever get married, we would begin our twenty-sixth family. But no! Beula Bogfrogl isn't to his liking! She is the eldest daughter of the B Bogfrogl clan leader. But

F. F. Bog Frog has an eye for Lillie Bogfrogl, the daughter of a second family instead of a first family. However, first families must marry before second families, so Beula has to marry before Lillie is eligible. And Gretta Bogfrogl is older than Lillie, so before Lillie can marry, Gretta has to get hitched too, but no one wants Beula or Gretta, so we haven't had a new family formed in more than twenty years."

After further discourse about the fact that Bogfrogls were Bogfrogls, and even though they capitalized Bogfrogl, they being the F Bogfrogls, F was their name and Bogfrogl what they were, Freddie invited Captain Favel and his "family" to Toure Fenait, as they called their floating island. Captain Favel and the others carefully stepped over onto the bed of swamp grass. It was spongy beneath their feet but did not give way to the extent they thought it might. Still, they felt as if at any moment they might break through the grass and slide into the dark waters below. It took them some time to get used to to the strange environment of the grass island.

The island, basically nothing more than a desolate mass of swamp weeds, stretched about a half mile in diameter, and its shape appeared to be more or less round. Scattered over the midsection of the island, five beaverlike houses formed a small village, the village of the F Bogfrogls. The mud houses were larger than they had appeared from a distance and were quite roomy inside.

"How do you occupy your time?" asked Kander inquisitively. He could not imagine living such a drab existence as the Toure Fenait appeared to offer. There seemed to be absolutely nothing to do.

"Ah, we do live the life, by muck and by mud," declared Freddie Bogfrogl with a wild wave of his hand. "We talk and laugh. But then, a' course we talk and laugh. Who doesn't talk and laugh? By the bog, there is nothing better than to talk and laugh. But we also fish. Tasty! Tasty! Gotta' eat, ya know. So when we fish, we talk and laugh. We swim a lot too. A' course, when we swim, we laugh and talk. Talk and laugh, laugh and talk, that's the life!"

Xzwindra broke into Freddie's explanation at this point. "You swim?" she exclaimed. "What about the snakes?"

"Snakes?" Freddie slapped his knee. "Why, bog snakes are harmless. They eat fish, not Bogfrogls."

"Tell em' about the popheads!" interjected one of the Bogfrogl children.

"Yes! Yes! The popheads!" laughed Freddie excitedly. "Nothing like riding a pophead. By the bog, they're fun!"

"What are popheads?" asked Kander.

"Oh, by mud and by muck, you don't know what a pophead is?" declared Freddie with disbelief written on his face. "Well, come along. I'll show you."

Freddie led the way out toward the lake. The Bogfrogls did not really walk. They put one foot in front of the other but seemed to gambol with a hop-lope motion. As they stepped, they would sort of hop from one foot to the other. And when the children were in a hurry, trying to keep up with the lope of the adults, they would spring forward with both feet rather like a frog. The whole clan went along for the show. When they came to the edge of the lake, a fellow carrying a small basket stepped forward. It wasn't long until one of the muddy-brown with an antler-like horn and shining yellow eyes – a fish the King's Company had seen earlier – popped its head up out of the water and gazed at them. The Bogfrogl with the basket tossed the pophead a fish. The pophead caught it, mouthed it once, and then gulped it down whole.

"You ride those things?" said Sergeant Tandrak. He shook his head in an expression of disbelief. "I'll believe that when I see it!"

Even as he spoke, F.F. Bog Frog kerflopped into the lake. Not a jump. Not a dive. A true to life kerflop! But then, what Bogfrogls lacked in coordination they made up for in pure joy of living. As F.F. Bog Frog hit the water, the entire clan broke out in laughter. They hooted, hollered, and slapped their knees as F.F. swam up behind the waiting fish, latched onto its horn, and squatted on the fish's back. Using his webbed feet to hold on, he gave a hitching movement as if to say, "Giddy up." Instantly, the pophead took off. The fish did not dive. It stayed just beneath the surface of the water, and F.F. Bog Frog laughed wildly as he appeared to skate across the surface of the lake. The pophead swam in a wide circle. As it approached the island again, F.F. pushed himself off the pophead and came skimming across the water on his belly, laughing like a child playing tickle bee. The whole time the clan was chitter-chattering amongst themselves and laughing joyously.

Once rid of its rider, the pophead twisted about, came to a stop, and gazed expectantly at the fellow with the basket, who in turn tossed him his reward. Then one of the small children jumped in and took a turn, after which Freddie tried to talk his guests into giving it a try. "Take a turn, by muck and by mud."

They all graciously declined, except Lrondie. Much to everyone's surprise, with a smile on her face and a twinkle in her eye, she slipped into the water and dog-paddled over to the waiting fish. As best she could, she wrapped her legs around the fish's body, grabbed onto its horn with both hands, and off they went! Lrondie's legs immediately pulled away from the pophead's slick skin, and she flew skidder-scudder over the water on her belly. By the time the pophead made its circle, Lrondie's initial sensation of breathless wonder had passed, and she was laughing uncontrollably—a laugh of pure delight. It was the first time the King's Company had heard her laugh. It was indeed the first time she ever had laughed. And she laughed so hard that it brought her to tears. The whole clan of Bogfrogls waved their hands, hooted and hollered, and laughed with her. They were delighted! And from that time on they treated Lrondie like one of their own.

"Bogfrogl runs in her blood, by mud and by muck!" declared Freddie with another stinging slap to the side of his head. "By the bog, she's a gamer! Hooray for Frondie!" he shouted. And to the F Bogfrogls that became her name.

The rafters, held hostage by the grass island, stayed with the F Bogfrogls for nearly a week before a strong wind began to blow out of the southwest. As the wind increased in intensity, the Toure Fenait slowly began to move away from the shore of the lake. Captain Favel and the King's Company reluctantly returned to their raft. Because of the heaviness of the logs and the protection provided by swamp willows and brush at the edge of the lake, they had to hoist their sail and pole the raft away from the shore. As they drifted out, the wind caught the sail, and they were off. Not at any great speed, but they were on their way again. Freddie Bogfrogl sent F.F. Bog Frog with them to guide them across the Murkmere and through the waterways leading to where the south fork of the Savage River exited the Marshmoor.

"It's tricky, by mud and by muck" Freddie had explained. "You will have to pole your raft through the bogway, a maze of channels that braid their way through a land of water willows that we call Wander Wood – 'cause you could wander there for days and have no idea where you were a wanderin'."

"Grandfather, I would like to see the world beyond the Bog of Murkmere," declared F.F. Bog Frog. "I've been as far as the great river. I can show them the way. And if Baruch wills, someday I will return to marry Lillie."

"It is forbidden!" cried his grandfather. "The Bog is our curse. We are no longer free to walk in the world beyond the marsh. You know that, Fiffle Bogfrogl, so why do you press me on the matter, by muck and by mud?"

"Because the time has come, Grandfather," said the smiling F.F. Bog Frog. "Two days ago Baruch came to me in a dream. I stood at the edge of the bog looking out on the world, and he beckoned me to go, and walk, and learn."

"You and your confounded dreams!" spat Freddie Bogfrogl. He still smiled, but for the first time, he displayed an air of open irritation. "By swamp grass, your dream doesn't mean a thing! As if our curse isn't bad enough, you seem determined to bring a worse curse on us!"

But F.F. Bog Frog would not be daunted, and finally, with a line of swamp-lingo expletives (swamp grass, mud, muck, snakes and the like) his grandfather gave in.

"It'll be a curse to us all, by muck and by mud, you wait an' see, Fiffle Bogfrogl!" Were Freddie's final words as F.F. Bog

Frog joined Captain Favel and the King's Company on the raft.

"I'm off to see the world!" shouted F.F. Bog Frog, as he wildly waved good-bye to all the F Bogfrogls, and they wildly waved good-bye to him.

Once out on the lake, the raft, with its makeshift sail, moved more swiftly than the flat, heavy Toure Fenait. The Toure Fenait slowly and steadily drifted toward the northeast. Using the sail, Captain Favel and Sergeant Tandrak directed the raft more toward the north. They passed the Toure Fenait and the waving Bogfrogls, caught the river current, and then turned the log boat toward the northeast again, and shortly after midday, they bid the F Bogfrogls a last farewell wave. Turning from the Toure Fenait, they cast their gaze to the distant lush green willows of Wander Wood.

Kander gazed at Wander Wood and wondered what dangers it held. What would they face next? Still, he held hope in his heart that their quest would succeed and the heir would be found.

Chapter 44

General Bodrak, determined to win the hearts of the people of Zwexdrof, required his Pagyn troops to maintain a low profile inside the city, and he lowered taxes – slightly – from the exorbitant level to which Xvardris had raised them. He lowered the price of bread and made more bread available in the marketplace. Xvardris had driven up the price of bread by requiring a large quota of all bread baked in the city to go to his troops.

The people applauded the changes, but still they did not trust the Pagyn ruler. As far as the people were concerned, since General Bodrak was not an Xzwendarian, he did not belong on the throne. However, few dared express their opinions in public.

"A good man, for a Pagyn, but there be not a royal drop a' blood in his body!" grumbled one old man.

Further, despite his efforts to win over the people of the city of Zwexdrof, General Bodrak still pushed the Pagyn war machines on toward Havenholt. So as the King's Company sailed across the Murkmere, the Pagyn war machines reached the halfway point in their slow, tedious crawl toward the Resistance stronghold, but there their drag-along pace came to a halt. The slaves, Findr and Boger, saw to that.

The war machines consisted of two giant rams, four large and six small catapults, and four armored scaling platforms each several stories high. Slaves and horses worked together to pull the war machines through the forest inch by inch on immense wooden wheels, while other slaves and horses worked to clear charred stumps from the war machines' path. Still other slaves and horses leveled the ground over which the heavy siege devices would pass.

The war machines were originally constructed of heavy, damp green logs. But the weather had been warm and dry for months. The now exsiccated logs put a smile on Findr's face.

He, Boger, and six other slaves slipped away from their slave camps in the middle of the night. Come evening the guards were more interested in drink and games than watching slaves. It had been months since anyone had tried to escape one of the slave camps, and the fools who had tried were caught, hung by their feet, and whipped until dead. A punishment all the slaves were forced to watch – and learn from. But what they learned was to hate their taskmasters.

The eight subversive slaves used pitch for accelerant. They dumped the pitch on the rams. They didn't have enough pitch for all the machines, so they piled charred brush under each machine, including the rams, set them on fire, and hoped for the best. The pitch-covered rams quickly became great balls of flame. The other machines burned more slowly. Guards came running, but so did slaves, the latter doing what they could to hinder the former. Water wagons were brought forward, sometimes at the cost of slaves crushed beneath their wheels. Soldiers, and some slaves, manned the buckets, while other soldiers manned spear and sword to keep insurgent slaves in line. More than one hundred brave slaves died in the fray, including Boger.

Wounded, Findr fled into the charred forest where he hid and watched. Wearing a satisfied smile, he tended to his wound as best he could. The battering rams had burned and toppled in a heap, a total loss. One of the scaling platforms had burned to the ground. Flames had severely charred the other two platforms and one of the large catapults, while damage to the other machines appeared to have been minor. But all in all, it would take months to repair the towers and even longer to build new battering rams and start them moving forward again.

"Bought some time—six months or more," Findr mumbled as he got to his feet and made his way toward Havenholt. "It'll be at least nine months to a year before they'll be able ta begin their assault on the fortress."

He thought of the slaves who had died, including Boger. "A high price," he breathed, "but then the price the slaves have paid has been high anyway, serving under the crush of the Pagyn heel."

As he made his way through the blackened forest, he wept for his friend and the other slaves who had laid down their lives for their country. "After this war is over, I will build a monument to those slaves right there in the middle of Tangle Wood," he promised himself.

Findr was not just a slave. He was a captain in the Resistance. Boger had been an officer in the Resistance as well. It took Findr two-and-a-half days to make Havenholt. Along the way, he met others who had fled after the battle by fire.

All total, two hundred and twenty-six slaves escaped to the Resistance stronghold. With the dead, they accounted for most of the Xzwendarian slaves. And from that day forward General Bodrak used only Pagyn slaves to repair and once again to move his war machines forward. In all, he brought in nearly three thousand Pagyn slaves, promising them freedom once his army breached Havenholt. General Bodrak had no further problem with slaves hindering the work. With eyes that looked beyond the walls of Havenholt to freedom, the gullible wretches willingly put their shoulders to the ropes.

Chapter 45

Wander Wood, a labyrinth of dense water willows and dark waterways, mocked the King's Company. The river current, dividing between numerous waterways, became exasperatingly random and impossible to follow because often the flowing waters simply passed under tangled tree roots that formed a barrier to further passage, which meant backtracking against the current.

"Tough work, by mud and by muck!" said a smiling F.F. Bog Frog after they had ignored his directions for the second time.

But the second time was the last time they ignored their gangly guide. And so he directed them hither, thither, and ultimately through the bogway and back to the open river. Smiles all around, and slaps on the back – and thanks to F.F. Bog Frog for coming along.

"Never would have made it without you, Fiffle." Captain Favel shook the Bogfrogl's hand (not that F.F. had any idea what that was all about). "You're welcome to continue with us, but it's not too late to make a small punt and head back to the lake if you've changed your mind."

"I must pursue my dream," said the smiling F.F. Bog Frog. "By the bog, I will not turn back. I'll not return until I can marry sweet Lillie!"

Slowly, the rafters meandered the snaking river, generally toward the north and then generally toward the west, until finally they left the Bog of Marshmoor behind them. Before them lay a windswept grassland that seemed to stretch for mile upon mile. The Wilderwarr, through which the South Fork of the Savage River snaked, swept westward to the great Neverwood Forest and eastward to Warrwood Forest.

Down the Savage River floated four men, two women, their horses, and a wide-eyed, smiling Bogfrogl.

"What lies beyond this flat land?" Kander brushed back his blowing hair to no avail.

"Pegran's map shows a town named Warrz down where the Savage River is joined by the Kener River that flows out of Neverwood." Captain Favel's clothes whipped at his body. "We'll have to stop there for supplies."

"What can you tell us about Warrz, Grey Wolf?" asked Sergeant Tandrak whose whiskers shivered with the wind.

"We are beyond the lands I have roamed." Grey Wolf stood as if untouched by the wind, except that the shiny gray hair of the wolf headdress fluttered in waves like the grass. "I have heard of Warrz, but I know nothing about the town or the people who dwell there. The pictures do not speak of Warrz."

"Perhaps F.F. Bog Frog knows something?" Xzwindra's long hair whipped about her face.

Sergeant Tandrak addressed his question to Fiffle, who shrugged his shoulders and gestured with his hands out to the side. He had never been beyond the edge of the Marshmoor nor had any of the other Bogfrogls.

"What about you, Lrondie?" asked Captain Favel. "Did your people have any contact with the people of Warrz?"

"All I know is that the Heather Hags did not like the leader of the people of the Wilderwarr." Windblown and sitting on the supplies, Lrondie looked almost normal. "He is said to be a very ugly-looking man. My mother hated Char Face because he feared Baruch and would endure no evil, though she claimed he was a Pagyn. Mixed words. However, I do know that there are people who live at Warrz and trade with the Heather Hags in goods—and slaves. Tundruli said that if Char Face were ever to find out, especially about the slave trade, six men near to him would probably pay with their lives. Char Face hangs lawbreakers – so they say."

"Any laws about intruders?" Sergeant Tandrak grinned as he spoke.

"That, I don't know." Lrondie brushed back her hair, then looked from Sergeant Tandrak to Captain Favel. "But if Char Face discovers that I am a Heather Hag, my life is forfeited."

From behind her, Grey Wolf laughed for only the second time. "I assure you, your life will not be forfeited, Lrondie. You are not a Heather Hag. In fact, you never were a Heather Hag. They are what they are because of their perversions. You are not what they are because you refused to participate in their perversions. You are as I am, an orphan and a wanderer. Make claim to no more than that."

"Kind words, Grey Wolf. However, when the people of Warrz look on my twisted form, they will know." Sadness brimmed Lrondie's voice. "What I am cannot be hidden."

"What you are is a brave woman who stood for what is right." Grey Wolf remained undaunted. "Baruch will reward you for being who you are. Remember, despite your physical features, you are not, and never have been, a Heather Hag. You are a child of Baruch. Trust him, Lrondie."

"I will." She spoke quietly, her head bowed. Grey Wolf momentarily laid a gentle hand on her shoulder. She smiled, and then he turned away.

When the King's Company came to Warrz, men waited at the quays to haul them ashore. Their progress across the Wilderwarr had been watched for days. Soldiers tied their raft to a large dock. They led the horses ashore and took them to a nearby stable. Men with crossbows and swords instructed the rafters to follow them. The soldiers looked at Lrondie with malice in their eyes, and they gazed on F.F. Bog Frog with great wonder and a sparkle of amusement. Grey Wolf elicited questioning looks and fear. When the soldiers spoke, they spoke to Captain Favel because he had identified himself as the leader of the group.

As the group reached the street, Captain Favel held up a hand. His company came to a stop. The soldiers turned their weapons toward them.

"Before we go any farther, we would like to know where are you are taking us." Captain Favel spoke as if unintimidated by the display of weapons. "We request audience with the clan lord called Char Face."

"You will see Char Face, all right," said the leader of the soldiers. "He's been awaiting your arrival since you were sighted floating down the Savage three days ago. And the gallows is ready besides."

"The gallows?" insolence edged Kander's voice. "Why the gallows? Is there no justice in Warrz?"

"You travel in the company of a Heather Hag," said the soldier. He cast Lrondie a disapproving glance.

Grey Wolf gently wrapped his fingers over her shoulder to comfort her. The bend in her back, and her limp were obvious. In her heart, she cried out to Baruch, not for herself but on behalf of the others.

"Have no fear," whispered Grey Wolf.

The soldiers led the detainees to a large square building in the middle of the village. Inside, the leader told them to wait in a hallway just outside two massive doors. Of course, with guards surrounding them, they had no other choice. The leader left them, passed through the doors, then after several minutes, returned. The doors swung open, and Captain Favel and the other rafters were ushered in. Grey Wolf kept Lrondie toward the back of their group where she would not be easily seen. And although he was ready to defend her innocence, he knew that any attempt at physical resistance would be futile in the face of the great array of weaponry.

Char Face sat in a thronelike chair at the far side of the rather bare and cold-feeling room. Beside him stood a tall, fairly handsome man who had a noticeable scar running down his cheek. The man with the scar smiled as the group approached. Char Face did not.

Char Face was as ugly as Lrondie had indicated. He had no hair whatever, and his face, badly scarred, had a distorted look about it. But the man's eyes glared bold and fiery, and his presence was commanding. He addressed Captain Favel. "Why have you come to the Wilderwarr?"

Captain Favel explained as best he could, but Char Face remained skeptical. Why had they come from the south out of the great swamp? And what was this strange creature they had brought with them? He had Fiffle step forward so he could take a closer look.

"Every word Captain Favel has spoken is true, by muck and by mud!" F.F. Bog Frog thought that being asked to step forward gave him the right to address the man who sat before them. "By the fen, these are people a Bogfrogl can count on. And by the swamp grass in the bog, you'd do well to count on em' too. Lrondie says you believe in Baruch. Well, so do all of us. So there, Mr. Char Face. What will you do with that, by muck and by mud?"

Fiffle's boldness took Char Face by surprise. The ugly-looking man broke his sculpted pose, and burst forth in laughter. "Well, quite a tongue for a frog!"

"A Bogfrogl," reprimanded Fiffle. "The name is F.F. Bog Frog, to be exact."

"Well, F.F. Bog Frog, if you want to talk about muck and mud, tell me this." Char Face turned and winked at the man with the scar. "If these friends of yours are believers in Baruch, what are they doing consorting with a vile Heather Hag?"

Char Face raised his voice as he spoke and came to his feet. "You, girl, the one standing by the funny-looking fellow with the paint on his face and the weird hat on his head, step forward and explain yourself."

Reluctantly, the others stepped aside so that Lrondie could limp forward. But to everyone's amazement, she stood perfectly straight when she stepped forward and did not limp. Her twisted leg appeared to be as straight as any normal leg, and her arms hung naturally at her sides.

"Gildus, are you sure this is the one?" Char Face grimaced as he turned to the soldier who had brought them. "She doesn't look like a Heather Hag to me!"

"My lord, her back was bent. Her leg and one arm were twisted," declared Gildus anxiously. "You can ask the others. They saw her. I... I don't know what to say, my lord."

"Well, what do you have to say for yourself, girl?" demanded Char Face as he turned to face Lrondie.

"Sir, I am not a Heather Hag. I am an orphan and a wanderer. I am a child of Baruch." She bowed meekly.

"So what is this stir about you being all bent and twisted like a Heather Hag?" Char Face leaned forward in his chair as if to intimidate Lrondie.

"Sir, you see with your own eyes what I am, and that I am not what I have been accused of being." Her demeanor remained sweet and gentle.

"Well, yes." Char Face sat back and leaned his chin on his hand, watching Lrondie thoughtfully. "I can't deny my own eyes, can I? Still, this report disturbs me."

"Sir, if I could have audience with you in private, I would gladly tell you more." Lrondie looked up and caught his eye. "But please, sir, do not press me further in front of these others."

"What's your name, girl?" Char Face wrinkled his browless forehead.

"Lrondie," she replied, dropping her eyes again.

"Very well, Lrondie." Char Face almost smiled. "Your audience is granted. Gildus, take the others outside for a time. And the rest of you can wait outside as well. I will talk with Lrondie in private. Be gone now!"

When they were alone, Char Face sat down again and beckoned Lrondie to speak.

"Sir, moments ago I spoke true words. I am not a Heather Hag. I truly am an orphan and a wanderer." She sighed softly. "However, sir, when I walked into your court, I was bent and twisted in the very way poor Gildus described me. Nevertheless, in my moment of need, Baruch healed me. Please hear me out, sir." Char Face had started to speak. He nodded, and Lrondie continued. "My mother, Tundruli, leader of the Heather Hags, disowned me many years ago. I have no idea who my father might have been. But I refused to participate in the perversions of the Heather Hags, and for that, and because I believed in Baruch, I was cast out into the forest to die. I have wandered Marshwood for more than ten years, nurtured and kept alive by Baruch until the moment of my delivery."

Char Face stared at the girl momentarily. "An interesting story," he said. His eyes seemed to smile, though his face did not, probably could not. "I believe you. You shall not die. Thank you for telling me all. You are a brave woman. Nothing further need be said about this matter. You are not a Heather Hag."

"But sir, more must indeed be said, though it is not pleasant and will not please you." Lrondie spoke gently but firmly.

"Speak on."

Char Face leaned forward, for Lrondie spoke softly lest others beyond the doors should hear.

"The Heather Hags keep male slaves for the purpose of breeding," she whispered. "This you must know. Before my mother cast me out into the forest, I heard her talking with her. . .friend, and she said that there were six men close to you who were trading with the Heather Hags, both in goods and in human lives. And over these ten years that I have lived alone in the forest, I have watched boatmen come and go from the Wilderwarr bringing the Hags both goods and male children. The boatmen wore masks. But as they approached the forest, I saw the face of one boat rider just as he was donning his mask." She stopped. Her hands trembled as she folded them against her breast.

"I have long suspected as much, Lrondie. So tell me, have you seen that rider since you arrived here in Warrz? Do not withhold the truth from me."

She looked up, and their eyes met.

"Sir, the rider in the forest was the man standing beside your chair when we entered the chamber," whispered Lrondie. "The man with the scar on his right cheek."

"Welkner?" The color drained from Clan Lord's face. His eyes became dark with anger. He had to consciously control his voice. "That man has been a trusted friend and advisor for more than twenty years. Welkner? Surely, Lrondie, it was someone else you saw."

"I am sorry, sir." Lrondie dropped to one knee. "I can only tell you who I saw. And it was the man with the scar."

"Lrondie, just a word further, if you will." Char Face stood and lifted her to her feet. They talked briefly, and then Char Face clapped his hands loudly. He had his minions usher the other rafters back into the chamber. This time Char Face welcomed them as friends and offered to help them on their journey in any way he could. They thanked him for his offer of hospitality. The whole time that Char Face and Captain Favel talked, Lrondie stared at Welkner. He noticed her gaze and became uncomfortable.

"Sir." Lrondie turned to Char Face and broke into the conversation. Urgency rode her voice. "There is something else I must tell you. It too has to do with the Heather Hags, and I think you will find it extremely interesting."

"I will speak with you in a bit, girl." Char Face spoke curtly, as if he did not like being interrupted. "Welkner, take the girl to my private quarters. I will speak with her there when I finish discussing the provision of supplies with Captain Favel."

Welkner forced a smile, but Lrondie saw a dangerous glint in his eye as he motioned for her to follow him. She protested, but Char Face pressed her to stop interrupting and to wait in his chamber, once again dismissing her and the man with the scar. Hesitantly, she followed Welkner out of the room.

The Clan Lord's personal quarters seemed rather simply appointed for someone of position. A thick curtain divided the large room. The doorway by which they entered led into the Clan Lord's bedchamber, austerely furnished with a bed, a storage chest, a table and chair, and an oil lamp. A finely woven rug covered the floor. Welkner and Lrondie passed beyond the curtain to the living chamber, where two comfortable-looking overstuffed chairs sat before a hearth and an inviting fire. In a corner off to the right, a table with chairs formed a dining area. Farther to the right of the dining area, another door provided entrance to the chambers. Lrondie wondered if perhaps it might not provide access to a kitchen area. She could smell the aroma of food, but the table stood bare.

Welkner gestured for her to sit in the chair to the left of the hearth. He sat in the one between Lrondie and the door. "Well, girl," he began with an encouraging tone, his hands together and fingertips dancing against each other nervously, "what is it you wanted to tell Char Face? Perhaps you can tell me, and I can save you the bother."

She smiled. "No. What I have to say is for his ears alone and especially not for yours." Lrondie hugged the far side of her chair as if trying to keep as far from Welkner as possible.

Welkner's face flushed. He stared at Lrondie and shifted uncomfortably in his chair. "Tell me, why were you staring at me when you came back form meeting with Char Face?" His smile had the look of a sneer. "Perhaps you have seen me before? Perhaps in Marshwood?"

"Please, I wish to talk only to the Clan Lord." Terror filled Lrondie's eyes. "I have nothing to say to you."

"Look, girl, you have plenty to say to me!" Anger rode Welkner's low, raspy voice. He rose from his chair and moved toward Lrondie, his demeanor intimidating. "Now, you're going to tell me exactly what you have in mind to tell Char Face!"

"I saw you there!" Fear rode Lrondie's voice. "I saw you bring slaves to Marshwood. You sold male children to the Heather Hags!"

Welkner laughed quietly. "You saw me, huh?" As he spoke, venom tinged his words. "Well, I tell you what, hag. If you whisper a word of this to Char Face, I'll see that you hang on that gallows you passed when you came into town. You see, in essence, you just admitted that you are one of those forest queens. And, if I tell Char Face that you are a Heather Hag, he will believe me. He believes everything I tell him. So if you know what's good for you, keep your mouth shut! You just forget all about what you saw in Marshwood, and you'll ride out of town with your friends unharmed. But I warn you. . ."

At that moment, Char Face stepped from behind the curtain.

Welkner turned to face the Clan Lord. His face drained of color. He tried to speak, but no words came out.

"So it is true." Char Face locked eyes with Welkner. "My trusted friend and advisor. Welkner, how could you? All these years? You break my heart, good friend."

"You're a gullible, self-righteous fool, Char Face!" Welkner moved toward the door. "I have never been your friend. I have simply used you all these years, and you were blind, Char Face, blind!"

Welkner broke for the door. He threw it open and came nose to nose with the tip of Gildus' sword.

"Yes, all these years," repeated Char Face. A deep sadness rippled his voice. "Arrest him, Gildus, and find out who conspired with him. I'm sure one of the others is Palkup. Pick him up too. He's tight with Welkner and has been living rather high for a farrier. He's not one who will want to swing alone. You can bet he'll readily implicate the others."

Gildus and his soldiers left with Welkner clasped in chains.

Char Face stood at the door and watched. He turned again, a tear wetting his cheek. He made an effort to smile at Lrondie. "You played your part well, Lrondie. Thank you." He grimaced and sighed deeply. "You are a courageous woman. But please, all of you leave me. I would be alone with my grief. I will see you again tomorrow."

The rest of the King's Company had entered the chamber with Char Face. With a twinkle of the eye and a nod of the head, they all told Lrondie that they were proud of her. She stood to her feet, and Grey Wolf put an arm around her and gave her a gentle hug as they left Char Face to his inner struggles.

A page named Pipkin showed them to the inn where they would be staying. He also told them where their horses were being kept and where they could pick up supplies. "You are free to come and go as you please," he said. He bowed slightly and left.

Kander flopped on his bed, and his thoughts went to the ugly Clan Lord. A Pagyn who believes in Baruch. The thought perplexed him.

Chapter 46

The next day Char Face held a feast in honor of Lrondie and the other guests. Lrondie sat to the Clan Lord's right and Captain Favel to his left. Char Face proposed a toast to Lrondie for her courage demonstrated in uncovering Welkner's vile conspiracy. The clink of chalice against chalice followed.

As the feast progressed, Captain Favel asked Char Face how he had become Clan Lord of the Wilderwarr, and, "Is the report that you are a Pagyn accurate?"

"Ah, now that's a story!" said Char Face, without smiling.

The hall suddenly became quiet. Most who were present had heard his story before. But they never tired of it.

"The truth of the matter is, I have never been a Pagyn," explained Char Face. "However, I was born in the land the Pagyns now possess, in a town called Netrag. The Pagyns killed my parents, and burned my home – with me in it! Look at my ugly face!" He nearly shouted the words. "Burned beyond recognition! A wonderful young girl named Warzella snatched me from the flames. Our town and our realm are named in honor of her.

"At the time of the fire, I was but a wee child. Warzella fled to Prauge with me in her arms. However, the people of Prauge did not take to an ugly child. 'Cursed!' they said. 'The child must die!' To protect me, Warzella fled to the mountains.

"An outlaw named Rylan found us and took us in. He married Warzella and became my stepfather, so to speak, since Warzella had for all intents and purposes become my adoptive mother. Well, eventually the Pagyns forced Rylan to seek refuge beyond the mountains to the east. The Pagyns pursued Rylan because he was an outlaw. He was an outlaw because he believed in Baruch. So seeking a home, Rylan brought Warzella, me, and a band of renegades with him to this great plain.

"Fifty-five years have swept by since he established this village and named it Warrz and since he declared the Wilderwarr his homeland and himself Clan Lord. Twenty years ago, Rylan died and I became the Clan Lord. My dear Warzella died just ten years ago."

"But why do you go by the name Char Face?" Lrondie squinted as if in pain as she spoke.

"Char Face," he muttered through a sigh. The Clan Lord folded his arms and leaned back in his chair. "Throughout my years of growing up, other children mocked me—'Char Face! Char Face!' they would cry. Now I wear the name proudly, for that is who I am. My birth name was Brokre, but I use it no more. I am Char Face."

After a moment of silence, those seated around the table broke out in applause. The guests joined in.

Char Face stood and bowed graciously. "But another story begs to be told!" he cried as the applause died away. "Our new friend, F.F. Bog Frog, surely must have a tale to tell. Stand up, good friend, and tell us of your people!"

Fiffle stood up, bowed three times, and smiled at everyone.

"Well, by the bog, I had not expected such an honor." F.F. put one hand over his heart and swept the other wide in a flamboyant gesture as he began his story. "Actually, you see, this is the first time in over three hundred years that a Bogfrogl has ever left the bog. By muck and by mud, it has been a long time coming, hasn't it?"

Everyone laughed, which delighted Fiffle to no end.

"By the bog, you are a most gracious group of listeners. Indeed, you are!" Then F.F. told the enraptured listeners how 319 years back in time, the bogfrogls had been men like themselves. Four families, all dirt poor, had gone to the mountains in search of gold. What mountains? Where? "No one knows," he said. Then F.F. assured the listeners that the four families were humble—"very gentle people, and before leaving on their venture, they sought Baruch's blessing. Baruch appeared to the head of each family in a dream and promised to bless their endeavor. So Fogerty, Bander,

Landau, Gudmar, and their families left the city—what city, I do not know—and made their way up into the mountains where they found gold in abundance. They built their own small village and hoarded their gold in a vault that Gudmar built in the side of the mountain. 'By rock and by pick, it was their gold!' he declared.

"Well, Fogerty, Bander, Landau and Gudmar became proud because they were the blessed of Baruch. They also became greedy, wanting more and more gold to stack in their storehouse. And they became selfish, allowing no one else to live in their village or to share in their abundance.

"After a time, by pick and by shovel, Baruch came to their village in the guise of a weary traveler. And so it was that that fateful night he went to each man's house, and knocked on each man's door. Fogerty looked on the traveler with a scowl engraved on his face. The traveler asked for a piece of bread, a drink of water, and shelter for the night. Fogerty responded curtly, 'I'll be a frog in the bog before I share my bread and water with such as you!' and he slammed the door in the traveler's face.

"Baruch approached Bander's door. Bander answered in kind. "Why, I'll be a frog in the bog before I have anything to do with the likes a' you!" He too slammed his door in Baruch's tear stained face.

"Landau proved a bit more tolerant than Fogerty or Bander, but no less selfish. 'I do wish I could offer you a slice a' bread, and a cup a' water – but my children! I cannot take bread from my poor children to feed a stranger. One must provide for his own, you know. And I will be a frog in a bog before I take from my own to give to another. There is a stream in the valley for drink, and many a tree for shelter from the dew. So, good-day, sir.' And Landau too shut his door in Baruch's face.

"The weary traveler went to the last of the four houses. Gudmar saw him coming, threw open his window, stuck his head out and declared, "I'll be a frog in the bog before I open my door to some wretched beggar. Don't even bother knocking! Turn your feet to the road and be gone!

"That night as Fogerty, Bander, Landau and Gudmar slept Baruch again appeared to them in a dream, and the four were greatly troubled, for he appeared to them in the form of the weary traveler who had visited their village. Tears trickled down Baruch's cheeks. 'You sought my blessing, and I blest you,' said Baruch gently, lovingly. 'Yet, today I came to your door asking for no more than a piece of bread, a cup of cold water and shelter from the elements, and you closed your door in my face. Of your own free will you have turned my blessing into a curse. You have become proud, greedy and utterly selfish. Thus, as you have declared, so it shall be.'

"'What did we declare?' their minds echoed in response to the visitant.

"'You said you would be a frog in the bog before you would share your blessing with me.' said Baruch. 'It shall be so. When you wake in the morning your wealth will be gone, the mountains will have disappeared, and you will find yourself in a great bog. It is the destiny you have chosen. From this night forward you will be known as bogfrogls.'

"Did Baruch transport them, by mud and by muck, from the mountains to the bog?" asked F.F. in behalf of those listening. "Did the mountains sink and the bog rise during the night?" He jacked a shoulder. "Questions we have — but no answers."

When F.F. finished his tale the chamber remained silent. Those who sat at the Clan Lord's table did not applaud, although Fiffle had told a wonderful story. In fact, no one in the room had ever been touched so deeply by a story.

"Such a terrible curse your people have endured," Char Face finally stammered. A great sadness weighted his voice. Heads nodded, and numerous sighs of agreement followed.

"No! No! No!" F.F. waved his arms wildly, and laughed light heartedly. "By muck and by mud, as I see it, when we were blest we made the blessing a curse. And when we were cursed, the curse became our blessing! I tell you, by the bog, Baruch is loved by every bogfrogl in the marsh. Joy and laughter echo across the Murkmere. Pride? What's to be proud of? And greed? The only thing we could hoard is swamp grass. Selfish? Not any more. We are a simple people, and we have learned to share what little we have – though we seldom have anyone to share it with. By fen and by marsh, we are indeed a blest people!"

Fiffle tossed his froggish head back and laughed that kind of laugh that is infectious. Others began to laugh, and then the room exploded with thunderous applause. In fact, F.F. Bog Frog received the first standing ovation ever given (so now you know where the standing ovation originated).

When F.F. Bog Frog realized that the people laughed and clapped for him, his greenish face grew dark with embarrassment, and he waved a wild hand as if to say, "Please, I am not worthy of such adulation." Poor F.F. swallowed his laughter, sat down, and wept.

When the applause ceased and knives and forks were clinking again, Char Face turned to Fiffle, put his hand on his shoulder and said, "Thank you, F.F. Bog Frog. And I tell you this, your people shall ever be looked upon with great esteem in the realm of Wilderwarr. I would count it a privilege, F.F. Bog Frog, if you would allow me to call you friend."

"By the bog!" Fiffle flapped his hands together jubilantly. "I would be delighted to be your friend. Wouldn't want it any other way!"

The next day Captain Favel and Grey Wolf met with Char Face to discuss their journey to Eknard.

"We would know more about the way that lies before us," said Grey Wolf.

Char Face nodded. "The Outmoor is a pleasant land," he began as he looked from one to the other. "The road from here to Eknard is well traveled. I know, because I do considerable business with a merchant who goes by the name Ferret. Although I don't like doing business with Pagyns, I have little choice. Anyway, the road follows the river to the Draw Gulch. It winds down into the canyon to the great Spanway Bridge, twists up out of the gulch again and straight to Eknard.

"However, the people you're looking for are probably not at Eknard. The Pagyns send the banished to Xziland Isle, to a town called Krock, where they pay the Chameleon to house their exiles for them."

"Is the Chameleon a Pagyn? Is he one with them?" asked Captain Favel.

"No, the Chameleon serves only himself. For that reason he can be bought. You might say that he serves the highest bidder." The Clan Lord attempted a smile. "You will have to make contact with the Chameleon through a fellow called the Weazel, and you'll have to have something to bid with, gold, silver, jewels, something of value."

Captain Favel and Grey Wolf gave each other one of those "now what do we do?" looks. They obviously didn't have anything of value with which to bid for the Chameleon's services. Char Face laughed knowingly, and told them that if they could find the bogfrogls' gold they would be in business. At that they enjoyed a good laugh together.

"Well, I guess we'll cross that bridge when we get to Eknard." Captain Favel shook his head. "We can promise much, but our ability to pay will depend on the restoration of the heir to the throne. If we can get the Chameleon to do business on that basis we have plenty of bargaining power. We shall see."

"Very doubtful." Char Face shook his head, offering little hope. "I've never known the Chameleon to deal in promises. He prefers cash he can see to a promise he cannot see. But who knows. Perhaps you will be lucky. He likes the Pagyns' gold and silver, but he despises them otherwise. Anyway, when you get to Eknard you will need to make contact with the Ferret. He will tell you where you can find the Weazel."

"And how do we find this fellow you call the Ferret?" asked Grey Wolf.

"He is not a fellow." Char Face laughed good-naturedly. "The Ferret is a woman. She's tough as brass nails, but she can be trusted. Down by the docks you will find a warehouse with a large sign painted on its face: Outmoor Enterprises. Inquire for her there.

"If you don't find her at the warehouse, check at the Dock Side Inn. The owner is a fellow named Dinkin. He'll know where you can find her. I'll have my men accompany you as far as the warehouse. We have supplies to pick up, and that way you won't have to worry about possible trouble along the road between here and there. After that you're on your own."

So the next day, accompanied by three wagons, and twenty Warrz horsemen, the King's Company set out again for Eknard.

Chapter 47

*T*he journey to Eknard proved long and tedious but uneventful until the crossing of the Spanway. There the travelers met a column of soldiers coming from the west with their faces set toward Eknard—forty men with spears and shining helms riding warhorses that pranced proudly along the road. As the soldiers drew near, a contingent broke away from the orderly column and met the captain of the horsemen of Warrz at the northern end of the bridge. Words passed, and the soldiers inspected the wagons, then turned and rode off to rejoin the column.

Captain Favel had watched the column of soldiers as they rode along the north ridge of the gulch toward the Spanway. He had led the King's Company aside into a copse of sheltering trees where the Pagyn riders could not see them. After the column passed on toward Eknard, he and the others rejoined the horsemen of Warrz.

Captain Cadman met them grim-faced and eyes flashing. "Eknard will not be a safe place for you." He nodded toward the road ahead. "They didn't say who or what they were looking for. However, they asked if we had seen any strangers, travelers from the west. They took a good look at each of my men. Our dark hair and brown eyes mark us well. Your fair hair and light-colored eyes mark you well. They will be waiting and watching at Eknard."

"How much farther is Eknard?" asked Captain Favel. He too gazed down the road to where the Pagyn soldiers had disappeared.

"Four or five days, depends on how things go." Captain Cadman raised his eyebrows and tilted his head in a gesture that said, Who knows?

Captain Favel pulled out his map. He pointed a finger toward the forest that lined the northern ridge of the gulch. "The road runs along the eastern edge of Thiswood." Captain

Favel turned again to Captain Cadman. "What if the seven of us were to go through Thiswood into the foothills west of Eknard, while you and your men take the main road? We could camp there, and later one or more of us could slip into town under cover of darkness."

"As far as I know, no one is living out in the foothills. It's a barren place." The captain of the horsemen pursed his lips thoughtfully. "And it wouldn't do for us to be seen together anyway."

After a moment's thought, the captain reached back and took a curled ox horn from his saddlebag and handed it to Captain Favel. "We will be in Eknard for three days. Should you get in trouble, give a blast like this." Captain Cadman blew the horn softly, lest he alert the column of Pagyn soldiers. The horn pealed forth a low but resonate note. Then the horseman of Warrz put his finger over a hole near the curve of the horn, and the pitch rose considerably. "Waa-eee! Waa-eee!"

"However, you will want to blow it for all you're worth." Captain Cadman handed the horn to Captain Favel. "If we are in or near the village, we will hear and will come to your aid. But after three days, we will be gone, and you will be on your own."

That afternoon when they came to Thiswood, the two groups parted company. Captain Cadman and his men continued along the main road to Eknard, while Captain Favel and the King's Company passed through the arm of Thiswood into the hills. Through the woods, they cautiously continued on toward Eknard. They camped in a well-hidden ravine a few miles southwest of the city.

When darkness finally enveloped the hills, Captain Favel, Sergeant Tandrak, and Kander slinked off toward the lights of Eknard. Xzwindra argued her right to go as well, but Captain Favel would not hear of it.

"We can't all go," he said. "Finding the child is Kander's responsibility. And Sergeant Tandrak is the only one of us with dark hair and brown eyes. You are along to help in whatever way you can. And right now you can help most by being patient and waiting for us right here."

She unhappily complied.

The others made no protest. Fiffle was perfectly content to wait at the base camp, as were Grey Wolf and Lrondie. Grey Wolf had gladly helped them find their way, but the quest fell to them, not him. "As you wish," he responded.

Captain Favel, Sergeant Tandrak, and Kander circled the city, which was more like a large village, to the north. The south would certainly be watched. They dropped down to the sea and approached the wharf from the beach. The tide was out. The wet sand reached back under a twenty-foot bank where hanging roots and sod formed a partial tunnel. The undercut took them to a large building standing on barnacled pilings that protruded over the water. Beyond the building, they found a ladder leading up to the wharf.

Sergeant Tandrak climbed up first to see if the way was clear. But at the top of the ladder, he came face to face with two inquisitive sailors. "Hey, mates!" he declared loudly. "Did ya see 'er? She were a beauty, she were!"

"Did we see who?" asked one of the sailors curtly.

"Merdela!" said Sergeant Tandrak as he stepped to the wharf with a slight stumble. "A mermaid she were. The finest lookin" mermaid I 'er set me eyes on, mates."

Sergeant Tandrak stumbled sideways and fell on a pile of ropes. He mumbled incoherently, as he sprawled out on the coils and pretended to pass out.

"Mermaid!" groused one of the sailors.

"Drunken fool!" said the other.

Tandrak watched through nearly closed eyes as they walked off toward the city. Once they were gone, he called down to Captain Favel and Kander who quickly joined him.

"Nice work!" laughed Captain Favel.

"Merdela?" Kander shook his head disbelievingly.

Sergeant Tandrak laughed with them but with an eye toward the city.

Dark clouds had rolled in from the sea at sunset. Lightning suddenly lit the shadows where they moved along the wharf looking for the warehouse Char Face had told them about. Rain began to patter on the wooden docks and on the cowls that hid their faces. They passed a few people moving here and there through the night. None showed any signs of interest. After all, what could possibly be construed as unusual about people passing in the dark on a rainy night?

When they finally found the warehouse, it was engulfed in darkness, and the doors were all locked. They knocked, but no one answered.

"Well, it's on to the Dock Side Inn," said Captain Favel.

They had little trouble finding the wayhouse. Captain Favel and Kander waited in a dark alley behind the Inn while Sergeant Tandrak went inside to find Dinkin. But as the burly sergeant entered, his eyes immediately found the two sailors from the quay sitting at a table with two Pagyn soldiers. The sailors recognized him as well.

He stumbled into the room with his face twisted in a goofy sort of smile. "A bottle fer da mermaid, Merdela! Mos' beautiful a women!" he muttered as he lumbered over to the bar. "The bes' in the house!"

The two sailors whispered to the soldiers. The four of them laughed mockingly.

"So, ya saw the mermaid Merdela, did ya sailor?" called out one of the soldiers. "Where did ya see her? Inside the bottle a' cheap liquor you were suckin' on?"

The whole place broke out in ribald laughter.

Sergeant Tandrak laughed the hardest of all and stumbled backward onto a bar stool, almost landing in another sailor's lap. "She crawled right out onta the brim a' the bottle an kissed me smack on the lips!" He waved a hand wildly above his head.

Again, laughter echoed through the inn.

The only one not laughing was a giant of a man in a white apron whose thick, wavy hair was parted in the middle. He stood behind the bar polishing glasses. His thick mustache hung in a frown.

"All right, sailor, back out to the street!" declared the giant. "Go find yerself a hole ta crawl in till ya sober up. I'll have no drunks given my establishment a bad name."

"A bad name?" Sergeant Tandrak turned to face the giant. "The Wharf Inn Dock ain't no bad name. No, sir. An' I tell ya what, I ain't leavin' the Wharf Inn Dock till I've had a roun' fer the mermaid, Merdela!"

The giant did not answer a word. With quickness beyond his size, he came around the counter, caught Sergeant Tandrak by his cowl and the seat of his pants, and headed him for the street. The sailor, whose lap Sergeant Tandrak had almost fallen into, jumped up and opened the door. Once out on the walkway Sergeant Tandrak whispered, "From Char Face. I'll be in the alley."

The giant launched him out into the mud in the middle of the street. "And don't come back till yer sober!" he shouted angrily as he turned to the door again.

Back inside, one of the sailors sitting at the table with the Pagyn soldiers waved the giant over. "Hey, Dinkin, who is that souse?" Suspicion edged his voice. "I don't recall seeing him around here before."

"A recluse from up the coast who likes to think he's a sailor," lied Dinkin. "He doesn't come around much. Once in a blue moon, and only when he's drunk. Probably makes his own. An' when he does come around, he always carries on about Merdela the mermaid! He'll probably crawl back to his hole an not show his face fer another six months."

The sailors and soldiers laughed, shook their heads, and made further snide comments about the wretched sot, and then things returned to normal.

Dinkin shined the rest of his glasses before quietly slipping off to the backroom.

"Tolm, my lad, I'll be out fer awhile. It's all yours." Dinkin put on his coat, tipped his hat to his helper, opened the back door, and stepped out into the alley. He shifted his eyes to the right then to the left, but no one was in sight.

"Over here." The voice broke silence from the shadows on the opposite side of the alleyway.

"Follow me!" said Dinkin. He led them along the dark corridor of back walls, through a wooden fence and into a large woodshed, appropriately stacked with firewood. Dinkin lit a lamp and took a good look at his guests.

"So you're the reason the soldiers are hangin' about the town. Cadman told me to watch for ya." Dinkin turned to Sergeant Tandrak. "I must say, at first ya even had me fooled when ya came stumblin' inta the inn that way. The sailors asked about ya, an' the soldiers were listenin' careful, but I covered yer tracks. They didn't ask yer name, but if they do, I'll tell em it's Dogmar. So go by that name. It's a cover most of the people here in Eknard are familiar with. Ya live in a hole of a cabin north a' town. Ya got no family. Ya think yer a sailor, but you've never sailed a day in yer life. An' here's a bottle. Half full. Ya always carry one in yer pocket. Ya make it yerself."

"What about the Ferret?" asked Captain Favel. "Where can we find her?"

"Don't know right off." Dinkin pushed back his cap and shrugged his shoulders. "But I'll find out. Meet me here this same time tomorrow night." Dinkin paused, and his eyes shifted warily toward the door. "Did you hear that?"

They hadn't heard anything. Dinkin stepped outside and shut the door behind him. Five minutes later, he returned. "Guess I'm a little jumpy." He tipped his hat. "Tomorrow."

Dinkin blew out the lantern, and they all cautiously left the shed.

Tolm waited outside wedged behind the side of the shed and the fence. When the light went out, he scurried through the shadows, slipped in the alley door, and went straight to the table where two sailors and two anxious soldiers awaited his return. He told them what he had heard, and they passed him five gold coins.

When Dinkin returned to the inn, the sailors and soldiers were gone. He gazed toward the now deserted table and felt a twinge of apprehension. He brushed it aside.

Tolm had told the soldiers that Dinkin had talked to strangers out in the woodshed at the end of the alley.

"How many strangers?"

"Couldn't tell, but there were at least two different voices. . .maybe three. Couldn't see nothin' and couldn't hear a whole lot either. But hear the strangers say they would meet Dinkin at the woodshed same time tomorrow night."

"Could you tell if one was that drunk?" asked one of the soldiers.

Tolm nodded. "Yes, one of the voices sounded a lot like the drunk Dinkin threw out in the street."

The soldier lifted an eyebrow. "Still drunk?" he asked.

Tolm shook his head. "No. He didn't seem to be drunk anymore. He spoke clearly."

The soldiers grinned and gave the lad a wink as they slipped him the coins. Once outside, the soldiers paid off the sailors and went on their way.

Captain Favel, Sergeant Tandrak, and Kander returned the next evening. They arrived early. Slipping through the still night—the sky had cleared, and stars sparkled above the village—they made their way to the old woodshed. There they waited in the dark, silent, listening for Dinkin's heavy footsteps.

Down the alley, Dinkin removed his apron, turned things over to Tolm, and headed for the back door. But as his big fingers reached for the doorknob, he suddenly stopped. A prickly feeling ran up his spine. "Something's wrong!" he mumbled to himself. "Can feel it in my bones!" He turned from the door and went to the window. Slowly, quietly, he cracked the window open enough to allow him to see out into the alley. He looked to the left. "Soldiers!" he whispered. He looked down the alley toward the woodshed. Soldiers were coming from that direction as well. He slowly shut the window.

"Hope they're runnin' late!" he mused as he turned and headed out toward the commons.

Tolm watched nervously as Dinkin stalked past the bar and out the front door. As the door banged shut, Tolm's nerves jumped, and the glass he had held in his hand shattered at his feet.

In the alley, the Pagyn soldiers closed in on the woodshed. Slowly, silently they passed through the wooden gate. Then, with the woodshed surrounded, the leader approached the door. But the soldier's footsteps did not fall with the same weight as Dinkin's. The Pagyn placed an ear to the door and listened, but he heard nothing. He grasped the handle and pulled. The door was locked. He rapped on the door, hoping those within would think Dinkin had arrived. He could hear the scuffing of feet.

The soldier knocked again. No answer. "We know you are in there. We have the place surrounded." This time the Pagyn beat on the door with his fist. Bam! Bang! Bam! "You may as well come out peacefully, 'cause there's no place for you to go!"

"Well, in that case, I guess you'll just have to come in after us!" Captain Favel boomed in return.

"Don't be fools!" rejoined the Pagyn. "Lay down your weapons, and come out empty-handed, and you'll live to see the dawn. But if we have to come in after you – well, let's just say, there is no need for you to die useless deaths!"

"We may die, but our deaths will not be useless, Pagyn!" shot back Sergeant Tandrak, "Many of you will die with us! So break down the door, and face the wrath of Baruch!"

Outside the soldier swore.

Inside, Sergeant Tandrak put the curled ox horn to the small open window and blew for all he was worth. "Waa...eee! Waa...eee!"

The captain of the Pagyn soldiers stumbled back from the door shaken, by the terrible blast of the ox horn of Warrz.

His men trembled with fear. They looked about, expecting a supernatural host to suddenly appear. But the host did not materialize.

"It's nothing more than an ox horn!" shouted the leader. "Bring the battering ram!"

Four soldiers came charging through the gate with a long, wooden pole at the ready, but as they neared the old woodshed door, the ox horn of Warrz again exploded the night air. The soldiers dropped the ram and fell back.

The echo of the ox horn passed beyond the village and was swallowed by the night. The leader of the Pagyn soldiers urged his men forward.

"It's only an ox horn, though a mighty one! Do not let it strike fear! Stand like men!" he cried. "Now, break down the door and destroy both horn and man! To the ram! To the ram!"

Four brave soldiers hurried forward and picked up the wood pole. And when the great horn peeled its final call into the night, the soldiers stood their ground, drove the ram forward, and with a terrible cracking sound, the wooden door shattered.

TWANG-TWANG! Arrows felled the first two soldiers.

TWANG-TWANG! Another volley drove back the second two soldiers.

As the soldiers fell back, Captain Favel and Sergeant Tandrak exploded out the door, swords flashing in the moonlight. Two more Pagyns fell. Yet, the Pagyns seemed legion. They were everywhere! Flashing blades pressed Captain Favel and Sergeant Tandrak back into a corner where the woodshed butted the high wooden fence. There the two valiant Xzwendarians momentarily held the Pagyns at bay, steel smashing steel.

While the soldiers pressed in on Captain Favel and Sergeant Tandrak, the leader of the Pagyns and two of his men slipped into the shed. Were there only two Xzwendarians? Had there not been three?

Inside, the soldiers met no resistance, only silence, except for the clang of swords outside. One of the soldiers lit the oil lamp that hung near the window. Swords at the ready, the Pagyns examined every crook and cranny. "There were only two of them!" the leader declared. The Pagyn soldiers hurried outside again. "Take them alive!" shouted their leader.

However, a commotion in the alley drowned out his words.

"The horsemen of Warrz!" cried one of the Pagyn soldiers.

The thunder of hooves filled the night.

"Take the Xzwendarians!" shouted the captain. His men drove forward. At the cost of five more lives, the Pagyns finally overpowered Captain Favel and Sergeant Tandrak. Captain Favel took a blade to his right upper arm. His sword fell from his hand. A spear flashed and gored Sergeant Tandrak's left thigh. He blinked, and as he did, the butt of a Pagyn sword came down on his head. The leader thrust open the side gate and the two Xzwendarians were dragged out into the street and tossed into a cart that immediately trundled off to another part of town. The Pagyn soldiers followed, forming a rearguard to protect the cart's escape.

The horsemen of Warrz broke down the wooden fence and engaged the retreating Pagyns. The noise of rattling sabers moved toward the wharf.

Back in the alley, a new turmoil arose. Dinkin and a band of thirty men came tramping through the night brandishing clubs and whatever else they could find to use as weapons. Outside the shed, they found the bodies of the fallen Pagyns and saw the path taken to the street. With a raised hand and a shout, Dinkin silenced his men. They could hear the distant sound of battle.

The giant noticed the lamp left burning in the shed. "Jolkie, you and the others go on ahead. I'll catch up after I douse that lamp."

Jolkie and the other angry men hurried down the street to join the fray, while Dinkin ducked into the woodshed to check out the place and put out the lamp. "Stupid Pagyns should know better than to leave a lamp burning in a woodshed! Careless fools!" grumbled the giant. "Tolm musta' squealed! He'll pay, he will!" Just as he was about to put out the lamp, he stopped. Ay! What's that? He turned and looked toward the door. Am I hearin' things, or is one a' the dead not so dead? Poor soul.

"Help me!" the muffled voice cried again. Then the woodpile began to quiver as if it were alive. "Under here!"

"I'll be!" Dinkin hung the lamp back on its peg and began removing the wood. "Shoulda' noticed it wasn't stacked the same as I had it piled!"

Beneath the wood, he found a dirty and slivered Kander. "What in the ocean's depth are you doin' buried 'neath all this wood?" Amazement brimmed Dinkin's face and then his eyes narrowed. "Ya didn't cop out on yer frien's, did ya?"

"No! If it had been up to me, I would have stood side by side with them against the Pagyns!" Irritation rang in Kander's voice. "But our mission is to return the heir to the throne of Xzwendaria, and I am the one responsible to see that it comes about. So they buried me beneath the wood with the idea that despite whatever might happen to them, I would still be able to follow through on our mission."

Kander dusted off his clothes and looked at the broken door and the dead soldiers just outside the door. "What happened to Captain Favel and Sergeant Tandrak? Are they all right? Did the horsemen of Warrz get here in time?"

"They are not among the dead," said Dinkin. "But beyond that I can't tell you a thing."

"How did the Pagyns find out about our meeting?" Kander shot the giant a wary glance.

"My helper, he's been actin' a mite guarded since last night," said Dinkin. "When I thought I heard something last night, musta' been him listening outside the window. For a few gold coins, some people would sell out their own mother. That's Tolm. Money be more important than principle or integrity, either one. Sad, isn't it?"

"Sad, yes. Perhaps tragic in this case. Let's go find the others." Kander headed for the door, and Dinkin snuffed out the lamp. However, once outside Dinkin headed the opposite direction of the broken fence.

"We'll let the others worry about yer friends." Dinkin motioned for Kander to follow. "While the Pagyns are preoccupied, you had better come with me. The Ferret's waitin'."

Kander protested. He wanted to see to his friends, and then there would be time to see the Ferret! But Dinkin would have none of it.

"Listen, they put their lives on the line so that you can finish the mission ya were sent on," said Dinkin. "The mission must come first. An' chasin' after yer friends could jeopardize your mission. An' ya don't want ta do that, do ya?"

Kander caved in to reason and the giant's overpowering gaze. Dinkin led and he followed as they slipped through the shadowed streets of Eknard, out of the village and into the hill country to the north, to a small cabin nestled in a narrow vale. Smoke rose in wispy streamers from the chimney, and warm rays of yellow light beckoned from the windows.

The Ferret appeared to be nearly six feet tall. She was slender, had black hair, and powerful brown eyes. She exuded confidence. She seemed almost pretty, yet a hardness that she wore like a garment detracted the eye. Her pursed lips and the set of her square jaw indicated that she was all business. There was nothing soft about her.

"Why did Char Face send you to me?" Her fiery eyes made Kander feel uneasy. And her curt tone didn't help either.

Kander explained his mission in some detail. "We must get to Xziland, find the heir, and return him to Xzwendaria. Will you help us?"

"Chameleon will need more than a nice story if you expect him to turn the heir over to you." The Ferret's laugh was harsh. "The Pagyns are no doubt paying a handsome price for the Chameleon to keep the boy and his mother. So...what do you have to barter with? Gold? Silver? I can't imagine that you could have anywhere near the resources the Pagyns have."

Kander cast the Ferret a half smile. "Fact is we have no resources in hand." He shrugged sheepishly as the Ferret shook her head in disbelief.

"I'll talk it over with the Weazel. But I really don't see why we should help you," she responded grimly. "Since you have nothing to barter with, we could jeopardize our operations by helping you, and for what? The Chameleon only speaks the language of jingling coins, a language you apparently don't speak."

"We have no silver or gold in hand, but once the heir regains the throne, all of the resources of Xzwendaria are at our disposal." Kander spread his arms. "For now our promise will have to do."

The Ferret seemed unimpressed but told them to return the following night for her answer. "I can't say one way or the other till I talk to the Weazel. He'd be taking the greatest risk. We'll see."

When they got back to Eknard, Dinkin took Kander to his apartment. "Humm. Now what do I do?" he muttered. He glanced at Kander. "Can't have ya here in town lookin' like that."

A knowing smile suddenly spread his face. "Come on," he said. He took Kander into another room where he dyed Kander's hair black. Light-brown just would not do! He used a cream to darken the pigment of Kander's skin, and he covered each eye with a gray patch that Kander could see through, though poorly.

"You're my blind nephew," said Dinkin. "A ship, the Blue Belly, came in today, and you arrived on it. The captain's a friend a' mine. The ship left already, and no one will know the difference, since most folks know I have a blind nephew up at Dill. Well, for now you're him! Name's Binkie."

"Binkie?" said Kander in disbelief. "You can't be serious?"

"I most certainly am!" Dinkin scowled and crossed his thick arms. "Your name is Binkie, and that's that. At least, it's easy ta remember and easy ta pronounce."

Kander groaned. "What about Tolm?" he said. "Won't he be suspicious?"

"I'll take care of Tolm." Dinkin's scowl deepened. "He'll not be a problem."

The next day when Dinkin opened the inn, Kander sat at a table off in a corner by himself. People stared, asked questions, and at first seemed truly delighted to meet Dinkin's nephew. But Binkie was soon forgotten. Talk turned to the events of the previous night.

"Hey, Tolm!" called one of the sailors. Tolm's mood was grim, but he forced a smile. "What went on out in the alley last night? Hear there were a big fight between the Pagyns and the horsemen a' Warrz? How did things turn out?"

"Don't know," said Tolm, and he curtly turned away.

"You usually know jes' about everything that goes here in Eknard," said the sailor with a laugh. "Yer slippin,' Tolm!"

Tolm wiped tables, and Dinkin stood behind the counter smiling broadly. Kander wondered what Dinkin had told his young helper. Whatever it was he had taken it hard.

"You musta had a bird's-eye view of the ruckus, Dinkin." The inquisitive sailor turned his attention to the giant. "They say the horseman broke down yer fence and that near a dozen bodies were dragged from yer yard this mornin."

"Nine bodies ta be exact." Dinkin shined another glass. "And yes, someone broke down my fence, and someone even splintered the door ta my woodshed – wretched rascals! I heard the ruckus, but by the time I rounded up a few a' the boys, whatever the excitement was, it was over. I understan' that Jolkie and the lads followed on down ta the wharf. He'll be by affer a bit. I'm rather anxious ta find out what happened myself."

He no more had spoken the words when a rough-looking fellow with disheveled hair, bushy eyebrows, a missing front tooth, and bulky, hairy arms came swaggering into the inn. He glanced at Dinkin and winked, and then he turned to the others who waited anxiously for the news.

"Well, Jolkie, what's the word? What happened last night?" asked the inquisitive sailor.

"We had a whale of a street brawl, that's what happened!"

"Well, who won and who lost?" asked a second sailor.

"Humm, I'd say the Pagyns lost," said Jolkie. "Forty a those soldiers beat up a couple a' fellas who had come up from Warrz. The soldiers cornered em in the alley behind Dinkin's place here. Dinkin heard the scuffle goin' on and rounded up the lads, but by the time we got ta the alley, twenty horsemen of Warrz had answered the call of the ox horn. You heard it too, I bet!" The soldiers and a number of other patrons nodded. "Well, we followed the fray down ta the wharf an' waded in on the side a' our friends from Warrz. 'Parently, the Pagyns were tryin' ta kidnap the two fellas. We rescued the poor blokes, but they took quite a beatin'. On the other hand, this mornin' the Pagyn's is buryin' their dead an lickin' their wounds. An' there ain't as many of 'em as there were, by about half. But I imagine they'll send a rider off today, an' the place 'ill be crawlin' with Pagyn soldiers in ten, twelve days or so."

"Where are the fellas who took the lickin' in the alley?" asked another patron. "Don't know the answer ta that one," laughed Jolkie. "Probably trundlin' back ta Warrz wi' the horsemen. They left early this mornin' wi' smiles on every face. They didn't lose a man—nor did we. Those Pagyns is no match fer those horsemen and not fer our lads, either!"

"This is a story that will be told in Eknard fer years to come!" declared one of the old-timers with delight ringing in his voice. The folks who lived in Eknard were not particularly fond of the Pagyns, who tended to usurp authority at their pleasure.

Kander breathed a sigh of relief, though he still felt anxiety for the welfare of Captain Favel and Sergeant Tandrak. It concerned him that they had taken such a thrashing. Also, he was sure they had not returned to Warrz as Jolkie had surmised. He would find them back at camp.

Before Jolkie left the inn, he had a word in private with Dinkin, and Kander could see that the giant was pleased with what he heard.

Chapter 48

When Jolkie left the Dockside Inn, he headed west toward his cabin in the hills. A broad smile stretched his face. Word traveled fast in Eknard, and soon the Pagyns would know that the men they had tried to mob had been rushed off to Warrz. At the least, it would buy some time.

The chimney of Jolkie's cabin, nestled in a wooded vale well off the beaten trail, sent up a feeble rise of smoke that could barely be seen. He only burned well-dried wood. Horses tethered in the shelter of the trees behind the cabin indicated that it was a bit crowded inside.

After bringing Captain Favel and Sergeant Tandrak to his cabin, he had followed Captain Favel's directions to their camp and had brought Grey Wolf, Xzwindra, Lrondie, and F.F. Bog Frog as well. As Jolkie entered, he shook his head. It was not like him to get involved in the affairs of complete strangers, but Dinkin had asked, and he had jumped in with both feet. For some reason, he was glad. It felt good to help someone in need—and to be one up on the Pagyns! "Well, how are the patients?" he asked.

"They're sleeping," said Xzwindra. "Both are feeling pretty sore. And one thing for sure, Captain Favel won't be swinging a sword with his right arm for awhile, and Sergeant Tandrak won't be runnin' any races for a day or two. But they'll be all right, thanks to you."

"Oh, don't thank me. If ya want ta thank someone, ya can thank Dinkin and the Horsemen of Warrz." Jolkie waved his hand as if to brush their praise aside. "Me and the lads didn't do much."

"You have opened your home," said Grey Wolf. "We are grateful. But what about Kander? Why did you not bring him with you?"

"He's with Dinkin." Jolkie grinned. "He'll be okay."

"What about the meeting with the Ferret?" interjected Captain Favel, who had awakened at the sound of voices. Sergeant Tandrak had come to life as well. They waited for Jolkie's answer.

"After last night, things have changed." Jolkie sat down at the table. "Dinkin told me to have you sit tight, that he and yer friend would take care of things."

"Kander is going after the heir alone?" Wariness edged Captain Favel's voice. "I don't like it."

"You have no choice." Jolkie leaned cross-armed on the table. "The shape yer in, ya wouldn't be much help anyway, and after last night, Dinkin said he'd have ta be more cautious. He's come up with a cover for Kander, but how would he cover for any of you?"

"One of us should be with Kander!" said Xzwindra. "Why not me? I doubt the soldiers are looking for a woman."

Jolkie leaned back in his chair and laughed loudly. "You would stand out like a sore thumb in Eknard! Fair skin, light-colored hair, blue eyes. You don't belong, if ya know what I mean. Besides, it's too late. Dinkin's plans are laid. He says wait, so unless ya wanna spoil everything, you'll do jes' that. You'll wait."

None of the company liked the arrangement, but they had no choice. They simply had to hope that Dinkin's plan, whatever it was, would work and that Kander would return with the heir. But would he?

Chapter 49

Kander sat in the corner of the commons and watched sailors and town folks come and go. He listened to stories and rumors. He listened to the telling and retelling of the events of the night before. By midafternoon the story had taken on the trappings of legend. Nigh unto a hundred soldiers subdued by thirty of the town lads and a handful of men from Warrz! Kander smiled. He wondered how the story would be told a year from now.

As one of the lads finished retelling the story again, a donkey brayed outside the door. The bray brought a sudden burst of laughter in anticipation of the fellow they expected to come lumbering through the door at any moment.

"Well, if it ain't Maggot the Diamond Delver!" Dinkin called out in greeting as the wide bottomed, humpbacked prospector came trundling through the door. "Tell me old fella, did ya strike it rich yet?"

"Keep a civil tongue there, Dinkie!" declared Stekner testily. Again the place echoed with laughter. Stekner looked around the room with a satisfied smile. As he did, his eyes fell on Kander and stopped, then deliberately moved on. "Who's the stranger in the corner, Dinkie?"

"Okay! Okay! You win, Humpy." The giant shook his head and laughed. "Call me Dinkin, an' I'll do my bes' ta avoid referrin' to ya as Maggot. An' that's Blind Binkie, my nephew."

"Well, the lad looks lonely sittin' there all by his self." Stekner sauntered toward the corner. "Don't mind if I keep him company fer a spell do ya, Dinkin?"

Dinkin hesitated, and then forced a nervous smile. "No, no, that's fine. I'm sure he wouldn't mind yer company for a bit. But don't bore him too long with yer tales a' gold, silver, and diamonds. He might get foolhardy and want ta run off ta the gulch."

Laughter rumbled the place again. Humpy trundled over to Kander's table and sat down across from him. He stared hard at the gray patches over Kander's eyes, then smiled and winked as if to say, "Glad to see you made it." He called for food and drink for both of them. It wasn't long before Humpy was forgotten and the commons was once again abuzz with a confusion of voices.

"Where are the others?" whispered Humpy. "Have ya got what ya come fer yet?"

"They're camped outside of town," said Kander under his breath. "And no, we haven't found the heir yet, but Dinkin is trying to help us with that."

"Figured as much by the disguise." Humpy laughed quietly and tweaked his head to make sure they were going unnoticed. "Blind Binkie? That's worse than bein called Maggot!"

"Yeah, thanks, Humpy."

The prospector nodded. "Glad to oblige ya, Binkie. Anything I can do to help?"

"Ya' can give me a pile of gold so I can buy off the Chameleon," sniggered Kander in response. "That's our biggest obstacle right now. He trades in cash, not promises. But promises are all we have to trade with."

"So what are ya gunna do?" Humpy looked around yet again to make sure no one was listening.

"Whatever I can," Kander whispered. "I'm hoping he dislikes the Pagyns enough that he will listen to reason and accept our promises of future payment when the heir is returned to the throne. It's our only hope. But first I've got to convince the Ferret that it's worth her while to put me in contact with the Chameleon." He shrugged his shoulders. "In that I don't have any cash, she's not too keen on the idea."

"Sounds like you got yerself a problem, boy." Humpy laughed congenially. "As the old saying goes, 'Eat yer meal and drink yer brew; you'll feel much better when yer through.' I wish ya the best, lad. Sure wish I could be of help."

"Thanks anyway, Humpy," said Kander. "It'll work out. It has to."

They finished their meal. Humpy got up. "Business ta tend to," he said and then left.

Kander found himself hoping that he would return. But he didn't. Kander spent the remainder of the day sitting in the shadows waiting – particularly for the Ferret's answer.

"Well, Blind Binkie, you've had a long day sittin' an listenin' ta the wind blow from this direction an' that." Dinkin laid a hand on Kander's shoulder. The commons still hummed with activity. "Tolm can take care of things here. Let's head for home."

Dinkin took Binkie by the arm. As the giant passed Tolm, he gave him a stern look. Tolm's face turned red, and he forced a smile. Dinkin and Binkie went to the alley and on to the innkeeper's apartment above an empty warehouse. A half-hour later, Dinkin blew out the lamp, and they slipped off to meet the Ferret.

Clouds hid the moon as they stole from town. Dinkin led Kander to a little cabin enveloped in darkness. They entered without knocking. Dinkin lit a lamp then lit a fire in the hearth.

"I hope Maggot doesn't cause us any problems," he declared somberly. "I suppose he gave you what to since he's the only one around who's ever met my nephew, Binkie."

"Oh, you don't need to worry about Humpy!" laughed Kander. "We're friends. We had a good talk. He'd help us out if he could."

Dinkin let out his breath in relief. Humpy had been the only thing that had not gone as planned. "He's a dreamer," said Dinkin with a smile and a shake of his head. "Always going to strike it rich but only finds enough stones ta barely maintain a stock of supplies."

A gentle knock drew their attention to the door. Dinkin cracked a curtain and peeked outside. His eyes showed surprise. The giant unbolted the door, and in walked the Ferret and behind her trundled Humpy.

"Humpy, what are you doing here?" Kander blinked as if he thought the prospector might just be an apparition.

"Humpy and I are old friends," answered the Ferret. Her gentle voice contrasted with her steel-like eyes. "He has persuaded me to help you."

"How in the world did he do that?" Dinkin wrinkled his brow in disbelief.

"Let's just say he convinced me it would be worth the effort," replied the Ferret. "Anyway, the Weazel is waiting with a boat on the north side of Devil's Spit. He'll take Humpy and Kander to Xziland to meet with the Chameleon. You'd better leave now. I'll take care of the lamp and fire."

With Dinkin leading the way, the three unlikely companions cautiously twisted their way through the hills toward the sea. Humpy complained all the way beneath his breath that the night was long, and they didn't need to be in such a hurry. Dinkin's stride was long and deliberate, while Humpy's short stride with an uneven hitch made it hard for him to keep up. Dinkin walked. Kander hurried. Humpy lumbered at a near run, and his donkey trotted along happily.

"Pookshaw, I'll be glad when we get ta where we're goin!" Humpy complained between puffs and wheezes. Dinkin just laughed and kept to his tireless stride.

Devil's Spit was a rocky arm that hooked out into the sea. It began as a rugged high wall and tapered away into a series of rocky islets. North of the spit, a narrow path led down to the beach and a makeshift wharf. There a small sailing ship waited, and beside the ship stood the Weazel.

The nickname, Weazel, fit the man who anxiously awaited their arrival. Tall, slender, yet graceful and deliberate in his movements, he had shaggy hair, beady eyes, a small mouth, and a short pointed nose. His shifty, nervous appearance fit the picture Kander had weaved in his mind. As they approached, the Weazel raised his head, looked this way and that, wrung his hands, and impatiently shifted his feet.

"About time you were getting here!" he groused in a high-pitched squeaky voice. "The tide's going out. We need to cast off and be on our way." Suddenly, his frown deepened. "What's with the donkey? I don't like animals!"

"He goes wi' me," said Humpy without apology.

"Is 'at you, Humpy?" The Weazel's tone almost had a squeak of pleasantry to it. "It's been awhile. Come on aboard, both a' ya." He looked from Humpy to Dinkin. "Meet ya here a week and a night. Take care now."

The Weazel ignored the donkey as Humpy led the animal carefully across the narrow wooden plank followed by Kander. The Weazel came after. One of the Weazel's mates pulled in the plank. They waved to Dinkin as the little skiff slowly pulled away from the rocks. The Weazel's sea dogs hoisted sail, and they ran the choppy, windblown sea toward Xziland.

"Three days ta Krock," squealed the Weazel above the howl of the wind. "Then you'll have two days ta take care a' business. I order a furled sail the third day. Don't be late. 'Cause as you know, Humpy, I'm an impatient man."

"Once we get to Krock, how do we find the Chameleon?" Kander shouted against the gale.

"He'll find you!" returned the Weazel with an eerie laugh. "His men will be crawlin' the wharf. Yer newcomers. An' all newcomers are taken to face the Chameleon. Nobody comes ta Krock without facin' the Chameleon. An' I warn ya, he's a hard man who drives a hard bargain. An' ta tell ya the truth, if ya get what yer after, I'll be surprised."

"Just what I needed to hear," mumbled Kander.

The Weazel laughed.

Humpy waved off the Weazel as if his opinion was somehow skewed and encouraged Kander not to give up hope. But Kander's frown seemed sculpted into his face.

At the wharf outside of Krock, men dressed in green met the Weazel's skiff. Yellow belts and boots adorned the green outfits, and silver swords hung at the soldiers' sides. They wore yellow hats topped with shiny, brownish-green plumes. The soldiers acknowledged the Weazel with nods and curt words of greeting, and then they demanded that Kander and Humpy "come along."

The Chameleon sat in a large green chair. He almost seemed a part of the chair with his verdant clothing, variegateed greenish-brown hair, and his olive skin. His smile welcomed but did not disarm.

"The Weazel brought you over, huh?" he commented. "What's your business in Krock, and what do you have to do business with?"

They were in an outdoor pavilion, and numerous people were standing about. Obviously reluctant to state his business openly, Kander gave the milling people a questioning glance.

The Chameleon laughed. "Well, yes, one never knows whose ears may overhear a delicate conversation." His face acknowledged that he understood Kander's concern. The Chameleon excused all but two guards.

"So it's that kind of business, eh? Well, my price is high, and neither of you look like the type who can afford to do business with me. But then, the world is full of surprises."

"The Ferret sent us," said Kander.

"Of course, she did." said the Chameleon. "You came with the Weazel, so you obviously did business with the Ferret. So what? Does that mean you can do business with me? Not necessarily, although I must admit that the Ferret usually sends reliable clients. However, that's neither here nor there. The question is, are you reliable clients? You either are or you aren't. So let's hear your business and see your cash."

"My business is a woman and her son," said Kander. The Chameleon lifted an eyebrow. "The Pagyn, Xvardris, sent them to you nearly ten years ago. They are Xzwendarians, and we have come to petition you for their freedom."

"Petition me?" Mockery edged the Chameleon's laughter. "So I was right. You have come to do business with empty hands."

"Not entirely." Kander tried to regroup. "The boy is the heir to the throne of Xzwendaria. Once he is returned to the throne, the wealth of the mines of Xzendr and Luxurd will be at his disposal. Then we will be able to reward you handsomely."

"But Xvardris already rewards me handsomely," laughed the Chameleon. "So why should I throw away gold already in the bag for a mere promise? And I might add, a promise with no guarantee. Your offer amuses me, but I'm afraid it lacks merit."

"Xvardris is a Pagyn. By keeping the heir in exile, you aid and abet him in his efforts to usurp the throne of Xzwendaria," argued Kander.

"And what do I care whether the gold in my purse comes from the hand of a Pagyn or the hand of an Xzwendarian?" replied the unsympathetic Chameleon.

"Because the Pagyns purpose to rule all realms, including this one," said Kander. "Your land may indeed be the last to fall, but fall it will. Once the Pagyns rule the entire continent, then they will come to your island. It is inevitable, and you know it. As long as they are occupied with Xzwendaria, your island is secure. But if the Xzwendarian Resistance is broken, Xziland stands in jeopardy."

"A plausible argument," acknowledged the Chameleon. He grimaced and rubbed his chin. "And indeed, in spite of my harsh words, I am sympathetic to your cause. But still, I must have cash up front to show good faith that when the heir is restored, I will receive final payment, for I am also a pragmatic man. So go to your mines. Bring me gold, silver, jewels, and I will gladly release the boy to your custody. But not for a mere promise." He shook his head. "It just can't be done that way."

"So the boy and his mother be here, hey?" Humpy ran a hand over his stubbly chin and looked the Chameleon in the eye. "Afore we head back ta the mines ta dig out whatever it's gunna cost us, we would like ta see the merchandise in the flesh. Ya don't buy goods without knowin' what yer buyin'."

"Ah, a man of business has accompanied the diplomat. That, at least, is an encouraging development." The Chameleon smiled, and raising his hand above his head snapped his fingers. One of the guards stepped forward. "Benevar, bring the woman and her child. They are in guesthouse five."

The guardsman bowed slightly and hurried off. Chameleon noticed the anxious look in Kander's eye. He watched thoughtfully. "So, am I correct in thinking that there is more to this business than simply the return of the heir?" he pried.

Kander's face turned red. Humpy looked at him questioningly. "Is there sumpin' I don't know?" he quizzed.

"I don't think so." Kander stumbled over the words. "I mean, I have only seen her once, and that was ten years ago. I've never even spoken to her, but I've been looking for her and the child all these years, and I guess it's become a personal thing with me. I don't even know them, but I feel like they're family."

"This is getting interesting." The Chameleon sat back and shifted his gaze from Kander to Humpy. "Of course, you know it's one price for him but another for her. I'll accept a good faith down payment for the heir because it's to my advantage. But before I can allow the woman to go free, I will have to have payment in full."

Kander's face drained of color while his eyes flashed anger, but before he could speak Humpy intervened.

"An' jes' how much are we talkin' here, Mr. Chameleon?" He stated the question pointedly. "How much fer the boy an' how much fer the girl? State yer price, man, so we know the terms we be dealin' with."

"Xvardris is paying a one-pound measure of gold per year for me to keep them in exile," responded the Chameleon. "Half covers expenses involved and half is pure profit. That means for ten years, their worth is a five-pound measure of gold. Our contract was for twenty years. That's a ten-pound measure. But what are they worth today? That is the question, isn't it? After all, the boy is heir to a throne. That certainly increases his worth. So up front cash for the boy? A ten-pound measure of gold or its equivalent. And let's say a five-pound measure each year for the next ten years. The woman, a twenty-pound measure straight across. Those are my terms, and they're final!"

"Whew! You drive a hard bargain!" Humpy scratched his hoary head and spread a jolly smile. "Ya coulda' left a little room fer dickerin'! What fun is doin' business if it's all cut and dried?"

"All right. Make me an offer," challenged the Chameleon. "But when we strike a deal, you had better be good for it!"

"Humpy, are you out of your mind?" asked Kander, after regaining his composure.

Humpy waved him off nonchalantly. "If we have to, we'll borrow what we need from the Ferret." Humpy rubbed his hands together in anticipation of the bartering process.

The Chameleon laughed. "And where would the Ferret come up with that kind of wealth?"

Humpy shrugged a shoulder. "Don't know," he said, and then he and the Chameleon began haggling over the price. They both fully enjoyed what to Kander was a senseless process. And as the minutes passed, Kander grew more and more aggravated with the bickering that Humpy called dickering.

"Done!" Humpy gave his knee a triumphant slap. "If they're who we're lookin' fer an' they're in good health, we'll pay ya a fifty-pound measure a pure gold within the week. If we're unable to pay, the two of us become your property ta do with as ya please. Draw up the contract!"

"Humpy, are you crazy?" Kander's face drained of color. "This is stupid! I'll not be party to such an agreement!"

"Do ya want the woman an' boy or not!?" spat Humpy. "Sign yer name right there!"

Humpy would brook no protest, and in spite himself, Kander signed his name next to Humpy's.

The Chameleon's eyes sparkled. He liked the deal he had made. Kander and Humpy would increase his bargaining power and profit margin.

They had no more than signed the contract when Benevar returned with the woman and her son. Kander's heart skipped into rapid motion. Patrexna was more beautiful than he remembered. Her child was handsome, his features strong. Still, he was just a boy. He held tightly to his mother's hand.

"Well?" said the Chameleon to Kander.

"Yes, she's the one we're looking for." He let his eyes drift to meet hers. Surprise mingled with fear shouted back from

Patrexna's eyes. Kander smiled kindly. "What's the boy's name?"

"Tarkedrx," said Patrexna, though her tone was wary.

"As you can see, they are healthy," said the Chameleon. "Many have offered to buy her, but they couldn't pay my price. You have a week."

Humpy wasn't paying attention. He had stepped outside the pavilion and was scrounging in the sidepack on his donkey. "Pookshaw!" he complained. "I have more junk in here!" Then he pulled out a large, heavy leather bag, stepped back under the pavilion, and plunked the bag on top of the contract. "Now, where is your measure?" he asked.

"What do you mean, where is my measure?" The Chameleon came to his feet. "What are you up to?"

"I'm up to payin' my debt!" answered Humpy.

"You're what?" The Chameleon's eyebrows shot upward. "You mean you had the cash with you all along?" Humpy just smiled. The Chameleon shook his head. "Well, I do believe I've met my match!"

Kander watched in stunned disbelief as one of the guards measured out the gold. Patrexna and her son were confused. The Chameleon's face reflected his delight. And a look of triumph stretched across Humpy's face—ear to ear. The guard weighed out fifty pounds of pure gold in odd-sized ingots. A crowd had gathered again, and all eyes were wide with wonder.

The Chameleon's treasurer arrived, examined the gold and declared that he had never seen better. Humpy took up his leather pouch, pulled out another ingot, and added it to the pile. "For a night's lodging for four," he said.

"You can all stay in guest house number five." The Chameleon gave a slight bow. "You'll be free to leave with tomorrow's tide. And I must say it has been a pleasure doing business. It's not often I take it on the chin and still make a profit."

The Chameleon took Humpy aside and presented him with some "extraordinary business opportunities," as he put it. A boat? A good slave? Perhaps a good horse to replace the donkey? What about a carriage? But Humpy had finished with business. Would they share a meal? Indeed, they would gladly share a meal. One of the Chameleon's guards would summon them at the appropriate time.

Benevar led them off to guest house number five.

Patrexna, still confused, assumed that she and her son had been sold into slavery. Kander saw questions in her eyes, and once they were alone in the house, he told her the whole story from when he saw her in the temple to the highlights of their journey.

"Tarkedrx is the heir to the throne of Xzwendaria. We have come to return your son from exile and to crown him king of Xzwendaria," explained Kander. "But the way that lies before us is fraught with danger. Will you return with us?"

"Will we return?" Distrust quavered in Patrexna's voice. "Do we have a choice? You have bought us. We are indebted to you. We are your slaves."

"No, Patrexna!" Kander looked in her eyes and spoke emphatically. "We did not purchase you. We purchased your freedom. Yes, your son is heir to the throne, but whether or not you come with us is up to you. We ask you to come, but it must be of your own free will."

Patrexna held Kander's eyes as she weighed her decision. She longed to return to her home and family. She shifted her eyes to the window. Somewhere outside a child's laughter rang. She took a deep breath and nodded slightly. "We will return with you." Her voice cracked as she spoke. "I am sorry about Thaxndar. He was such a kind man."

"The kindest man I ever met." Kander momentarily looked off into space and then back at Patrexna. "And I apologize for eavesdropping."

"I'm glad you did." Patrexna blushed, then reached out her hand and touched Kander's arm. "No one would have known about me or my son had you not. I am grateful, Kander."

Their eyes met momentarily, and then they looked away uneasily.

Humpy and Tarkedrx came in from outside and broke the tension.

"Humpy's got lots of gold!" The excited boy pulled at his mother's arm. "Oh, Mom! You should see! Look!" He held out a small shiny nugget.

"What did you do with the gold, Humpy?" Kander glanced out the door to make sure no one was listening to their conversation.

"We hid the gold!" the boy declared before Humpy could open his mouth. "And we ain't tellin' nobody where! Not even you!"

"Just as well," laughed Kander.

The boy turned to his mother. "It's under the manure pile in our stable," he whispered loud enough for everyone to hear.

"We keep a cow." Patrexna glanced momentarily at Kander. "It provides milk, cream, and butter. I'm sure no one will look for the gold in the manure pile." She turned back to Tarkedrx. "But do not mention the gold or where it is hidden to anyone, under any circumstances, Tark. Not to me. Not to anyone. Do not even whisper it ever again. Do you understand, Tark?"

"I understand, Mother. I won't say nothin' about it, ever again! Not to anybody, anybody, anybody!" he promised. And it was a promise he kept.

"So it's Tark, is it?" Kander smiled approvingly.

"Of course my name's Tark! Always has been Tark." The boy struck a defiant pose with his feet spread and his hands on his hips.

"Then, Tark it is," said Kander. "And I'm Kander, and you already met Humpy."

"Yes, I've I met Humpy! He's already my friend. Aren't you, Humpy?" The boy's sparkling eyes turned and possessed the old prospector who instantly broke into a broad smile. He gave Tark a wink and a nod.

That evening Benevar escorted the four guests to the feast that had been proclaimed in their honor. They ate, told stories, listened to stories and had a delightful time.

The Weazel even showed. Unaware of what had transpired, he watched with wonder. And the next morning as they made their way out of the harbor, their mission accomplished, the Weazel expressed his amazement. Frankly, he had never expected them to pull it off. But when they got back to Devil's Cove, and Humpy paid him with a gold ingot, for all his troubles, enlightenment dawned. "So that's how you pulled off the deal!" laughed the Weazel. "You spoke the Chameleon's language—gold! Ha! Ha! Ha! You had us all fooled, Humpy!"

Humpy smiled, put his arm around Tark's shoulders, and walked away from the boat and up the rocky shore. Kander, Patrexna, and the donkey followed.

Chapter 50

Humpy had paid the Ferret before making the trip to Xziland. Once back at Eknard, he paid Dinkin for his trouble and the damage done to his woodshed and fence. He slipped Jolkie a nugget as well.

"You couldn't possibly have found all that gold prospecting in the Draw Gulch!" said Captain Favel as Humpy unloaded his donkey. "So tell me, Humpy, where did you come up with it?"

"To get past the Pagyn barricade, I cut across the mountains between Deepwood and Thiswood," he explained as he untied his bedroll. "An' in a valley deep in the mountains, I came to a ghost town, or what was left of a ghost town—a broken-down cabin wall here and there, four toppled chimneys, an' an old wooden fence. The place has been deserted fer years piled on top a' years. Anyway, I looks around at the town that once was, an' it strikes me funny that anyone would build a town way out there in the middle of nowhere. 'Why build a town here?' I says ta myself. I gave the question some thought. Then a light comes on. Gold! An' I began searchin' the hills. An' pookshaw! I foun' a cave, an' pokin' around in the cave, I foun' the gold. Can ya believe it? They deserted the town an' left the gold behind!"

Captain Favel and the others could hardly believe their ears. They looked at F.F. Bog Frog for his reaction. His eyes sparkled with delight, and his mouth hung wide with wonder.

"Anyway," continued Humpy, "I looks toward the heavens and says ta Baruch, 'Why after all these years da ya ha' me strike a mother lode? You know I ain't got no need fer all this gold!' Well, right away I thinks a you an' yer mission ta bring back the heir. An' I bats myself in the head an says, Humpy, this ain't yer gold! This be the king's gold! An' so it is!" He smiled broadly. "How 'bout you keepin' it fer him, Kander?"

Humpy handed Kander three bags of gold that weighed more than fifty pounds each. He turned to Captain Favel and the others, gave them a wink and a smile, and then clapped his hands and declared, "Now I can get back ta prospectin'. It's me callin' ya know." He grinned, eyes twinkling. "A course, I did keep a nugget or two so's I can replenish me supplies an' all. Sort of a finder's fee, if ya will."

They all laughed as they left Humpy's donkey to graze and headed inside Jolkie's cabin, except F.F. Bog Frog. His mood was pensive, thoughtful. Humpy's revelation had touched him, heart and soul.

"By the bog, my people are more a part of this quest than they know." F.F. Bog Frog swung his hands wildly as he walked through the door, and excitement edged his voice. "By mud and by muck, I'm glad I came along ta see our curse become a blessing. Why, one might even say that we Bogfrogls ransomed the king. By the bog, that's exciting!"

Humpy, Patrexna, and Tarkedrx looked at F.F. dumbfoundedly. And without missing a breath, he told them the story of his people. Humpy believed every word of F.F.'s story. Patrexna wiped away a tear and offered the gold to Fiffle to take back to his people. "It is their gold," she said.

"Why, I would not even touch the wretched stuff! Not me, nor my people! Bogfrogls have no need for gold." F.F. waved his hands in front of his face as if warding off a curse.

"F.F., I would like to visit your people someday," said Tarkedrx. "They sound—interesting."

"By muck and by mud, that would be an honor!" said Fiffle with a flamboyant gesture, "And I could introduce you to my grandfather, Freddie Bogfrogle, and all the F. Bogfrogls. And then I would introduce you to the B. Bogfrogls, and the G. Bogfrogls, and the L. Bogfrogls too. By the bog, that would be a proud day!"

"Well, it will have to wait," interjected Kander. "Right now our mission is to get Tark back to Xzwendaria. And the sooner we leave these parts, the better because in another day or two Eknard will be crawling with Pagyn soldiers."

"Humpy, can you take us back across the mountains the way you came?" asked Captain Favel. "If Jolkie's plan works, they will think we have gone south to Warrz. And once news reaches them that we have Patrexna and Tark with us, they will do everything possible to keep us from getting back to Xzwendaria. If they are looking in the wrong places, it will buy us some time."

Kander, for the first time in weeks, let his mind wander back to the clandestine meeting he had witnessed between Captain Favel and Zedria outside of Havenholt. With the ransom of the heir, the problem of the spy resurfaced. Kander gazed at Captain Favel as he talked. Could it be the man has changed? Kander questioned within. He has been a trusted ally and friend. He shifted his gaze to the boy. But a spy is adept at pretending, he mused thoughtfully. I must be wary. I must make sure Tark is never alone with Captain Favel. But surely, he would never. . . Then his thoughts were interrupted.

"Kander, you and Tark can sleep over there." Captain Favel pointed to a couple of mats that lay to the left of the hearth. Then he pointed to a corner off to the right where a makeshift screen stuck out from the wall. "Xzwindra, Lrondie, and Patrexna can sleep in that corner. The rest of you know where you're sleeping. Get a good night's rest."

He turned to Jolkie. "We will leave tomorrow morning. We've disrupted your life enough. Thanks for putting up with us. In fact, thank you for everything you've done. I don't know what we would have done without you and Dinkin and the others."

"Oh, it was nothin'!" Jolkie grinned and waved him off. "Glad ta be of help. An' my door's always open if ya ever find yerself in these parts again."

They rolled out their beds and snuffed the lamp. A wisp of smoke rose from the lamp's glass chimney, catching the moonlight shining through the window. Kander wondered how many moonlit nights would pass before they would be back in Havenholt. Would they make it back safely?

Captain Favel, Humpy, and Jolkie hunkered about the table in the middle of the room studying the map by candlelight. After they were finished, Captain Favel went to the window and looked out toward the mountains. He too was wondering what lay ahead. When he turned from the window, his eyes followed the moonlight to Kander and Tark. He smiled. Their rhythmic breathing told him they were sound asleep. Captain Favel gazed at the boy. The moonlight made Tarkedrx's face look as pale as a corpse. Captain Favel's face fell to a frown. Quietly, he moved closer. Yes, the boy was breathing. Kander rolled to his side, and Captain Favel turned and slipped silently over to his own bed across the room. He crawled in and lay with his hands cupped behind his head staring up at the ceiling. He felt deeply troubled.

The next morning, they waved good-bye to Jolkie and headed south through the foothills toward Thiswood.

Tark rode with Kander. He had taken to Kander like a little boy to a big brother or a child to his father. In fact, although he did not speak a word of it, Tark wished that Kander were his father. And deep inside, the boy wished that Zandirxn was not his father and that he was not the heir to the throne of Xzwendaria. He wished he were just a normal boy with a normal father. And there were times when nighttime came, that he would lay his head on Kander's shoulder and cry in his sleep. He was not aware that Kander could feel the dampness of those tears and that Kander's cheeks were wet as well.

A week and two days after leaving Eknard, the King's Company arrived at the ghost town where Humpy had found the gold. Fiffle, deeply moved by the decayed remains of his people's past, examined every wall, chimney, and fence and made a map of the town in his mind. Humpy offered to show F.F. the cave where he had found the gold. Everyone expressed interest in visiting the cave, everyone but Tark. Weary from the long day's ride, he had no interest in hiking up the mountain to an old cave.

"The rest of you go ahead," urged Captain Favel. "I'll stay here with Tark. I'm rather weary myself."

"I'll stay with Tark," said Kander. He tried to act detached. "You can go ahead with the others, Captain Favel. My turn to prepare the stew."

"You stick to the boy like glue," laughed Captain Favel. "It won't hurt to share his company. I'd like to spend some time with him too, and I really am too weary for a hike up into the mountains. You can do dinner when you get back, Kander."

"That's fine." Kander forced a smile. "You can spend some time with Tark, but you'll spend it with me too. I'll not allow the boy out of my sight."

"Back to the matter of trust, are we?" said Captain Favel with an understanding smile and a shake of his head.

Kander raised his eyebrows as if to say, yes, that's the way it is.

Patrexna urged Kander to accompany them to the cave, and he very much wanted to, but he was not about to leave Tark alone with Captain Favel. The growing tension affected everyone. Even Grey Wolf and Humpy encouraged Kander to loosen up, but to no avail.

That night the King's Company slept in the shelter of one of the ancient walls.

In the middle of the night, awakened by a sense of impending danger, Kander rolled over and came up on one elbow next to Tark's sleeping form. An apparition stood in the shadows at the corner of the wall. The blade of a dagger flashed in the darkness as the phantom slipped away. Kander did not sleep the remainder of the night.

In the morning as they broke camp, Captain Favel smiled and asked Kander how he had slept.

"Well enough, I suppose."

The two men stared at each other and then parted.

Xzwindra witnessed the brief confrontation. She came up behind Kander after Captain Favel was gone and laid her hand on his shoulder.

He looked at her and smiled wearily.

"There are a lot of miles between here and Xzwendaria, Kander." She gave him a kind look. "If Captain Favel is the spy, don't you think he would have tried something by now? Did you ever think you might be making something out of nothing?"

"It's all a matter of opportunity, Xzwindra," said Kander. "Fact is, last night he stood at the corner of the wall with a dagger in hand. I awoke and he hurried away. But I saw him, and I saw the dagger."

"And you're sure it was Captain Favel?"

Kander bit his lip. "Not exactly," he muttered.

"So what do you do now, stay awake every night, or just trust your instincts to wake you up?"

"I don't know." Kander's shoulders sank as he spoke.

"Tark could sleep with his mother, Lrondie, and me," she suggested. "Sleeping between us, he would be well-protected. That way you can get some sleep. You'd be near Captain Favel, where you could keep an eye on him."

"I hesitate to let the boy out of my sight. But you're right. I can't stay awake night after night." Kander tied his bedroll behind his saddle. "I'll give it some thought and let you know."

That day they left the ancient village of the Bogfrogls and pressed on westward through the mountains. When evening came, they camped in the shelter of an overhanging bluff.

Kander forced himself to stay awake through the night. He chose a position for himself and Tark where he could see Captain Favel and the others. And as Kander expected, Captain Favel awoke in the middle of the night. Kander pretended to be asleep. Captain Favel sat up, looked about the camp, and for a time just sat there staring at him and Tark. Then he lay back down and did not stir the rest of the night.

The next day, Kander fought to keep from falling asleep in the saddle. He felt awful. Xzwindra rode up beside him late in the day and tried to encourage him.

"Xzwindra, I think I'll take you up on your offer tonight," he said. "I'll not be able to stay awake. And if I fall asleep, I'm afraid I'll really be out of it and would not be able to wake up if the need should arise."

Xzwindra smiled understandingly and agreed to keep a watchful eye on Tark that night.

"Is that all right with you, Tark?" asked Kander over his shoulder.

"I'm not afraid," responded the boy with his jaw firmly set. "Why are you so worried about me anyway?"

"You're the heir to the throne of Xzwendaria, Tark. But there are people who don't want you to return to Xzwendaria to become king," said Xzwindra. "It's our responsibility to see that you are kept safe from those people."

"And you think Captain Favel is one of those people?" Tark shook his head. "I like Captain Favel. He would never hurt me. He told me so himself."

Kander scowled. Xzwindra forced a smile. Tark reluctantly agreed to sleep with the women. But he liked being a man.

In the late afternoon, dark clouds rolled in from the north. Humpy began thinking about shelter. Grey Wolf went ahead to see what could be found. By the time he returned, the storm's forward edge had reached them. A cold wind whipped at their cloaks and tossed their hair. Large raindrops tapped them on the shoulders warning of more to come.

"There's a large cave up ahead," shouted Grey Wolf above the wind. "It's a bit out of the way, but it's shelter!"

"Let's do it!" Humpy picked up the pace. The others willingly followed. For the moment shelter was their first priority.

Before they could reach the protection of the cave, the storm broke with intense fury. Lightning ripped the fabric of the sky and boomed angrily as if warning them to get under cover. They pressed forward and up the side of the rugged hill, but rain sheeted down from black clouds driven by gale-force winds so that by the time they reached the cave, they were wet to the skin and chilled to the bone.

Grey Wolf had had the forethought to lay in a supply of firewood before returning for them. Thus, it was not long before a roaring fire provided much-needed warmth and comfort.

They sheltered the skittish horses at the back of the cave. After a warm meal, they dried out their wet clothes. Then the women and Tark made their beds on one side of the cave, while the men laid out their bedrolls on the opposite side. Kander bedded down next to Captain Favel, who gave him a questioning look. Kander just smiled and crawled in hoping to get a good night's rest.

As Kander laid his head on his saddle, he felt pleased to see that Captain Favel looked frustrated. Kander smirked as he glanced across the cave one more time. The women and Tark had turned in for the night. Satisfied that Tark would be safe, Kander snuggled back into his bedroll and fell asleep almost instantly.

As the night deepened, the storm intensified. Peals of thunder shook the night air. Suddenly, lightning struck just outside the cave, jarring Kander from his sleep. He turned, and with heavy eyelids, looked at the dying embers that had been their fire. He felt chilled and pulled his bedding in tight about his neck. Boom! Lightning lit the cave again. Alarm jolted Kander fully awake. The bedroll beside him lay open and empty.

Kander slipped from his bed and slid his sword from its sheath. Boom! The cave shook, and light momentarily filled the cave. With a quick glance, Kander spotted Captain Favel standing near the far wall, watching the women and Tark. The sudden return to blackness frightened Kander. His heart pounded, his eyes fought to see through the darkness. Boom! Again light flashed through the cave. Relief! He saw Xzwindra awake, kneeling at Tark's side, keeping watch. Darkness returned, but his hand relaxed its death grip on the hilt of his sword.

Boom! Again, momentary light. But in the blackness that followed, Kander felt a sudden flood of confusion. What had he seen? A splash of light off the blade of a dagger? A dagger in Xzwindra's hand, not Captain Favel's? Xzwindra? No! It couldn't be! Xzwindra, a conspirator with Captain Favel? Was she also a spy? Kander lunged across the cave, though he felt like he was moving in slow motion. His head pounded with his heart. Boom! The storm again lit the cave. He was close enough to see tears on Xzwindra's cheeks. The shiny dagger lay in her lap. Captain Favel stood at her side.

"Tark!" Kander shouted. But the black night again enveloped the cave.

"Hold, Kander!" Captain Favel's voice broke the silence engulfed in the storm.

Only then did Kander realize that he held his sword above his head, ready to kill. Boom! He looked into Captain Favel's eyes. He hesitated. He is my friend. The thought raced through his mind. But he is a traitor. His sword flashed as darkness again engulfed the cave. The deadly blade sliced the dark night air.

"Kander, the boy is fine!" cried Captain Favel. "He's not in danger! Hold your sword, friend!"

"I'll not hold my sword! I'll not listen to your traitorous lies!" shouted Kander. Sweat beads rolled down his brow.

BOOM! Captain Favel had escaped the first blow, but now lay helpless at Kander's feet awaiting the death blow. But the sword stopped in midair. A strong hand gripped Kander's arm.

"Easy, Kander! Easy!" said Grey Wolf as he removed the sword from Kander's hand.

Confusion and fear awoke in the darkness. The cave stirred with life.

Sergeant Tandrak added wood to the fire to shed light on the situation.

"What's wrong?" Tark's quavering voice reached Kander's ears. The fire flared. A frightened mother held her child in her arms. Kander looked from Patrexna to Xzwindra.

"I couldn't do it! I just couldn't do it!" Xzwindra wept in her hands.

"You were in cahoots with Captain Favel all along!" Kander"s anger still had the best of him. He looked around at the others. There were no indications of sympathy. "You were all in on it?"

"You're acting the fool, Kander." Xzwindra looked up at him and wiped her tears. "I'm the spy, not Captain Favel. Not the others. Just me."

Kander didn't know what to say. He turned from Xzwindra's tearful face and met Captain Favel's unflinching eyes. Kander's head seemed to swim. He felt confusion. Lightning flashed. Boom! Thunder shook the cave. Kander shook his head, trying to clear away the mist.

"But I saw him. . . " Kander tried to argue.

"It was not Captain Favel you saw the other night. It was me," confessed Xzwindra.

"But at Havenholt, before we left..." Kander stammered as he turned again from Xzwindra to Captain Favel. "I saw you. I saw you meet in secret with Zedria. You have to be the spy!"

"So that's it!" said Captain Favel said with a laugh. "You should have told me. We could have settled this long ago, at least between the two of us. After returning to Zwexdrof, Zedria happened on some startling information. She did not say where she picked it up, but she found out that Xzwindra was in reality the daughter of the Pagyn priestess, Wazrxna, and that she was the spy."

"Is that true?" snapped Kander.

Xzwindra nodded affirmation.

Kander glared at Captain Favel again. "Then why did Zedria tell you instead of Major Targndel?"

"Because she also found out that Major Targndel was Xzwindra's father." Captain Favel cocked an eye at Xzwindra. Her tears stopped, and her eyes went wide in wonderment. "Zedria was not sure if Targndel had been compromised by the situation or not. I talked to Jentrxn before leaving. He was sure that Targndel was not aware of having a daughter. Jentrxn told me not to compromise Xzwindra, that it could jeopardize our mission. He ordered me to watch her closely, but he hoped that she would prove loyal to the Resistance in the end. I'm not sure where her loyalties are, but when it came down to it, she did not have the will to kill the heir."

"And what if she had?" flared Kander.

"I was standing in the shadows with a crossbow aimed at her heart." Captain Favel ground his teeth and gritted. "The moment she lifted the dagger, I would have killed her. But I am glad it did not come to that."

"You could have told me!" Kander continued his glare.

"No, I could not have," said Captain Favel with a negative shake of his head. "You would have demanded proof. You would have demanded that we not allow her to come along. To tell you would have jeopardized our mission as well. I'm sorry, Kander."

"Jentrxn put a great amount of trust in you, Captain Favel." Kander's scowl broke into a half smile. "What if he had been wrong? You could just as easily have been the spy as anyone else. The story about Xzwindra could have been a setup. He took quite a chance, if you ask me."

"Jentrxn knows me better than I do!" Captain Favel chuckled. "He is my older brother. I assure you, he would have known if I were false. He has always been able to read me like a book. But few people know we are brothers. He prefers it that way, lest people think he shows me favoritism because of our relationship."

"But his father's name was Hendred, and yours was Beldrxin," muttered Kander. He shook his head as if to clear away the confusion.

"Yes, but Lindzella was his mother and mine." A smile flickered across Captain Favel's face. "After Hendred died, our mother remarried. I was the child of her age, born of Beldrxin, her second husband. And although we had different fathers and Kartxn was some fifteen years older, still, we were close. In fact, he loved me more like a son than a brother."

"He speaks the truth, Kander," broke in Sergeant Tandrak. "Every word is true."

"Captain Favel?" Xzwindra let her dagger fall to the ground as she rose to her feet and took hold of his arm. He acknowledged her with his eyes. "Is Major Targndel really my father? Are you absolutely sure?"

"I didn't think that you knew." Captain Favel put his hand over hers. "Yes, Major Targndel is your father. But again, he doesn't know he's your father."

"I don't understand. Mother said that my father was a Pagyn prince and that he died shortly before I was born." Sadness edged Xzwindra's voice. "Wazrxna told me that if my father had not died, he would have been king of Xzwendaria instead of Xvardris. She told me. . . .she told me so many things."

Boom! The thunder rolled at a distance now.

"I'm sorry, Xzwindra, but she told you lies so she could use you." Captain Favel moved his hand up around her shoulder, and drew her in close to his side. "Your mother seduced Major Targndel with her charms. She came to Zwexdrof pretending to be a Pagyn slave girl named Walzara, who had been adopted by an influential family in Avard. They had supposedly sent her to Zwexdrof to receive a formal education. Targndel courted her for a month. They were secretly married, lived together for several months, and then Walzara disappeared. Targndel looked everywhere for her. Interestingly, the school she claimed to be attending had never heard of her. He traveled to Avard and looked up her family. He confessed that he had secretly married their daughter, only to be told that they had no daughter, and no, they had not adopted a slave girl named Walzara. Targndel found no trace of her. It was as if his wife had never existed."

"Yes, I remember mother laughing and saying that she had gone by that name at one time." Tears trickled down Xzwindra's cheeks.

Captain Favel gave her a slight hug. "According to Zedria, Wazrxna hoped to use the relationship to eventually compromise Targndel as head of intelligence. But Xvardris usurped the throne before she had opportunity to connive her way past Targndel's defenses. But you proved to be an unforeseen opportunity. She could raise you to be her own personal spy. You had retained the Xzwendarian features instead of her Pagyn features—the light-colored hair and eyes. You fit in."

The firelight revealed a look of indignation. "My own mother!" she murmured.

"I hate to say this, Xzwindra, but when you get back to Zwexdrof, you will want to be careful. You may be Pagyn, but you also have Xzwendarian blood. I assure you that once you are no longer of use to your mother, she will not hesitate to destroy you. She will not want anyone to know that she gave birth to an Xzwendarian."

"She may hate Xzwendarians, but I'm her daughter!" Despair cracked her voice.

"Has she ever told you that she loves you?" Kander had gotten over his glare. He spoke softly. "Did she ever touch you? Did she ever hug you or show any affection?"

Xzwindra felt like her heart had suddenly been ripped from her breast. Tears flooded down her cheeks. "Never," she whispered. A word never seemed so heavy.

"How did she treat you differently than the other people she used?" Kander said what had to be said.

The others stood silent. The fire cracked and popped.

Xzwindra gathered her thoughts and then slowly shook her head. "I wanted her love and approval." She let out her breath. "And I blinded my eyes to the truth." More tears ran down her cheeks. "You are right, but it hurts to admit it."

"Yes, Xzwindra, it hurts terribly." Kander's eyes filled with tears as well. "But you are not alone. Most of us have suffered the same kind of pain you are feeling. We've been there. We do understand, at least to some degree, Xzwindra."

Captain Favel folded Xzwindra in his arms, and she vented her tears on his shoulder.

Then Lrondie put an arm around her waist and led her aside, speaking words of comfort. She understood Xzwindra's heartbreak better than any of the others, for she too had been rejected by her mother and did not know her father. Previously, Xzwindra and Lrondie had just been two people traveling in the same company, but that night they became fast friends.

The next day, Kander approached Captain Favel. "I apologize for not trusting you. And I must say I'm glad I was wrong about you. Despite myself, I have appreciated your friendship. I trust that my actions last night will not change that."

"I have no bitterness in my heart, Kander." A smile broke across Captain Favel's face. "You did what you had to, and I would likely have done the same had I been in your shoes. But that's behind us, and I am glad it's behind us. Let's leave it there." He held out his hand, and they clasped wrist to wrist in a gesture of friendship.

The others expressed their approval with smiles and nods. No longer would they have to deal with the distraction and tension of distrust. Facing the enemy without would be challenge enough.

Chapter 51

Wazrxna paced the dark hall of the Black Chancel, waiting for her servant to arrive with the sacrifice. To conjure a vision of Bayl required the blood of innocence—of a child yet unweaned. In Athos she would go to the temple and approach Bayl directly. However, here in Zwexdrof, she could only make contact by way of a conjuring, and a vision was necessary. In no other way could she discover the fate of the heir. She needed to know if Xzwindra had succeeded in killing the child.

"She is my daughter," she muttered to herself as she paced. "The wench would not dare fail me!" Yet, nagging doubt whispered other words in the recesses of her mind. But she is of mingled blood. Did she not inherit the wretched features of her Xzwendarian father? Perhaps she... The arrival of her servant interrupted her thoughts.

"Was the child taken fresh from his mother's breast?" she snarled as she grabbed away the whimpering babe.

"Yes, my lady, milk still dripped from the orifice after I pulled the child away." The servant lowered his shoulders in a half bow. "I left the mother weeping. However, I must say I am not sure if she wept in sorrow at the loss of her child or in joy for the silver coins."

"The latter, no doubt," she said dryly.

She examined the child's organs just to be sure. Wazrxna preferred the use of male children for the purpose of sacrifice. She dismissed her servant with a wave of her hand. She turned and entered the chancel.

High on the altar hungry flames danced in anticipation of the offering. The five darklings waited at the foot of the altar. They too were anxious to avenge their brothers. They hissed and muttered bloodlust as the priestess walked to the top of the dais, the male child squirming in her outstretched hands.

On one side of the altar, the fire burned. To the left and above the flames, the place of sacrifice awaited the child. She killed the sacrificial child with a stone dagger. Innocent Xzwendarian blood drained down onto the fire creating a rancid smoke, for it was in the hideous stench of death that Bayl would come to the vile priestess of darkness. To Bayl the death of the innocent rose as a sweet, compelling smell.

As the awful smoke swirled upward before Wazrxna, she held up her hands and began her incantations.

In the smoke, Bayl came to her, his serpentine features convincingly real. "Sssilence, Wazrxna!" breathed the angry apparition. "Your ssspy hasss failed. Ssshe hasss gone over to the Ressistancesss. The heir livesss, and they return to Xzssswendaria. They mussst be ssstopped. The heir mussst be dessstroyed. Sssend the darklingsss. Give them the ssscent of the child, and they will find him."

"And if the darklings should fail?" Wazrxna's voice cracked. "What then, Lord Bayl?"

"The darklingsss will not fail usss," hissed Bayl. "They mussst not. If the heir returnsss, then you mussst call forth the horssseman from the pit of blacknesss. The horssseman isss our lassst hope. But he cannot be controlled. He leavesss death and dessstruction in hisss path. He mussst be called forth only asss a lassst resssort."

"Yes, Lord Bayl," answered Wazrxna with a tilt of her head. "I will send the darklings."

"The ssspy mussst die asss well!" slurred the terrible apparition. "Ssshe hasss causssed usss great grief. Ssshe hasss defied me. Give the darklingsss her ssscent asss well."

"I will, Lord Bayl," returned the priestess. Her sneer indicated that such had been her intent all along.

The apparition faded. As it languished, it met Wazrxna eye to eye and adjured, "Do not fail me in thisss, Wazsssr-xzsssna. Do not fail me!" Bayl's ethereal presence passed, but the threatening look of his eyes lingered in Wazrxna's consciousness as she turned and descended the altar.

The darklings watched and waited her coming. Anticipation danced in their vile black eyes. Lust for blood appeared to drip from their fangs. They maintained an intense murmur-like hiss. Wazrxna beckoned them to follow her. Obediently, they left the chancel and entered the hall, trailing her to a small closetlike chamber from which she produced a blanket such as one might use to wrap a baby. The darklings ran their faces over the cloth sniffing and sensing. Wazrxna produced another mantle, even older than the first. It had been Xzwindra's favorite. The vile creatures of death hissed and sniffed until they had the scent.

"Go. Destroy them both," barked the evil priestess with no regret in her voice. "They are yours, body and blood. All that Bayl requires is their death. Avenge my sons, your brothers, my true children. Let no one stand in your way."

"Ssshe isss our sssister!" grated one of the darklings.

"She is not like you," shot back Wazrxna. "The blood of Bayl does not run in her veins. She is a vile Xzwendarian. She is a misbegotten, a curse to you and to me. She must die, even as the boy must die."

"Yesss, priestesss mother," answered the darkling softly. "To rid our family of thisss curssse will be our pleasssure. Her blood will be deliciousss. It will give usss life."

On moonless nights, the darklings slithered through the streets of the city, leaving behind unexplained bodies, drained of blood and paralyzed by venom from a snakelike bite on the neck. But now the streets of Zwexdrof would be safe—until they returned.

Chapter 52

Hiding out in the foothills, the King's Company watched as soldiers tramped south toward Ograf, a column a hundred strong. After the Pagyns passed beyond sight, Captain Favel warily led his small band down from the hills and westward into Deepwood. Grey Wolf lingered behind to cover their tracks. He caught up with them later in the day.

"Well, now that we're beyond the road to Ograf," grunted Humpy as they made camp that evening, "we can make our way to Draw Gulch and then on west."

"Nay, friend Humpy," responded Grey Wolf. "It is one thing to move a company such as ours downriver in the gulch. But upriver is something else. We would fair better edging Deepwood to the Barrier Horn, traversing the horn to Deadwood, and then on to the headwaters of the Savage River. There, where the Savage begins, an ancient pass cuts across to the Murkwold. It will save many days."

"It would save months!" broke in Captain Favel. "If there is such a pass, then indeed, that is the way we must go."

"There is such a pass." Grey Wolf looked off into the distance and spread a hand. "I have stood on its height and looked down on the green expanse called Murkwold."

Captain Favel looked at Humpy to get his response. He shrugged his shoulders but smiled approvingly. "Sounds good ta me," he said. "But as you know, I've got work ta do in the gulch. So, you all continue on ta the west wi' me blessing, but in the morning, I'll be breakin' off an headin' south. Wouldn't do ta let me pick get rusty."

They urged Humpy to return to Xzwendaria with them. But the crusty prospector waved them off, emphatically declaring that he had seen enough civilization for a while. But they were welcome to visit the Draw Gulch any time.

The next morning, with a broad smile creasing his weathered face and a friendly wave to them all, Humpy headed south, glad to leave adventure behind and return to his prospecting.

After a last good-bye to Humpy, Grey Wolf led the others westward through Deepwood, a five-day trek to the Barrier Horn.

They passed across the horn by way of a high, deep-cut canyon that at times narrowed to where they felt as if like they were squeezing through a crack in the mountain. But after two days, they came out on the westward side of the horn. Before them stretched Deadwood, a parched, desolate-looking forest. Though not petrified like Parchwood, it appeared just as lifeless. Leafless trees pointed accusing fingers toward the cloudless sky, while other trees lay dead on the dry ground. A twenty-year drought had caused the forest to become its name.

They followed the rim of the gulch and the southern edge of the forest westward. On two occasions, they actually watched once-stately trees give up their battle with the sun. The fall of the trees struck a sad blow to the traveler's hearts.

"The forest is much like our homeland," murmured Captain Favel, "destroyed by an outside influence, with its children dying before their time. A beautiful place that has become a desolation."

"Will life return to the forest?" Tark cocked an inquisitive eye at Captain Favel.

"It is dead." Patrexna cut off any answer Captain Favel might have made.

They rode on in silence for a while, no one willing to pursue the subject further as they pondered the implications for their country. Would life return to Xzwendaria?

"Look at the clouds." Kander broke the silence. The others followed his finger that pointed off to the north. "The promise of rain, of hope, of life. Are the clouds but an illusion? Laughing, do they pass over this land only to leave the forest languishing and its thirst unsatisfied?"

"Yes, many times the promise of rain has passed over Deadwood." Grey Wolf gazed at the distant clouds. "They mock the dead, then turn to the east and give life to the living, to Deepwood instead. So is the way of the rain clouds." Grey Wolf fell silent.

The King's Company rode on.

Later in the day, the wind suddenly swept down from the north, cooling the hot sun's life-robbing rays. Suddenly, lightning danced across the darkening sky and boldly laughed at the dead forest. But then the laughter turned to tears. Drops of rain rode on the wind. The travelers' dour faces broke into smiles as cool droplets refreshed their parched skin.

Flash! Crash! The heavens split open, dumping the glut that had been held back year after year. Water rained down in blinding sheets. The travelers, caught unawares, were wet to the skin before they could get into their rain gear. For three days and nights, white bolts ripped the sky and rain watered Deadwood Forest. And through the deluge, the travelers trudged on. Then, after the third day, the sun fought back the clouds.

On the fourth day, as they reached the western end of the forest, wonder of wonders! "Look!" burst out Tark. He pointed to a fallen, rotting tree. On top of the tree, several green sprouts seemed to mock the dead forest that surrounded them. Casting about, they discovered even more sprouts breaking through the parched ground. With hope rising in his chest, Tark declared, "Perhaps the forest will live again!"

"Perhaps." His mother offered a heartening smile. "And perhaps there is yet hope for our people."

Kander looked at the boy, and the corner of his mouth lifted upward. He too is a green sprout in a parched land, he thought and then said aloud, "Yes, there is hope."

That night they camped in the hills west of Deadwood, glad for a dry camp and warm fire but still feeling exhilarated by the life they had witnessed in the dead forest.

"In three days, we will reach the Place of Crossing." Grey Wolf gestured toward the heights. "From there we will be able to see the Murkwold, and from there I will point the way. The Place of Crossing must also be our Place of Parting."

Lrondie quietly gasped for breath. Stunned disbelief flushed her face. Her heart raced. She had not thought about partings. And the one person she did not want to part from was Grey Wolf, for Lrondie only now understood the feelings she held for the gentle desert warrior.

Grey Wolf sensed Lrondie's change in spirit. He looked at her and smiled knowingly.

A tear rose to Lrondie's eyelid. "Why must you go?" she whispered.

"The Savage Lands are my home," replied Grey Wolf calmly. "Their home lies beyond these mountains, but I belong here in the land of the ancients."

"And where do I belong?" murmured Lrondie as she gazed at the dancing flames of the campfire. "I have no home. Suddenly, I am lonely. I have no place to go."

"They will care for you," Grey Wolf reassured her.

"But my heart is not with them." A great sadness filled Lrondie's voice. "My place is not in the land that they call home."

"Well, by muck and by mud, and we've had plenty of that lately," broke in F.F. Bog Frog, "why, anybody can tell yer heart's on this side of the mountains with old Grey Wolf here. The two of ya make a fine pair, if I do say it myself. I mean the obvious is the obvious. By the bog, anybody can see that!"

A brief spurt of smothered laughter caused Lrondie to blush and brought forth a round of meager apologies followed by an uncomfortable silence.

Grey Wolf broke the silence.

"Fiffle, you are right." The man of the wild spoke his heart. "But I am not a whole man. Many years ago when I was sold into slavery, a cruel taskmaster cut away my manliness. I cannot be a husband, for I cannot father children. I arn not worthy of Lrondie."

Grey Wolf turned to Lrondie. His eyes spoke volumes. His smile tenderly caressed the tears that trickled down her cheeks. "If I were a man, I would ask you to be my wife, Lrondie. But I have nothing to offer. I assure you, beyond the mountains you will find someone worthy of your love and worthy of your hand, someone who can be a husband and give you children."

"Grey Wolf, you are a man whether you can father children or not," whispered Lrondie. "No one could be a better husband to me than you. I have no desire to cross these mountains. My only desire is to spend the rest of my life with you, Grey Wolf. My desire is to be your wife."

"Well, Captain," Xzwindra broke into the conversation and gestured to Captain Favel. "You have the authority to perform a wedding don't you?"

That night before the dancing flames of an open fire beneath the stars and the moon, Captain Favel joined Grey Wolf and Lrondie in the bond of marriage. And in that bonding both man and woman found joy beyond expectation.

The next day they began the ascent to the Place of Crossing. Three days later, they arrived at the summit. After pointing the way and after emotion-filled good-byes, Grey Wolf turned Sterling Grey back to the Savage Lands. With Lrondie hanging on tightly behind him, he rode east then south to Rest Mere. There they made their home in the great cave of the ancients.

Chapter 53

The Murkwold was unlike any forest the King's Company had yet experienced. It grew thick not only with trees but also with bramble, vines and thickets and tangles. Once they entered the forest, the forest seemed to dictate their path. Although they tried to ride southwest toward Yeps, the forest continually turned them northwest and pushed them toward its center.

"By muck and by mud, this is a demanding forest! Always has to have its own way!" muttered F.F. Bog Frog. "You go where it tells you, or you don't go at all!"

The moment of laughter that followed helped break the weight of frustration that lay heavy on the group. Fiffle had a way of making heavy things lighter.

"Fiffle, I think your calling in life is to cheer the weary heart," laughed Captain Favel. "You are a fresh breeze in a stale forest."

F.F. Bog Frog responded with a quizzical look. However, the others all agreed with Captain Favel's assessment. But F.F. Bog Frog did not understand. He shook his head. "I'm just me and by the bog, me is who I am. What else could I be? But cheering a weary heart is something you do, not something you be," argued Fiffle. "But you're telling me what I am doing, when really I am just being me. And if I'm being me, I am not doing. So I just don't understand."

Again, they all broke out in a fresh breeze of laughter.

Captain Favel briefly argued the point with Fiffle but finally gave up. He decided that whether Fiffle understood did not really matter. What mattered was that F.F. Bog Frog was the way he was. And that he was what he was made them all glad. And one thing they did not want was for F.F. Bog Frog to be any different.

"Look!" burst out F.F. Bog Frog with surprise exciting his voice. "By muck and by mud, it looks like an ancient wall or building or something."

He pointed through the trees to what indeed looked like a vine-covered wall. As they drew near they determined that it was in fact a wall, the remains of some ancient fortress. The vine-enshrouded stonework stood some fifty feet tall. They slashed their way through the brush that grew between forest and wall, and then worked their way along the edge of the wall until they cleared a path to where they found a gate. And beyond the gate, they lifted amazed eyes and looked on an ancient fortress castle, forsaken and as thickly overgrown with bramble and vines as the great wall itself.

They tethered their horses in a small clearing of ankle-deep grass and let them graze while they explored the ancient structure.

"These halls must have been truly magnificent in their day," mused Xzwindra as she looked about in wonder.

"It's spooky, if you ask me," grunted Patrexna. "I don't like this place at all. There are so many dark halls and corridors."

"It is a massive place," agreed Captain Favel. Awe edged his voice.

"It's wonderful!" Tark gazed about wide eyed and with his jaw hanging open.

A peel of thunder rumbled in from outside.

"Rain?" Kander raised a surprised eyebrow.

"We had better get the horses inside and find a good room to make camp in," barked Sergeant Tandrak. "Then we can get our fill of exploring."

Captain Favel agreed. So they brought in the horses and bedded them in an ancient stable, where they also discovered a supply of old pitch torches. They were overly dry and burned too fast, but at least they burned.

"Now to find a place to set up camp for the night." Captain Favel began unpacking supplies and encouraged the others to do the same.

"Let's camp up in the tower!" suggested Tark with boyish enthusiasm edging his voice. The boy's idea didn't set well with Captain Favel. It would mean dragging supplies up several flights of stairs. "Please, Captain!" pleaded the boy. "Please let's camp up in the tower. I'll carry your things if they're too heavy for you."

Captain Favel smiled. Laughed burst from the others. So they trekked to the tower. And Captain Favel carried his own saddle, pack, and bedroll, while the others made a not so successful effort at holding back their smiles. They made a second trip for other necessary supplies. Several times over, while trudging up and down the stairs, Tark expressed his delight, and Captain Favel cast him a less than honest smile.

Outside, the violence of the coming storm intensified.

Kander stood at the edge of the tower's covered balcony to watch the lightning display and wait for the rain he could see dripping from the onrushing clouds. He looked down on the darkening courtyard as a bolt of lightning flashed its momentary luminosity. Kander's heart leaped to his throat. The storm revealed a serpentine creature, like the one they had found dead in the cave out on the Stakz. But this creature was alive and had just entered the fortress by way of the same gate they had entered. Kander's spine turned cold as ice.

Not waiting for another bolt of lightning, he turned on his heels and sought out Captain Favel. "One of those snakeman has entered the ruin," he whispered sharply.

Captain Favel followed him to the balcony.

He watched the dark courtyard. For a moment, he thought he saw movement near the entrance to the castle, but he could not be sure. Sheet lightning came to his aid. The courtyard stood empty. The sky crackled with wild laughter.

"Are you sure?" murmured Captain Favel.

"I'm not one given to seeing visions, especially of such a vile nature," snapped Kander. "It was definitely one of the snakemen."

They returned to where the others stood waiting in bated silence, having sensed that something was amiss. With cocked eyebrows they looked from Captain Favel to Kander.

"So by the bog, what's up, Captain?" F.F. Bog Frog broke the quiet.

"We have an unwelcome visitor—a snakeman." Captain Favel gritted his teeth, and his eyes swept the room. "Where is Sergeant Tandrak?"

"He went to check on the horses." Xzwindra clasped a nervous hand to her chest.

Captain Favel paced to the door of the tower room. The hinges were rusty but the door proved functional, though the metal rod that served as a lock was so corroded with rust that it wouldn't slide. With water and his dagger, Captain Favel freed the bar.

"Bolt the door behind me," he commanded as he slipped out of the room. "And keep your weapons handy. Kander, watch the balcony. The snakeman may be able to crawl up the wall. Can you use a weapon, Fiffle?"

"A weapon? A weapon?" grunted F.F. Bog Frog. "By the bog, the only weapon I ever used was a pointed stick to spear peddle fish. But by muck and by mud, give me a sword, an' I'll do what I can!"

Captain Favel nodded toward the supplies.

Kander reached into a leather pouch, pulled out a sword, and gave it to F.F. Bog Frog. It was the black sword with a long wavy blade that they had taken from one of the dead snakemen out on the Stakz.

With torch in hand, Captain Favel disappeared down the circling stairs in search of Sergeant Tandrak.

Kander took a deep breath, closed the heavy tower door, and slid the big iron bar into place with a clink. Then Kander listened with his ear against the door, but the only sound he could hear was the thump, thump of his own heart.

Beyond the door, Captain Favel padded silently down into the darkness, sword at the ready and longbow draped across his back.

Back in the tower, Xzwindra put Patrexna and Tark in a protected corner and assigned F.F. Bog Frog to stand guard over them. Then she went to the balcony to check the courtyard. Large, cold raindrops, blown by a stiff breeze, spattered on the rail and at her feet.

In the darkness below, a darkling inhaled the night air, his eyes turned upward, locked on the figure that leaned over the baluster searching the night. The darkling lurched noiselessly through the gloom to the tower wall and began to climb inch by inch. Lightning stroked the ebon sky, and thunder shook the ancient fortress. The creature momentarily froze in place, eyes fixed on the balcony. "I sssmell them," it whispered.

The darkling had not been seen, nor his low hiss heard. The deadly venom that dripped from its fangs fell on a vine. The vine shriveled.

"I don't see anything out here," snarled Xzwindra. "Do you think Captain Favel and Sergeant Tandrak are all right?"

Kander did not attempt an answer. He gritted his teeth, cranked his crossbow and placed an arrow. His hands, wet with sweat, felt cold. He glanced out to where Xzwindra leaned against the railing like a statue in silhouette against the nighttime sky. He felt a sudden sense of fear for her. He crossed toward the balcony. The rain now fell in sheets. "You'd better come on in out of the rain." He spoke softly, controlling his fear. "We've no fire to dry you out if you get soaked. Besides, it's safer inside."

"I suppose." She left the balcony, her eyes staring through the darkness at the bolted door across the room. "I'll be glad when Captain Favel and Sergeant Tandrak return. Should we go look for them? They might need our help."

"They're soldiers. They'll be all right." Kander didn't really believe it, but he said it anyway. Then he added, "Besides, our responsibility is to protect Tark and Patrexna. Captain Favel and Sergeant Tandrak know what they're doing."

"By the bog!" croaked Fiffle as he leapfrogged past them with his sword projected outward. Kander and Xzwindra whirled about. Dripping rain, a snakeman crawled over the balcony rail, hood flared, tongue flicking in and out, and its eyes steadily fixed on Xzwindra. Patrexna and Tark huddled trembling in their dark corner. Kander and Xzwindra both raised their crossbows, but Fiffle had come between. The snakeman hissed a violent warning, followed by the clang of sword on sword.

"By muck and by mud, you're a quick one!" chattered F.F. Bog Frog. Then he cried out in pain and tumbled head over heels, landing at Kander's feet.

TWANG! Kander loosed his arrow. THUNK! It lodged in the ornate doorpost inches from the beast's right shoulder.

Xzwindra could not control her shaking hands. TWANG! SMASH! Her arrow shattered against the wall. Before either could set another arrow, the darkling assaulted Xzwindra, his sword flashing like the sheets of lightning that lit the sky without. Xzwindra dropped to the floor avoiding the snakeman's first blow that had been aimed at her neck. She rolled to the side. The creature's tail swept around, taking Kander's feet from beneath him and blocking Xzwindra's escape. The darkling raised its sword intent on killing Xzwindra, but its eyes went wide when the wavy black blade of F.F. Bog Frog's drove into its vile body. Venom ejected from the beast's fangs fell on Xzwindra's leg, and burned the skin.

Kander, having regained his feet, drew his sword. The silver blade sliced the night, air cutting through the darkling's hooded neck and driving half way through its spine. The creature crumpled to the floor.

F.F. Bog Frog, having leaped aside, stumbled and smashed against the wall. He slowly slid down the cold stones to the floor.

Xzwindra hurriedly crawled to his side. "Fiffle, are you all right?"

"F.F. Bog Frog! F.F. Bog Frog!" cried Tark. He fled his corner to the bogfrogle's side.

"By the bog, that fellow was quick!" whispered Fiffle through pained lips. He grimaced, and for the first time his forever smile looked like a frown. His left arm hung loosely at his side. His shoulder drooped and was saturated with blood.

Tark fell on Fiffle's lap, wrapped his arms around his waist, and sobbed .

Kander cut away F.F. Bog Frog's shirt with his dagger, revealing a deep puncture wound. Fortunately, the darkling blade had missed the heart. With Xzwindra's help, Kander dressed the wound, while Fiffle did what he could to comfort Tark.

Patrexna joined them momentarily, then stepped aside where she could watch the balcony while the others did the doctoring.

"I wish Captain Favel and Sergeant Tandrak would return," groused Xzwindra as Kander dressed the burn on her leg. She gazed at the door and wondered what was happening in the darkness beyond.

Chapter 54

When Captain Favel left the tower loft, he hurried down the spiral stairs. He did not want Sergeant Tandrak taken unawares. The stairway led to a long hall lined with doors that opened to the right and left. His torch cast eerie shadows that jerked his eyes one direction then another and caused his heart to leap. Halfway down the hall, he turned to the left and stole down another flight of steps to a large chamber adjacent to the stable. As he reached the bottom of the steps, two snakemen slithered forth from the shadows. Black swords sliced the air. Captain Favel's silver blade flashed in response. Sparks flew like lightning and the crash of blades rang like thunder.

One of the darklings circled Captain Favel to the right, while the other shuffled to the left. And when Captain Favel shifted his eyes to the right, the snakeman to the left brought his tail across the floor like a whip. Captain Favel heard the tail swish over the stone floor and leaped even as he parried a blow from the other darkling's sword. As his feet came down, he lurched forward between the two darklings, rolled, and came to his feet, torch and sword still in hand. He made for an alcove from which one of the monsters had originally stepped into the light of his torch. Standing in the arched doorway of the alcove, he kept both darklings in front of him. The narrow opening to the nook nullified the use of their tails.

At about the same time in the stable down a hall and beyond closed doors, Sergeant Tandrak was giving the horses grain when he noticed a slight movement among the shadows across the room. At that same moment, his ears picked up the distant clash of swords. He feigned ignorance of both, though his eyes shifted toward the crossbow he had laid in the manger, now out of reach and on the other side of the horse. "Easy boy, let's check and see if there's any hay in that manger," he muttered. He patted the horse on the neck and slipped under to the feeding trough on the opposite side.

As Sergeant Tandrak reached into the manger and wrapped his fingers around the butt of his crossbow something moved between him and the torch on the far wall, casting its shadow over him. Instinctively, he swung around with the uncranked bow extended to meet the falling blade of the darkling sword. WHAM! He parried the black blade off to the side, rolled backward under the horse's neck, and came up on his feet, cranking his bow. With a singular fluid motion, he set a quarrel.

Yet another snakeman slinked out of the shadows from behind the horse, even as the first darkling slipped beneath the halter rope that tethered the rearing, agitated horse.

Sergeant Tandrak jerked up his crossbow and pulled the trigger. The powerful horse let his rear hooves fly, sending the second darkling rolling across the stable floor.

But the first darkling struck even as Sergeant Tandrak let his arrow fly. The snakeman's black blade impaled Sergeant Tandrak's side, slicing through and protruding out the back. The darkling released his grip on the sword and stumbled backward, slumping to the floor with an arrow protruding from its chest.

Sergeant Tandrak winced in pain as he cranked his bow and turned to face the second darkling that had regained its feet. The black sword sliced downward as Sergeant Tandrak triggered his bowstring.

In the chamber beyond the stable, Captain Favel parried one darkling sword, turned, caught the second snakeman off guard, and drove his sword home.

The darkling convulsed to the side, wrenching Captain Favel's sword from his hand. Instantly, the first snakeman moved in for the kill.

Captain Favel dropped to the floor as the black blade sliced air above his head, smashed against the wall, and broke off at the hilt. Captain Favel leaped from the doorway. The other darkling had stumbled away and now lay sprawled on the floor with the instrument of death protruding from its chest.

Captain Favel lunged for his sword. However, the living darkling brought its tail around, wrapping Captain Favel's ankles and pulling his feet from beneath him. He hit the floor, rolled to his back, but before he could regain his feet, the snakeman was on top of him. Fangs bared, the viperous creature struck, and Captain Favel could do nothing to stop him. But as the darkling's white fangs flashed, TWANG!—a bowstring sang its song. THUD! An arrow drove into the snakeman's forehead, lifting it up and away from Captain Favel's neck. The captain shoved the creature aside and sprang to his feet. He scooped up the torch that had fallen just out of his reach.

The darkling shuddered. Its hood flared and its mouth writhed, hissing agony and spitting angry words, and then it fell silent.

Captain Favel turned, and the light from his torch fell on Sergeant Tandrak, who stood near the far door, leaning heavily against the wall. CLANK, CLATTER! His crossbow dropped to the floor.

Face covered with blood and with a darkling sword hilt extruding from his side, Sergeant Tandrak reached out a trembling hand as if seeking help.

Captain Favel rushed to his side, grasped his waiting hand, and put an arm around him to hold him up, while being careful to hold the cresset out and away. Their eyes met and the affection that soldiers share passed between.

"Can you make it to the tower?" Concern edged Captain Favel's voice. His eyes swept the shadows.

Sergeant Tandrak forced a smile and gave a grunt of affirmation. Leaving their weapons where they lay, the comrades staggered back to the tower, knocked at the door, and stumbled inside when it opened.

The glancing blow Sergeant Tandrak had taken to his head, though bloody, was superficial. The sword in his abdomen was another matter. "It's not the kind of injury one lives to brag about. Hurts bad." Sergeant Tandrak chuckled horsely then sucked air and gritted his teeth.

"It has to come out." Captain Favel gripped Sergeant Tandrak's shoulder as if to say, "You know that, don't you?" He blinked back the tears. Although he was a soldier hard as nails, he was also a man of compassion.

"Well, friend," said Sergeant Tandrak as he set his jaw against the pain, "there is no time like the present."

The two soldiers' eyes met again, and the love, not merely of comrades, but of friend for friend passed between them. Although the others stood by the two soldiers seemed to be alone. Sergeant Tandrak nodded toward the hilt of the sword. Captain Favel slowly wrapped his hand around the haft, gritted his teeth, and then with an even pull, he extracted the black blade. Sergeant Tandrak shuddered, his teeth ground, and his eyes rolled back in his head. As the sword came out, he sucked air again and forced a grim smile. Captain Favel hurriedly dressed the wounds and wrapped his midsection with part of a blanket Kander had torn for him.

"Why did those snake things attack us? Are there more of them?" snapped a teary-eyed Tark.

"They came looking for you, Tark," breathed his mother. "The Pagyns do not want you to be king. They will do whatever they can to stop you from returning to Xzwendaria." She arched her eyebrows and raised her hands to the side. "And I do not know if there are more."

"I doubt there are any more of the creatures," said Captain Favel. "They would have come to the aid of the others or attacked separately by now."

Tark looked at Sergeant Tandrak. An angry grimace sheeted his face. "When I am king, I will drive the wretched Pagyns from our land!" He raised a clenched fist as if defying the darkness. "Truly, I will! Every last one of them!"

Sergeant Tandrak's eyes sparkled, and he let out an anguished snigger. "He will make a good king," he mused. Captain Favel nodded his agreement. The sergeant added weakly, "How is F.F. Bog Frog doing? Looks like he fared about as well as I did."

"He'll be all right," said Xzwindra. "What about you?"

"Well, blood's not bubbling up through my throat yet." He rasped, then winced in pain. "Only time will tell, huh?"

"Only time will tell," repeated Captain Favel as he prayed to Baruch for his friend.

Tark was the only one who slept that night, and he did so in spite of himself. They did not allow Sergeant Tandrak or Fiffle to sleep. "Stay awake, and keep fighting," they told them.

As the night passed, Sergeant Tandrak became more and more thirsty. They wet his lips but would not let him drink. When morning approached, he smiled. "Ya know, Captain, I just might live through this ordeal." Though weariness strained his voice, strength reflected in his eyes. "Give me a skin a' water. If I'm destined to die, I'd just as soon it wasn't from thirst. I'll live with the results. Besides, it will let us know how serious things really are."

Reluctantly, Captain Favel agreed.

Xzwindra brought a water skin, lifted it to the patient's mouth, and let him drink.

"Ah! Now that's good water, even if it does taste like leather!" sighed Sergeant Tandrak. He wiped his mouth with the back of his hand.

A broad smile crept across Captain Favel's face. His friend would live.

With the dawn and Captain Favel"s approval, they decided to allow the two patients to sleep. "The danger of their slipping into unconsciousness is past," he judged.

Xzwindra and Patrexna did what they could to make the two patients comfortable, and soon, breathing rhythmically, both were dead to the world.

Kander, Captain Favel, Xzwindra, and Patrexna slipped out to the balcony. The storm had passed, but dark clouds threatened another outburst. They scanned the courtyard. It was empty and quiet.

"So how many of the snakemen were there?" asked Kander as he plopped down on the broad balcony rail and leaned back against the ivy-covered wall.

"One up here, and four down below." Captain Favel shifted his eyes from the courtyard and twisted the corner of his mouth upward. "Are there more somewhere? That I don't know, though I wish I did. And I must say that it's rather discomfiting to realize that the wretched creatures climb walls."

"Well, according to Grey Wolf, three of the snakemen died out in the desert, and we came across two more in the Stakz," reflected Kander. "That's ten all total. How many more could there be?"

"I don't think there are anymore," broke in Xzwindra. The others fixed their eyes on her. "My mother used to speak of the ten Bayl creatures. She called them darklings, even referred to them as her "children." They were in her command. And I believe she sent them, not only to destroy the heir, but to kill me as well. The darkling that crawled up the wall seemed focused on me rather than the heir."

Kander nodded in agreement. "Yes, the "darkling," as you call it, was definitely trying to get to you."

"What did you do with the carcass?" grunted Captain Favel.

Xzwindra leaned out over the rail and pointed to the brush below, where a darkling tail draped the overgrown bushes and snaked out onto the grass.

A grin flickered across Captain Favel's lined face. He turned toward the door and motioned for Kander to follow him. "Can you help me clean up the mess down there?" He turned to Xzwindra. "I think it's safe to assume you are right about the number of these darkling creatures. But still, bolt the door behind us, and keep a close watch."

Using one of the packhorses, Captain Favel and Kander dragged the five darklings out into the forest well beyond the fortress gate where their stench would not be so bothersome. They brought in dirt and covered the bloodied floor, saw to the horses' needs, and then returned to the tower.

Although the darkling blade had missed Sergeant Tandrak's vital organs, he had lost a lot of blood, and his wound was not a minor thing. Healing would take time.

And as for F.F. Bog Frog, after three weeks, all that was left of his wound was a scar.

They camped in the ancient fortress for six weeks and a day. It was then that Sergeant Tandrak, although not yet having regained full strength, assured Captain Favel that he was able to ride again.

The King's Company mounted up and left the ancient ruin. They threaded their way south, seeking to escape the encompassing Murkwold.

Chapter 55

The war machines General Bodrak inherited from Xvardris moved ever closer to Havenholt. Soldiers and slaves pressed forward side by side until they could be seen from the fortress walls.

"At this rate, they will reach the trenches we dug tomorrow," grated Jentrxn. "Is everything ready, General Vandwert?"

"All that is left is to give the order. But we'll have to act tonight. Our scouts report that the main army is only a day behind. We must strike and then retreat before they can come forward."

Jentrxn looked to Razrdris, Prior Forknedrn, and Targndel for their approval, then instructed General Vandwert to give the order. The general left to make preparations for the coming night.

"What about the King's Company?" asked Prior Forknedrn. "Any news?"

"Not since Private Sedrnal got word to us that they had passed beyond Luxurd," snapped Targndel. "His report was not encouraging. Said he'd be surprised if they made it. As you know, he remains at Yeps, watching and listening."

"His report came in more than nine months ago," retorted a despondent Jentrxn. "I do wish we would hear something more."

"They will return with the heir," stated Razrdris with an air of confidence. The others looked at him with questioning eyes, wondering if he knew something they didn't. He shrugged and added, "Baruch promised a perpetual heir. He will keep his promise."

"He made the promise long ago in another time," groused Targndel. "And perhaps what has been passed on to us as a promise is nothing more than a king's wish. Maybe Xtrakan simply presumed he would always have an heir. In fact, how do we know someone who lived after Xtrakan didn't make up the story about Baruch promising a perpetual heir? It's possible, you know."

"Always the skeptic," muttered Razrdris. "But I tell you, the heir will return."

"Razrdris, are your men ready to launch the initial attack come morning?" interjected Jentrxn, more to change the subject than to hear the answer he already knew. "The day's waning, and we have much to do before the dawning of another."

While the council met, men and even some women hauled buckets of pitch and baskets of rocks up to the rampart. A multitude of hands stacked spears and stockpiled arrows at strategic locations along the high wall. They placed firepots and pitch-readied arrows where they would be available to every fifth archer. Throughout the fortress, people scurried here and there, making preparations for the coming battle.

When darkness fell, the gates quietly swung open and two battalions of cavalry galloped out into the night. One battalion rode to a staging area north of the Pagyn war machines. The other battalion of Resistance soldiers thundered south. Also, two hundred foot soldiers crept out into the forest of blackened stumps where they hid in holes dug for the morrow's battle. When the enemy woke with the dawn, they would see the same blackened stumps that had been there the day before, but behind or under each stump would lurk a Resistance soldier.

So the night passed. And with the dawn, the Pagyn war machines creaked slowly forward once again.

When the enemy reached the trenches, Razrdris ordered the front gates opened, and with footmen following, he rushed forward to a mound built on the fortress side of the trenches.

The Pagyn soldiers who were with the war machines moved forward to defend it, while their slaves worked to bridge the first of the three trenches.

The Pagyn soldiers were met with a barrage of arrows. And once the arrows were loosed, the bowmen retreated out of the Pagyns' range. The Pagyn soldiers passed over the first ditch only to meet another hail of arrows as they reached the second ditch. The second barrage of arrows expended, Razrdris and his men retreated back inside the gates of the fortress, while bowmen up on the wall kept the Pagyn soldiers from advancing on the retreating guardsmen. As the gates in the wall shut behind the archers, a horn sounded on the rampart. Resistance soldiers came out from behind and under every stump. The startled Pagyns turned to face the ambush. As they did, the gates of Havenholt swung open again and horsemen rode forth to the attack.

The ram's horn wailed again, and the two battalions of cavalry waiting in the staging areas to the north and south behind the war machines thundered forth. The riders did not carry bows; rather they conveyed pitch and fire.

Most Pagyn slaves scattered. The few who stood their ground died. It was not long before fire and smoke could be seen rising above the forest.

The Resistance had successfully crushed the forward guard of the Pagyn army.

When the main army saw the rising flames and billowing smoke, they rushed forward to join the fray. But by the time they arrived, the Resistance had retreated. Slaves who had come out of hiding tried to put out the fires, throwing dirt, beating the flames with rags, and shouting for water—but there was none. So the Pagyn war machines temporarily ground to a halt.

The siege of Havenholt had begun.

Chapter 56

Wazrxna awoke from her dream in a cold sweat, her body trembling. In her dream she heard the cries of her dying children. And as the last wail of her darklings died away, a sword fell to the earth. The sword became a gravestone, a marker that stood in deathly silence outside a castle wall in a distant forest. She awoke as the gravestone suddenly shuddered and sank into the ground.

Dread gripped Wazrxna's heart. She dressed, called her servant, and sent him out into the city. Then she left her room in the castle and hurried down the dark street toward the Black Chancel.

She paced back and forth at the foot of the altar until her servant appeared with a crying male child in his arms. She grabbed up the sacrifice, with a curt bark dismissed her servant, and ascended the altar stairs. At the apex, she performed the required ritual. As the stench of death rose above the altar, Bayl appeared to her, his eyes red with anger. He struck out at her with his fangs dripping venom. And although this was only a vision, she recoiled in fear.

"The darklingsss are dead!" spat the serpent god. "Our children have failed usss. The blood of a god ran in their veinsss, but they were weak becaussse of your mortality. They have been ssslain in the Murkwold. Now you mussst loossse the horssseman. The heir mussst be dessstroyed. He mussst not return to Xzwendaria. It isss your lasst chancssse, Wazsssrxsssna. If you fail, you will die with the othersss. Loossse the horssseman!"

"Yes, Lord Bayl," murmured Wazrxna, her eyes downcast. And with trembling voice, she added, "I will loose the horseman. But once he rides free and the heir is destroyed, how do we bind the horseman again?"

Bayl chortled. "Oncssse the horssseman isss loosssed, he cannot be bound. He will do your bidding in exssschange for the loosssing. But when he hasss dessstroyed the heir, he will do hisss own bidding. It isss the pricssse we mussst pay for your failuresss. Yet, he will ssspare you, for you are hisss doorway to freedom. But be careful, for he isss feral."

"I will heed your words, Lord Bayl." Wazrxna's voice quivered as she spoke, for she feared the horseman named Diabolus. Indeed, Diabolus's eyes brought fear to the stoutest of hearts. He wielded a fiery sword called Hades and rode a horse named Dread, whose breath went out into the world, striking fear in the hearts of men. The horse and rider were one. They were Death, and no one could stand before him.

Wazrxna stumbled down the steps of the altar. Her head felt light, her legs weak. At the foot of the altar, she collapsed to the chancel floor, where she spent the remainder of the night. There, with the coming of the dawn, her servant found her sprawled on her face. He touched her shoulder. She sprang awake, rolled to her back with a start, her eyes wide with fright.

The horseman had ridden through her dreams, terrorizing her mind. A shudder ran the course of her spine. She brushed her hand across her forehead, wiping away the cold sweat that had come with her servant's touch. "I will not loose the horseman!" she muttered.

Instantly, the image of Bayl appeared in her mind, his eyes flashing anger, and his fangs dripping venom. Coiled and threatening to strike, he hissed in her thoughts, "Loose the horseman! Loose the horseman!"

She shook her head to clear it of the vision and command.

"Are you all right, my lady?" her servant asked. She nodded and tried to smile, but the smile would not come. She got to her feet, shivering.

"You must be cold, my lady."

"Did you hear the voices?" she murmured.

The servant's eyebrows cocked upwards.

"Never mind." She bit her lip, then glanced up at her servant and tried to smile. "The gods speak. They demand a sacrifice."

Her servant's face went tight, and he nodded as if her words explained all.

"Tomorrow is the sixth of Steedra, the month of the horse," she mused as they left the chancel. Then gritting her teeth, she turned to her servant and declared, "I'll need six babies, and each must be six days old tomorrow. Have them ready for sacrifice by the sixth hour of the morrow's night—three male nurslings and three female nurslings. Buy them if you can, take them if you must. Bring them to the lower chancel, the Pit of Darkness. They will be offered on the Deep Altar, on the Obelisk of the Abyss."

The servant bowed and hurried off to do as he had been instructed. He had learned long ago not to question Wazrxna's commands, but this time he obeyed reluctantly. Not because of the number of babies required, but this time he felt an inner sense of terror. He feared participating in this vile machination. He felt a deeper sense of evil than ever before. Still, he was no fool. Because he valued his life, he did her bidding, not knowing which evil might be greater as far as his own welfare was concerned.

Before nightfall on the sixth of Steedra, Wazrxna's servant brought six six-day-old babies to the Black Chancel to ready them for sacrifice. On their foreheads, he branded them with the number 666 in black. He branded their chests with a black heart inside a five-point star. Beside each crying babe, he placed a black-bladed dagger.

He prepared the nurslings in a side chamber of the lower chancel. Prior to the sixth hour of the sixth Steedra, Wazrxna appeared, took a male child, and entered the chancel. In the middle of the chancel, she approached the altar. This altar was the exact opposite of the altar in the upper chancel. The Deep Altar was a replica of the High Altar except that it was cut into the floor extending downward rather than upward. The altar above was mass, but the altar below was nothingness, the Pit of Darkness.

Wazrxna walked down the steps of the altar with the child in her hands. At the bottom of the altar was a black stone that stood waist high, the Obelisk of the Abyss. The obelisk stretched six feet across. A hole cut in the center of the stone—the Bottomless Pit—emanated light and heat, as if coming from the fires of Hades far below. Wazrxna laid the sacrifice on the Obelisk of the Abyss. The child levitated above the hole—the Bottomless Pit. At the sixth hour, she silenced the child's cries with the black-bladed dagger. Fire flared from the pit in a giant column, consuming both the sacrifice and the dagger.

At the seventh hour, Wazrxna offered a second babe, a female child. At the eighth hour, she offered a male child, and so on until the twelfth hour. When the twelfth hour came, the sixth nursling, a female child, levitated on the air and heat that came from the altar. The black dagger fell, and the flame leaped upward, consuming the sacrifice. Suddenly, Wazrxna saw a fiery devil staring back at her from above the altar. She fell away in fear.

The demonic apparition laughed. "You have offered the Hecatomb of Releasing," snarled the apparition. "The Pit of Blackness has opened. Who would you release?"

"The horseman," blurted the shaken priestess. As she spoke the words, a great dread filled her heart.

The demonic apparition burst forth in vile laughter and clapped his fiery hands. Thunder shook the chamber, throwing Wazrxna to the floor.

When she looked up, the apparition was gone. Wazrxna ran up the altar stairs and out of the Pit of Darkness, out of the Black Chancel, out into the dark street. She stopped, spun on her heels, and stared. She sucked air, but her breath caught in her throat, for she heard the sound of hooves pounding over the face of the earth, keeping rhythm with the beat of her heart. She trembled.

Her servant, who had followed her from the chancel, now stood beside her. He took her by the arm. She leaned on him, too weak to stand on her own. A desire to flee gripped the servant's heart, but he stayed by the side of his mistress. They shuffled along the street, somehow finding their way home where they threw themselves on their beds.

But for Wazrxna sleep did not come. The horseman did. Wazrxna, terrorized by hoofbeats approaching from of the north, held her pounding chest. Her eyes stared into space as Death flew like the wind, his hooves rumbling. Fear went before Death, riding the breath of his steed's flaring nostrils. The hammering hooves stopped. Wazrxna knew the horseman was near, but her eyes would not focus. Terror wrenched at her heart.

"What service do you require?" Death's voice rumbled out of the night. "Whatever recompense you ask is binding. But once your desire is fulfilled, I am unbound. So tell me, what do you require of me? Speak, and it shall be done!"

"The life of the heir to the throne of Xzwendaria!" rasped Wazrxna into the darkness. "You must destroy the heir, the grandson of the great king, Xtrakan!"

"It shall be done!" The voice broke through the night like a violent breeze. Then in a vision, Wazrxna's eyes focused on the horseman, and her heart quailed. Diabolus's eyes shined immeasurably deep and red with the fire of hatred. The number 666 scarred his forehead. And his fear-breathing steed emanated blackness deeper than night, as did the robe that enshrouded Death. And rider and steed seemed as one. A black sword filled the horseman's right hand, and the edge of his sword danced with black fire. Before the horseman stood a mountain, as if restraining him. With great power, he brought Hades down on the mountain, and the mountain vanished.

The vision faded, and Wazrxna trembled upon her bed.

Chapter 57

Although the dark of night enshrouded Havenholt, everyone suddenly stirred to life, their hearts filled with fear. They leaped from their beds and ran to the walls to man the parapets. Men gazed out on the killing field of the previous day. Nothing stirred. Eyes turned to the north. Did they hear the sound of beating hooves? Sweat broke out on every brow, and every hand trembled.

Beyond the killing field, the Pagyn aggressors also came to life as fear swept through their camp. They scurried from their tents, swords and bows atremble in their hands. Surely the enemy had ridden forth from the fortress and was upon them! They peered through the darkness toward Havenholt. Moonlight revealed gates still shut and a killing field barren and silent.

"A horseman comes!" someone shouted. All eyes turned toward the north.

The hoofbeats stopped. And although warriors' hands ceased their trembling, fear did not give up its grip on their hearts. Men on both sides of the killing field no longer felt themselves the courageous soldiers of the day gone by.

So it was, when dawn spilled out unto the killing field and the enemy armies engaged in battle, the awful intensity of the previous day could not be found. Somehow the day's battle seemed unimportant. Each soldier found his or her thoughts engaged by a presence to the north.

Chapter 58

*T*he King's Company crossed the Yeps Corridor protected by the night. They camped at Pinnacle Peak, the same campsite from which they had started their journey across the Savage Lands. When morning came, Kander wanted to continue on to Havenholt.

Captain Favel shook his head. "First, I must go into Yeps." He looked down toward the village. "We need to find out what has transpired in Xzwendaria while we trekked the Savage Lands. For all we know, the Resistance may have fled Havenholt. I don't think we want to go rushing headlong into Xvardris' waiting arms. And further, I would have a word with Private Sedrnal. He may be waiting for us at Yeps."

With an impatient grimace and a nod of his head, Kander acknowledged the right of it. Still he protested, "But there will surely be soldiers at Yeps, waiting and watching. Dare we take the risk?"

"Not we, Kander. You will stay here," rejoined Captain Favel. "You are responsible for the heir. Xzwindra and I will go into Yeps. We will be back tomorrow, midmorning at the latest. If we do not return by noon, continue on to Havenholt with great caution. We must not let the heir fall into Xvardris's hands."

With a laugh, Kander protested that Xzwindra was his woman, not Captain Favel's. Xzwindra cast him a disapproving glance. He shrugged, then helped Captain Favel with a new disguise. Wearing a broad grin, he shaved the captain's head, including his eyebrows, then pasted on a curly black mustache and beard, attached a large ring to his ear, and fitted him in blousy pants and shirt. "Yes!" he mumbled. "Yes!"

He turned his smile on Xzwindra. Although she bristled, he set to work on her as well. He dyed her hair black and ratted it so that it sprang up and out like a fountain, after which he sprinkled it with glitter. He attached large rings to her ears and snapped a ring around her neck. Her clothes were similar to Captain Favel's but more colorful.

"You two are Vandarian Rovers from the south," stated Kander. "You would like to go to Luxurd to entertain the miners—a price, of course."

"What if they ask questions?" shot back Xzwindra. Doubt filled her eyes.

"Tell them you are supposed to meet with a miner named Pegle to make arrangements," responded Kander. "He won't mind, and they'll probably recognize his name and think you're legit. You, Xzwindra, will go by the name Rosa. Captain Favel, you are Borga."

"We are entertainers," affirmed Captain Favel. "What kind of entertainers?"

"Well, not singers, that's for sure!" replied Kander. "How about puppeteers? And your puppets are at the docks at Belem to be shipped once arrangements are made."

So Borga and Rosa rode into Yeps, turning every eye.

Pagyn soldiers seemed to be everywhere. Soldiers stopped them at the edge of town to check them out. They were checking everyone. In fact, inquisitive Pagyn soldiers stopped them on the streets. "Who are you? Where are you from? Why have you come to Yeps?" "Puppeteers?" The soldiers laughed and mocked, pretending to dance puppets on a string. But on each occasion, they let Captain Favel and Xzwindra pass, satisfied with their story.

As Borga and Rosa, they gadded about town, eventually arriving at the Twin Spur Inn at midday, and nary a customer was in the place. They sought out an inconspicuous corner from which they could eye everyone who came and went.

The curious innkeeper probed, nodded, and cocked an eyebrow, but he seemed to accept their explanation.

"No, Pegle's not in town. Ain't seen him anyway. An' if he were in town, I'd a' seen him because he hangs out here," grunted the innkeeper. "But if yer expectin' him, I'm sure he'll show. Pegle's one a' those ya can count on. More 'n I can say for some a' those who hang about the town. Know what I mean?"

They tipped their heads in affirmation and explained that they were actually two days early. The innkeeper laughed and told them that Pegle was the kind who wouldn't be late but wouldn't be early, either. They chatted for a while longer and then ordered the most expensive meal on the menu. The innkeeper went away from their table smiling.

"At least, he didn't recognize us from the last time we were here," whispered Xzwindra.

Captain Favel bristled and cast her a disgruntled glance. "And would you recognize us in these ridiculous outfits?" he groused.

Xzwindra did her best to smother her laughter.

A THUMP! THUMP! THUMP! on the hardwood floor diverted their attention. Both Xzwindra and Captain Favel gazed at the door. Just inside the doorway stood Pegran and Private Sedrnal. Pegran stood perfectly balanced on a fine, varnish-shined wooden leg.

"Either a' you men named Pegle?" barked Captain Favel. Both heads snapped in his direction, eyes alight with recognition, not of the face but certainly of the voice. Private Sedrnal broke into a broad, knowing smile, and then with a gentle elbow from Pegran, he stuffed it.

"No, but I be acquainted with the fellow," rumbled Pegran. "Can we join you? A friend a' Pegle's be a friend a' mine."

With a welcoming gesture, Captain Favel motioned toward the empty chairs.

THUMP! THUMP! THUMP! Pegran and Private Sedrnal crossed the room. They stood momentarily staring at the Vandarian Rovers and repressing laughter.

Exasperated, Xzwindra broke the quiet. "Sit down!" she snapped. They gave a nod and took a chair. "I'm Rosa and this is Borga."

A rumble of laughter momentarily came to the surface. Pegran shot Private Sedrnal an accusing glance. Then with eyes aglitter, he turned back to Rosa and Borga. "Mus' be

Kander's work!" he whispered. "But more importantly, did ya find the heir?"

In quiet undertones, Captain Favel told them all. And the sparkle drained from Private Sedrnal's eyes when Captain Favel told how Corporal Mifstern succumbed to temptation in the Witherdeep—and how he had died. But both Private Sedrnal and Pegran sat intrigued as Xzwindra told the story of the Bogfrogls.

"For meself, I can't wait ta meet this F.F. Bog Frog," mumbled Pegran. "Sounds ta be an interesting feller."

"He is at that," said Captain Favel, as he glanced about the room. "But what about the situation in Xzwendaria? Any news of the Resistance?"

Private Sedrnal filled them in on everything from the death of Xvardris to the siege of Havenholt. "But as far as we know, the fortress has not yet fallen into the hands of the Pagyns." He paused and looked down at his hands before continuing. "Xvardris had Zedria executed."

Captain Favel and Xzwindra's faces went white, and tears came to their eyes. "The Pagyns will pay!" grated Captain Favel.

"How have you avoided being taken by the soldiers, Sedrnal?" muttered Xzwindra, changing the subject.

"As you can see, I'm dressed like a miner." He spread his arms in self-display." I'm a friend of Pegle and Norgran and was sent to Yeps for treatment of miner's lung. I cough a lot, and the soldiers avoid me. They seem to think it's catching." Finally, their laughter broke free. And Sedrnal decided he would cough for the benefit of the innkeeper.

"Well, we had better be goin' our way," said Pegran after Sedrnal's display. "We don't want people getting' suspicious."

"We'll be making our way back to Pinnacle Peak after dark." Captain Favel addressed Private Sedrnal before turning again to the old prospector. "You going to join us, Pegran?"

"Don't rightly know." He gritted his teeth, momentarily lost in thought. Then added, "I'll come with Private Sedrnal tonight. Let you know then. After all, I do have to see this bog-frog! fellow!"

That evening as the night isolated Yeps, Captain Favel and Xzwindra slipped out of town and stole through the shadows back to camp.

An hour later, Pegran and Private Sedrnal quietly rode out of town. Free of the prying eyes of Yeps, they circled up into the hills and rode into the light of the campfire. A pleasant reunion followed. And both Pegran and Private Sedrnal got their first look at F.F. Bog Frog, who seemed as fascinated with Pegran's wooden leg and patched eye as Pegran and Private Sedrnal were with his unusual features.

"By the bog, I've never seen such a strange-looking leg in all my life!" croaked F.F. Bog Frog. He waved his arms wildly, then pointed and added, "Look! No foot!"

"And look here!" crowed Pegran. He unsheathed his broad-bladed knife, and without flinching, stabbed his leg. F.F. Bog Frog winced, drew in a deep breath, and nearly fainted. Pegran let go of the knife, and it stayed where he had stuck it. Fiffle's eyes shot as wide as the top of a goblet. But Pegran had mercy on the poor fellow, and with laughter riding his voice, he told him how the decrodile had bitten off his leg and that a wooden one had been attached. Fiffle slapped his knee and laughed long and hard.

"To more serious things," interjected Captain Favel. "With Havenholt under siege, where do we take the heir?"

"There is no other place to take him," muttered Private Sedrnal. "Besides, what good would it do to hide him in some safe haven if one existed? If Havenholt falls, it seems to me our hope of restoring him to the throne is all but lost."

"The presence of his Majesty at Havenholt may, in fact, give renewed energy and strength to the Resistance fighters," put in Kander. "And when word gets out that the heir has been crowned king at Havenholt, then perhaps the people in the villages will be encouraged to rise up and join the Resistance against their oppressors."

"But at Havenholt the heir would be in the place of greatest danger," protested Xzwindra. "That doesn't seem prudent to me."

Patrexna listened. Fear gripped her heart. She bit her lip. They must not send her son to Havenholt!

Tark could feel his mother's emotions. He looked up at her and saw the fear in her eyes. He laid a comforting hand on her knee and squeezed it, smiled, then he rose and stepped forward. "I will go to Havenholt," he announced with a firm voice. "That is where I belong."

Tears poured from his mother's eyes as she wept in her hands.

Kander gazed on the young king with pride shining in his eyes.

The others responded with brow-raising surprise, for the ten-year-old boy spoke like a man—like a king.

With the coming of the midnight hour, silence suddenly engulfed the company. Each thought they heard distant hoofbeats, or was it just the hammering of their hearts? The moment of dread passed, and they grabbed their weapons, thinking that surely soldiers had followed from Yeps. Facing the darkness, they surrounded the king. Nothing! Cautiously, they circled the bluff and looked down on the Yeps Corridor. Lights blinked in the village below, but they saw no signs of soldiers. But then, out of the north came the sound of a horse riding southward, hooves pounding like thunder. Fear whelmed the King's Company. Hands trembled, and knees quavered.

"A horseman comes! We must away!" barked Captain Favel. With hurried urgency, they broke camp, leaving their campfire blazing in the night. And so it was that Pegran's mind was made up for him. He fled south toward Havenholt with the King's Company. Dusty, Pegran's swayback nag, ran like a yearling, fear having renewed the old cob's youth.

And when the thunder of hooves no longer beat in their ears, they still felt the evil presence to the north. The dread of it pushed them on until at last they came to Havenholt, weary of their saddles and their hearts still filled with fear.

The return of the heir brought momentary hope to the Resistance. A shout of joy and triumph rose from the great stone fortress that caused the enemy to withdraw from their siege of the walls of Havenholt.

And among the enemy, in spite of General Bodrak's ranting, his men no longer had the will to press the battle. They ran quaking to their tents, waiting, watching for the dread rider out of the north.

Within the walls of Havenholt, after the initial shout of triumph at the coming of the king, despair returned to haunt the soldiers of the Resistance as well. Quavering at their stations on the wall, they too anticipated the arrival of the rider.

Also, the day the King's Company arrived at the fortress, the ruling council met and determined that Tark was in fact the rightful heir to the throne of Xzwendaria. The presence of the heir brought a new day to the land. A trumpet sounded in Havenholt, and the coronation began.

However, a pall of dread encompassed all who attended the grand occasion, for "the horseman comes!" whispered one soldier to another.

Chapter 59

As word filtered into Zwexdrof that the heir had returned and had been crowned king at Havenholt, a sliver of joy pierced the shroud of fear that enwrapped the people's hearts. The news even brought a smile of delight to Wazrxna's sculpted face. She commandeered a coach and with her servant headed for the camp at Havenholt to await the horseman that no man could stand before, that no man could conquer, for the horse and rider were Death, and the words were truth.

At Havenholt the king summoned Captain Favel, Xzwindra, Kander, and F.F. Bog Frog to join him and Jentrxn in waiting before Baruch. He also invited Sergeant Tandrak, but the journey south had taken its toll on the wounded warrior wracked with pain. The physicians confined him to his bed.

Prior Forknedrn presided over the sacrifice of a lamb. Then they all bowed before Baruch and waited. After four hours of unbroken silence, a vision came to them and set them atremble, for their widened eyes looked upon the terrible horseman and his fiery sword. "I am Death!" echoed in their minds. "And no man can stand before me! The end of all things is at hand!" But then a great black sword rose out of a murky sea and struck the horseman. Death died, and Diabolus fled to the Bottomless Pit. Hope returned.

The vision changed. Out on the killing field lay the black sword, and the horseman came. From the wall of Havenholt came a shout, "Who will wield the sword?" And no man was found who could wield the sword called Darkness and face Death. Tears rained down from heaven, and despair whelmed their hearts once again.

A voice suddenly broke upon the vision. "Build an altar before the gate of the fortress. And you, King Tarkedrx, place the sword of the darkling on the altar. He who is able to remove the sword from the altar shall be your champion." The vision passed.

The king commanded an altar to be built outside the gate. He took the sword Kander had taken from the darkling in the Murkwold, placed it on the altar, and stepped back. BOOM! Thunder rolled in the cloudless sky. CRACK! A bolt of lightning struck the sword and altar. An eerie silence fell on the fortress. After the silence passed, the king approached the altar, staring. The blade of the black sword appeared to have melted into the stone. He spun on his heels and shouted in his young voice to those gathered at the gate, "Who will be my champion? Step forward, and remove the sword from the altar!"

General Vandwert strode forward. He grasped the hilt of the sword in his powerful hands, but try as he might, he could not remove the sword from the altar. Jentrxn stepped to the fore. The sword remained in place. Targndel , Razrdris, and Captain Favel all tried and failed. Xzwindra reasoned that if a man could not slay the horseman, then perhaps a woman could. But to her dismay she too was unable to remove the sword—nor could Patrexna. Kander tried. The sword remained immovable. Man after man and woman after woman came to the altar, grasped the hilt of the darkling sword, but no one was found who could take up the sword of Darkness.

The sound of weeping rose to the heavens from the gates of Havenholt.

Indeed, that noise reached the encampment of the Pagyns. Wazrxna's eyes sparkled. She burst forth in laughter. Then the horseman! Fear heralded his coming. Death and destruction marked his passing. He left forests and villages burning. Men, women, and children fled before him. And now Diabolus came thundering onto the killing field, where he reined Dread to a halt between the two terror-stricken armies.

Death's eyes sought out Wazrxna, who stood beside General Bodrak at the head of the prostrate Pagyn army. And although his mouth seemed not to move, the horseman's voice echoed forth—deep, hollow, resonant—real yet unreal.

"I have come," Death snarled. "And as you have requested, the heir shall be destroyed, consumed by the fires of hell.

Yet, priestess of Bayl, once my deed is done, all that you possess will be mine. I will rule all realms. All people will do my bidding, or I will consume them by the black fire of my sword. And you, lady, shall be my slave."

"Yes, Lord of Darkness," murmured a tremulous Wazrxna. "We ask only that you destroy the heir. We are your servants."

The horseman slowly turned and faced the great fortress called Havenholt. The men who lined the rampart trembled. Those within the gates sought a place to hide from Death, but even hidden from Death's dread gaze, fear still gripped their hearts.

Courageously, the quaking king stood on the wall. His mother stood at his side as he looked down on the altar.

Jentrxn stood behind the king. He placed a trembling hand on the boy's shoulder.

Tears ran down Tark's cheeks, for he knew that Death drew nigh.

Yet, within the walls of Havenholt, one person did not quake in terror. When the others left the temple room, F.F. Bog Frog stayed behind. There at the Altar of the Lamb, overcome with the wonder of Baruch, F.F. wept before him confessing his sins and the sins of his people.

Suddenly, Baruch filled the temple with his glory.

Overwhelmed with reverence and awe, F.F. Bog Frog cast himself prostrate before the altar.

Baruch reached out from his glory and touched F.F. Bog Frog.

For the first time in his life, Fiffle felt clean, pure, whole. The glory faded, and F.F. Bog Frog rose to his feet with tears of joy running freely down his face. Then he realized that the others had left.

Out on the killing field, the horseman once again spoke without speaking. "I am the Lord of Darkness. I am Diabolus and Death. No man can stand before me. Send me your king, and the rest of you shall live."

In spite of their intense terror and unbridled fear, the soldiers of the Resistance refused to open the gates. Instead, with trembling hands, they took up their weapons and prayed for courage. But courage seemed but a distant memory, something they once knew but knew no more.

Death cried out again, "Open the gates! Yield your king!"

Leaders and followers alike fought back the desire to obey the commanding voice of Death, and swallowing fear, they stood their ground.

The horseman raised his shrill voice in rage. Fire danced in Diabolus's eyes. He lifted his dark, flaming blade and commanded the destruction of Havenholt's gates. Black fire exploded from his sword, shattering the gates of the fortress, opening the way for Death to seek its prey. As the smoke dissipated, the horseman cantered across the killing field toward the fortress.

The king appeared in the charred gateway. He walked to the altar, clinging to his mother, weeping like a child, though standing like a man. His mother's tears wet his blond hair.

Dread breathed a blast of chill air into the fortress. Stricken with fear, each man and woman stood at the ready but unable to move.

Then from the temple, F.F. Bog Frog loped across the courtyard. He hop-frogged through the still-smoldering gate, past the altar, and stood between the horseman and the king.

The horseman peered at Fiffle through fiery eyes. "And what is this monstrosity that dares stand in the face of Death?" boomed the horseman. And on Death's words rode laughter.

"I'm F.F. Bog Frog!" croaked Fiffle.

"Ah! So you are one of Baruch's many mistakes. Well, frog, he gave you a bad body and a foolish mind. My quarrel is not with you. It is with the king. Out of my way!"

F.F. Bog Frog leaped back and cast about for some weapon. He saw the darkling sword on the altar, grabbed the hilt, and turned on the horseman again. "By muck and by mud, if you want Tark, you'll have to come through me to get him!"

Laughter rolled across the killing field like thunder.

"No, I will not waste my power on the likes of you, frog except to strike you with fear and then let Dread run you into the ground."

The horseman dug his heels into blackness, and Dread sprang forward, hooves shaking the ground and its chill breath flowing freely. Death bore down on F.F. Bog Frog.

But F.F. Bog Frog stood firm, a smile spreading his face. Other than the incident in the Murkwold, Fiffle had never used a sword. A spear? A dagger? Yes. He looked at the black sword, for it felt strangely light in his hand. The brave bogfrogle shrugged a shoulder, stepped forward and hurled the Sword of Darkness with all his might.

Too late, the horseman saw the black blade hanging on the air. Too late he pulled back on the reins. The blade drove to Death's heart as Dread trampled F.F. Bog Frog beneath his pounding hooves. Then, dust flying, Dread skidded to a halt before the altar and the king.

"No man can stand before me!" sputtered Diabolus. Then he pointed his sword at the king and cried, "Igni crematus!" But Death's command fell to the dirt of the killing field unanswered.

At that moment, a clarion voice exploded out of the north. "Return! Return!" The earth quaked, and darkness whelmed the killing field. The horseman cast his empty eyes toward the north and struggled to remove the darkling sword from his chest, but his strength was gone. The ground beneath trembled. "Return!" growled the voice from the north. Dread turned, and Diabolus fled back to the pit from whence he had come.

As light returned to the killing field, it revealed the Pagyn army advancing, led by General Bodrak with Wazrxna at his side. The enemy descended on the crumpled body of F.F. Bog Frog.

Between the enemy and the body of their brave friend stood Captain Favel, Xzwindra and Kander. Private Sedrnal bolted from the fortress to join them.

"I will have the body of that wretched monstrosity!" snarled Wazrxna, pointing a trembling finger. "I'll tear the fool creature limb from limb and boil its hide in oil! It has spoiled everything!"

The contingent of King's Company stood firm.

With a violent gesture and a shout, General Bodrak commanded a company of his best soldiers forward to dispatch the four who stood over F.F. Bog Frog's body. But as the Pagyn swordsmen stepped to the fore – SWISH – SWISH – SWISH. Captain Favel notched arrow after arrow, dropping a Pagyn fighter with each. Xzwindra and Kander were not as efficient, but they too felled their share. Private Sedrnal nearly matched Captain Favel arrow for arrow. Yet, for every Pagyn who fell, another appeared. On they came.

Captain Favel notched his last arrow, but as he pulled the bowstring, an enemy arrow drove deep into his shoulder. He loosed his bowstring, but the arrow twanged wide of its mark. The quarrel he took spun him sideways. A second arrow pierced his back. He fell across F.F. Bog Frog's legs and struggled to rise, but he could not.

An arrow sank into Kander's thigh as he cranked his crossbow. His bowstring twanged, and the soldier who shot him fell. But as Kander pulled the trigger, a second arrow grazed the side of his head. Gritting his teeth against the pain, he reached for yet another arrow. His fingers fumbled at an empty quiver. He heard the swish of an arrow, felt the jolt, and then a burning pain in his chest. Driven backward, he stumbled and fell.

Xzwindra's eyes arched wide as she watched the black arrow drive into Kander's chest. She had dropped her own bow and was struggling to pull an arrow from her right arm. At the moment she saw the black arrow pierce Kander's chest, she felt the sudden impact of a Pagyn spear. She gasped air as blackness engulfed her.

Private Sedrnal, riddled with arrows, wobbling on his feet, tried to catch Xzwindra as she fell. His efforts proved useless. She slipped through his hands and sprawled on the killing field. Another black arrow hit home. Sedrnal stiffened. "War is an awful thing," he murmured, and staring blankly into space, he slipped to the dust beside Xzwindra.

A shout of triumph issued from the Pagyn soldiers as the last defender fell. The enemy surged forward. But as they approached the fallen of Xzwendaria, arrows rained down on them from the ramparts of Havenholt and forced them back. As the hail of arrows ceased, a column of horsemen broke from the gap that had been the fortress gate. Led by General Vandwert, the Resistance army drove into the enemy ranks like a wedge into wood, splitting their defenses asunder. A great wave of foot soldiers followed the horsemen, and the killing field became the stage of the bloodiest battle in the history of Xzwendaria.

While General Vandwert pressed the battle to the Pagyns, Major Targndel retrieved the bodies of the fallen heroes. He and his men carried them to the infirmary where an anxious Sergeant Tandrak ranted and raved, demanding release so he could join the battle. But when Major Targndel brought in Captain Favel, Sergeant Tandrak fell silent. His face turned white, and for the first time in his life, he felt repulsed by the violence of war. "Is he dead?" he gasped, his eyes fixed on the shaft protruding from the captain's chest.

"Not far from it," offered Major Targndel. "Appears the arrow lodged in the breastbone but didn't reach the heart. It's the quarrel in his back that concerns me most."

Sergeant Tandrak forgot the battle. He swallowed his pain and began assisting the healers as they cared for Captain Favel and the others.

F.F. Bog Frog lay unconscious with multiple broken bones and gashes and the side of his head badly bruised. But a healer told Sergeant Tandrak that none of the wounds appeared to be life-threatening. "If he regains consciousness in the next couple of days, he should make a good recovery."

Xzwindra, having taken a broad-bladed spear just below the rib cage, had lost a lot of blood, but she had recovered consciousness. However, her pulse was weak, and she seemed to be fading.

Kander's wounds, though severe, did not appear to be life-threatening. On the other hand, Private Sedrnal was not brought to the infirmary. Sergeant Tandrak wept like a child when he heard how the young soldier had died.

On the other side of the infirmary, a healer feverishly plied his art to Captain Favel's wounds, while Jentrxn held his brother's hand and with bowed head prayed to Baruch for him and the others. The physician removed the arrow that Major Targndel had broken off and left in Captain Favel's back, and then dressed the wound. "Not as bad as expected," mumbled the healer. "He'll live." And moments later, Captain Favel opened his eyes and slowly shifted them to his brother. The corners of his mouth turned up slightly, and Jentrxn saw a sparkle in his eyes. Only then did he feel assured that his brother would make it.

Major Targndel stood by Xzwindra as another healer tried to stop the bleeding of her wound. Xzwindra coughed and winced in pain. Blood trickled from the corner of her mouth. She looked up at Targndel and forced a smile. "What about the others?" she whispered.

Major Targndel took her hand and gave it a tender squeeze. He explained to her how each of the others was doing. The smile vanished from Xzwindra's face. She looked up into Targndel's eyes. A tear welled in hers. "Did you know?" she asked with a groan, her teeth clenched against the trauma of her wounds.

"Did I know what?"

"That I'm your daughter?" The words rattled from her throat. She coughed. More blood trickled down her cheek, but she did not remove her eyes from his.

She felt Targndel's hand turn clammy and saw the color drain from his face. His mouth moved, but all that escaped his lips was "Walzara?" He reached out a trembling hand and wiped the blood from her lips.

"She never existed," rasped Xzwindra. She sucked air, gritted her teeth, and then added, "Your Walzara is Wazrxna, the priestess of Bayl. She hoped. . .to compromise you and get the king killed. That was accomplished in other ways. I didn't know...you were my father, as you didn't know...I was your daughter. I'm glad you're my father. I hope you're not disappointed." Her face went red, and a tear fell from her eyelid. "I was...spy. I am sorry...Fa...Targndel."

Targndel found his voice. "Call me father, Xzwindra. And you've no need to be sorry. I'm delighted that you're my daughter. And I'm proud of you. In the end, you did what was right." He reached out his other hand and gently brushed back her hair. "You've always been special to me. Perhaps my heart knew what my head did not." Hot tears fell on his daughter's cheeks and mingled with hers.

She smiled and squeezed his hand. "I love you...Father."

Through blurred eyes, he looked at her and returned her smile. "And I love you, my daughter."

Xzwindra's grip tightened further as pain wrenched her body, and then her hand went limp.

Targndel wrapped his daughter in his arms and cried as he had never cried before.

From somewhere out on the wall came a trumpet's bray.

Chapter 60

Out on the loathsome killing field, General Vandwert sat astride his sweat-lathered charger, casting a grim eye at the carnage. An unbidden tear slipped from the corner of the general's eye. He hurriedly wiped it away.

In the distance, enemy troops fled the field of battle in disarray. General Bodrak lay sprawled in the dust at General Vandwert's feet, slain by the sword that hung heavy in the old soldier's hand. His eyes ranged the lists for sign of the evil priestess. "Escaped the noose!" he mumbled. He let his gaze focus again on the wanton reality of war. His lip quivered in spite of himself as he noted man after man who had fought at his side, who now lay silent on the hard, cold earth tinted with scarlet. Here and there able-bodied warriors of the Resistance attended the disabled, both their own and those of the Pagyn army.

Razrdris commanded the second battalion that poured forth from the splintered gate to pursue the fleeing Pagyns. Their job was to make sure the enemy did not regroup or return to Zwexdrof and hold the city hostage. Razrdris took prisoners of those who yielded, but all who opposed fell by the sword. Some fled into the charred forest and sought refuge in its shadows.

When General Bodrak fell, defeat seemed imminent, and Wazrxna abandoned the killing field. She fled into the blackened woodland. Stumbling aimlessly through the unfamiliar forest, bone-weary and fearing for her life, she finally crawled into the hollow of a partially burned tree. Although she felt compelled to find her way back to the safety of Zwexdrof, she could not. Her strength spent, she collapsed on a bed of dried leaves. As darkness spread its protective cloak about her, she remained awake, listening to the noises that broke the quiet of the night and continuing to quake in terror.

Hours later when Wazrxna finally fell asleep, in the shadowlands she relived the coming of the horseman. As Diabolus rode from the pit, the froglike creature appeared and hurled his sword. Wazrxna shrieked in rage. Her cry echoed into the night. She turned, and before her stretched the killing field. Hope rose in her heart. Her army surged toward victory. However, hope soon fled, for a shining sword flashed like lightning. Thunder shook the earth. General Bodrak fell from his charging steed. And then her reflective dream became a nightmare. She saw herself fleeing through the forest with a rider pounding the earth at her heels. Although utterly spent, she dared not stop. Gasping for air, she pressed on. The thunder of hooves drew closer. She turned and her eyes went wide, for she looked into the grim face of Major Targndel. He brandished a bloodied rapier and sat on his steed laughing at her. "I did love you!" she called out over her shoulder. "Truly I did, but my soul belonged to Bayl. Spare me, Targndel! Forgive me. I beg you to forgive me!"

The rider stopped. Tears ran down his ashen cheeks. He stared into space, no longer threatening death. Now he stood on the killing field surrounded by carnage, and in his arms he cradled their daughter. Xzwindra's lifeless body hung limp, and blood ran from her wounds like water from a spring, covering the ground. . .becoming a stream, then a river. Wazrxna's hands felt suddenly warm. She let her eyes drop. Her hands dripped with her daughter's blood. The river rushed down upon her and swept her away—to the city, to the temple of Bayl. Wazrxna fled into the chancel seeking refuge. Weary beyond measure, she crawled up the steps of the altar, blood still dripping from her hands. At the top of the altar, her strength gave way and she collapsed.

Bayl eyed her from his place above the dais. "Do not fail me, Wasssrxsssna! Do not fail me!" The words hissed in her ears as she watched the serpentine god slither down from his perch, his fangs bared and his eyes burning with anger.

A ray of sunlight burst through the hollow she had crawled through to get to her hiding place inside the charred tree, waking her with a start. Her heart hammered violently in her chest.

Sleep fled, but the nightmare did not, for at the moment of waking, a deadly viper slithered down out of the darkness above her and dropped onto her chest. The snake sensed her terror and felt her heartbeat. She sucked air and tried to pull away. The viper struck. Wazrxna's scream echoed out into the charred forest.

Razrdris and a contingent of soldiers, searching the wood for stragglers, heard Wazrxna's cry. As he rode up to the hollow tree, a five-foot viper slithered out into the sunshine. Razrdris arched an eyebrow. He had never before seen such a snake in Tangle Wood. He slew the serpent, then found Wazrxna lying in the bowl of the tree, trembling with fear and weeping.

Razrdris brought Wazrxna out into the sunlight. There, propped in his lap, she told her story and died in his arms. He wept for what she could have been.

He had his men bury Wazrxna in an unmarked grave, then gathered the rest of his troops and returned to Havenholt, his heart heavy with grief. At the fortress, he found Major Targndel, and in a shadowed corner of the fortress, he told Targndel Wazrxna's story.

Major Targndel was never quite the same after those events. He became a softer, gentler, kinder man. And tears came more easily than they once did. He did not smile often, but his heart was not filled with sadness. He was just more thoughtful, more reflective.

As news that an heir of the royal line now reigned as king in Xzwendaria reached into the countryside, villages, and cities, the people took up arms and drove their oppressors from the land. In a time yet to come, King Tarkedrx would drive the Pagyns from Amity and destroy Nefarious Reach.

A week after what became known as the Battle of F.F. Bog Frog, King Tarkedrx rode into Zwexdrof flanked by Jentrxn and General Vandwert and leading the proud Resistance army. Lining the streets, cheering men women and children hailed the king of Xzwendaria.

Baruch had kept his promise. He always did. And once again a king of the line of Xtrakan, a king who bowed before Baruch, sat on the throne in Zwexdrof. And no king before or after Tarkedrx ruled with such extraordinary wisdom and justice. He had a heart for Baruch and for Baruch's people.

Pegran rode into the city flanking the king just behind General Vandwert. During the whole debacle at Havenholt, Pegran had stood with the king, sword in hand, having taken to himself the role of personal protector. He felt responsible to the boy and his mother, since he had accompanied them when they were taken into exile. And, of course, Tark found the one-eyed man with a wooden leg intriguing. After Tark took the throne, Pegran stayed on in Zwexdrof as Tark's unofficial, adopted grandfather.

Prior Forknedrn also returned to Zwexdrof as a more conscientious and believing priest than when he left. But before leaving Havenholt, he stopped by the infirmary and apologized to Kander for his lack of kindness over the years they had known each other. Upon returning to Zwexdrof, the prior immediately began dismantling the Pagyn Black Chancel and rebuilding the temple that Xvardris had destroyed.

Shortly after the king left Havenholt, Major Targndel mounted his horse and rode south to Aynek. He felt a need to get away for a while, and word had reached him that the people there had arrested Jelknerd and would not accept his explanation that he had been a spy working for the Resistance. He had sent a messenger to Havenholt pleading with Targndel to come to his aid, "lest they take me out and hang me!"

Razrdris stayed at Havenholt where he retained a garrison and was commissioned to maintain the fortress as the king's retreat. The king also charged him with the reforestation of Tangle Wood.

F.F. Bog Frog eventually recovered from his breaks and bruises, although he never did walk quite the same. His right leg had a slight twist to it. Several months after the others had left Havenholt, he traveled to Zwexdrof in the company of

Kander, Captain Favel, and Sergeant Tandrak. In a public ceremony at the palace, King Tarkedrx awarded F.F. Bog Frog the King's Medal of Honor for his extraordinary act of bravery in facing the horseman all alone on the killing field before the gates of Havenholt. The king also awarded others for their acts of heroism during the Battle of F.F. Bog Frog.

Captain Favel and Sergeant Tandrak were granted medical discharges from the military. The sergeant never had a day free of pain, though he gritted his teeth and endured. The arrow in Captain Favel's back affected the nerves in his legs, making walking difficult. He too lived with constant pain, and when he lay down at night, his legs often twitched and jumped. He squared his jaw and smiled anyway.

F.F. Bog Frog stayed with Captain Favel and Sergeant Tandrak in Zwexdrof for nearly a year. However, after a time, he longed for the Marshmoor and his grandfather, dear old Freddie Bogfrog. "By muck and by mud, I must return to the bog and tell my dear old grandfather all my grand adventures," he declared one bright sunny day.

"Well, by the bog, you're not going alone!" responded Captain Favel. Sergeant Tandrak agreed. And a week later, the three friends waved good-bye to the others, mounted their steeds, and headed for the Marshmoor.

Kander saw them off. "Sure would like to be going with you," he glummed.

"You take care of that new wife of yours!" said Captain Favel with a laugh. "You know, we started our adventure with your saying that you never did anything right. Well, I'd say that this time you did something right. And in the end, I guess you got the best reward of all!"

Kander smiled and put his arm around Patrexna's shoulders. A tear rose to his eyelid. His only regret was that Thaxndar had not been there to perform the ceremony. He and Patrexna waved as their friends rode away, and Kander smiled as he reflected on the adventure they had lived. Yes, he had done something right, and it had changed his life. Indeed, he had come a long way from where he had been when he tried to steal a loaf of bread from a wily priest.

Tark stood on the palace balcony, watching Kander and his mother. Tears wet his eyes, for at last he had a father. And although Jentrxn advised the king concerning matters of state, Kander, his new father, had a profound impact on the young man's life. And it was primarily his influence that molded Tark into the finest king to ever rule the realm of Xzwendaria.

And so it was that Baruch kept his word of honor.

APPENDIX

NAME PRONUNCIATIONS

Andrapegran or Pegran (andra-PEEG-run) – Rogue drifter
Bander (BAN-der) – A gold miner
Barkus (BAR-cuss) – Man living in Netrag
Baruch (BEAR-ook) – God, the Presence, the Majesty
Beldara (bell-DAR-ah) – Slave girl
Belka (BELL-kuh) – Trevr's mother
Benevar (BEN-nuh-vahr) – One of Chameleon's guards
Bindel (BIN-dull) – A Resistance soldier
Blind Binkie (obvious) – Cover name
Bodrak (BOW-drek) – a Pagyn general
Boger (BOW-ger) – Undercover as a slave
Borga (BOAR-gaa) – Cover name
Brokre (BROE-ker) – Child saved by Warzella
Burggen (BURR-gin) – A sailor in Avard
Cadman (KAD-men) – Captain of Horsemen of Warrz
Char Face (Ch as in channel) – Warrz Clan Lord
Diabolus (die-ABB-oh-lus) – The horseman
Dindrikin – (din-DRIK-en) – One of Xvardris' men
Dinkin (DINK-en) – An Innkeeper
Dogmar (DOG-marr) – Cover name
Dollfig (DOLL-fig) – Man living in Netrag
Dorkin (DOOR-kin) – Kander's mother's landlord
Drandek (DRAN-deck) – Trainmaster
Dulandr (duh-LAN-der) – One of the Ancients
Egrnal (EE-ger-nall) – Government official from Aynek
Elprinda (el-PRIN-duh) – One of the Ancients
Elraydik (el-RAY-dick) – a Xzwendarian general
Elthexn (el-THEX-in) – The last great king of Fairlander
Favelthex or Favel (FAY-vill- thex) – Captain, Regent's Guard
Fendrik (FEN-drick) – A miner
Fiderdink (FIDDER-dink) – False name
Findr (FINN-der) – Undercover as a slave
Fogerty (FOE-ger-tee) – A gold miner
Forknedrn (fork-NED-ran) –High priest after Thaxndar
Fragn (FRAY-gin) – Man out fishing

Gildus (GILL-duss) – One of Char Face's men
Gorlon (GORE-len) – A miner
Grandex (GRAN-dex) – A Pagyn soldier
Grey Wolf (obvious) – The desert warrior
Gudmar (GUUD-mar) – A gold miner
Heferndal (HEFFERN-dall) – High Priest time of Xzadrk
Jelknerd (JELK-nerd) – Merchant spy
Jentrexn (jen-TREX-in) – King Xzadrk's advisor/ Regent
Jolkie (JOEL-key) – One of the men of Eknard
Jorfindel ((JOR-fin-dell) – Patrexna's father
Juflek (JEW-fleck) – A miner
Kanderxn or Kander (kaan-DIRK-sin) – Street thief
Kardis (KAR-diss) – Slave girl
Kavadren (kav-VAY-dren) – Captain of a ship
Landau (LAN-dowe) – A gold miner
Leftrip (LEF-trip) – One of General Vandwert's soldiers
Lrondie (el-RON-dee) – The daughter of Tundruli
Lurndrin (LEARN-drin) – A Pagyn soldier
Markta (MARK-tah) – Patrexna's mother
Merdela (mer-DELL-ah) – An imaginary mermaid
Mifstern (MIS-tern) – A Corporal in the Guard
Narfin (NAR-finn) – A guardsman
Norgran (NOR-gren) – A miner
Patrexna (puh-TREX-nuh) – Violated by Zandirxn
Pegle (PEE-gull) – A miner
Razrdris (ra-ZER-driss) – Captain of Palace Guard
Rosa (ROW-zah) – Cover name
Rylan (RYE-lin) – An outlaw
Sedrnal (SEE-der-nall) – A private in the Guard
Snarl (obvious) – Wild Man from the North
Stekner or Humpy (STEK-nerr) – A prospector
Tandrak (TAN-drek) – A sergeant in the Guard
Targndel (TAR-gen-dall) – head of intelligence gathering
Tarkedrx or Tark (Tark-ED-rix) – heir to the throne
Teldrinda (tell-DRIN-dah) – Ancient picture writer
Thaxndar (THAX-in-darr) – High Priest after Heferndal
Thedrix (THED-rix) – A beggar
Tolm (TOLLm) – Dinkin's helper
Trevr (TREV-er) – Boy sold into slavery

Tundruli ((toon-DROO-lee) – Leader of the Heather Hags
Vandwert (van-DWERT) – Commander of Resistance Army
Vilkina (vil-KINE-ah) – Slave girl
Warzella (war-ZELL-ah) – Girl who saved Brokre
Wazrxna (wa-ZERK-sna) – Priestess of Temple Tenebrus
Welkner (WELK-nerr) – One of Char Face's men
Wendark (WIN-dark) – A Pagyn lieutenant
Werfex (WERE-fecks) – Puppet king of Nefarious Empire
Wilgrin (WILL-grin) – Boy out fishing
Xtrakan (X-tra-kon) – The first king of Xzwendaria
Xvardris (x-VAR-dris) – Nefarious Empire ambassador
Xzadrk (x-ZAY-rick) – King of Xzwendaria after Xtrakan
Xzwindra (x-ZWIN-druh) – Intelligence operative
Zandirxn (Zan-DIRK-sin) – King Xzadrk's son
Zanzxra (zan-ZEX-ruh) – The Black Assassin
Zedria (ZED-ree-uh) – An informant

OTHER PRONUNCIATIONS

Bellem (BELL-um)
Bogfrogls (BOG-frog-gulls)
Decrodile (DECK-row-dial)
Fairlander (FAIR-lander)
Luxurd (LUX-erd)
Ogremen (OH-ger-men)
Pagyns (PAY-gens)
Phantazia (Fan-TAY-shuh)
Stakz (Stacks)
Tenebrus (Ten-EE-brus)
Toure Fenait (Tour-fen-ATE)
Xzendr (ex-ZEN-der)
Xziland (ex-ZIE-land)
Xzwendaria (EX-zwen-DAR-eeuh)
Zwexdrof (ZWEX-droff)

fbk – From the Beginning of the Kingdom

About the Author

Born in Battle Creek, Michigan, John grew up in East Leroy, a small town just to the south. He graduated from Athens High School, and served in the Army during the Viet Nam War era.

After his stint in the Army he graduated from Appalachian Bible College and Berean Christian College, majoring in pastoral ministry, teaching and theology. He has been a Christian school teacher, a youth pastor, pastor, assistant mission director, mission director, and has been writing Christian fantasy fiction since his two sons were knee high to a gnome.

John was a member of a sci-fi fantasy writer's group in Seattle for twelve years, and now leads a Christian writer's group in Pahrump, NV, a sprawling town in the Mojave desert, where he lives with his exceptional wife, Sue—also his proofer.

John is the author of Wanzalara's Cottage and numerous e-books.

Explore his website: faithfantasyfictionebooks.com

Made in the USA
Lexington, KY
21 November 2014